Suzanne
Thanks for
the support.

Hungry Ghost

Tales of the Pack: Book Two

ALLISON MOON

Enjoy! · Allison Moon

Lunatic Ink

ISBN 978-0-98383093-1
Library of Congress Control Number: 2013900971

Learn more:
www.TalesofthePack.com

Contact the Author:
moon@talesofthepack.com

Printed in the United States of America

For Hans

THE HEADLINE DECLARED THE MOST recent death in all capitals: MISSING WOMAN FOUND MAULED. Lexie's naked feet picked up the ink from the newsprint as she tip-toed across the pages spread out over the carpet of her new bedroom.

The girl's death was news to no one. Even the police chief's statement at the end of the article sounded more resigned than revelatory: WE REGRET THAT THE YOUNG WOMAN APPEARS TO BE YET ANOTHER VICTIM OF A RARE WOLF. WE CONTINUE TO ADVISE ALL CITIZENS TO MAINTAIN A TEN P.M. CURFEW AND AVOID UNNECESSARY FORAYS INTO THE FOREST.

Just below the quotation was a picture of Governor Blackwell at a press conference discussing plans for a new highway project, his teeth and tie too straight to be natural. The caption read GOVERNOR BLACK-WELL EXPECTS NEW HIGHWAY TO DISRUPT RARE WOLF TERRITORY AND PUT AN END TO RARE ATTACKS "ONCE AND FOR ALL."

The paint fumes were getting to Lexie's head. She would need three coats of the pumpkin orange to cover the cayenne color of the walls that had once belonged to Renee. She enjoyed smoothing the paint onto the walls; it was a cleansing act declaring clear endings and new beginnings.

A chill wind gusted through the window, half-open to keep Lexie from passing out. Tiny flakes of snow fell, barely enough to stick, covering the grass beyond like a light dusting of talc. The sun cast the room in the same orange as the fresh paint, breaking below the cloud line for a few moments before diving to its death behind the trees.

Lexie sighed at the recollection of autumn nights watching the sunset through cedar needles, warm and naked, tangled in Archer's arms. Maybe orange was a bad choice.

Outside her bedroom, Lexie heard the shuffling of coats in closets and the jangling of keys in pockets. She poked her head out of the door.

Hazel skipped through the hallway, ruffling the lime-green tulle beneath the skirt of her black and white polka-dotted dress, looking like a gothy anime character.

"She lives!" Hazel shouted, flipping her sleek, black ponytail over her shoulder.

Lexie heard Renee sigh from the foyer.

"Where are you guys going?" Lexie asked, creeping to the top of the stairs.

Renee stood below in the foyer, pulling on a burgundy leather jacket. "Out. The holidays were rough. Classes start next week and I'm T.A.-ing for four classes plus managing the animal labs. Mama needs a little R&R to prepare."

"What about the new mauling?"

"Dead girl gonna stay dead," Renee said, checking her wallet for cash. "I need a little life."

Lexie knew Renee to be clever, but never so callous. Maybe she was just deflecting; that was more her style. "What about you, Hazel?"

"I'm pulling a shift at Luscious," she said, smearing a layer of lip gloss on her lips. The fake vanilla scent drove a sugary dagger into Lexie's head.

"Since when are you a stripper?" Lexie asked.

"Since two years ago, dummy. It's my first night back since before I joined the Pack. Blythe wouldn't let me dance."

Renee sat on the stairs, pulling on a pair of short-heeled brown leather boots. Her hair was pulled back into a perfect black puff at the crown of her head, and black eyeliner accented her wide, brown eyes.

"Wow. Hot date?" Lexie asked.

"Yes ma'am," Renee answered.

"Oh my god, you should come!" Hazel clapped and did a small leap.

Lexie flinched. "What? Why?"

Renee slumped her shoulders. "Christ, Hazel."

"What?" Hazel said. "She's depressed." Hazel looked to Lexie as though she were staging an intervention. "You need to get out of the house. You haven't put on underwear in four days."

"Why would I need underwear to go to a strip club?"

"You don't need it," Renee said, standing, "but it helps."

"I'm not twenty-one," Lexie said.

"Doesn't matter," Renee said to her reflection as she smeared her own sugary, black cherry gloss on her lips.

Hazel whined. "Come on, Lexie! It's my first time back, and I need support. Plus, it'll help you get out of your break-up mope spiral, which is kind of a drag." Hazel placed her hands on her hips, making her look like a bossy fourth-grader. "It's not like you have homework or anything."

Lexie groaned and buried her face in her hands.

"What?" Hazel asked.

"I forgot to register for classes," Lexie whined. "I'm going to get stuck with a bunch of Victorian Literature crap."

"Dude," Renee said. "Registration was three *months* ago."

Lexie peeked through her fingers. "I was a little . . . distracted then."

"Face-down in werewolf snatch, you mean," Renee said, checking her hair in the mirror.

"See?" Hazel said. "It's a sign! Have a little fun tonight. Get out of the Den. Live a little. You can deal with registration and all that tomorrow."

Lexie was coming up with a myriad of excuses, her skills of evasion well-honed. She was preparing to utter the first when from the end of the hall, behind Corwin and Sharmalee's door, came passionate moans and screams. The girls all paused at the interruption.

"Uh..." Lexie laughed nervously.

"Is that them?" Hazel asked with a scrunched nose, edging down the stairs.

"No," Renee answered. "They've been watching that porn on repeat for days."

"That's porn? I thought that was just...them." Lexie said, making a face.

"Blythe wouldn't let us watch porn either," Hazel said. "We're all off the leash a bit, I guess."

As the performers' shouts of climax faded into sighs of satisfaction, Corwin and Sharmalee's own sounds ramped up. Lexie widened her eyes and said, "So...Luscious."

"It's a super queer-friendly venue," Hazel assured Lexie.

"Yeah, half the crowd is dykes," said Renee. "It's actually pretty cool. Hazel's right, you should come."

"Really?"

"You can be designated driver. Just don't crush my mojo."

Lexie cleaned herself up, removing her flannel pajamas and unbuckling the knife from her hip. She tied her auburn hair into two braids and put on the only clean t-shirt, underwear, and jeans she had. She restrapped her mother's knife to her hip and yanked the hem of her t-shirt over it, the bottom of the sheath just peeking out.

The knife had lived there day and night for the three months since the night Renee killed Blythe. Since the night Archer left. Since the night Lexie tried to change and couldn't. Since she discovered her mother was dead.

Its continued presence soothed her. She found that meditating on her mother's memory kept her calm, as though calling forth that lineage, no matter how hazy, kept her breathing.

At least for now. The full moon was coming up in less than two weeks and Lexie didn't look forward to it like her packmates did. Her wolf always stalked beneath the surface, like a parasite that wriggled in tiny but nauseating ways. It didn't beg or plot. It merely paced, eager to kill—and more distressing, readily able to do so. Lexie didn't know how to unlatch the cage, but she knew she didn't want to, regardless. She hoped that the wolf would never return, hoped that her monthly blood proved as much. While the rest of the women of the Pack went running on each moon, Lexie wrestled with tampon strings and stained sheets. Despite the pain and loneliness, she knew this to be the better deal. She wasn't ready to revisit the feeling she had only once, when she made love to Archer beneath October's full moon. She discovered two bodies that night: Archer's and her own wolf form that followed. Four perfect, wicked bodies in the space.

Lexie didn't need to feel that way again. Blood was the way for now.

She gave her image a once-over and decided she looked strange but fine. Her skin didn't suit her anymore, but it was all she had. She knew she'd never be as glamorous as Renee or as stylish as Hazel, so she didn't try.

The parking lot was full of cars and smokers. It did feel nice to be human again, away from the Den and the ever-present mixture of anxieties it offered, though the wall of cigarette smoke at the club's entrance undid all the good of her recent shower. Layers of oil, sweat, liquor, and sugar oozed out the front door, so thick as to suffocate. Renee breathed it in and gave Lexie a slow nod. *It's all part of the illusion*, her eyes said. *Look human.* Lexie hid her disgust with a wary smile.

A leggy, mahogany-skinned woman in tight jeans and a tube top waved at them. Her red-painted lips parted to reveal a gap-toothed grin, her shellacked nails twirling a strand of hair that looked expensive, if not real. She leaned like a greaser's girl against a vintage Mustang, a display of dangerous curves. Renee urged Lexie toward the door, abandoning her and Hazel to greet the pin-up with a kiss.

Lexie held her breath as the bouncer made fleeting eye contact before waving her through the door. Inside, Hazel bounded for the bar, throwing herself at the bartenders for hugs. She knelt on a stool as the enthusiastic staff caught her up on all the dirt of the past two years. Lexie found a chair between the bar and the stage and warily scanned the crowd: an even mixture of men's and women's faces, and plenty inbetween. To the right of the stage hung a blackboard listing women's names in chalk: Athena, Lolita, Octavia, Jezebel, Bijou, and Valencia. Lexie shifted on the spooled oak chair and wondered which one was Hazel. She guessed "Jezebel" because of the z rather than the biblical myth, which Lexie didn't know the details of anyway.

Fumes like ethanol pushed at her eyeballs, and she felt as though a migraine would soon follow. Lexie tried to snuffle out the tumult of scents pummeling her sinuses. Renee approached, trailed by the girl from outside, and offered Lexie a cold can of Pabst Blue Ribbon.

"I can't drink in here," Lexie said with a furrowed brow, hiding her voice behind the blare of the jukebox. Renee shoved the can into Lexie's hand and sat, pulling her girl onto her lap. The girl smiled tightly at Lexie through those red-painted lips. Renee introduced her as Nina. Her hair was glossy black and swooped in rigid architectural curves. Her breasts threatened to spill out of the simple tube of fabric that supported them. Lexie wondered where Nina's jacket was, or if she actually went out on a February night in the mountains of Oregon in nothing but a goddamned tube top. Lexie smiled back without showing her teeth.

Hazel hopped over from the bar.

"I gotta go change. Get out your singles and make me look good."

Hazel didn't need their help to look good. Growing up riding show horses, first on her grandfather's ranch and then on a small carnival circuit, Hazel had developed both an elegant flair and extraordinary quad muscle strength. Lexie sipped her beer as Hazel, or as the club's DJ announced, "Bijou", stepped across the stage in five-inch heels and a black ruffled "skirt" that didn't even attempt to cover her backside. She wore a tiny vest over a black and white-striped bikini top.

Renee reached into her pocket, pulled out a single dollar, and gave it to Nina. Hazel danced to a loud rock song that Lexie couldn't identify, though she guessed it was from one of those ambiguously sexualized rock bands of the 80's. When Hazel reached the brass pole at the center of the stage, she gripped it and whipped her body around it twice. Then she climbed it to the ceiling, wrapped her legs and fell back. Dangling upside-down, she removed her vest from her body and let it fall to the floor. She giggled, shaking her small breasts with a naughty smile. The crowd hooted and cheered.

Lexie leaned toward Renee's ear. "No wonder Blythe was so against Hazel dancing."

"Oh, yeah," Renee groaned.

Hazel lowered her legs, locking the pole beneath the crook of her knee, and spun with her arms outstretched. Several people whistled at the difficult-looking move, and wadded dollar bills bounced onto the stage.

Renee stroked Nina's bare shoulder, her eyes glued to Hazel's contorting, hip-swaying figure. "Blythe was always telling us what was or wasn't feminist based on her own ideas of everything. But it's hard to watch Hazel and not see how authentic this whole sexy display is for her, you know?" She shrugged. "I think it's kind of sweet." She wadded up a dollar bill and tossed it onto the stage.

Hazel gripped the pole with her hands again and swirled to the floor, where she spread her legs wide and dropped her heavy heels to the stage with an attention-grabbing thud. Clearly her preternatural strength had kept her in shape during her time away from the club. She stood and walked to the edge of the stage to flirt with the customers.

"Sweet." Lexie nodded, scanning the crowd and finding a mix of hipsters in flannel, grizzled mountain men, and a smattering of dykes. "Okay."

Nina held her dollar bill as though she were presenting a ticket to a train conductor. Hazel squatted so that her crotch was at Lexie's eye level. She winked as Nina placed the bill in the garter she wore high on her thigh.

Lexie looked away, embarrassed. Though the Pack members' various sex sounds were becoming a regular fixture in the Den, Lexie wasn't prepared to see any of the girls grind their pelvises to bad rock music in front of a cheering crowd. Hazel stood and strutted, unfastening her skirt and wrapping it around her wrists, faux-tying herself to the pole. She writhed, and the crowd roared.

Lexie scanned the audience, taking shallow breaths to avoid inhaling too many of the pheromones wafting through the cramped space. Still, they teased their way into her bloodstream, cycling through her body and reminding her of the desires she'd spent three months dampening. She could be lying beneath Archer somewhere, looking up at warm stars, running at her side beneath the full moon, chasing rabbits. Instead, Lexie was living in a house of seven alpha-less werewolves, all trying to figure out how to live without Blythe the oppressor, and how to live with Renee, her murderous replacement.

At the far end of the stage, a woman with a cougar's grin caught Hazel's eye. Hazel lowered herself to all fours to crawl to the woman. The stranger held a single between two fingers like a cigarette. With a stoic grin that Lexie decided was the standard expression of strip-club arousal, she teased it along Hazel's arm and chest. Hazel rolled onto her back, letting the woman caress her torso with the bill as she stroked her own thighs to the music. The woman leaned forward and slid the bill into Hazel's thong. Hazel arched up and kissed the woman lightly before returning to the pole. She whipped off her bikini top to expose tiny sequined pasties as the big finale.

Twenty minutes later, Lexie was at the bar picking up two beers and two tonic waters when Hazel bounded over. She'd changed into a new costume— cotton-candy boy shorts and a teal bra. *Not much to strip out of,* Lexie thought.

"What'd ya think?" She scooted onto the vacant barstool next to where Lexie leaned.

"You're really good," Lexie said, unsure if that was the best adjective to use, so she revised. "You're strong. Like, that hanging stuff was incredible."

"Thanks! That was so fun! Man, I missed this place!" Hazel said.

"Good job then. Here. Tonic for you."

"Sweet, thanks. I have to go work the room for a bit and then I'll be back for my next number. You having fun?"

Lexie nodded with a shrug.

"Cool. Ta-ta."

Renee and Nina were kissing when Lexie returned with the drinks. Lexie scanned the room to find Hazel sitting on the lap of the woman at the end of the stage, chatting. The woman wore a crooked smile that reminded Lexie of Archer. She sighed and looked for a distraction.

"I'm going outside for a smoke," Renee shouted over the blaring music. "Wanna come?"

Outside, the air was crisp and damp, as though the sky couldn't tell whether it wanted to rain or snow. Blessedly, it did neither for the time being. Renee shook a cigarette out from her pack and lit it.

"That's bad for you," Lexie said.

"No shit, Sherlock."

"I meant that as a question," Lexie said. "Is smoking bad for you, or does it not matter?"

"It's bad for everything," Renee said with a chuckle. "I'm mortal Lexie, so are you. So are all werewolves."

"But stronger."

"Stronger, sure. Longer life, if we're lucky. Better lots of things. We aren't like some vampire bullshit, already dead. We're the pulsing, sweaty, throbbing heart of life, feeding, fighting, and fucking til we drop. We get to smell, taste, and feel more than anyone. We are more alive as werewolves than we were as humans."

"Which also means we can get cancer," Lexie said.

"It's the bitch of living." Renee shrugged and offered the open pack to Lexie. "Dulls the olfactory sensors. Might help."

Though Lexie had never smoked a cigarette before, she was willing to try anything that promised to dull her sense of smell. Renee held the flame to the end, and Lexie took a long, thick drag. Corwin had introduced her to the glories of marijuana only a month earlier, so Lexie used the technique Corwin had taught her: she inhaled deeply and held it.

After five long seconds, Lexie exhaled with a cough. Her head pounded even worse than before.

"Hey, I want to talk to you about the peacespeaking thing. I want to try and explore your powers."

"Now?" Nausea tugged at Lexie's throat. She staggered, bolstering her back on the brick wall of the club.

"You okay, Lex?" Renee asked.

She nodded vigorously and swallowed in an attempt to keep the limited contents of her stomach from spewing forth. "I just...uh...need to sit down." She slid to the ground, breathing as much of the cold, clean-ish air of the night as she could.

Renee flicked her cigarette into the parking lot. "You sure you're okay?"

"I just…need a sec," Lexie mumbled.

Renee gave her a wary look. "I'm going to go back inside then," she said. "We can talk about this later back at the house." Lexie nodded in acknowledgement.

Lexie was beginning to regret coming out to the club. She'd thought she wanted people and connection, but it only drew bold lines around how lonely and disconnected she was these days. She held her head in her hands while the thin line of smoke trailed up and away from her forehead. She thought about Archer's cabin, and how nice it'd be to go light a fire in the fireplace, cozy up on the lambskin, and sink into a dreamy sleep there. Only, there was no more cabin, there was no more Archer. Lexie groaned and pressed the heels of her hands against her closed eyes.

"Can I bum a smoke?" asked a raspy voice. Lexie opened her eyes and saw a pair of black leather motorcycle boots standing in front of her. She followed the boots up past ripped blue jeans to a black t-shirt and leather jacket, all the way to the woman's face. It was the same woman who had been lavishing so much attention on Hazel as she danced.

"You can have this one." Lexie held her cigarette aloft, and the woman took it with that crooked grin. She squatted against the wall next to Lexie, dragging heartily on the cigarette. Lexie expected more conversation but none came; the woman leaned and smoked. She was tall and lean, her black hair cut short and shaved on the sides, where a spray of silver mingled with the black. The rest was greased back like a sloppy dorsal fin. Lexie found it impossible to guess her age, somewhere between twenty-five and sixty.

"How do you know Hazel?" Lexie asked.

"Who's Hazel?" asked the woman.

Shit, Lexie thought.

"Oh, you mean Bijou?" the woman said.

Lexie flinched and nodded.

"Hazel, huh?" the woman said. "That's pretty."

Lexie knew there was some unwritten rule about sharing strippers' real names. She hoped she hadn't just given Hazel up to a stalker.

"I play down the road at a place called The Cat Club. I used to come here after my sets and watch my...ex, I guess, dance."

"Which one is she?"

"Oh, she's not here anymore. Turned out to be a cocksucker and took off for Seattle on the back of the prick's bullshit rice rocket." She flicked the cigarette into the parking lot with a short sigh.

"Yikes."

"Bijou and she were buds. Nice to see her back. It's been a bit." The woman gazed out into the nighttime parking lot, her eyes soft and cloudy as she assessed the memories.

"I'm Randy," she said, holding out her hand for a shake. A faded orange flame tattoo peeked out from the edge of her sleeve.

"Lexie."

"Whoa," Randy said, pulling her hand back. "That's quite a side-arm."

Lexie tugged at her t-shirt, though the leather sheath still peeked out from below it. She knew it made her look eccentric, but Lexie hoped Randy would dismiss it as a quirk of Oregon white trash. God knew, there were weirder habits among the townies. Randy must've seen Lexie's embarrassed flush. She changed the subject.

"If you're around next weekend, come see my set. It's mellow, but good, I think."

"I bet it is. Good, I mean."

Randy smiled. On her sharp, long features, the expression looked sly. Her eyes crinkled deeply at their corners.

The door burst open and Renee slid out with Nina leaning on her shoulders. The scantily-clad girl was giggling and fanning herself with her hand.

"All right, Mama. Let's hit the road," Renee said to Lexie. She thought she heard Renee slur a bit, but she could have just been saying "lez."

"What about Hazel?"

"She's getting her stuff together."

Randy stood and slapped the dirt from her thighs. "Well, nice meeting you."

"Yeah, you too."

"I wasn't kidding about the Cat Club. Check it out. I'm there every Wednesday." Randy held out her hand again and Lexie took it.

"Nice hands," Randy said, squeezing Lexie's.

Warmth flooded Lexie's cheeks.

Hazel ran through the parking lot, her heels clattering against the pavement with sharp shocks, pummeling Lexie's eardrums. Renee warmed up the car.

"Yay!" she shouted. "That was SO FUN!"

Lexie slipped into the driver's seat, and Hazel leapt into the passenger's side, bouncing like a child on her way to an amusement park. "I made seventy-three bucks in tips!" She held out the handful of wrinkled bills. They stank up the car with smells of people and their grubby hands. Lexie rolled down her window.

"You have fun, Lex?" Renee asked from the back seat.

Lexie looked at her in the rearview mirror and shrugged. Renee squeezed her shoulder before returning her hands and attention to Nina.

The grunts and moans of Renee and Nina's love-making drifted down the hall. Lexie tried to bury her head in pillows, to stuff her ears with plugs and cotton, but nothing silenced the pleasure of others while she squirmed. Lexie cursed her own arousal at the sounds, wishing for an emptiness to drag her into the mindlessness of sleep rather than the numb tugging at her genitals and fingers. Three months since she lay with her love. Three months since Lexie felt loved. Three months since Blythe's death and Renee's vengeance. Her fingers crept to her groin. She rubbed herself furiously, a punishment for her poor choices. She could be lying beneath Archer's body somewhere right now, watching the crescent moon cut the silhouette of her breast. Instead, she lay in her fume-laden bedroom, trying to forget.

But forgetting Archer's face was easier than forgetting her own mistakes. Archer was gone, and that was Lexie's fault. The admission made her cringe. She commanded herself not to cry, not to pity her own idiocy. She told herself that she was too young to trade in a life for a lover, too disillusioned by the horrors of the fall to believe that Archer could treat her as an equal instead of a puling little beta 150 years her junior.

Her orgasm came and went. Still, she couldn't sleep, and she wouldn't until every last girl in the house was unconscious.

She rose and dressed. She had to get out of here, away from the stink of paint and sex and memory. Lexie was in the mood to mourn.

2

IT WAS STUPID TO GO running alone. Though the moon was slim, full-blood Rares still lurked. The most recent death was evidence enough of that. But Lexie needed silence. She needed peace. She needed her treehouse.

As she climbed the stoic cedar, the nausea of an eager sob clung to her insides, awaiting release. The dark blue night fogged her vision, and the scents of memories glowed in her brain like ghostly beacons. She snuffled them out of her nose like dust.

Lexie resisted the urge to inhale deeply, to take in any lingering particles of Archer that clung here. She soaked in the silence and explored the tiny differences of the space since her last visit. Frost covered every surface, including the undersides of the cedar's needles. She reached her fingertips to one spine. The frost warmed and disappeared beneath her touch. She turned to the tree trunk, wrapped her arms around it, let warmth and wood seep into her. After a while, Lexie knew she felt it hugging her back. It was the most touch she had known in a while, but she was willing to make do with a hug from a chilly, seasonally-lethargic tree.

Lexie circled to the far side of the platform, not ready to approach the sheepskin that lay abandoned in a gray, sodden lump at the center. Instead, she sat at the edge of the treehouse and faced inward. She wanted to pray to Archer, as though she were a ghost or a god. But she was neither of these things; she was merely gone.

Lexie picked at splinters on the platform, trying to figure out what to feel. What would it be like, to see a pair of mismatched eyes looking back at her? Archer left. Archer gone. Archer driven away.

Tears would be appropriate, but she felt immune to their charms. Tears she'd had enough of. She was done with them for now. What then? Fear? Resentment? Despair?

There was something clawing at Lexie's insides, but it was none of those things. Her upper lip quivered with the realization. It curled into a snarl. The fury of betrayal seized her jaw. Lexie was fucking angry. She wanted to growl, to howl, to shout and rage. She wanted to curse Blythe's arrogance that demanded allegiance before cooperation, the same arrogance that led to the deaths of three boys at the jaws of Renee. She wanted to curse Blythe's ego and her death and the tailspin it caused in everyone. Lexie wanted to curse her own passion for Archer, her willful ignorance of Archer's fraught connections to the Pack. She wanted to tear Archer apart for thinking she knew better than anyone, and for the unceremonious way Lexie learned of her own mother's death. But she saw herself from the outside and felt foolish. All that was in the past, and everyone seemed to have moved on. Except for Lexie. She bit her tongue until she tasted blood.

She thought this would be different, college.

A rustling in the branches pulled her attention outward. Nestled in the lowest branch, one that Lexie's hands had once gripped in passion, was a nest. Two fluffy birds clung to each other, sharing warmth. Beneath them, Lexie saw the merest curve of an egg. A new family was repurposing this lonely place.

Lexie pulled off her shirt, the winter air slithering against her skin. She leaned back against the tree trunk, pressing back into its coarse touch. She squirmed against the velvety rough edges. Bits of wood skidded across her flesh, while other, smaller bits splintered off to lodge within it. It all felt like touch to Lexie. She couldn't discern pain from pleasure anymore. She scratched harder, until strips of her flesh peeled away to be replaced by the tiniest shards of her tree. A moist connection followed, her bleeding skin sticking to the tree's bark. She scraped harder, grateful and angry at the cedar for hurting her so.

She sneered at the birds' nest. Her claim to this territory was stronger than theirs. She fell to her haunches within reach of the sheepskin. She wanted to rub it against her bloody back, to stain it with the rest of the story. She didn't. She sat in silence, her bloody back drying her to the tree. Then, she jerked herself away, ignoring the tiny stings of reopened wounds, and climbed down to the forest floor.

She walked with eyes cast downwards, following her own scent trail back to the Den. A different scent on the breeze made her stop. She reached for her blade. No growl followed the shadows. Lexie stood still, trying to track the creature's intent.

But there was no stalking creature to match the scent, just the odor's own presence, clinging to the trees like sap. It smelled like power: musk and earth and stone. Vertigo assailed Lexie. The scent threatened seduction, willing her to lose control.

She ventured into the shadows, where thick boughs kept even the starlight from finding its way to the forest floor. She inhaled deeply to make up for her weak eyesight. The scent told a story of strength and solitude. She wanted to bathe in it, to take some of its essence as her own. It was ennobling and intimidating all at once.

Logic struggled against instinct—take it, flee it. She gave in, pulling it inside her, holding her diaphragm out to keep it in. She fought dizziness and euphoria. The darkness around her filled with colored shapes, as though her eyes were squeezed shut even though they were wide open. Lexie was getting high on this scent, this invisible seducer that carried her from anguish to bliss in the space of a few breaths.

A breeze cut through the brush and boughs, tugging away Lexie's invisible intoxicant, carrying it off into the night. The thieving wind brought a new scent to replace it: sickly and strong, half putrescence and half sugar-sweet.

Lexie dropped to all fours, the sobering scent knocking her brain back into working order. She resisted taking it in, wishing to savor the last delicious remnants of the scent that teased her to this place, but the new scent bullied its way up her nose, tinny and saccharine at once. This odor she could trace back to its source, at least.

Lexie stalked the scent, letting it dance a ribbon across her face as it drifted downwind. The sugary odor expanded, becoming a lake rather than a rivulet. She knew she was close—close to the scent, and close to the Den. She crept around tree trunks and found the source in a clearing.

A crumpled corpse lay sprawled in the clearing. Lexie stared at it in ambivalent shock—run to it, or run away? She crept toward the body. It had been a quick and efficient kill: one swipe across the throat and another across the belly. The girl's pale skin reflected the meager light of the stars and the new moon. Her tongue poked between her lips, a slice of still-pink beauty among the wreckage. Lexie leaned toward the girl's face and recognized her. Her name was Bree Curtis, a classmate of the straight-A, squeaky-clean variety. She wore eye makeup, smeared and running from dried tears, and a heavy coat as though she had been preparing for a long night outdoors.

The fresh death fascinated Lexie more than it repulsed her. She reached out to the gash that nearly severed Bree's head. She reached, but didn't touch. A tickle of a sound just beyond hearing shocked Lexie's brain back into wariness. With one last glance at Bree Curtis' blue, bloodless face, Lexie ran.

Nobody followed, but Lexie ran as though all the Rares in Oregon were after her. She ran from an invisible foe and the dark reality of this life. Bree Curtis had been killed by a Rare. Another dead girl. Twice in as many weeks. Lexie's present and future, laid out before her in the form of a girl's corpse.

Lexie stopped at a dark and lonely gas station on Red Hill Road and called 911. She muffled the receiver with her hand and gave as many details as she could without giving herself away.

When the dispatcher started asking her questions, Lexie hung up the chilly receiver with a clunk. The interplay of treehouse, memories, and desire was gone; all that was left was Lexie's shame and one more corpse. She threw it all into the cage behind her heart, feeding it to her dormant, silenced wolf. And when it was gone, she brushed herself off and ran home.

3

IT WAS EARLY DAWN WHEN Lexie emerged into the backyard of the Den. Black silhouettes of the hot tub, lawn chairs and deck reminded her of the barbeque when she first met the Pack. She'd been intimidated then. She'd thought she would do anything to be accepted, but as it turned out, she'd been wrong. Now, the patio furniture stood as ebon relics, their stoic shapes highlighted by white dusting of snow. Summer, and so much more, was long gone.

Lexie stripped in the yard and hosed off the smeared blood and saliva that marred her skin. She didn't want to enter the Den stinking of blood, tears, and another corpse. Cleanliness would preserve the illusion of her sanity. Not that she thought any of the Pack would be fooled.

The ice water shocked her skin, but it left her feeling appropriately penitent. She climbed back in through her window. She didn't like to take the stairs when all the girls were home. They creaked. She landed softly on her carpet and nearly jumped back out the window when she saw Hazel perched on her desk, waiting.

Lexie grabbed her chest. "What the fuck, Hazel?" Lexie said in a stage whisper, trying to express her shock without waking the house.

"I just wanted to talk."

"Hazel," Lexie pleaded. "I'm tired. We can talk later."

"You always say that."

Lexie dropped her ruined clothes in a heap on her floor and moaned, yearning only for her mattress and blankets.

She crawled into bed, folding back the top blanket for Hazel. "Come on then."

Hazel threw off her robe and wriggled into bed alongside Lexie. She rolled over, presenting her back to Lexie. A smattering of tiny beauty marks rode high on her shoulders. She shivered at Lexie's touch, hot skin pricking with goosebumps.

Lexie reached her arms around Hazel and pulled their bodies tightly together. Lexie was used to being the small one. She liked feeling big and strong in relation to the tiny Hazel. She nuzzled her nose against Hazel's head. Her black hair smelled like gardenias and vanilla.

"Do you miss her?" Hazel asked, finally.

"Yes," Lexie said. "Every day."

"Me too."

Lexie must have misunderstood. She almost spoke, but Hazel continued.

"Blythe, I mean," Hazel whispered. "You only really got the worst of her. And that was bad, for real. But, for a long time, she was pretty rad. I mean, she helped me own things that I didn't even know were there. She was really good to all of us."

"I'm sorry," Lexie said.

"It's not your fault. It's neither of our faults," Hazel said. "Ego, right? Sheesh." Then, after a long pause, "I'm worried about Renee."

"Do you think she's taking it hard?" Lexie asked.

"Duh. How would you feel if you killed someone?"

"Someone? Or Blythe?"

Hazel let her restless leg shake. "Fair. But I don't think Renee is managing."

"She sounded like she was managing just fine tonight."

"She's in denial," Hazel said.

"Whatever you say," Lexie said. She wanted to care, to help, but she was tired. Her heart was in the woods at the treehouse, and her mind was still with the body she'd found in the clearing. She didn't have anything left for Hazel; she didn't even know how to divine what Hazel might need. Everyone in the Pack seemed to need something from one another, but no one would say so directly. Instead, it was constant shots across the bow: indications, double-speak, and lingering silences. Perhaps the girls, having known each other so long, were able to parse this type of communication. Meanwhile, it only left Lexie feeling stupid and disconnected.

Hazel grasped Lexie's wrist and drew her even tighter. She curled like a squirrel into the space formed by the crescent of Lexie's body.

"I don't think what she did was wrong," Hazel whispered, a confession.

Lexie didn't know whether she was talking about Archer, Blythe, or Renee.

"Neither do I," she replied, absolving them all for past sins.

She stroked and nuzzled Hazel as if it were the next logical step, but as Hazel's sigh became a snore, Lexie too let herself drift off.

4

"IS THERE ANYTHING TO EAT?" Lexie asked, blinking bleary eyes and stifling a yawn. Bree's death-slackened face had jolted her out of her dreams throughout the night. She wished she could keep sleeping, but she had to try and score a seat in some classes today.

Jenna stood in the kitchen wearing a cotton sundress despite the chill. She punched a wad of dough that would soon become a loaf of sourdough bread. The morning sun was stuck behind impenetrable layers of cloud, and Jenna used the opportunity to warm the kitchen with the preheating oven.

"I just made some hummus. And there are some flax crackers in the cabinet."

"Meck," Lexie said.

"Well fuck you very much, too."

"Sorry. I just need more heft. Meat."

"There's still some of the jerky I made in the fridge," Jenna said. "Go for it."

Lexie smiled and retrieved her snack.

"You should really eat something other than jerky. That's a lot of sodium. Bad for your heart." Lexie shut the fridge door on another flash of Bree's face: her waxy skin and blind, staring eyes. When to tell the Pack? Lexie didn't know. She didn't know how to deliver such news without callousness or chaos.

"Nothing else you make tastes as good," Lexie said, her salivary glands bursting into overdrive with the salty-sweet meat.

Renee staggered into the kitchen in shorts and a bra. Her hair was smooshed and poofed in weird shapes, and she searched for the coffee pot through half-closed eyes.

"Morning, sleepyhead," Jenna teased. Renee woofed a greeting.

"Where's Nina?" Lexie asked.

"I drove her home last night," Renee replied.

"Already?" Lexie said. "She allergic to dog hair or something?"

"I'm allergic to sleepovers."

Renee filled her mug and found her way to the living room sofa, where she pulled out her phone to check email.

Jenna smiled sweetly and continued to throw her fists into the dough with tiny grunts. "You going to come running with us on the moon?" she asked Lexie, not looking up from her hands. "It's next Friday."

Lexie shook her head. "Nah. I don't think it'll happen."

"You just have to let the moon do her thing. She'll take you."

"You said that last month, and the month before," Lexie groaned. "I'm like a one-shift pony. I can't change anymore."

"I don't think that's true," Jenna said. "Mother Moon is stronger than any earthly magic keeping you from changing. She'll take you when the time is right."

"Well, I hope the time is never right. I don't think I'm cut out for the werewolf business." Lexie tore a bite from the leathery meat and chewed noisily.

"Why would you say that?" Jenna looked genuinely hurt.

"It's too..." Lexie regretted telling the truth, and reminded herself not to speak of such things to the girls again. "Raw."

She didn't know if the word referred to her heart or the nature of the creature. Either way, the word felt apt.

"It's not really as dramatic as you make it sound," Jenna said with a faint giggle.

Lexie gnawed on her jerky. "What do you guys do when you go out?"

Jenna bopped her head from side to side, shaking her curls, as she considered. "Just run around mostly."

"Run around?"

"Yeah, we chase things, wrestle, rough house. You know, like girls do." She shrugged.

"Girls do?"

"Sure," Jenna said with a cherubic grin.

"Sex?" Lexie asked after a pause.

"Sometimes," she shrugged again. "We get excited sometimes, and once you erase certain cultural stigmas the rest follows quite easily. But sex doesn't really overshadow the overall experience. Plus, lesbian werewolf sex is kinda weird," she said with a laugh. "Too much fur. Long claws. It all just gets in the way."

Renee snickered from the living room and Lexie bit her tongue.

"I mean," Jenna continued, directing her attention to her hands, "kidding aside, what we do, it's really intimate and nurturing. We get to share a very private side of ourselves with each other. It's far more vulnerable than sex, and it brings us so close each time. Plus, it's only once a month, so we need to take advantage when we can. You should come running with us. Just try. It's healing."

Lexie tried for a sympathetic smile. "The change doesn't feel healing to me. It feels…." From what Lexie could remember of that singular event, it was that she was betrayed by her body once again, another in the long series of betrayals womanhood offered. Her whole young life, Lexie had run and leapt and dangled from tree branches, played in dark rivers, and stomped through nighttime forests. Then, when she turned twelve, everything changed. Her body became gangly and weak, and the world was populated with new threats. The rivers were no longer wondrous, but filled with leeches, snakes, and parasites. Her body became a thing of blood and guts, never to be economical again. "…Messy," Lexie finished. Like her menstruation, like her cramps and odd digestion, her pimples and tears and odd moistures and odors. Puberty ruined her. If anything, her lone transformation into a wolf

during her first shared orgasm only served to remind her of the unwieldy grossness that was endemic to being so much flesh and blood.

Jenna kneaded her dough in silence for a moment. "Almost all of
us found our wolves through violence. You know that, right?"

Lexie watched Jenna's hands flex and pull at the dough. She had
remarkable strength in her forearms for someone so soft. "Blythe told
me. But she said a lot of crazy things that night. I didn't really know
what to believe."

"Well, that part is true. Running together helps us remember the
gift of survival. What seeing the edge and living past it does to a
woman. I've changed in many ways since my attack. But of all those
ways, my wolf was the one thing that kept me together.

"I'm not saying you to have to suffer to find your strength," Jenna
continued. "But if you don't find it when you do suffer, you won't get
out alive."

Lexie thought back to her first experience of violence in Septem-
ber, when she was attacked by the full-blood Rare in the Barrens. She
remembered her meager defense of flailing paws and sharp jaw snaps,
her all-too-easy surrender. She chuckled at herself out of shame.
Sometimes she summoned that memory, staring into it as one might
a deep canyon, seductive in its fatality. She shook her head, as if that
would rid her of the memory.

"The change," Lexie said. "It doesn't feel good. It makes me feel
weak."

"To be a woman is to change, constantly, frustratingly. Our moods,
our weight, the water we carry, the sadness and joy we possess in turn.
To be a woman is to be in flux. That's not the problem. Weakness is
always at the joints. I'd guess that your wolf form isn't weak, just like
your woman form isn't. It's the in-between space that scares you. The
dreamtime, when your consciousness loses shape."

"Wow," Lexie said. "That was pretty profound."

Jenna giggled and punched the dough into the bread pans. "It was,
wasn't it? I wish I had a tape recorder. I've never said it that eloquently
before. Not that I have many people to tell."

Jenna opened the oven, and warmth swelled in the kitchen. "But
true, right?"

"I guess. I can't say," Lexie said. "The only in-between space I felt was when I was...you know, cumming." Lexie drew swirls in Jenna's leftover flour. "Which I kind of figured was part of the experience."

Jenna nodded at her dough. "Would you do it again?"

"Have an orgasm? I sure hope so."

Jenna giggled. "No, silly. Find the in-between space. Let your physical self dissolve?"

Lexie took a deep breath and exhaled slowly. "I don't think I know how."

Jenna shrugged and slid the loaves into the oven. "Maybe just try moving toward the darkness rather than running from it."

Lexie gnawed on the stringy strap of jerky, considering Jenna's suggestion. Hazel walked in and dropped her backpack on the kitchen table. She propped a foot on the edge and adjusted her stockings.

"You shouldn't hold it back," Hazel said. "It's not healthy. It'll give you cancer or something."

Sharmalee and Corwin clattered down the steps and into the kitchen, laughing. Corwin wore a sarong and a white tank. Sharmalee was in her panties and bra. Corwin wrapped her arms around Sharmalee from behind.

Jenna put on water for tea. "Having fun up there?"

"Oh my god, yes." Sharm giggled, her brown eyes nearly hidden behind her plump cheeks.

"We're watching a movie," Corwin said, squeezing Sharm.

Lexie raised her eyebrows.

"A *porno*," Sharmalee said in a stage whisper.

Lexie pulled a face, and Sharmalee said, "No, it's like super progressive queer feminist porn."

"It's like all gender queer and fierce femme," Corwin said. "There's hair in all the right places, and some of them are fat, and it's fucking rad."

"And seriously girls, it's werewolf-themed." Sharmalee spoke like it was a dance, all waving hands and exaggerated expressions. "It's called *Horny Like the Wolf* and the special effects are *ridiculous*. You have to watch it."

Corwin pulled her blond dreadlocks back into a high bun. "Yeah, the women are just basically wearing these Halloween costumes. They look like sexy Lon Chaneys."

"Ew," Jenna tittered.

"But it's cool, because they get to keep their thumbs," Corwin said with a silly grin, wiggling her fingers. "And we all know how important those are, don't we Lex?" She punched Lexie in the shoulder.

Lexie made a face and batted Corwin's hand away. "I didn't know you liked porn."

Sharmalee squealed. "Me neither! I had never seen one before."

"We should invite Mitch to watch it. The bellies would totally work for—" Corwin cut herself off and raised a brow. "—What is Mitch calling Mitchself these days?"

Jenna greased another bread pan. "Mitch is a 'he' all the time now, remember?"

Sharmalee groaned, and Corwin rolled her eyes.

"Mitch is a part of our family, ladies," Jenna scolded. "I don't know why this is so hard for you to grok."

"It doesn't make sense that Mitch is doing this," Corwin said. "Why should I have to accommodate her baggage?"

"Because he's your sister. It's not about making you comfortable. It's about making Mitch feel safe."

"Men are safe everywhere," Sharmalee said.

"Not trans men," Jenna said.

Corwin pursed her lips. "As long as she—*fuck*—*he* doesn't get up in my case when I fuck it up, which I will because this is like the third fucking time Mitch has changed pronouns in, like, two months."

"Yeah," Sharmalee said. "It's not like this was a long time coming. She just out of the blue is demanding we call her a boy."

"So what?" Jenna said, barely raising her voice above speaking tones, which for Jenna was akin to yelling. "Shapeshifting is a legitimate form of self-expression."

"Yeah, woman to wolf. That's easier to understand than woman to man." Corwin ran her fingers through Sharmalee's long, chestnut hair.

"All she's doing is abandoning her gender for an easier one," Sharmalee agreed.

Their conversation was shocked to silence by a loud slam upstairs.

Mitch shouted from his room, "I can hear you, you know!"

The girls all flinched.

"I'm still a wolf!"

"We know, sweetie," Jenna called back. "We're just sisters having a concerned conversation. We'd say these things to your face, too!"

"You don't have to yell!" Mitch shouted. "I have the same hearing as all of you!"

"We'll stop yelling when you do, sweetie."

"I'm yelling 'cause I'm angry, not because I can't hear."

"Oh," Jenna said. The girls exchanged sheepish glances.

"Fucking Health Services," Jenna sighed, seemingly apropos of nothing.

The girls looked to one another, no answer coming.

Jenna whispered, "They denied Mitch testosterone. They cited budget cuts, but it's clearly transphobic."

"Clearly how?" Sharmalee asked.

"Milton Health Services is still offering boner pills and condoms, but they cut birth control subsidies, HPV vaccination, and any sort of transition services. It's horrible."

"We should protest," Hazel said.

"Over testosterone?" Corwin asked. "There's too much of that in the world already. Why the hell should we protest for them to make more?"

"It's not about making, it's about sharing." Jenna pushed the remainder of the dough into a bread pan. "I'm doing some research into herbal substitutes. Apparently there are some options growing right around Milton."

Lexie found a patch of sunshine in the front room and stretched out in it, ready for a nap before she tried to win over Professor Rindt of Indigenous Linguistics of the Americas. The front door's slam shook her awake. Renee entered the kitchen with more slamming sounds: keys, books, something that whumped like a purse. Jenna greeted her with mock singsong. "Welcome hooome, darling!"

"Where's Lexie?" Renee asked.

"Napping. What's up?"

"We need to talk. This is getting out of hand."

"Weren't you just the one that ordered us all some R & R?"

"That was before I saw this. Look," Renee said.

Lexie listened as Jenna read silently. "Oh no. Another one?" Jenna's voice cracked with the onset of tears. Lexie curled into a tighter ball and buried her face in her arms. Renee's Google Alerts had let her off the hook.

She listened to Renee's paces. "She was found less than two miles from here in the Western woods."

Jenna sighed. "There's nothing out there. No trails, just trees." She read under her breath, skimming the article. "She was dating Rory Blackwell? The Governor's son?"

"Exactly," Renee said. "Why would Bree Curtis, a nineteen-year-old valedictorian from New Hampshire, wander around those woods alone in the middle of the night, especially when she's got some stud of a boyfriend waiting at home?"

"Who knows?" Jenna opened a cabinet and fished around the tea bags. "A girl's got a million reasons to court danger. Postmortem psychoanalysis won't get us far."

"I don't buy it. The Blackwell kid could be a Rare." Renee threw her phone on the counter and sighed. "I need to get at Lexie. Her peacespeaker sight has to help us in some way."

"We don't know that," Jenna said, rummaging through a drawer for a tea ball. "She obviously doesn't know how it works, and we don't even know if she could reproduce the effects. It's not like there's a guidebook for seeing werewolves while they hide in human form."

"Well, maybe I'll have to beat it out of her."

"Seriously?"

"What?" Renee said.

"I don't know what she needs, but it's not that." Lexie held her breath, wanting to escape, but knowing she'd be spotted. So she kept playing dead.

Renee returned to pacing. "We have *another* dead girl on our hands and a werewolf that we should have killed by now."

"Even if Lexie did help us find a werewolf, Blythe was always the one who led the hunts," Jenna said. "Without her, I don't even know how we'd begin to capture and interrogate him."

Renee stopped pacing. She slumped into a chair, defeated. "We don't need Blythe." It sounded almost as much a threat as a promise.

"It's winter. We're hibernating."

"Wolves don't hibernate."

"We're mourning, Renee. Some more than others. Just let it happen. Nothing you can do will force the issue."

Renee half-snarled.

"Maybe we need to process," Jenna offered.

"We don't need to process."

"Maybe we do," Jenna insisted. "Everyone's miserable, no one trusts you, Lexie can't even find her wolf, and we don't know what the hell to do. We're getting sloppy, everyone stepping over shit like this."

"Shit like passive aggression? Or shit like corpses?"

"Both."

Renee shoved away from the table and grabbed her stuff. "You know where to find me for the latter, but I'm not down for any group healing lesbian circle bullshit."

Three hours later, the Pack sat in the living room, in a circle around the low table. It reminded Lexie of that first party: kissing Renee, warmed by candlelight, the first of so many things. But that stormy night felt like years ago, not months.

Renee looked the least happy of the bunch, which was quite a feat, considering how dreadful the rest seemed.

"I'd like to share," Sharmalee offered.

Jenna nodded.

"I miss Blythe, but not really," Sharmalee said. "I miss what she was to me, but not who she was in the world, not toward the end at least. And that makes me feel really sad. That's all."

"Thank you for your share," Jenna said. "Anyone else?"

No one spoke.

"Okay, yeah. I'm worried," Hazel said finally. "I'm really freaked out a little bit. I'm just gonna say it."

"Thank you, Hazel. Anything else?"

Hazel nodded, her whole body rocking with the force of her enthusiasm. "I mean, we know we let one half-blood go free."

"You mean *Lexie* let go free," Corwin muttered.

"No cross-talk," Jenna scolded.

Hazel continued, "And we know there are more. Like how many? At least two, right?"

The girls looked to one another. Renee answered, "Well there's the half-blood Milton student who we—Lexie—let go."

"Stefan," Hazel interjected.

"Right, Stefan. And," Renee continued, "the full-blood that attacked Lexie near the barrens, the one who mauled the girl last week, and the one who killed Bree, which could be the same one. That's all I'm aware of."

"But it's gotta be the tip of the iceberg," Mitch muttered.

"You're right," Sharmalee said. "Those woods are too big to be hiding one measly full-blood."

Hazel nodded. "So then what the hell are we doing?"

"That's what I'd like to know," Corwin growled.

"Okay Corwin," Jenna said. "Let's let Hazel finish."

"I'm done. I guess," Hazel said. "I'm just wondering. Like I'm happy to have a normal life right now, really happy. I'm happy I can strip again, I'm happy we're not all walking on eggshells because we're afraid we'll be the 'wrong' kind of women or feminists or whatever. But it feels like a lie. Nothing's normal. Another girl died."

"We let her die," Mitch mumbled.

"It wasn't our fault," Lexie said, so quietly no human would have been able to discern her voice above the crackling fire.

"Well you're the one who let Stefan live, so I guess you're right. It's your fault," said Corwin.

"Corwin," Jenna scolded, "we have no proof that Stefan was responsible. It's just as possible Bree was killed by a different Rare. Or by a full-blood."

"Great, so it could be a *bigger* werewolf, which means we're even more screwed."

Sharmalee slumped in her chair. "It's still not fair to blame Lexie."

"None of this is fair!" Corwin erupted. "Blythe is dead. Renee's in charge, which hasn't exactly been a smashing success, and another girl died on our watch."

Renee shot Corwin a look. Corwin met it, not backing down.

"Thank you, Corwin," Jenna said. "We hear you, and you're sharing some important feelings. Let's just try to keep this constructive. Why don't we talk more about our feelings around Blythe's death?"

Everyone shifted uncomfortably and Renee held her temples. A full minute of awkward silence passed before Lexie finally spoke.

"I wish I could speak on behalf of Archer," Lexie said. "I don't know what she'd say. I never really knew what was going on in her head. But I do know that she cared about you all and what you were trying to do. She wanted to stay, to help. But I wouldn't let her."

"Fucking genius," Corwin said.

Jenna shot Corwin a cold look.

"I could never be the woman I needed to be as long as Archer was around. If that's selfish, then fine, I'm selfish. But I know that you feel the same way about Blythe. She helped you all to grow, but then when you were strong enough, she held you back. She demanded your allegiance when she should have been encouraging you."

"You don't know shit about Blythe," Corwin said, standing. "You knew her for what, three months? She saved my fucking life, all of our lives, not to fulfill some ambition, but because she cared. Don't project your ex's personality defects onto Blythe. She stuck around. Your girlfriend bolted, and you, I don't even know why you're here!"

"Corwin, chill!" Renee shouted. "I'll tell you why she's here, but first you gotta stop acting like a stuck up bitch!"

The girls gasped. The b-word had been verboten when Blythe was around, and now Renee was the first to use it against one of their own.

"We all need to take a breath," Jenna said. "Renee, please use your 'I' statements."

"Fine," Renee said. "*I* think Corwin's being a bitch."

Jenna sighed.

"That wasn't what she meant," Mitch mumbled.

"Listen," Renee said, sinking back into her chair. "This circle shit is killing me. Just let me say my piece and I'll shut up for the rest of it, alright?"

The girls looked to each other. Jenna waved an exasperated hand.

"This is what I'm seeing," Renee said. "We're all happy Blythe is gone and we're ashamed to say so. You need to blame someone for killing her, and it should be me. Because I did kill her, with my own fucking jaws. So let's leave Lexie and Archer out of that.

"I'm sorry she's dead, only because she was a good lover to you, Mitch, a friend to the rest of us, and a leader when we all needed one. But don't you dare doubt that I killed her because she would have killed us."

The girls sat still as Renee stared into the eyes of each member of the Pack. "You get that?"

Mitch chewed on his lips. Sharmalee hid her body behind her knees. Corwin stretched her fingers. Hazel twisted the tips of her hair into tight coils. Jenna scrunched up her mouth at the sudden loss of formal process, and Lexie shifted a mouthful of air back and forth between her cheeks.

"Blythe didn't know how to improve our odds, so she decided to start killing humans by profiling them—poorly. With that much heat on us, we'd be found out in no time. Tracking half-bloods and waiting for them to harm someone is not only a losing game, it's unethical. But taking out humans we only suspect to be werewolves is just as bad. Either way, innocent people die. We need a way to figure out who really is a werewolf without having to wait for another girl to end up like Bree. We need Lexie."

Lexie, whose mind had been wandering during Renee's speech, sat up as all eyes fell on her. She forced an uncertain grin.

"Lexie is a peacespeaker," Renee continued. "She has an ability we don't. She can see the wolves while they're dormant in human forms. With her help, we can spot them and take care of them before any more innocents have to die."

"Why isn't she called a peace-seer, then?" Sharmalee asked.

Renee paused and they all looked at Lexie, who shrugged.

"We don't know," Renee continued. "This is all fairly new to us. As far as we know, Lexie's all there is. Her mother died in the battle with the Morloc full-bloods, and unfortunately, she was the only one who had the knowledge. What we've got to work with is the some-what-questionable powers Lexie's gleaned through her dreams and memories."

Lexie fidgeted, pretty sure there were better words for it than the ones Renee used, but she didn't know what they were.

"Whoa whoa whoa," Corwin said. "We're relying on prophetic dreams to decide our strategies now?"

Sharmalee said, "She's right, Renee. How do we know Lexie isn't just crazy? No offense, Lex."

"S'alright," Lexie mumbled.

"We're going to put it to the test."

"What?" Lexie said.

"I've been trying to talk to you about it for a month now, Lex, and you've dodged me every time," Renee said. "I'm introducing some accountability. You've got to pull your weight around here if you want to stay. Let's take your powers for a test drive."

She walked to Lexie's side. "We'll find someone using your vision, we'll capture him, we'll wait for the moon, and then we'll know."

"Are we sure this is the best approach?" Jenna asked.

"Blythe took those boys' innocence when she ordered their deaths, but she also took ours. She made us murderers. Now, we are free from her tyranny and we have the chance to think for ourselves. The issue now is how we decide who we are as a pack without her telling us," Renee said. "Another girl has died, and I see no end and no easy solution. We are the only ones standing between these wolves and the women of this town."

Renee's energy increased as she spoke. She sat up straight, leveled a finger and swept it over the group. "I'm calling an end to innocent deaths. Beginning after the next full moon, the Pack plays offense."

5

LEXIE HADN'T PLANNED ON MAKING the drive out to The Cat Club. The club was smoky by design, flagrantly bucking Oregon's anti-smoking laws to provide a safe haven for the addicts. Lexie liked it, feeling that this was what a real urban venue must have felt like once, when smoky clubs were still smoky.

It was a thin crowd. She ordered a can of club soda and grabbed a chair at a table halfway between the bar and the stage. Randy walked on soon after, a single spotlight on the microphone. She wore a plaid shirt, a fedora with a red feather, and a black guitar. She greeted the crowd with a few words and began to strum. Lexie liked being able to observe Randy in this way. Acutely aware she was being watched, she seemed to actively disengage from that reality by focusing nearly all of her attention on the sounds she made. Lexie found herself rocking back and forth in her chair, plucking the soda can's tab in rhythm with Randy's downbeats.

Randy was an assertive player, though not aggressive. She hit each string with precision but no preconceptions. It took her a while to lean into the mic and sing.

I hate you for loving me so well. You've forced me to reevaluate my imaginary hell...

Lexie nodded with the lyrics and continued to sway in time. Randy's grin, no matter how wide or shrouded, always looked sly. Something about her narrow jaw and the creases around her eyes made her look as sharp and brash as a coyote. Her voice was raspy but elegant. The mic was old and warm, the amp filling the space with music like heat from a wood furnace.

After the set, Randy walked over and knelt next to Lexie's chair.

"You came," Randy said. Her hair was damp with stage-light sweat.

"Yeah," Lexie shrugged. "I try to say yes to nice invitations."

"Adventuresome?" Randy asked.

"More like a spiritual practice," Lexie joked, and Randy nodded in appreciation.

"You came alone?"

"Did you want me to bring people?"

"No, it's fine. Last week it just looked like you ran with a tight little posse."

"Oh. I guess. I mean, we're friends. We're supposed to be...more I suppose. I guess I don't really know why they want me around. I'm not sure if I belong."

"A common problem." Randy swayed back and forth, her elbows on her knees, squatting in her black leather boots and slacks. She had removed her outer shirt to reveal a white tank top and suspenders. Their black lines cut a shadow along the whiteness of her shirt, a curved band that stretched from her hips across meager breasts to her slim, rounded shoulders. Tattoos began at her jaw, stretched in swirls of black and red lines down her throat and across her chest, and joined up with a colorful chestpiece: a red heart with angel wings, stretching from sternum to shoulder in each direction. Her hat cast her eyes into shadow.

"You want anything?" Randy asked, gesturing to the bar.

"Nah, I'm good."

Randy left and returned with a non-alcoholic beer a minute later, pulling up a chair beside Lexie.

"Do you have class tomorrow?"

"Yeah."

"Bad girl," Randy said with a crooked grin.

"Are you kidding?" Lexie asked.

"I don't know, am I?"

Lexie shrugged.

"I suppose 'bad' doesn't really describe you."

"It's not obvious?"

Randy relaxed into her chair, resting her ankle on her knee, her black leather motorcycle boot catching the dim club lights in its shine. "You've got something in you, that much is true."

"Something?" Lexie squirmed, thinking about Jenna's encouragement and Renee's decree. Was her wolf so close to the surface it was detectable even by norms? Whatever piece of her willed away the wolf worked twice as hard to shove it further down.

"A thirst, maybe? For adventure, risk?"

"Thirst?" Lexie mocked.

"I can tell you're looking for something."

"Yeah, small talk."

Randy laughed, keeping her eyes on Lexie. "Fair enough."

After three seconds of silence Lexie spoke. "Where are you from?"

"Heh," Randy shrugged and pulled the brim of her hat further over her eyes. "Seattle," she said. "That's where I met the, ah—"

"Cocksucker," Lexie offered.

"Yeah," Randy smiled. "Her."

"Gotcha."

"How about you? You ever get your heart broken?"

Lexie nodded, stretching her jaw against the tightness that threatened any time Archer came up. She opened her mouth as wide as she could and let her tongue hang out. She wiggled it and stretched her lips with a long "Bleh" sound.

"Sorry," she said, finally. "I'm not being very articulate."

"And yet you're saying so much," Randy laughed.

"I'm still kind of...getting over someone."

"What's her name?"

Lexie plumbed her mind for the answer, but her name was no longer a mere denotation of a person in a space. The word "Archer" had come to attach itself not only to that woman, but a myriad of memories and systems that tangled Lexie's insides, squeezing like ratchet straps across her heart.

"It's not—" Lexie said.

"It's cool."

"Yeah."

"So then, you chasing this one still?" Randy asked.

Lexie plucked the top of her can. "I'm the one who sent her away."

"Why?"

"Good question," Lexie said, bending the can tab back and forth. "I thought it was ambition, but now I think it may have been fear." At Randy's incredulous expression, she asked, "Does that make sense?"

"You're asking the wrong person. I'm kind of a burnout, though I can appreciate ambition in theory."

"In theory?"

"Sure. I see ambition like I see a really beautiful naked man. I can appreciate the aesthetic and potential, but I'm not going to go chasing it down."

"You're pragmatic," Lexie said.

"Or a burnout," Randy laughed.

"The kind of girl my mom wouldn't have let me play with."

"Nah. Moms love me. I remind them of their wild pasts."

"Wild woman?" Lexie asked. She was flirting; it was strange.

"That's me." Randy said with a tip of her hat. Lexie assessed her and wondered what she meant by wild, now that Lexie understood a whole new definition of that word. Drinking and dancing it was not. Not anymore.

"Oh, sorry," Lexie said. "I didn't even ask, do you use female pronouns?"

"Hell yes. I'm all woman," Randy said. "A dying breed."

"Women?"

"Butches."

Lexie snorted.

"True fact. Seventy-five percent of the dykes I used to ride with are now dudes. It's the end of an era that never even really got to start."

Lexie fidgeted. She thought of Mitch and his new predilection for masculine pronouns. She thought of mentioning it, then resisted.

Randy left to begin her second set, and Lexie contemplated leaving. It would have been an easy thing to do had the club held more people. Instead, whenever Randy glanced up from her hand on the fretboard, her eyes caught Lexie's, trapping her in her seat. She squirmed with the attention, but the heat of Randy's glance held her in place.

After her set, Randy walked Lexie back to her truck.

"How did you know my ex was a 'she'?" Lexie asked. "Is it obvious?"

"Straight girls tend to be more afraid of me."

"Really?" Lexie said with a snicker. "And they don't drive out on a school night to see you, huh?"

"No, ma'am."

"So I'm either a bad girl or a not-straight one."

"Either way you win," Randy said as Lexie hoisted herself into the driver's seat. Randy stepped forward to fill the space Lexie left behind. "And me too, maybe."

Lexie smiled. "Maybe."

On her drive home, humming the refrain of Randy's song, Lexie told herself that she'd likely never seek Randy out again. In the telling, though, she knew was lying.

6

LEXIE AND RENEE WALKED ALONG Milton's main drag, the heels
of Renee's red cowboy boots clacking on the sidewalk. They stopped
under the neon sign of Uncle Mao's.

"I can't afford to go out to dinner," Lexie said.

"Don't worry. We'll be in and out. Enjoy yourself. Relax," Renee
said.

"Sure. Relax. It's what I do best."

"Har har. Do you have your knife?"

"Always."

"Cool, let's do this." Renee held open the door and ushered Lexie
inside, but Lexie hesitated.

"What if I forgot how to see them?" Lexie asked.

Renee cocked a hip and gave Lexie an incredulous look. Lexie
shrugged.

"Alright," Renee said, releasing the door and leading Lexie toward
the neighboring darkened storefront. "Try it out on me."

Lexie pulled her knife from its sheathe, holding it tight in her fist.
She closed her eyes and took a breath. When she opened her eyes, the

form in front of her rippled and shifted, like a reflection in a half-dim glass, part Renee, part wolf. She softened her gaze and let the two images merge, ghostly superimpositions.

"Got it?" Renee said, her wolf jaw moving comically with the human words.

Lexie sheathed her knife and snapped the cover closed. "Got it."

Lexie ordered a green tea and let Renee buy enough Szechwan lamb for both of them. They sat at the bar with a view into the kitchen.

Renee scanned the room and whispered, "I've been wondering about one of the line cooks here. Whenever he works the late shift, he always leaves early."

"Maybe he's got kids."

"We can speculate all we want, but you've got the ability to tell me if I'm full of shit. So let's do this, alright?"

"I'm not just going to whip out my blade in the middle of a crowded restaurant," Lexie whispered.

"You don't have to, do you? Just like, finger it or something. Get into the groove."

Ah yes, the groove.

Lexie hoarded another fork full of spicy lamb into her mouth and wiped her hands on her jeans. She let one hand rest on the handle of her knife, took a deep breath, and tried to relax.

"There he is," Renee whispered. A dark-haired man appeared at the kitchen counter. He was a small, round man with a patchy mustache, and he had to reach above his shoulders to deliver the meals to the counter for the waitstaff. He shuffled from task to task, neither frantic nor slow, just taking care of business as it happened.

"Him?" Lexie asked, incredulous.

"Just look."

Lexie narrowed her eyes trying to catch a good look at his face through hanging utensils and steaming pots. As soon as she focused on his face, he ducked behind boiling pots and full dish racks. When he stopped to garnish a plate, she drew in a breath through tight lips and tried to reach into the space between the layers of her vision. She squinted and glared, trying every trick, until a headache pressed against the backs of her eyeballs.

"No," Lexie said, shifting in her seat and picking up her fork. Her phone buzzed, and she saw a missed call from Dean Fern's office line. She pressed delete and shoveled another mound of noodles into her mouth.

"You sure?"

"Yep," Lexie said around her mouthful of noodles.

"Look again," Renee said.

She glanced toward the kitchen and shook her head.

"You're completely sure."

"Sorry, dude."

Renee sipped her tea. "You're positive?"

"No, Renee, I'm lying. The line cook and I are in cahoots to turn Milton into a new werewolf empire. He will build a wonton army, and I will rule as his lo mein queen."

Renee blew the steam off her tea with one arched eyebrow. She kept her eyes on the cook. "Don't you mean wanton?"

"I was making a Chinese food pun."

"Mm," Renee said.

Renee paid the bill, and they headed for the exit.

Lexie was staring at the back of Renee's head, trying to read her mind, when she shuffled and tripped into the back of a waiter carrying a loaded tray.

"Shit!" Lexie said, too late to course correct. Her shoulder smashed into his back. He struggled not to lose his platters of peppered squid.

"Sorry!" she cried. Renee yanked her out the door. The waiter was too distracted with recovering the heavy platter to respond, but she heard him mutter "bitch" as the door swung shut.

Through the glass pane of the door, as hazy as a mirage, a wolf form rippled at his periphery, then disappeared.

Lexie pressed her nose against the restaurant's window and fogged it with her breath.

"What are you doing?" Renee snapped.

"Him," Lexie said.

"What?"

"He's a werewolf."

"The skinny waiter?" Renee asked, peering over Lexie's shoulder. "Hardly."

"Oh, but the line cook is? Aren't I supposed to be the one with the fancy gifts?"

Renee wiped away the fog of their mingled breaths. "I'm going to go sniff him," she announced and headed into the restaurant.

Lexie watched Renee weave her full hips, covered in black leggings, through the restaurant. Lexie's eyes caught Renee's muscular haunches as she strode among the tables of townies and faculty. Her brain darted to memories of warmth and wetness, strength and stillness. She was telling her brain to shut up when she felt a heavy hand on her shoulder.

"Hey!"

Lexie jumped, her heart in her throat. She turned to see Duane Ward.

"Christ, Duane!" she shouted. "Are you really so stupid that you sneak up on girls at night on this campus?"

Duane flinched and looked to the ground, sheepish. "Sorry. I was excited. I thought you'd be happy to see me."

Lexie studied him. He looked like hell, and not just because his expression bore more angst and fear than she had ever seen on him before. He looked terrible, or at least terrible compared to what Lexie knew to be his usual, glowing self. His rich brown skin had turned sallow, his untended hair formed little naps, and the sharp flash in his eyes had gone dull. This was not the Golden Boy she had grown up knowing. She wrapped her arms across her chest and softened her voice. "I am, Duane. Just no more surprises, okay?"

He nodded, staring at his feet.

"Where have you been?"

"Kind of on lockdown. No media, no internet. My therapist said it'd be best if I eased back into things and avoided triggers for now, which isn't really easy to do in Milton." He chewed on his lips and Lexie felt a stab of shame for her own involvement in his trauma.

"Duane," Lexie flinched over his own memories of the scene, of finding Duane in that broken heap. "I'm really sorry."

He shook his head, hard, changing the vector of the conversation. "You're in Comp Lit, yeah? Want to be study buddies?" His breath was stale, but Lexie hoped it was just her overactive sense of smell and not a sign he was even worse off than he looked.

"You missed class today," she said.

"Why I need a study buddy," he half-grinned. "Don't worry, once I get my stride again, you know I'll be the one you lean on."

Duane's smile was so earnest, so wary, she couldn't say no.

"Besides, Bree Curtis and I were supposed to be partners, but her phone's been going straight to voicemail."

Lexie nearly laughed until she saw his quizzical look. He didn't know.

"Wait, really?"

"Yeah, we were study partners in the Women's Studies class that you never came to last semester. We worked well together so we're going for another round."

Lexie looked at his fragile face and took a deep breath. "She...uh...died."

Duane's face went blank. Oh god, she'd broken him.

"Duane?" she asked.

His face froze in an expression of confused horror. She reached out, but she feared touching him would trigger a cascade of trauma he wouldn't be able to contain. So she stood, arms outstretched as Duane rode out the panic her news had triggered.

Finally, he choked, "How?"

Before Lexie could answer, Renee burst out the door, "He smells totally—hey."

Duane yelped and recoiled.

Renee slouched and cast her eyes away, silent. Duane took stumbling steps back and likewise fixed his eyes to the sidewalk. Lexie hadn't even thought it was possible for people to attempt to out-omega each other, until she watched two of the most self-assured people she had ever met try to make themselves invisible.

"I'll see you this week okay, Duane? Comp Lit, right?" Lexie said finally, breaking the awkward silence.

"Sure, yeah," he said, his eyes glued to his shoes. He hurried away.

Once Duane was far down the block, Renee shook herself and opened her mouth wide, stretching her tongue. She cracked her knuckles and her neck.

"You okay?"

Renee nodded, though Lexie couldn't agree with her assessment. She looked caught in her own head.

"He'll be okay," Lexie said.

Renee laughed bitterly and shook her head. "Nope. He'll never be okay."

And neither would Renee, Lexie thought, watching her tumble over thoughts as they walked in silence through the town square.

"It's not your fault," she said.

Renee laughed again. "It is every bit my fault. That brother is barely clinging to his sanity because of me. And that will never change."

"He might forgive you someday," Lexie said.

Renee stopped and placed an index finger an inch before Lexie's sternum. "For him to forgive me, he'd have to know it *was* me, and for him to know that, he would have to know about werewolves. Please tell me you can see why that'd be the worst possible thing."

Lexie raised her open palms. "Okay, fine. I get it. Sheesh."

"No one—*no one*—gets to know about werewolves except for us. As far as Duane knows, a big Rare is responsible for the deaths of his frat brothers, and that's how it's going to stay, alright?"

"I didn't say we'd tell Duane about werewolves," Lexie mumbled.

"We've all got trauma, Lex. He'll deal with it just like the rest of us do," Renee said.

"How's that?"

"Time, distance, community, and activism," Renee sighed. "In that order."

Enough of Lexie's classmates at Wolf Creek High had parents stationed in Afghanistan and Iraq that the principal brought in a veteran to give a speech about PTSD. She thought about mentioning it to Renee, but as she struggled to keep up with each of Renee's long strides, she figured it'd be better to wait until later.

As they passed the plaque naming the park, Renee finally spoke. "He's totally gay."

"Duane? No way. He's just traumatized."

"Not Duane, the waiter. He's totally gay. I sniffed it on him."

"Gay? You can't smell gay," Lexie said. "...Can you?"

"No, but you can sure as hell smell vagina, and there wasn't a whiff of it anywhere near him. And there's no such thing as a celibate were-wolf." Renee took a sharp left. Lexie hurried after her. "You sure you saw what you think you did?"

"As sure as I can be about any of it. He couldn't have killed Bree, though. He's so skinny. And...gay. That doesn't make sense on so many levels."

"How many wolves does that make so far?"

"Three. The full-blood that attacked me, and two half-bloods, at least one of them gay."

"And then..."

"There's all of us." Renee and Lexie looked to each other for a moment, unwilling to follow that thought any further.

"Archer," Renee said.

"Who's been gone," Lexie said.

"True. We'd all be climbing the walls if we smelled her back here."

"We would?"

"Oh yeah. Purebloods will fuck your shit up. They smell like god having sex in a Jacuzzi filled with red wine and chocolate."

"That explains so much," Lexie said with wide eyes.

"Doesn't it?" Renee said.

"Besides..." Lexie said. "Archer couldn't."

Renee shook a cigarette out from her pack and stopped to light it. "Well, someone did."

Their footsteps echoed across the empty square, the fresh, foggy air fighting against the harsh perfume of Renee's cigarette. Lexie sniffed the air, just for something to do. Before she could stop herself, before she even thought about it, Lexie asked a question.

"Why am I here?"

Renee arched an eyebrow. "Like on this planet? Meaning of life shit?"

Lexie chewed on her lip. "No, like with you guys. Part of the Pack. Is it just because of these peacespeaking powers?"

"Partially yes," Renee shrugged. "But we like you. I like you."

The night of their kiss seemed long enough ago to be part of a remembered dream, not her life. Lexie snorted. "Why?"

Renee took a long drag from her cigarette before stubbing it out on the ground and placing the remaining filter in her pocket. "Let's cut through the quad." Renee reached into her jacket and pulled a fresh cigarette from her pack. "I think a better question is why you don't think you belong."

Renee's profile reflected the oranges, blues, and whites of electric lighting. Her brown skin added its own warmth to the slips of color that glanced her nose, cheekbones and forehead. Lexie liked Renee the most this way: standing tall, moving smoothly, her stride carrying her down a brick path as it would carry her through a grand hall or a fashion runway. She presented no airs, no different faces for public spaces versus private. The word that teased through Lexie's mind as she took in Renee's beauty was "integrity," in a literal sense.

Four months ago, walking alongside Renee, Lexie felt gangly, awkward, and ugly. She had witnessed her own self in reflection, drawing a forced comparison between their two disparate bodies. Now, after sharing a home, meals, and community with her, Lexie stopped seeing Renee as a mirror and began to see her as woman unto herself. Sometimes, like now, Lexie's insecurities would slither into the space between them, but she was determined to not let them mean anything. She would stop letting them seize whatever moments she and Renee might share.

"I've lived with you all for months, and I still feel like a stranger. An alien," Lexie admitted.

Renee lit her cigarette and took a hearty drag. "To be fair, you came into our home at a particularly squirrely time." Renee paused, and Lexie chuckled agreement.

"Blythe worked really hard to keep us unified. She was the common denominator for all of us. Now that's she's gone, we all trust each other less, but we like each other more. Does that make sense?"

"Probably."

"Now, we all have to work hard to stay unified. That's what real communities do. No mother figure telling us to kiss and make up. We have to prioritize it without anyone telling us to."

"But where do I end up in all that?"

"Honestly, if I had to peg you, I'd call you a lone wolf who never had a family. You're..." Renee chuckled. "...Undomesticated. You don't know if a pack like ours works for you. But if you're curious, you may as well give it a chance.

"The key is sticking around. We're working together on this. If, after we bag this killer Rare, you still don't feel like you belong, then I'll help you figure out where you want to go. How's that sound?"

Lexie smiled. "You're not going to fight for me?"

"I don't fight for people. I fight with them."

7

RANDY CALLED JUST BEFORE MIDNIGHT, just when Lexie was ready to give up trying to figure out the proper spelling of "hegemonic." She hoped she wouldn't have to pronounce it out loud tomorrow when she turned in her first essay for her Comp Lit class. She smiled when Randy's name blinked from her cellphone's glowing screen.

"You're terrible at responding to texts, you know."

"Yeah." Lexie smiled.

"I'm going to invite you somewhere, but I don't want you to freak out."

"Freak out? Why would I?" Lexie asked, doodling daggers on her empty notepad.

"It's a club called the Thorny Rose. Heard of it?"

"No." Images of English pubs or burlesque clubs flitted through her mind.

"Just Google it. But know that I have no attachments to it, I just think it might be good for you."

Randy had made it sound like shredded wheat or some fresh air, but when Lexie typed the words "Thorny Rose Oregon" into her web browser, she wasn't sure what Randy meant by "good for you." The website was red text on a black background, making Lexie's eyes ache from strain. Centered on the page was a single picture of a woman's back covered in lash marks, like red tiger stripes.

Below were testimonials: "A breath of fresh air for womyn in the scene." –DM

"Finally, a place where I can let myself go." -KD

She shut her computer and took a breath, scanning her empty room as if anxious of being watched. Was she on the school's network? She'd double check. But first, she reopened her computer and looked again at the website with the fair woman's damaged flesh. It looked as though her skin struggled to hold back something just beneath.

The computer beeped at her as an email from her linguistics professor Dr. Rindt popped into her mailbox.

DEAR MS. CLARION, it read, I WOULD LIKE TO SCHEDULE AN APPOINTMENT WITH YOU DURING MY OFFICE HOURS ON WEDNESDAY FEBRUARY 20TH AT 2PM. PLEASE CONFIRM BY REPLYING TO THIS MESSAGE.

Lexie pulled a face and deleted the email, just as her phone buzzed with a text: PICK YOU UP AT 9 FRIDAY, YEAH?

Lexie thought about the blessed pain of the tree cutting into her back, which carried deeper pains to her mind: the terrifying joy of feeling Archer's full hand within her, the stone pressing into her spine as Archer lay atop her, the steely regret of watching Archer drive away. Lexie reached back to stroke her shoulder where the tree's scars should've been. Her flesh was smooth.

Lexie stared at the computer screen and the faceless, proud woman. She picked up her phone and typed the letter "K," then pressed SEND.

8

THE DEN BUZZED WITH ACTIVITY, but Lexie stood in her closet, bereft. Sharmalee danced down the hallway, waving a stick of incense outside Lexie's room.

"Hey Lexie," she called.

"Hey," Lexie groaned.

Sharmalee poked her head through the doorway. "You okay?"

"I have a date. Trying to figure out what to wear."

"Tonight?! It's the full moon!"

"I'm not going to turn, Sharm. It's pointless to try, and I don't want to get stoned alone and watch YouTube videos all night like last time."

"Fair enough." Sharmalee entered and peered into Lexie's closet. The selection consisted of mostly a pile of dirty shirts and a few sweaters half-falling off their hangers. She cocked an eyebrow. "What are you going for?"

Lexie made a face. "Rebound?"

"Oh, yeah, totally. Forget this," Sharmalee said, dismissing the closet. "Wait here."

Sharmalee walked around the corner to her room, wafting the incense over her as she went.

Lexie turned to her mirror and sectioned her hair. She needed to look like she knew what she was doing, like she belonged among the motorcycle dykes and leather women. She was tying the first braid when Sharmalee reentered, clothes in hand.

"Nu-uh. Hair down."

"She's picking me up on her motorcycle."

"Hair in a loose braid, then. Undo it when you get to the club. Here, try this."

She threw a shirt at Lexie: a simple black-ribbed tank top with red floss serging at the edges. It was nothing too special, and it was soft.

Lexie tried it on while Sharmalee watched. It fit with just the right amount of give and cling, making even her boyish top look curvy.

"Yep," Sharmalee said, then threw a pair of jeans at her. "These haven't fit me since oh-six. You can keep them."

Lexie checked out her reflection and was weirdly pleased. Except—

"I look straight," Lexie said, grimacing.

Sharmalee giggled and flipped her hand, dismissing Lexie's concern. "You look like a baby dyke."

"Is that a good thing?" Lexie asked.

"Yes," Renee shouted from downstairs.

Lexie and Sharmalee laughed. Hazel bounded down the hallway and peeked through her doorway. "Baby dykes are the puppies of the lesbian world. Everyone's gonna want to pet you."

"Yep," Sharmalee said. "Shake out your hair and put on a little liner. It's perfect." Hazel nodded and ran back down the hall.

"What about a jacket? I can't wear a flannel." Lexie paused. "Right?"

Sharmalee looked Lexie up and down and wiggled her mouth, thinking. "Yeah, okay."

She gave the waning stick of incense to Lexie and walked downstairs to the hall closet.

"Renee!" she called. "Come here, please!"

Lexie stuck the incense in an empty soda can and dug around her limited makeup bag for some eyeliner. She stroked the pencil along her lashes in jagged, awkward lines. She grabbed for some tissues and tried to unfocus her hearing so as to ignore Sharmalee and Renee as they spoke downstairs.

Lexie was ambivalent about not running with the Pack tonight. Relief wrestled with hurt, and a whole mixture of resentments accompanied the contradictory emotions. She wanted to blame everyone for pushing her aside, even when it was she who had figured out a new and subtle way to exclude herself from their adventures. She tried to pretend she was doing better, stepping into her fears and becoming stronger, but she couldn't; it just wasn't true. She was running like always, and Randy was just a convenient excuse.

Lexie wanted to change her plans. She couldn't. She'd already said yes to Randy, and the girls of the Pack...didn't seem to care. She turned away from the mirror and dug for un-crunchy socks in the pile of dirty laundry.

A minute later, Sharmalee stood at the door frame, offering up a black leather jacket. "Here."

"Wow," Lexie said. "Really?" It looked expensive enough to make Lexie recoil for fear of somehow breaking it.

"It's no biggie, just try it."

Renee appeared and leaned against the doorframe to watch.

Lexie took it. The leather felt like velvet. She tried it on. It fit her perfectly, molding along the slopes and angles of her body when she zipped it up over her narrow frame. She shook her hair over her shoulders and glanced at the mirror, then away. She'd never thought she could look so stunning.

A scent curled up from the leather. She pulled the collar up to her nose: freesia and peroxide.

"Blythe?" Lexie asked.

Sharmalee nodded. Renee said, "It doesn't fit any of us. Her shoulders were narrow, like yours. Seems appropriate."

"Are you sure?"

"None of us are very sentimental," Renee said. "Take it."

Lexie stared at the mirror and caught the gazes of Renee and Sharmalee sharing her reflection.

"Are you sure you're going to need it?" Sharmalee asked. "The moon's like, right here."

Lexie shook her head and clipped her knife sheath to her belt, making sure the jacket concealed it. "No. I mean, I feel something, but not the irrepressible beast-something. Just a presence that I'll attempt to ignore for the next eight hours."

"Well, if you change your mind," Renee said, "we'll be running in the south woods."

"Archer's territory," Lexie said. Renee shrugged part of an apology that didn't need to happen at all. "Cool," she said. "See you in the morning."

Lexie could hear the exhaust pipe of Randy's motorcycle from two miles away. When she pulled up to the drive, the girls all went to the front door to peer out. Lexie wished she had been ready, so she could run through them, avoiding their eyes and questions. But she was lacing up her boots when Randy walked onto the porch and rang the bell.

Hazel answered. "Hi, Randy!"

"Hey, Bijou," she said with her permanently sly grin.

Hazel beckoned her in. Lexie called from the kitchen table where she was fumbling with her laces. Randy stepped into the kitchen. The Pack drifted in after her to resume their pregame preparations: Jenna making sandwiches and placing them in the fridge, Corwin bringing up fresh towels from the basement, and Mitch in the backyard, heating up the hot tub.

"Big night?" Randy asked.

Lexie offered her an awkward, closed-mouth smile. "Yeah. The girls like to tear it up once a month. Bonding."

"Did you want to reschedule? Spend time with them?"

"No, no, no." Lexie waved away the question. "I can't…handle it. It's not really my scene anyway."

"Lexie," Renee called from the basement, where she was taking fresh changes of clothes out of the dryer.

"I'll be one second." Lexie was almost relieved to leave Randy alone in the kitchen.

Downstairs, the laundry room smelled like heaven.

"We're going to try and catch some scent trails tonight," Renee said. "See if we can gather any clues."

"Be careful."

"We're going to avoid the Barrens, and the west where Bree was found, at least for now. But hopefully we'll get something farther to the east. I'll let you know what we get."

Lexie bit her lower lip and nodded. So much for last-minute re-prieves. She headed back up the stairs to her date.

They walked to Randy's bike. Lexie's shoulders tightened with each step.

Randy chuckled nervously. "You sure you're into this?"

Lexie nodded. "I just don't like leaving my truck behind. I like being—mobile."

"Do you want to take it instead of my bike?"

"No, I'm cool, I'm just..." She tried to wiggle it off. "Just a bit nervous, I guess."

"Well, you look amazing, and you smell delicious. I'm happy we're doing this."

"Me too," Lexie said, determined to mean it. "Is it going to be...?"

"You'll be fine, I promise. It's mostly bark, very little bite."

Lexie had never ridden on the back of a motorcycle before, and she wasn't keen on getting her first lesson in front of the Pack. Randy revved and Lexie squeezed the metal bar at her coccyx. The engine's vibrations rattled through her, and Lexie fought to suppress a squeal.

"Hold on," Randy said.

"I am," Lexie replied.

Randy laughed. "You're such a dude."

At the first turn, Randy made a sharp left. Lexie yelped and threw her arms around Randy's waist.

"That's better," Lexie heard Randy mutter beneath her helmet.

The Thorny Rose was nearly an hour's ride north, but the cool, dry night made the ride bearable, and the motorcycle's thrumming vibrations provided enough of a pleasurable distraction from Lexie's creeping anxiety.

Along the dark road, Lexie felt as though she were in a submarine, rolling with the curves, only able to see what the lone headlight illuminated. A low, chilly fog slithered through the trees on either side of the road. Above the forest to the east, the full moon rose. Something prickled under Lexie's skin, like an itch on the inside. She gripped her knife and swallowed hard.

She stared at the bold white disc and felt pulled to it, as though it were a Siren and she a hapless sailor, lonely, desperate, eager to feel the touch of beauty. She squeezed Randy tighter, tying herself to the mast that was this woman. She'd be willing to hold on forever if it would keep her from being rent apart on the rocks.

A few seconds later, Randy took a turn in the road, speeding past the beginnings of an on-ramp. A sign declared it part of Governor Blackwell's new highway project. For now it was just tamped-down dirt and construction barriers, but soon it would split the north woods in half. Crisscrossed along its path lay the fresh corpses of dozens of trees. Lexie's heart twitched, and she buried her face back in the leather of Randy's jacket to stifle her urge to howl their pain to the moon. The motorcycle passed the construction zone and the trees rose up again to cover the moon, freeing Lexie of its pull for the moment. She released her held breath, grateful for the respite.

The club was a cement warehouse. There was no sign and only a small, packed dirt parking lot. Lexie's anxiety welled within her. This didn't seem like the kind of place where good people would hang out.

Inside the black-painted lobby, a chemical odor punched through Lexie's sinuses, seized her skull like a vice, and pressed into a headache. She snuffed and sneezed, woozy.

"You all right?"

"Yeah, I'm just…sensitive to odors." Lexie couldn't place the smell—it was more toxic than rubber, more synthetic.

"This is a fragrance-free space. No perfumes or lotions. You should be fine."

PVC, Lexie thought in a flash. She exhaled forcefully through her nose. *Fragrance-free. Hah.*

The sounds of chains clinking and leather slapping on skin echoed from behind the next door, stealing Lexie's attention.

The lobby smelled like Freon and sweat, leather, steel, and grease. A chuckle came from the coat room.

"Well look what the cat dragged in." A spherical woman with a white crew cut and dead tooth emerged from the coat-check booth and pulled Randy into a bear hug. "Nice to see you, sweetheart," she said in a voice roughened by life and cigarettes.

Randy slapped the woman's back. "It's always great to see you. How's your boy these days?"

The woman grinned. "Blacking in the back if you want a shine."

Randy nodded. "This is Lexie."

"Well aren't you just a downy innocent," the woman said. "But not for long, eh?" She elbowed Randy in the ribs and laughed.

"You a hugger?" she asked Lexie.

"Uh...sure."

"I'm Glenda," she said, pulling Lexie into her plush torso. The smell of her freshly-polished leather vest made Lexie woozy.

"Welcome to the Thorny Rose." Glenda gestured grandly to the dark lobby. "This here's coat check. You can change out of your street clothes in the bathroom." Lexie unzipped her jacket. Glenda eyed the knife on her hip.

"We don't allow blood play here, sweetheart, but you can use your blade for intimidation and psychological play. Just be aware that a lot of folks run around barefoot, so be extra careful."

"Oh. No, I. Uh...Okay." It hadn't occurred to Lexie that they would take her knife away. She let her fingers glance the hilt for assurance.

Glenda escorted them through yet another set of heavy curtains. "Ready, youngblood?" she teased. She held the curtain back to reveal a room the size of a gymnasium decorated with chains, silver pipes, and leather. The sounds of smacks, cracks, whimpers, and moans filled Lexie's ears, so densely packed she couldn't discern one from the next. The scent of sweat assailed her, and she found her mouth pooling with saliva. She swallowed, embarrassed, though neither of the other women noticed.

A young, shorthaired person in a black leather chest harness hurried over to where they stood. "Glen, we're out of nitrile gloves in the makeout room."

"Ugh. Savages, all." Glenda grinned, that brown tooth shadowed in the low light. "Randy, I can trust you to give youngblood here the tour and rules and regs, yeah?"

"Aye aye," Randy said with a two-finger salute.

Lexie already felt overdressed in her black tank and jeans. The guests all seemed to dress by merely accessorizing their nude bodies with black leather. One severe-looking woman appeared fully dressed in a quasi-formal red latex gown, until she turned around and Lexie saw her complete rear exposed through a hole in the dress.

Randy wore a black dress shirt with a brown suede vest, pinstriped pants, and a fedora. Lexie only half listened to her reiteration of the rules, too captivated by the colorful setting to hear much beyond "Get permission before touching anyone."

The rules seemed easy enough to follow, especially since she couldn't imagine herself in the position of any these people.

"So, what are you into?" Randy asked.

Archer.

Lexie shrugged. "I don't know."

"Nothing?"

"What? I mean, puppies. Ice cream."

Randy laughed. "I meant more along the lines of—"

"I know," Lexie interrupted. "Just, I've never really put much thought into it. I like things as they come, and I guess I don't pay much attention until they're not around anymore."

The regret tied into that statement made Lexie bite her tongue.

"See anything you like?" Randy asked.

Lexie wiggled her jaw, whether out of discomfort or fear, she couldn't say.

In the corner of the room, a large cage sat empty. Lexie's eyes lingered on it until she realized she was staring. She diverted her gaze to a tiny, pale woman bound to a St. Andrew's Cross. An ample, brown-skinned woman in a black corset and purple latex skirt slapped the woman's breasts with a riding crop. The restrained woman shrieked and grunted, her skin swelling with purplish-red lines.

"Are those pleasure sounds or pain sounds?" Lexie whispered.

"Yes," Randy said.

"I don't know that I see the appeal," Lexie said.

"Give me your arm," Randy said. She placed the fingernails of her right hand lightly against Lexie's skin. "Does that feel good?"

Lexie nodded. Randy increased the pressure, so that her nails barely indented Lexie's flesh. "Now?"

Lexie nodded again.

Randy's nails dug further, burying themselves in the flesh of Lexie's upper arm. "Does it hurt yet?"

"A little bit," Lexie whispered, not wanting to draw any attention.

"But there's still pleasure there, too, right?"

Lexie nodded, watching the shadows Randy's fingers drew on her skin.

"Good," Randy said. "Feel into it. Where does the pleasure end and the pain begin?"

Lexie closed her eyes and concentrated on Randy's grip. She found the estuary in a cloudy and clear space: the pleasure a warm throbbing with a gentle tingle, the pain hard and sharp, the tingles becoming prickly shocks.

Lexie breathed into that space and savored the intermingling of those feelings. Randy dug harder, and Lexie was surprised to find not only the pain increase, but the pleasure too. It lurked just below the superficial sensation of pain. Her neck prickled as adrenaline trickled into her system. It ran through her veins, chasing the sensation, running it down and circling it. She drew air into her lungs, hard, fast. Her wolf stirred, rippling beneath the layers of pleasure and the tumult of pain.

"A little more," Randy whispered, her breath puffing at Lexie's ear, sending sizzles of pleasure down her arm to clash against the sharp cut of Randy's nails.

Lexie breathed deep through her nose, not wanting to cry out. She exhaled through o-shaped lips and felt her wolf begin the slow rumble of a growl.

But the pleasurable pain Randy inflicted confused Lexie, and in the space between the layers of pleasure and pain emerged doubt. She wasn't sure why she was here, what she was expecting to feel. She told herself she was fooling herself with this distraction. Randy wouldn't solve anything, this pain wouldn't heal her. She needed something else, more elusive, more personal, less carnal.

The prickly pleasure swelled again, and Lexie spoke. "Stop."

Randy's grip eased; Lexie's muscles relaxed. Her blood pumped hot where Randy had gripped her. Lexie looked at her arm and saw four crescent indentations. The white of her skin gave way to pink, then purple as her blood swelled to the damaged area.

She savored the adrenaline high that came with it—a mix of relief and high-alert. She rubbed her wound.

"All right?" Randy asked.

Lexie nodded, intrigued by this sensation, though she was not sure she was grateful for it.

"Cool. I'm gonna go grab a quick smoke," Randy said. "You okay alone?" Lexie smiled. "Take a look around. See if you find anything you like. Nobody bites. Unless you ask them to." Randy winked and headed for the front.

Below Lexie's feet were rubber mats that made each step spring. She had a flash of running through the woods with Archer, pine needles springing beneath each paw step.

She inhaled; her high dissipated into alertness. She wandered to the corner with the empty cage and stepped inside. She grabbed the bars over head and shook her weight. The steel didn't budge. This was no mere party favor. From behind her, Lexie heard a metal clang. She whipped her head around to see a woman in a sling struggling until her chains rattled. Her hands were bound behind her back, and her black hair matted to her sweat-streaked olive skin. What had once likely been beautiful makeup now streamed down her face in rivers of black mascara and a smear of red lipstick. A blonde-goateed person stood in front of the woman in jeans, a leather vest, and a leather motorcycle cap. Lexie was unable to discern the person's gender, even further confounded by the huge dildo that rose from their open fly. The person held the woman's hair in a tight fist and forced her mouth onto the dildo. Behind the dangling woman, a large, bald, bare-breasted woman slipped a purple latex hand between her legs.

The scene troubled Lexie, but the woman looked euphoric, even as she gagged and coughed.

"Tonic?" Randy said, making Lexie jump. She glanced back and forth between Randy and the strung-up woman and fumbled for a word.

"Thanks," she finally managed.

"You like this cage?" Randy asked. "I know the guy who makes them down in Cali. Kinky motherfucker. Does great work, yeah?"

"It's the real deal," Lexie said. "I don't think I could break this apart with a chainsaw."

"I suppose that's kind of the point."

"What do you mean?"

"Well, all this play is psychological, though some of it comes with physical sensation. If I locked you in a chintzy dog crate, you'd probably be more rapt with figuring out how to break it rather than surrendering to the experience. Most of this whole thing," Randy said, gesturing to the room, "is upholding the illusion so you can give yourself over to the experience."

"What illusion?"

"That you're powerless," Randy said, nodding to the black-haired girl in the sling. "Or, that you're all-powerful." Her gaze shifted to the person with the goatee. "Both are lies, but here, you can let yourself believe they're true. And that's where the magic happens."

Lexie watched the bound girl gag and fight against her restraints. Both her frustration and her joy seemed real, their synergy driving her to ecstasy.

Randy pulled Lexie into a kiss. Her practiced lips artfully tugged on Lexie's. Lexie opened her mouth wide and let Randy's tongue tumble onto hers. They kissed with the insides of their mouths, locked and playing with pressure, their tongues doing all the work. The sharp cracks of leather against flesh filled Lexie's ears, and she willed herself to relax into Randy's strength.

"C'mere," Randy winked. She dragged her fingernails down the tender flesh of Lexie's forearms to grasp her hands. She lifted Lexie's arms aloft and placed her hands on the top bars of the cage.

"Hold the bars," Randy growled. "If you let go, I'll stop."

Lexie's heartbeat quickened. The wolf paced, eager to confront the threat.

Randy pressed her mouth against Lexie's, hard. Her lips were cool and firm. Her kiss was like a sharp intake of breath: a dart and a dodge.

Lexie felt the heat of her dampening groin and the steel bars against her palms. The collection of screams, grunts, and moans in the room drowned her brain in the delighted anguish of strangers, allowing her to slip outside her own mind and hide in the cacophony.

Randy grabbed Lexie's hair in her fist and pulled, taking her exposed throat in her jaws. Not like Archer, Lexie thought. Not at all. She was rough where Archer was gentle, aggressive where Archer relented.

Randy was hitting all the right notes, but she wasn't listening to Lexie, else she would have noticed her hesitation, the passive resistance that kept her from giving in. Lexie tried to release Archer's tawny image from her mind, to replace it with the cool black and white of her new, leather-clad seducer. Randy's teeth bit into her neck: hard against soft skin, grinding muscles and tendons. They clenched in response. Inside Randy's jaws, she recognized the same power that teased her that night in the forest, the allure of strength that could overpower her. She felt the beginnings of panic, but Lexie told it to quiet and it did.

Lexie's breathing quickened. Randy's hand found the crotch of Lexie's jeans and pressed against the moisture there.

"Naughty girl," she purred.

Lexie rubbed her cheek against Randy's ear, wanting to speak the word "Yes," but failing. She removed her hands from the bars, and Randy flinched.

"Y'alright?"

Lexie scanned the room for curious eyes and found none; everyone was enraptured with their own scenes. She grabbed Randy's wrist and forced her hand down her jeans. Randy searched Lexie's face. Lexie met her gaze, returning her grip to the bar above her head. She closed her eyes and willed her mind to go blank—without allowing her wolf to take hold.

Randy made a sound that wasn't quite a chuckle. Her fingers slid against Lexie's flesh. The clinks of chains and slapping skin dissolved into the rhythm of Randy's breath in her ear. Lexie let herself fall into the sensation, releasing her memories and fears into precious white noise.

Lexie followed the trail Randy led her down, using her hips and her moans to push her ahead, and then running to catch up. She could run all night like this, mouth open wide and grinning, Randy's fingers coaxing her along. But something was catching up with her. It matched her steps, gaining ground with each pace. It was closing in. Lexie squeezed her eyes shut, willing it away as she had before. It didn't listen. She heard its paws breaking branches beneath its steps, its hoarse breath hot on her neck. Its teeth were just close enough to...

"Stop." Lexie released the bar and grabbed Randy's wrist.

Randy stopped but didn't remove her hand.

"You all right?" Randy asked, voice clipped.

"I just...feel a little out of control," Lexie said.

"That's kind of the point, sweetheart."

Lexie shook her head, and Randy eased her hand out of her jeans.

"I already feel out of control all the time," Lexie whispered. "I don't think I need your help making it worse."

Randy sighed and wiped her palms on her pants. "I'm gonna go smoke." She didn't wait for Lexie to offer to join her.

Lexie wandered to the front and poked her hand through the condom jar while the coat girl fetched her jacket. For a fleeting moment, Lexie wished she was in the woods with her sisters, running openmouthed through scattered moonbeams, pleasures chaste but meaty.

"How you gettin' on?" Glenda slapped a heavy hand on Lexie's shoulder. It released a little of the tension knotting there.

Lexie growled a bit under her breath.

"Randy not treating you right? Seemed like you were having a good time." Glenda set her fists on her stone-washed denim hips and gave Lexie a hard look under a concerned brow.

"She's fine," Lexie said. "It's me."

Glenda pulled a candy from her pocket and popped it in her mouth, listening.

"I feel a little out of control."

"Alcohol? Drugs?" Glenda asked with a no-nonsense, non-judg-mental tone.

Lexie grimaced. "No. Just me. My body. My mind. Stuff." She laughed again, embarrassed at airing such 'stuff' to a stranger.

"Well, you look pretty in control to me. Maybe a bit too much for your own good."

"How can you tell?"

"That's usually what brings people here. Well, it's number three on the list, after curiosity and a fierce need to get laid."

Lexie laughed. "Number two might be more like it. And number one too, I guess."

"Well, hate to say it, youngblood, but all three tend to go pretty well together. Randy's a good egg. I've seen her beat on ladies, and she's pretty dern excellent at it. She'd be a good one."

Lexie lowered her voice. "I don't know what I need, but I don't think it's that."

"Well then," Glenda said with another friendly shoulder slap. "I think when people get into a situation like yours, they know exactly what they need, they just aren't admitting it to themselves. You just gotta tell your brain to shut the fuck up and follow your gut."

"That seems dangerous."

"Usually is," Glenda said with a sure nod. "But that's the fucking point isn't it?"

"Of BDSM?" Lexie asked.

"Of life!" Glenda said with a hearty laugh. "Everything worth doing is a little dangerous. You'll see."

On the ride home, Lexie wrapped her arms tightly around Randy's torso and leaned into the curves. She didn't fight or shift her weight. She followed like a dancer guided across the floor by a skilled lead. She found the ride far more pleasant for it. The motor vibrated between her legs, and she sank her haunches around the seat, losing herself in the hearty thrum of the engine.

Randy hadn't said much between the cigarette and their depar-ture. Lexie knew she'd hurt Randy's feelings by ending their scene so quickly, but she didn't particularly care. She'd felt out of control with

Archer, but she had also felt safer. She knew she'd give herself over to Archer any time. Randy, not so much.

Lexie looked to the apogee of the sky, finding the white pearl of the moon. It found her back. The white light bathed them, its reflection adding a sheen to everything: chrome, leather, exposed skin, and the moonstone in her knife. The gem shone as though it were sentient, magical, somehow more than it appeared. A well of nausea crept up her throat. She buried her face into Randy's shoulder blade, hiding from the moon and what it begged her to become.

At a lonely stop sign five miles outside of Milton, Lexie raised her head. A metallic tang drifted through the cold, fresh air. Randy lifted her visor and said, "What's wrong?"

Before she knew why, Lexie said, "I need to get off."

"We're five minutes away from your place. Can't you hold it?"

Lexie removed her helmet and leapt off the motorcycle, running to the edge of the road. A deep ditch separated the pavement from an incline down to a large marsh dotted with young pines. She sniffed the air.

It smelled of wet rot, and running through it was a blazing throb of metal and salt. Blood.

She leapt over the ditch and into the mud. Randy shouted after her.

She ran, marking her pace with the trees, and stopped where the ground sloped down to a pond. A maggot-pale shape lay amidst the tall grasses: a dead man, his guts shining in the moonlight, a gash from a claw widened by feeding. The blood pooling in the chasm of his torso mirrored the pond just beyond, black and glimmering.

Randy shouted from the road. "Lexie what the hell—?"

Something rustled in the shadows at the curve of the pond. Lexie crouched, training her eyes on the shadow, struggling to find its scent.

A shaky growl burbled in the cold, dry air.

"Lexie?" Randy's shout echoed from the road.

Lexie drew her knife from its sheath, hopeful it would work on another wolf as well as it worked on her own.

"Lexie!" Randy shouted again. Lexie snarled and silently pleaded for Randy to stay where she was. *I got this*, she thought, willing it to be true. She didn't know where this bravery was coming from. Just months ago, her instincts would have told her to flee, but now a different, wordless voice goaded her to move toward the shadow with the will to fight.

She stepped forward and caught a whiff of the wolf's scent. He was restless, unsure whether to fight or flee. Lexie would decide for them both.

She faked; he braced. He growled a warning, but Lexie didn't flinch.

Her mind flashed to the dungeon, to the woman in the sling. *Dominate*, her mind roared, as if it were a simple concept. Dominate, because that is what you're meant to do right now. Simple as that. Lexie stood. The wolf flinched. He wasn't so big, Lexie thought. Only two-thirds the size of the one she fought before: four feet tall and maybe four-hundred pounds. The size she was when she changed.

Her grip tightened on the hilt of her knife. Piece of cake.

She leapt into the shadows. The wolf dodged and ran. The marshy ground made them both clumsy. She tried to track him with her nose, but the breeze kept slithering in odd directions. He hid behind tree trunks as Lexie stalked sideways. She heard her breath, and his, and Randy's nervous key-jingling back on the road.

The wolf lunged at Lexie from his hiding place, but he fell short. With a rabid cry, Lexie pounced, aiming her knife for his spine, but catching a bony shoulder blade. The knife glanced off the bone, slicing a gash through fur and skin. He squealed. Lexie slipped in the mud and fell. The wolf swung his heavy head at Lexie's prone body, sneering and snapping. Lexie raised her arms in defense just as he dropped to the ground in convulsions. His wolf form slipped and flickered, giving way to a human body.

In a moment everything silenced except for Lexie's heavy breaths.

The boy lay naked on his side, shivering, then crying.

Lexie turned to face him. His head rested on the marshy ground. The moonlight glanced off his corn-silk hair. Blood and mud caked the pale skin of his torso. She recognized the cluster of freckles at his temple and the smooth upward curve of his nose.

"Stefan?" Lexie whispered.

Stefan, the boy she let live when her Pack commanded his murder. Guilt stabbed her gut.

He raised his head, his tears falling freely.

"Oh, oh, Stefan." She crawled to him and took him in her arms, the knife still clenched in her left hand and the blade flat against his bare back.

Lexie groaned. "What did you do, Stefan?" she whispered. Had she made the wrong choice when she let him live? Should she have done what the Pack commanded and offed him before he hurt anyone else?

His sobs came freely. "If I told you he deserved it . . ."

Lexie sighed and stroked Stefan's naked back. He felt as fragile as an infant and as sinewy as a street cat. "Did he?" Lexie whispered.

Stefan nodded vigorously through his heaving sobs and pressed his cheek to Lexie's chest.

Lexie glanced over at the man's glistening viscera. "Okay," she said, wiping tears from Stefan's cheek. "For now."

Randy called out from beyond the trees, "Lexie? Are you okay?"

"We're okay," Lexie called. "Where are your clothes?" she asked Stefan.

Stefan gestured to a turnoff from the road hidden by trees. A silver Jaguar sat cold and still.

"Were you in it?" she asked. Stefan nodded, his face streaked with tears.

"He picked me up. And things got . . . wrong."

Lexie sighed hard. "Okay, Stefan, listen. If the cops find you, you say you met him online and had a date tonight, and that he dropped you off at eleven. Okay?" Lexie gripped his chin and stared into his eyes. "You got that?"

Stefan shook his head. "They'll find out."

"They won't," Lexie said, stroking his cheek. "No one knows about us. What we are. Okay? You'll be okay. The cops will come and they'll ask you questions but they'll know that a Rare wolf did it and *not you*, okay?"

Stefan whimpered and nodded.

Randy tromped through the marsh to where Lexie and Stefan lay together on the ground. She saw the corpse and stifled a shout.

"I'll explain later. Can we get him home?" Lexie said.

Randy stared aghast at Lexie clutching Stefan. "Not with that!" Randy said, gesturing to the corpse laying exposed in the moonlight.

Lexie shot Randy a cold look. "They were attacked by a Rare. We need to get Stefan home. Can you carry both of us on your bike?"

Randy seemed to have no choice but to nod, stunned and silent. She dropped Stefan at the back door to his house and took Lexie back to the Den. They stood on the creaky porch, the fog descending, a slow erasure of the sky and scenery.

"What was that?" Randy asked, finally.

"Bad luck. Bad timing. Bad wolf," Lexie said.

"Did that kid kill the man?"

Lexie chewed her lips. *In a manner of speaking.* "No. A Rare did."

Lexie zipped up her jacket as far as it would go and shoved her hands in the pockets. She didn't have any more words to address any of it. She was learning to just trust word and instinct. Integrity had a certain scent that Lexie couldn't parse, but she understood nonetheless. She'd smelled it on Stefan.

"Some night," Randy said, dropping her eyes to the porch and digging her hands in her pockets. She turned and wandered back to her bike, muttering something about needing a drink. Randy sped off into the night. Lexie watched from the porch, her breath fogging in the street-lamp glare.

Lexie was dreaming of drowning when a clatter shook her from her sleep, like hailstones hitting her window.

"Lexie," a muffled slur came from the backyard. Delirious, Lexie scanned the voices of the Pack, wondering who would be disturbing her so late. No one would even be home yet. There was still night and moonlight left. Another clatter hit her window. Not hail. Pebbles. A plea followed, and Lexie realized it was Randy.

Lexie stumbled to her window and looked out. Randy stood in the yard. As Lexie watched, she threw a fistful of gravel at Corwin and Sharmalee's darkened window.

"Randy?" Lexie called.

Randy started and swept her glance past all the windows before seeing Lexie eight yards to the right of her target. "Can you let me in?" Randy asked.

"Why?" Lexie asked.

"I just…. What was…? Can we talk?"

"We can talk," Lexie said warily, pushing open the window. She pulled her blanket tighter around her and leaned on the sill.

"Let me in."

Lexie knew it was a simple request, but it was too odd to be wrenched from her dreams like this, by a new, strange person, at her house, before the morning's frail hours.

"What do you want, Randy?"

Randy stumbled and whined. "What's up with you, Lex? What was that all about?" Her language was halting and clumsy. From the grass below, Lexie could smell a queasy mixture of whiskey and bile.

"It was…just a thing. Just part of who I am."

"Part of you," Randy repeated. "Please let me in. I'm scared."

Lexie hesitated and scanned her bedroom floor for a t-shirt. "I'll come out."

She crept down the stairs in a t-shirt and pajama pants, sliding open the back door and meeting Randy on the deck.

"Randy?" Lexie asked with more than a hint of concern.

"You scared me tonight, Lex," Randy said, her brow furrowed. "You were acting so weird. And so mean."

"Yeah, I'm—" Lexie wanted to come clean, but Randy was still too new in her life; she didn't know if she could trust her, though she wanted to. "I have things I should tell you."

Randy fell to her knees and wept. "I'm so confused."

"Randy, it's okay." Lexie patted Randy's head.

"No it's not. There was a dead guy…."

Randy clung to Lexie's legs like a koala. Lexie grew impatient. She wasn't sure if it was trauma or booze that was making Randy so maudlin.

"Come on. Stand up, Randy." She pulled her to standing and Randy shoved her mouth against Lexie's.

Lexie pushed her away. "Randy, quit it."

"Can I stay here tonight?" she begged.

Lexie pushed. Not hard, but enough to break the contact with Randy. "No. You need to go home."

"I'm scared," Randy said, reaching for her.

"You'll be fine. Come on, let's go." Lexie extricated herself from both Randy's grip and her sleepy misapprehensions. She pressed her palm into Randy's sternum and forced her to her feet. With another gentle push, Lexie forced Randy backwards down the steps to the grass. "Good night, Randy." Lexie stepped back into the house, closing and locking the sliding door.

Randy had no time to react before she was in the dark backyard, alone. She laughed once and then ran to the deck. "Lex, come on. I was just playing."

"Go play somewhere else," Lexie said through the glass.

"Come on. Lex, this isn't like you. Be nice."

"You don't know anything about me. Nothing real."

"I don't understand."

"Obviously," Lexie sighed.

"Please open the door."

"No."

"God! Why do you have be such a bitch!" Randy kicked the door with her heavy boot twice. The glass shuddered.

"If you're trying to get me to open the door, you're doing it wrong," Lexie said.

Randy sighed hard. "I'm sorry, Lex." She let her head rest on the door. Lexie felt the glass vibrate with Randy's breath. "Can't you just tell me what happened?"

Lexie shook her head. "No. I really can't." The truth of the admission twinged like a toothache.

"I'm a fuck-up," Randy said at last, her voice gravelly and shame-filled. "I'm a fuck-up. But with you—you make me feel like less of that. I felt cool tonight. I felt like you liked me. I like you."

Lexie sighed and squeezed her eyes shut. "We just met, Randy. I'm not the me you saw tonight. Not really. You like the lie of me."

"It's not a lie. You're wonderful. You're so much better than me." Randy placed her open palm on the glass, begging for Lexie to touch it.

"That's not true, Randy. And it's why this isn't going to work. Go home." She turned and ran up the stairs, back to bed.

The glass door rattled when Randy leaned against it and slid to the ground, where her sighs turned into silent sobs. Lexie curled up and pulled her pillow over her head.

9

"BIG NIGHT?" RENEE ASKED, A steaming cup of coffee in her hand, when Lexie stumbled into the kitchen.

"What?" Lexie asked, grimacing at the sunshine and Renee both.

"Why was there a person passed out on our deck this morning?"

"Oh, fuck," Lexie said, shuffling for the coffee pot. "Forget it. I can handle it."

"I know you can handle it. I'm just wondering why you didn't."

"I didn't realize she'd passed out."

"Regardless," Renee said, pausing to blow the steam off her mug, "when we got back this morning, I nearly clawed that bitch to death."

"Shit," Lexie said, filling her mug to the brim.

"If I wanted drunk assholes passed out in my hall, I'd live in a frat house," Renee said.

They both flinched as she said those last two words. Since the night it happened, no one had spoken directly about the Phi Kappa Phi brothers Renee killed in service to Blythe's insanity.

Now those words seemed to conjure their ghosts, and Renee's forehead creased with the their weight. Lexie wondered if she should say something to try to assuage Renee's guilt, but she feared saying the wrong thing, and she let that be an excuse to keep her mouth shut. Lexie thought instead of Duane, the one who survived.

"Just be more careful when you're bringing home strays," Renee continued.

"She's just a woman."

"This isn't a gender thing. It's a Pack thing. You can never know where a person's loyalty lies. You gotta look after your own," Renee said. "You dig?"

Lexie scrunched up her mouth, nodding. "I dig." She took a healthy, burning sip of the sweet and bitter brew, then set the mug down. She grabbed her hair at the nape of her neck and started braiding. "I don't want her to come back anyway, and I don't know how to say it."

"You just say it. You say it until they hear it." Renee picked up her phone and started texting.

"Easier said than done."

"Well yeah. Even more important then."

Lexie rubbed her still-sleepy eyes and dug through the refrigerator, pulling out a thick stick of salami and block of cheese. She unwrapped them both, holding them stacked one on top of the other in a fist, and bit. She chewed, slow and earnest, looking up, thinking.

The silence stretched on, broken only by Lexie's chewing and Renee's texting.

"I found Stefan last night. He killed a man," Lexie said.

"What?!"

"He said the dude was a bad guy. He insists it's the first time he's killed. Or, remembered killing, at least."

"Shit." Renee slammed her phone on the countertop and rubbed her forehead.

"And Randy saw the body."

"Double shit."

"Yeaaaaah," Lexie said, shoving the rest of the meat into her mouth to shut herself up.

"We can't let any more humans know about this."

"She doesn't know about the werewolf bit. I told her a Rare attacked them both."

Renee rubbed her lips together. "Regardless, if word gets around that werewolves are Rare wolves and responsible for these deaths..."

You're screwed, Lexie thought.

And Renee replied to her unspoken curse: "We're *all* doomed."

"Got it. I'll take care of it." Lexie recentered the cheese on the salami. "How about you?" she asked, noting the puffiness around Renee's eyes and the clear scent that she hadn't showered since the Pack's run last night. "Rough night?"

"Naw. It was all right. I'm just...I'm thinking about Bree. About what the Pack can do."

"Any ideas?"

"Thoughts, none of them solutions."

"Can't we just go after the one full-blood we know exists? The one that attacked me probably took out Bree, too."

"That's the thing. We've never hunted a full-blood before. Only half-bloods like us, only by catching them off guard as humans and forcing changes by beating the living shit out of them. I wouldn't even know how to go about catching a full-blood," Renee said. "They're much bigger, much stronger. Much more...everything."

"My dad was in the wolf-hunting business for twenty-some years. Why don't I ask—" Her sentence was interrupted by a beep and a buzz. Renee grabbed her phone from the kitchen counter. She read, smiling, and began typing a response.

Lexie sighed.

"What?" Renee said.

"Fucking phones," Lexie grumbled.

"You're no Luddite. You've got a cell."

"Archer doesn't," Lexie growled. "All day, every day, I watch people texting their friends or getting voicemail from their friends or fucking their fucking friends! And my girlfriend doesn't even have a fucking phone. Ex. Ex-girlfriend." She sighed. "I don't even know where she is, and I'm listening to everyone get laid around me all the fucking time. And I'm here dealing with drunken bullies on my back porch and a werewolf gone all feral and murder-y."

Renee held her breath for a moment, waiting for the end of Lexie's rant. "Um, A: Were you or were you not at a BDSM dungeon last night?"

Lexie rolled her eyes.

"And B: Did you not lose your virginity five fucking months ago?"

Lexie tried to protest, but Renee shook her finger in her face.

"With, C: One of the hottest women this town has ever seen, by the way. But whatever, you're magical or something. So instead I'll just mention that, D: You were the one who told her to straight-up get."

"Yeah, well, you all seemed pretty glad for it."

Renee raised her hands in mock defense. "And we didn't tell her to leave. But since you brought it up, she would have led us into battle headlong. Archer's a fighter, not a strategist. That's, if you don't mind me saying so, what got your mom killed."

"You're saying Archer killed my mom that night?"

"No," Renee said, "she's no more responsible than anyone, regardless of what Blythe said. But Archer let a lot of people make bad choices that night."

"What does that even mean?"

"It means strategy, Lex. Archer is a pureblood which means bigger and stronger than full-bloods like the Morloc, than half-bloods like us, than anyone. That's great for the big and strong, great for the lone wolves defending themselves and hunting, but for the rest of us, we just can't take what she can."

"So you'll be more careful than Archer?" Lexie asked.

Renee's eyes darkened. "I have to. We all do. Especially now."

Lexie cocked her head.

"I don't see an easy end to these attacks. The Rare that killed Bree needed a motive."

"It did?"

"There's no good reason to attack a lone woman in the woods."

"Why not food?" Lexie asked, cramming another wedge of cheese into her mouth.

"Duh. You should know," Renee said.

"People taste like soap."

"Exactly." Renee reached across the counter and took the salami/cheddar horror show from Lexie for her own hearty bite. "A Rare killed Bree and didn't eat her. What does that sound like to you?"

"A human killer, not an animal predator," Lexie said. "But she wasn't raped either."

Renee shrugged. "The reports said they aren't releasing the full details of the autopsy out of 'respect for the family', whatever that means."

"But nothing explains why Bree was alone in the woods at night in the first place."

"How do we know she was alone?" Renee asked.

Lexie nodded and chewed, hiding her thoughts behind a confused expression. She had waited too long to tell Renee about finding Bree, and to say something now would unravel the tentative trust that was forming between her and the Pack.

"Good point," Lexie said. "So then, an affair?"

"Why meet in the woods?" Renee asked.

"Maybe she was seeing a half-blood," Lexie offered.

"Bree Curtis was dating one of the most popular guys on campus, but she was slumming with a half-blood werewolf?"

"Well, apparently they aren't all trash. I mean, hello?" Lexie said, gesturing at the Den. "What else?"

"I don't know. But that seems pretty sordid for our town. Maybe a fight. Or she was set up."

Lexie shook her head. She unscrewed the top of the orange juice and tossed it back. She wiped her mouth with her bare forearm.

Renee took the orange juice from Lexie and finished the carton. "We should figure out who she was when she was alive. I'll start poking around, see if there's a link between Bree and the other girl. You go talk to Stefan. See what he knows. Just keep your head down. We don't need the cops sniffing up on us. All these attacks out of the blue, and they're gonna start paying attention to new things."

10

LEXIE LAY AWAKE IN BED, listening to the faraway howls of gray wolves and clutching her knife to her breast. The wolf inside her was anxious, wanting to sniff out the strangers and run or fight with them all. She let the howls lull her to sleep, pushing out thoughts of packs and conspiracies and desperation.

Above her, Lexie saw crisp stars break through the clouds. The sky was a deep blue, shadowed by looming pines. A breeze kicked up and the clouds began to travel and separate. In a moment, the sky was clear and broken only by clods of purple clouds.

She admired the winter sky for its clarity. Something about the cold made the night lights shine brighter. Just as she thought this, she felt teeth on her neck, sinking slowly, testing. Lexie froze. If she flinched, the wolf's jaw would tighten and tear. His musk made her eyes water, or maybe she was crying.

The alpha's teeth sank deeper, breaking flesh. Her blood cooled in the night air.

She nearly howled with the tension, but didn't have a chance. With a faint whimper and snuffle, the wolf freed her throat.

Lexie looked overhead, seeing the curve of the waning gibbous moon glint through the pine needles. A moment of shifting paws, then Lexie heard the wolf shuffle away. Lexie breathed slowly at the calm quiet before a hint of the foreign crept its way into her brain. She eased up on her elbows to see a shadow at the edge of the clearing. Her eyes strained into the darkness. The being moved into focus. It was a Rare wolf, gray and brindled, standing stoic in the shadows. She pushed herself to standing, frost cracking beneath her footsteps. A white plain expanded in all directions. Lexie stopped, listening to the wind. The sun joined the moon; the blinding landscape turned blue with a sudden solar eclipse.

The Rare didn't move, still, save for the breeze dancing across its fur. Lexie kept its eyes trained in hers, and in the periphery she saw her knife glint in the space between her body and the Rare's. Lexie looked at her knife and found she was no longer standing on frost but dried mud. The desert landscape was cracked like the skin of a long-dead corpse. Her toes dug at the dust.

The Rare stepped into the sunlight and its form receded, giving way to the lithe naked form of a woman. Archer. She stepped forward, her bare feet making no noise as they broke the caked mud into dust. Her skin glowed golden, radiating warmth into this cold, dark place. Her breath drew clouds though she didn't shiver as the breeze glanced off her naked flesh. She stepped toward the knife and placed her palm atop it. With that motion, her body returned to her true wolf form. She held her paw on the blade and beckoned Lexie over with a sweep of her heavy skull. Lexie felt chilly tears roll down her cheeks and the need for a thousand words she couldn't find. Archer silently gestured to the knife, encouraging Lexie to take it. Lexie placed her hand upon the hilt and felt the tears flow freely.

"I miss you," Lexie whispered through tear-stained throat. "So much."

She pulled the knife from beneath Archer's paw, and Archer shifted once more, back into her human body.

Archer stood, leaned to her, and pressed her lips, russet and hot, against Lexie's. The moisture of her skin made Lexie wince. Then Archer stepped away. The knife thrummed in Lexie's hands.

* * *

Lexie woke when a cello suite started playing—Jenna's alarm—and Jenna began rustling in her bed.

No one in the Pack could sleep far past the earliest riser, so Jenna's tendency for perkiness at dawn pissed everyone off before they were even vertical. Lexie buried her face in her pillows, knowing her efforts were futile. Maybe she should just give in. Go out. Experience what a dining hall breakfast tasted like.

Lexie hadn't even reached the sidewalk when she heard a car slow to meet her pace. She turned to see Randy, leaning into the passenger's seat to speak out the window.

"Lexie, can we talk?"

"I'm going to class."

"I'll drive you."

"It's less than a quarter mile away. It'll take you longer to drive." Lexie hurried down the sidewalk, but Randy kept pace.

"Please? I want to apologize."

Lexie sighed and stopped.

"I've been texting you like crazy for two weeks," Randy said.

"I'm not interested in manic drunkards right now."

"Is that what you think I am?"

"Is it?"

Randy threw the car in park and looked Lexie dead in the eyes. "That night was...crazy. Before that, I was sober for eight and a half years."

Lexie gave her a look.

"I'm not an alcoholic in the traditional sense."

"No, just in the modernist one," Lexie said.

Randy laughed. "That's funny. You're sharp."

Lexie rolled her eyes.

"Please?" Randy asked.

Lexie tugged at her braid and threw her backpack through the window, climbing into the passenger's seat.

Randy sighed and drove them toward campus.

"Okay, I just...you really freaked me out the other night, all right? I've never...seen a corpse before."

Lexie sighed. "You get used to it."

Randy laughed bitterly and shook her head. "What are you into?" Randy asked.

Lexie fidgeted with her hoodie's zipper. "A bunch of shit that you don't really want to know about."

Randy's nostrils flared, and she opened her eyes wide. Lexie feared the other woman was fighting back tears, or something worse. She just wished for a clean break so Randy would have a shot at finding a nice girl to play with instead of getting caught up in Lexie's various insanities.

"I don't want to be an accessory to... ." Randy shook her head and concentrated on changing lanes.

"You're not an accessory to anything," Lexie groaned. She gestured for Randy to turn right at the intersection and counted the seconds until they would arrive at a campus building—any campus building.

Randy shook her head. "I guess it explains a lot about you. I've been in the scene a long time and have seen some crazy-ass shit, but that was beyond."

"Wait," Lexie asked, incredulous, "are we talking about the sex, now?"

"In part, yeah. I mean, there was a lot going on between us—"

Lexie groaned.

"—a lot going on in you."

"What do you mean?"

Randy pulled herself toward the steering wheel and pushed back, nervous.

"I'm not going to say that you checked out, but you didn't really seem there anymore. I probably should've stopped a couple times when you didn't respond to my check-ins."

"Gross!" Lexie scowled. "Are you saying you thought I wasn't responsive and you *kept going?!*"

"Shit, Lex, you were having a real good time. Mega sub space. It's not like I...." Randy tightened her lips. "You weren't giving me the signs that anything was wrong until you told me to stop. Then on the way home...." She nearly chuckled. "I was not prepared for that."

"Neither was I."

"Are you kidding? You ran headlong into the dark with nothing but a seven-inch blade on you. It seemed like you had been training your whole life for something like that. That's what's got me freaking out. What the hell, Lex? Are you like a marine or a fucking ninja or some shit? That was fucking freaky."

"I'm not a ninja."

"What happened out there?"

"This is my class," Lexie said.

"What's going on with you, Lexie?"

"I don't know!" she shouted. "I don't fucking know! No one does. No one knows what my mom was trying to teach me when she sang me lullabies in dead languages. No one knows why I seem to stumble over corpses like it's my job. No one knows why I'm so fucking scared to let go of this knife! No one knows any of these things. The only one who did died when I was eight." Lexie felt the truth of her answer settle onto her muscles like a chill. "'I don't know' is the only answer I've got for you. And if that's not enough for you, then I don't know what else to say."

Randy's face was frozen in shock.

Lexie saw Randy's defensive posture and checked herself. She had whipped out her knife without even realizing, waving it in her right hand like a madwoman, feral and ready for a fight.

"What are you doing with that knife?" Randy asked in the forced evenness of someone trying to calm a wild animal.

Lexie looked at the blade, seeing her own reflection limned with honey-colored fur. She sheathed it. "I don't know that either."

The two sat in the car. An apology formed on Lexie's lips, but found no voice. Finally, she grabbed her backpack and muttered, "I have to go. I'm late." Despite not owing Randy anything, she still felt the lie bite her like an insect.

"I'll keep your secret," Randy said. "Whatever it is."

Lexie nodded. "I'll keep that in mind."

"Can we…?"

Lexie slammed the door and shook her head. "Sorry, no."

"I'll make it up to you. Promise I will."

But Lexie was already walking away. Randy hit the steering wheel with the heel of her hand then sped off.

Lexie loaded her plate with sausage, bacon, and eggs, scolding herself for taking so long to try out the whole "up in time for breakfast" thing.

She grabbed the Milton Gazette and sat alone at a round table by the windows. The dining hall was empty but for two tables. One was full of swimmers carbo-loading after their morning practice. The second was full of boys, Stefan among them. Stefan wore smudged eyeliner and his hair was streaked with glitter. He looked like he'd gone straight from the dance floor to the breakfast table. He reached to the boy next to him and tugged on his earlobe. It was the skinny waiter from Mao's. Lexie scarfed down her meal, keeping her eyes trained on the table. The waiter wore a tight white t-shirt and khakis. He giggled and batted Stefan's hand away. The boys were all playful and high energy, wolfing down their huge breakfasts and replaying scenes from the previous night.

She gripped her knife and squinted at them, needing confirmation, though she'd already held the evidence in her hands that night by the lake, in the form of Stefan's furry back. Her head hurt. She couldn't keep focus, and nothing happened, no faces within faces, just blurry boys.

None of the others noticed Lexie staring, and Stefan was making an effort to ignore her glares. She skulked until they took their trays and left. She returned to her table with another tray of eggs and bacon, with a little juice for nutrients, and flipped open the Milton Gazette to find about the new developments in the Bree Curtis case.

INVESTIGATORS ARE SAYING, the article read, MULTIPLE DIFFERENT KINDS OF WOUNDS ON BREE'S BODY INDICATE THAT HER INJURIES WERE NOT DUE TO ONE LONE RARE WOLF, BUT THE WORK OF A PACK.

11

LEXIE DOWNED THE REST OF her omelet and ran from the dining hall. She tracked Stefan's pack until they split off in various directions. She followed Stefan into Pierce Hall, one of the oldest buildings on campus, all heavy gray stone and carved redwood. His footsteps echoed on the grand staircase as he climbed his way up to the third floor. Just before he reached his classroom, Lexie collared him and dragged him into the elevator room.

"The hell?" he stumbled.

"Why didn't you tell me you ran with a pack?"

"No! I—You don't get it."

"Clearly."

"They're just some boys I hang out with." Stefan adjusted his glasses and backpack, glancing through the doorway of his class.

"Some werewolves, you mean?"

"Well…yeah," he whispered through a clenched jaw, begging her discretion.

"Is that really the first guy you killed?"

"Shh!!" Stefan covered Lexie's mouth and looked past her shoulder. "Jesus girl. Are you insane?"

"Stefan, what the fuck?"

"Lexie, I've got enough heat on me as it is, I don't need you broadcasting my business through the language hall."

"The cops came?"

"Hell yeah, the cops came, but not like the lame Milton cops. Oregon motherfucking State Police. They questioned me for forty-five minutes before Blackwell showed up."

"Wait, what? The governor?"

"Yep. Gucci-wearing son-of-a-bitch just stepped right in, palled around with the guys and then sent them away like it was N.B.D."

"Why?"

"The jo—the guy that picked me up was Governor Blackwell's senior advisor something something. Like his best guy."

"Whoa."

"Yeah," Stefan said.

"Wait," Lexie said. "If he was Blackwell's right hand, why did he send the cops *away*?"

Stefan scanned the hall outside the doorframe. "Must we hash this out in a public hallway?"

Lexie glared at him. "Yep."

Stefan groaned and stretched his neck. "Fine. That guy...the one I—you know—he was a notorious shitball. Some of the guys warned me not to go on a date with him, but I did, and...everyone was right. The boys wanted me to show him that we skinny fags aren't to be messed with, I guess."

"The boys? Who?"

"Just guys I work with."

"At Mao's?"

"That GMO soy shack? Hell no." Stefan lowered his voice to such a tiny whisper no human ears could hear. "The dude you found me with was a client."

"Client?"

"The guys I run with, my pack, most of us hustle."

Lexie had a vision of a bunch of Stefan's skinny friends hanging out in a pool hall. Then she realized what he actually meant and struggled to maintain her cool.

"Who else knows?" she asked.

"My whole—" Stefan halted when the elevator binged and a student in a wheelchair rolled out. Lexie and Stefan shared an awkward nod with the boy and waited until he was out of earshot to resume their conversation. "My whole pack knows I messed him up. Only Taylor and Otter know the dirt."

"And you trust them?"

He gave Lexie a hard look. "Every night with my life."

"How many more of there are you?"

Stefan shrugged. "Anywhere between five and fourteen, depending."

"Fourteen?! Are you fucking kidding me?!"

"What? What did I do wrong?"

"We're trying to figure out who killed Bree Curtis and you're sitting on fourteen werewolves?"

"Well not all at once."

Lexie rolled her eyes.

"They're not killers. They're not strangers. Not to me. Besides, only Tay and Otter live in town. The rest of them come down from Portland on the full moons to run."

The full moon had been a week off when Lexie found Bree's body, and she was barely cold. If Stefan was telling the truth, it meant some other wolf did the deed. "And when you run, do you remember?"

"In dribs and drabs. We probably could if we tried. But most of us don't want remember. We shift to forget. It's better than drugs, than sex, than any of it. We don't exactly try to stay lucid."

"How can you control yourself?"

"That's the point. You don't. You just have to trust that you'll have integrity, in the literal sense."

The threads were coming unraveled faster than she could cling to them. "So, if not you, then who?"

"Lex, I'm late for Arabic."

"Who, Stefan?"

"How the fuck should I know?" Stefan said.

"The coroner's report said Bree was killed by a pack, and there aren't any packs other than mine and yours."

Stefan groaned. "Why do you care so much about this? It's not like you knew Bree."

"As long as there's this threat out there, my life will never go back to normal." Lexie said it with conviction, but it didn't feel like the whole answer.

"Right. This is all about you. Thanks for the reminder," Stefan said. He sidestepped around Lexie. "I'm going to go to class now. Can you try not to get any of the rest of us killed while you play Nancy Drew?"

Lexie shrugged, her mind churning with claws and fangs as she contemplated the depths of her naiveté in expecting that Stefan would care. She watched Stefan step into his classroom and sit next to a stocky, square-jawed boy who greeted him with a smile and slap on the back.

Stefan gave the boy a coy smile and blushed. Lexie left.

Lexie arrived ten minutes late to her Indigenous Linguistics class and ditched out to go to the bathroom twice. She was fidgety and distracted, and Professor Rindt noticed. He was a visiting professor from Ontario, and one of the more beloved profs on campus, a straight-edge punk made good. He supervised the environmental group and led students on nature walks on weekends and evenings to give them booze-free alternatives. Tattoos peeked out from his shirt collar and cuffs, and Lexie couldn't help but think of Randy, though that was where the similarities ended. He wore a trimmed beard and a buzz cut. Most of the girls in class thought he was a dreamboat. Lexie only feared he was going to fail her.

Lexie wanted to care, to do a good job in this, if only this, class. But her mind was back outside, on Bree's waxen face, on Archer's burned-down cabin, on Stefan and Renee, and on whomever was doing this killing. She wondered what she would do, or if she would have to do anything at all. She didn't want to think about it, so she focused on the front of the classroom.

On the chalkboard Rindt wrote out the terms bilabial, velar and palatal, which Lexie supposed had something to do with pronunciation, but she couldn't be bothered to care beyond that. He drew a horse and led the students through homonyms in various North American languages. "Kawayo," he droned to the students who repeated in a mix of earnest and disinterested tones. "Kawayu" he said, with a new intonation. "Cahuayoh," he said, and they repeated again. A horse in three languages. Lexie tried to care, but it felt pointless.

Bridle, bits, muzzle, tack…

The teacher recited.

…mane, haunch, gait, gallop.

If she could ride her ambivalence like a horse, maybe she could make sense of it—guide it to some mutually-beneficial location, perhaps one in possession of clean water, and possibly oats.

But her problem wasn't a horse, bred, broken, and trained for thousands of years, docility and obedience the end goals. Her only option was her wolf and Lexie didn't want to think about where it would guide her if she let her guard down.

She dreamed about blood most nights, blood with a pulse. She woke up horny and exhausted, hungry and miserable. She used school and studying and the Pack and their daily dramas to distract herself, but it didn't do the trick. Her system was tricking itself. She needed something more, something more real, something real at all.

Lexie rubbed her eyes, fighting off the headache that clawed at her temples. Her eyes were fuzzy and strained, like she'd been watching an action movie out of focus.

"Ms. Clarion?"

Lexie started. The classroom had emptied out while she daydreamed. Professor Rindt stood alone at the front. He smiled tightly beneath his trimmed beard and gestured for Lexie to come forward.

"I have a question for you, Lexie." Rindt sat at his desk and gestured for Lexie to take a seat.

She tried to read his cool expression and sat. He continued. "You aced the placement test, but you have failed every quiz in the two weeks since. You didn't even bother turning in the first paper of the semester. Do you have any idea why that might be?"

Lexie shifted her weight from foot to foot, trying to figure out how to give him an answer that she didn't know herself. In her head they all felt the same. She shrugged.

"Can I tell you what I think this indicates?"

She bit her lip and shrugged.

"You have a great natural talent, or you know the material exceedingly well. But you don't care to do any work." He rested his chin on his thick hands. "Sound about right?"

Lexie shrugged again. "I guess."

"Melauak?" he said.

"Huh?" Lexie gave him a confused look.

"Kwayask? Eya?"

Lexie tittered nervously. "Was this part of the reading?"

"Kloosh?"

Lexie raised an eyebrow. That sounded familiar.

"Karout?"

Her head tilted with recognition, like a dog understanding a command. Professor Rindt inhaled sharply and nodded. "I see."

"What? What do you see?"

He smiled and pushed away from his desk, standing to erase the board. "I've got all I need. Thank you Ms. Clarion. You can go."

Lexie tried to stammer a request for clarification, but nothing came. Her face was frozen with a furrowed brow.

"Please do the reading. You're missing a lot of context. See you Wednesday."

Lexie walked through Milton, squinting at every warm body that walked past her field of vision, finally resting on a bench outside of the library. Had Rindt just popped her with a verbal quiz? Had she passed or failed? She stretched her jaw and rubbed her temples. She spotted the same stocky boy that Stefan had sat next to in class hanging with some friends over by the student union. He looked up, and she looked away before she could be caught staring. Her gaze landed on the doorway to Spohn Hall, clear across the quad. She saw two figures exiting the building. The outline of their bodies shimmered like an asphalt mirage on a summer day. She drew in her breath and straightened her back, sharpening her gaze to hold those forms in their protean shift. It was like trying to watch a dim star; the harder she looked, the less she could see the wolves. The hairy visages slipped away to reveal Stefan and his friend walking toward the library. Lexie sighed, disappointed with her lack of discovery.

As they walked past, Stefan placed his hand to his face, theatrically shielding himself from Lexie's gaze.

"Don't let that bitch see you," Stefan said in a stage whisper to his friend. "She's cray-zay."

"Fuck you, too," Lexie said with a sneer.

"Well sheesh," Stefan said. "I was just playing. This is Taylor."

Stefan's companion was the waiter from Mao's, a tall boy with delicate features, black hair, and linen-colored skin. He had long lashes that gave his face a demure air. He smiled wordlessly and rocked on his heels. Both the boys wore plaid shirts in different colors and sneakers to match.

"Who's that guy?" Lexie asked, pointing to the same rakish boy from Stefan's Arabic class—the one he'd fawned over—now sitting on the porch of the student union.

"Rory Blackwell," Taylor said. "He's Bree's boyfriend."

"Was," Stefan corrected.

"Right, was."

"Did you know Bree?" Lexie asked.

"Yeah. She was a real bitch."

Taylor laughed. "Oh my god, shut the fuck up." He shook his index finger at Lexie. "Princess didn't know Bree, he's just wet for her widower."

Lexie made a face.

"Shut up, Taylor," Stefan said.

"Is Rory a wolf?" Lexie asked.

"Princess wishes. He'd be easier to bone that way," Taylor said.

"Oh my god, I want to bite your face off." Stefan slapped Taylor's arm.

"So what was her story?"

"Bree? She was a good girl…mostly," Stefan said. "Wanted to be a diplomat's wife someday."

"We all can dream," Taylor sighed.

"Rory is political royalty around here. His dad is Governor Blackwell. Owned a bunch of local corporations and basically bought himself the governorship. Used to be the mayor of Milton and now there's all sorts of presidential hubbub around him."

Lexie's gaze slid back to Rory, who was digging through his backpack. "If he's so rich and powerful, why the heck is Rory going here?"

"Civic pride, probably," Stefan said. "Oregonians might give his daddy side-eye if Blackwell shipped him off to New England."

"Presidential hubbub," Lexie muttered, trying to imagine the kid in the tech vest and slouchy jeans wearing a fancy suit in Washington.

"I think Bree was trying to get in on the ground floor," Stefan said.

"Though he doesn't exactly look like a Kennedy," Taylor sassed.

"A Schwarzenegger more like it," Stefan said with a slight growl.

"Which is pretty much the same thing, isn't it?" Taylor asked.

"Oh my god, right?!" The boys laughed.

Lexie said, "And you were hoping to be, what, the pool boy?"

"Ugh, this skin doesn't tan," Stefan said. "Maybe like the stable boy or something. Whatever. Fuck it. He's straight."

"You're finally admitting that? Good boy!" Taylor golf-clapped.

"He's not like straight-straight. I had a chance."

"Straight-straight?" Lexie asked.

"He's got something going on. I think he's got some unique tastes. Bree wasn't all good, and there are plenty of pretty white girls on campus he could have had that are all good. But Bree had a wild streak. I think that's why he liked her," Stefan said. "Actually, I'm surprised he hasn't sniffed up any of your trees lately."

"The Pack? We're dykes."

"Exactly," Stefan said.

"Weird."

"There's more in heaven and earth, *Whore*-atio, than is found on your Kinsey scale." Taylor tittered at his joke and Stefan gave him props in the form of a delicate high-five.

Corwin emerged from the student union with a smoothie, scrolling through text messages. She hadn't seen Lexie and the boys when Rory shouted, "Hey Corwin, wait up!"

Rory leapt from the porch of the Union and chased her down the sidewalk. He was military-handsome: tall, broad-shouldered, with a strong, clean-shaven jaw and light brown hair. He looked well-fed and proud.

"Hm," Stefan said. "Spoke too soon."

Corwin smiled at Rory with an open grin Lexie hadn't seen from her before. Lexie and the boys turned their ears toward them, breathing lightly and tuning into the breeze-blown conversation.

"I'm going to go lift later," Rory said. "Wanna join?"

"Training already?" Corwin asked. "It's only mid-February. Doesn't your season start in March?"

"Yeah, well, my mom's Christmas cooking hasn't worn off yet and I don't want to be the only dude in the gym with a keg instead of a six-pack." He grabbed his belly and laughed.

"Six-packs are overrated," Corwin said with a curled lip, digging through her backpack and pulling out a bag of rolling tobacco and a lighter. "Everyone likes a little softness. Gives you something to grab onto."

Lexie struggled to hide her confused shock. Stefan wasn't nearly as successful. He leaned in Rory's direction with hanging jaw and incredulous eyebrows.

Rory and Corwin spied Lexie and the boys and headed in their direction. Stefan struggled to look nonchalant as they approached.

"And then I said," Stefan rushed, "why not the whole team? I've got nowhere to be! Right? Am I right?"

Lexie and Taylor rolled their eyes as Corwin and Rory stepped to them.

"This is my friend Lexie," Corwin said, twisting her freshly made cigarette and lighting.

"The Rare wolf hunter!" Rory said.

Lexie's heart jumped into her throat. Stefan shot her a look. "What?"

"You were the one those hunters shot when that wolf attacked you. Weren't you, like, tracking it or something?"

Lexie struggled for composure. "Oh, yeah. I was...trying to track it."

"It sucks that the Rare got that old guy."

"Hal Speer. Yeah. It sucks," Lexie said.

Rory shook his head. "Nasty fuckers. We should just carpet bomb these woods once and for all."

"Yeah, plants and animals, who needs 'em?" Stefan said.

Rory laughed. "Right?!" he said, smacking Stefan on the arm.

Stefan reddened and rubbed his arm. Lexie rolled her eyes.

Rory turned to Corwin and elbowed her in the bicep. "So, whad-dya say? You want to lift with me tonight? We could grab dinner after."

Lexie didn't try hiding her horror this time. She chattered to Corwin, so quick, quiet and subtle it would've registered to any normal person like a hiccup. *He's not wasting any time.*

Corwin glared at her then looked to the boys, who had been throwing shade but now tried to cover.

"Yeah, that'd be fun," Corwin said to Rory. Lexie stepped close to Rory and sniffed, trying to find a trace of him in her memory of Bree's scent.

"Cool." Rory jogged away. Lexie barely waited until he was out of earshot to launch in on Corwin.

"What the *hell* was that?" Lexie asked.

"Since when do you care, Miss 'Dudes aren't that bad'?"

"Dudes *aren't* so bad, but that doesn't mean you have to sleep with one. You've been the most ardent anti-dude person I know. You're even mad at Mitch for wanting to take testosterone."

"That's different. That's about solidarity. Rory can't help he's a man," Corwin said.

"But that doesn't mean you should sleep with him."

"No one said anything about sex. We're lifting together."

Lexie gave her a face.

"Christ, Lex. I'm curious! I used to sleep with guys before my attack and I kinda liked it." She looked sheepishly at the boys.

"Don't look at me, sweetheart," Stefan said. "I think guys are filth, and I still go bottoms up for them." He and Taylor nodded gravely to one another.

"Out of all the guys on campus…?" Lexie asked. "How do you know you won't get triggered?"

"In what universe is that any of your business?"

"Fine, it's not. But Sharm is. The happiness of my Pack is—"

"—*Your* Pack? Since when?"

Lexie rolled her eyes. "His girlfriend was murdered like *two weeks* ago. That's suspicious."

"And scary," Taylor said.

"Rory's not a murderer. She was killed by a Rare, and he's not—" Corwin cut herself off and looked under her heavy brow at the boys.

"They're cool," Lexie said.

"Yeah, we're totally werewolves," Taylor said with a flip of his hand.

"What?" Corwin said.

"Yep," Stefan said. "We are."

"It's true," Lexie said. "I caught Stefan munching on some dude the other night in a seriously unsexy way. I'll explain later."

"Christ, Lexie!" Stefan hissed.

"What?" she said. "It's like an open secret now."

"No, it's like a *secret* secret."

"Sorry," Lexie said. "Sorry to all of you, but *seriously* Corwin, everything about this is screaming Bad Idea to me. I know you can handle it, and it's fine if you want to kick it with men-types, but *that* one? Now? With the body count hopping up every day? It's just…it will destabilize the little stability we have left at home."

Corwin furrowed her brow and shook her head in disbelief. "Uh. Okay. Um. Well, Rory isn't a werewolf, though I guess he's the only non-Rare around here. Bree was killed by someone for some other fucked-up reason. She probably had something going on that none of us knew about."

"Like what?" Lexie asked.

"I dunno. An affair?"

Lexie made a face. "Ew."

Stefan made a sound in protest. "Don't knock it til you try it."

"But feel free to knock it immediately afterwards," Taylor said.

"You guys are grossing me out," Lexie said. "I just had three images of wolf peen race through my head and now I need a brain enema."

"The papers said she was killed by a pack," Stefan said.

"Well it wasn't ours," Corwin said, her cigarette stuck to her lips as she fumbled one-handed for her lighter.

"Not ours either," Taylor said. "Ick."

"Then unless we're way off base," Corwin said, "it'd have to be the Morloc."

Taylor shared a confused look with Stefan. "The whatnow?"

"Morloc," Lexie said. "It's the name of the full-blood Rares that live up near the barrens. Direct descendants of the original pureblood werewolves."

"Oh sure, I know those guys," Stefan said. "Big, scary, total assholes."

"That's them," Corwin said. She handed her smoothie to Lexie while she lit her cigarette. Lexie took a sip.

Stefan shook his head. "And they never needed a reason to kill anyone."

"See? Not Rory," Corwin said. "Let me handle Sharm. Our relationship has always been open, and we've talked about this kind of thing before. It's not going to ruin anything."

Forty-five minutes later, Sharmalee was sobbing in Jenna's arms, and Corwin was trying every tactic to smooth things over.

"I'm not choosing anyone! And if I had to, I'd choose you. This isn't about that."

"You're straight! You're straight, and you're a liar."

"I'm neither of those things. I came to you first! I could've snuck around on you, but I didn't because I love you." Corwin reached out to stroke Sharmalee's hair. "I love your body and your mind and your femininity. I love that you're a woman. I love our relationship. I'm just curious. We've been open since we got together, and I'm finally not afraid of men anymore. Why can't you let me explore that?"

"Because. I can't touch a woman who's been touched by a man." She batted Corwin's hand away.

"I had sex with, like, four guys before you and I even met."

"This is different!"

"How?"

"Because you never wanted to touch a man again when I met you."

"I was raped, Sharm."

"Well, that was good enough for me!"

"Wow," Corwin said. "That was a condition for our relationship? 'Must be traumatized by men so as to never want to be around them.' Nice."

"It was sympathy. Not many girls could understand what I'd been through."

"That's a *good thing*, Sharm. But if you're saying the only reason we were together was because of trauma empathy, that's hella fucked-up."

"It's not!" Sharmalee fell into sobs again.

Jenna spoke next, her soft tone cutting under the cacophony. "Everybody breathe. I know this is a lot for everyone to handle right now."

Hazel spoke up from where she was stretching on the living room floor. "Isn't he Bree's boyfriend?"

"Was," Lexie answered.

"Yeah, well, he's not a wolf, if that's what you're wondering," Corwin said. "I sniffed him out."

Sharmalee heaved a sob.

"Not really," Hazel said. "More wondering if he's a murderer or something."

Jenna spoke quietly, "Are you sure that's a good idea, Corwin? I don't have a problem with you being curious about boys, but this feels a bit suspect."

"He's harmless. He's a nice guy, he's not a Rare, and he had bad luck with a girlfriend who was probably cheating on him in the first place."

"Cheating?"

"Why else would Bree have been in the woods in the middle of the night?"

Lexie shrugged. "I think that's what the police are trying to figure out."

"Whatever," Corwin said. "Rory's one of the good ones, all right?"

Jenna sighed and stroked Sharmalee's hair. "I guess we'll all have to trust your instincts about this."

Lexie and Hazel shared a wary look. Corwin leaned close to Sharmalee, taking care not to touch her. She whispered, "I love you, baby, but I'm going. I'll be back soon."

12

"THE WORD VIRGIN COMES FROM the same root as Virile. There is little evidence to suggest such historically-significant women as Joan of Arc, Mary of Nazareth, and Queen Elizabeth, often referred to as virgins, were actually virgins in the modern sense. Rather, the term was more likely interchangeable with the male version of the word: virile, with which the term virgin shares a root. Read this way, the term virgin likely referred to the self-sustaining nature of these women's sexualities. A virgin, in this respect, refers to a woman whose sexuality is not claimed by a husband. Rather, she is her own guardian, her own master, and her own hero."

Lexie listened as Duane read aloud, her eyes crossing as she tried to follow along in her own book.

Duane uncapped his green highlighter and struck it across the page, perfect lines glowing in the library light.

"Okay," Duane said. "So if we apply this to the reading, are the 'unwomen' virgins or...prostitutes, I guess?"

Lexie drew a crescent moon with her yellow highlighter, and added heavy eyebrows and a frown with her pen.

"Lexie?" Duane said. "Hello?"

"I dunno."

"I doubt Professor Spencer will find that a compelling thesis statement."

Lexie sighed and rubbed her head. She looked forward to a future where she could deal with life without having to be burdened by five-page papers, if she made it that far.

"They sound like the same thing to me," she answered.

"How so?"

She sighed and rolled her head back, the ache burning behind her eyes indicating a need for sleep, food, or alcohol. "I don't know. But who's more virile than a prostitute? If the original virgin meant an unmarried woman in control of her sexuality, then a whore is the most virginal virgin who ever did virgin."

Duane cocked an eyebrow.

"The virgin/whore dichotomy isn't a dichotomy," Lexie continued. "They're both. They're the same."

Duane rested his head on his hand.

"Right?" she asked, suddenly unsure.

"I mean...sure. Yeah. We could make a paper out of that, easy."

"Awesome," Lexie said, slamming her book shut and tossing it into her backpack. "Can we talk about it...later, then? Tomorrow?"

Lexie cracked her knuckles and neck, wanting fresh air to purge the old-book smell from her nose.

"You want to get dinner?" Duane asked. "They're serving bacon cheeseburgers in Butler tonight."

Lexie's stomach gurgled.

"Whoa," Duane laughed. "I'll take that as a 'yes'."

Duane's smile was gentle, and she knew he cared, but a splinter of doubt shadowed his gaze, as though he needed the company more than he was letting on.

"Sure."

After long minutes of nothing but their footsteps and a few scattered voices from corners of campus, Lexie spoke.

"How are you doing, by the way?"

Duane cleared his throat and made a face, but a thread of tension ran under his lightness, like it was all a cover for a trigger.

"All right, I guess."

Lexie waited a few more silent paces.

"I mean—nightmares. Which is expected. And, you know, flashbacks or whatever."

Lexie nodded and gave him a sympathetic smile.

"It's just weird, because the Rare that attacked us was so...sentient. So smart. I would've expected an animal to be more impersonal, but it wasn't. And the fact that they haven't gotten it...I know it sounds stupid, but it just makes me feel like I've been targeted. Like he'll come back to finish the job."

She, Lexie thought, though she didn't correct him.

Duane shuddered. "We're all screwed, I suppose. Any word on the wolf that killed Bree?"

"Plural," Lexie sighed. "It was a pack."

"They run in packs?" Duane asked, blanching. "That means...there are more of them."

Lexie nodded.

"How many?"

"Too many," Lexie said. Duane's gaze shifted furtively across the quad as they walked. He was still so scared. Moreso than she was, more than she could even really understand. She felt cruel for not understanding, for not telling him everything right that moment, but the coming clean would surely destroy the tiny thread that held him together. "They don't know where they're from or why she was in the woods in the first place, but I have a feeling it's because of Rory."

"Rory Blackwell? No way. That guy's like a giant Golden Retriever. He'd never hurt anyone."

Lexie shrugged. "She was alone in the woods for a reason, and I can't imagine a girl ever doing that by choice."

"Uh...you used to hang out in the woods alone all the time."

Lexie wanted to counter, but Duane was right. She managed a small laugh.

He smiled in return, but it didn't last. "I was always one of the stronger guys, you know. I mean, I'm not huge, but I can run, I can jump, I can throw things. It just feels so terrible to be so weak, you know?"

Lexie couldn't help but laugh. "Yeah, Duane. I know. I'm a girl. It sucks."

"But I mean, to feel so vulnerable..."

Lexie scoffed. "Duane, that is like every woman's daily situation."

"Yeah, but," Duane continued, "it's not like you're constantly scared a monster's going to jump out from behind a tree and eviscerate you."

Lexie stopped walking to reassess the boy she was just starting to consider a friend. The boy who had four teenage sisters. The boy who survived Renee's jaws and Blythe's orders because he was one of the good guys.

"Dude, did you know that when I enrolled at Milton, I got a little pamphlet with all my forms that told me not to drink and to travel in groups so I don't get raped? It told me to be 'conscious' of my dress and to be careful about being 'overly flirtatious.' Apparently they send it to all the female students. Did you get anything like that?"

"How Not To Get Raped pamphlets?" Duane chuckled.

"How about How Not To Be A Rapist pamphlets? Did it tell you not to drink so you wouldn't accidentally rape someone? Or to travel in groups so your friends can stop you from raping someone?"

"No, of course not," Duane laughed.

"*Of course not.*"

"Okay, okay, okay, I get it."

Sure you do, Lexie thought. They continued their walk to the dining hall in silence. It glowed like a lighthouse across the quad. Her fingers grazed the hilt of her knife, and she took comfort in the simple power of carrying a weapon in a space where most people did not. Even better was knowing, however slightly, how to use one. Duane was beautiful, smart, and fit. He could excel in nearly any setting, rising by sheer force of will and charm. But there was one place where his wits and composure failed him—indeed where they were impediments. And that was the place where Lexie survived. When she tugged at her ill-fitting clothes and cracked her wily knuckles, she remembered: in the mundane world, where Duane had once moved like a would-be hero,

Lexie failed at five-paragraph papers and the myriad subtle cues of proper human female behavior. But in the woods, where Duane lost his innocence and very nearly his life, Lexie had fought and lived.

Their footsteps echoed against the faces of silent buildings.

"So..." Duane said, in an awkward attempt to redirect the conversation. "You been..."

Lexie quickened her pace, trying to deflect whatever he was about to ask, but Duane matched her steps and kept on. "I mean...are you seeing anyone?"

Lexie bit her lip, hoping the darkness would hide her reddening ears and cheeks. "Yeah," she admitted finally. "I guess. But not anymore."

"Is he a student?"

Lexie held air in her cheeks and released it like a broken balloon. "Ah...She was not."

"Oh." Duane's eyebrows rose. "Huh. Cool."

"Well, not really. It didn't end well."

"I'm sorry."

She shrugged.

"Are you like...fully lesbian?" He laughed and rubbed his stubbly jaw. His round, brown eyes caught Lexie's and then dropped away, only to seek them out again. Lexie couldn't help but laugh at the awkward phrase. She wondered what that might mean: 'fully lesbian.' Golf-playing? SUV-owning? Married and cat-breeding?

"I don't know. I think so. Probably. Why?"

Duane's face lost its usual composure. He struggled with expressions Lexie couldn't place.

"Just. I've known you for a long time. It's kind of surprising."

"To me too, I guess." Lexie wiggled her mouth.

"Though I guess in retrospect it makes sense. I mean, you are fairly..."

"Fairly what?"

Duane shot her his movie star grin, and she had to tease him.

"Fairly what, buddy?" she goaded.

"You know..." he chuckled and made an ambiguous gesture with his hands.

Lexie tipped her head and gave him a daring look. "You're batting a thousand right now, bucko, so you may as well spill."

Duane shrugged, laughing at his own loss of composure. "Like, woodsy. I mean, you never really dressed like a lot of the girls at Wolf Creek High. And you, like, hung out alone in the forest a lot." He laughed nervously. "I'm going to shut up now."

"Uh huh," Lexie said with a grin.

They walked together in more thick silence.

"Woodsy, huh?"

Duane smiled. "Sooo…bacon cheeseburgers?"

Between gargantuan bites, Duane tried to get more details about the wolves that attacked Bree, but Lexie, regretfully, had none. None that she could share with a boy who thought Rares were animals and nothing more. The last thing Lexie needed was for Duane to start suspecting that the townspeople of Milton were other than human. If he even got an inkling that Renee was involved in his own attack, so many things would topple over.

Lexie shook the thought away and squeezed more mustard on her plate.

"Good call on these," Lexie said, her mouth full of meat. "The Den never has good stuff. It's all tempeh and mushroom bullshit."

"I could go for a bit of that. Phi Kappa Phi is overloaded with bread and cheese. It's killing me."

"Maybe you and I could both benefit from time outside of our lives."

Duane sighed and smiled. "That sounds terrific."

Lexie shoved another hickory-smoked bite into her mouth. "Do your brothers feel like real brothers?"

"You mean the Phi Kappa Phi guys?"

Lexie shrugged and chased her burger with a glass of water. Her stomach gurgled with joy.

Duane shook his head and made a moue. "Not really. The frat experience is really deep for a lot of the guys, but I have a family already, and the two don't feel like the same. Girls or not, my sisters will always be more to me than these guys will. PKP is like most frats I guess; it's just a presumed family by proximity. I love a lot of the brothers, but they're not, like, capital 'B' Brothers." Duane took his own hearty bite. "What about you and the Pack?"

Lexie made a face. "Nah. I'm not really like them. I think we all want me to be, but I feel like a different species. I'm like the weird half-sibling from Dad's secret family. None of them really know what to do with me. And I don't know what I want done with myself."

Duane nodded sagely and they finished their burgers in silence. "I do actually dig Rory, though. He's been having a pretty hard time of it since the guys died."

Lexie wiped her hands and stacked her empty plate. "Well, Bree too, right?"

Duane shrugged. "Yeah, of course. But I think he was more torn up about their breakup before she died."

Lexie's hand slipped. Dishes clattered. "Wait, what?"

"What?

Lexie gave him a hard look. "They broke up?"

He nodded. "Yeah, he broke up with Bree the week before she died."

"Do you know why?"

"He wouldn't say, but it sounded pretty dramatic. Lots of yelling and crying. I do know that his dad didn't like her."

"Governor Blackwell?"

"That's the guy."

Lexie cleaned her side of the table with a napkin and tried to think of a casual way to phrase her question. She gave up. "Do you think you could find anything else out?"

"What will I get in return?" Duane asked, raising his eyebrows.

"Ick."

"Oh, stop. You're the gross one," Duane said. "How about being my research subject for Abnormal Psych?"

"I'm not even taking that class."

"Better if you aren't."

"Will I have to wake up early?" Lexie asked.

"No."

"Show up anywhere on a regular basis?"

"No."

"Homework?"

"No."

"Fine. Dig up some juicy dirt on Rory, and I'll fill out all the surveys you want me to." Lexie curled her hand into a fist and met Duane's with a friendly bump.

13

ONLY MITCH WAS HOME WHEN Lexie returned. He sat in a pool of yellow light, reading next to the empty fireplace.

"Hey," he said.

"Hey," she said.

Lexie felt bad for Mitch; his position as the Pack's whipping boy was now fully in effect. She didn't know what to say to him, or what to ask, though her mind was aswirl with questions. The fact that most of the questions started with the word "Why" was enough to convince her to keep her mouth shut.

"How you doing?" Mitch asked.

Lexie shrugged. "I'm getting kind of worked up about the whole Bree thing."

"Why? You scared?"

"Not scared. I think I just feel this strange affinity. Like I want the Pack to help her out of a sense of sisterhood—" Lexie flinched. "I mean, sibling-hood, or..."

"I can be your sister."

Lexie nearly laughed. "That doesn't make sense."

"Why should it have to? None of this makes sense. Us being werewolves doesn't make any sense, and the Pack treats it like it's totally normal."

"I wouldn't say normal."

"What's the point, is what I'm saying. Why the hell should we, of all people, be saying what's normal? If I become a dude, use a male pronoun, start looking to the world like I'm a guy, does it change who I am? More than me turning into a wolf every once in a while?"

Lexie picked at the frayed corner of the couch. "It's different."

"How?"

"It just seems...god this going to sound awful, but it seems unnatural. Like, being a girl is hard, but that doesn't mean you have to become something else."

"Yeah, being a girl is hard, but I bet you don't think about it as much as I do. I mean, you have your hair and your clothes. When people call you 'she', you don't flinch. You don't think that there's something wrong, something off, about you that they can't see."

"You sure about that?" Lexie said, raising her eyebrows.

"Fair." Mitch nodded. "Moving through the world as a man just feels more right to me. It's almost like when I run as a wolf."

Lexie snorted. "The idea of running as a wolf feeling 'right' is so far from my reality."

"Being a wolf is a kind of magic. You don't force it. It's part of you. It's effortless. I want my gender to be the same way. A synergy, a harmony so tight you can't even tell it's a bunch of different notes smooshed together."

Lexie had never known Mitch to be so eloquent. It indicated that perhaps he'd thought more about all this than she had. It gave her a stab of shame for ever doubting him. "I don't think I know that feeling."

"But what if you could? What if your wolf could feel as true to you as it does to me?"

"I'd probably be a lot happier."

Mitch shrugged. "There you go."

"But you're talking about changing your body chemistry."

"Renee and Sharm are the closest things to scientists we have in the Pack, and they don't understand the werewolf thing, either. How should we know whether werewolves are magic or science? Does it matter? Magic is just science we don't understand, right?"

"I've heard that," Lexie said with a faint grin.

"Listen, all I'm saying is that masculinity has always been part of me. Longer than my wolf has. I was a butch since I was old enough to hold an ax. I think society's just starting to catch up with people like me. Why can't I use science, and a little bit of magic, to turn myself into something new, something that feels more right for a reason that no one really understands?"

Lexie didn't want to argue with Mitch, and couldn't anymore anyway. He had a point. She nodded. Mitch picked up his book and continued reading. Lexie cracked her neck and grabbed her backpack, ready to finally do some homework.

She put on a kettle and settled into the corner of the couch with the newest novel in her Gender and Literature class while she waited for it to boil. The kettle screeched at her just as she struck her highlighter across the words, "Truth is a matter of the imagination."

"Tea?" she asked Mitch, who still had his head buried in his own book. He grunted an affirmative. Like a dude. Lexie was still smiling over that when she handed Mitch a mug of chamomile.

She curled up on the couch with her book, but a creeping discomfort wouldn't let her sink back into reading. She tried to shake it off, knowing her subconscious was merely distracting her from her work, like always. After reading the next sentence six times without absorbing a word of it, she dropped her book and sighed. The ill feeling remained. Lexie took a sip of her tea, but it wasn't enough. She needed a snack.

She headed to the kitchen, going for the fridge, when a tiny crunching sound tickled her ears. She glanced out the back door and saw a shadow at the edge of the woods in the backyard. She flinched, then bristled, a whine low in her throat.

"What?" Mitch asked.

The shadow slid into view and Lexie saw it was a person, stumbling. A person she knew.

"Holy shit."

Mitch jumped to the window. "Oh no."

They ran to the door and out onto the deck.

"Sharmalee?" Lexie smelled blood. Heavy like iron and salt, the odor lay thick in the air.

Mitch ran to Sharmalee and draped her arm around his shoulders. She leaned on him, limping, cringing with each step.

They lowered Sharmalee to the living room floor atop a pile of pillows. The soft glow of the lamps gave them a better view of her wounds. She had a deep gash across her abdomen that had just started to crust. Bite wounds punctured her shoulder, front and back. Dried saliva—Lexie prayed it was saliva—crusted on the tatters of her shirt and jeans. Blood soaked the purple satin of her top, dying it a putrid brown. It clung to her skin, making her look like a burn victim with flesh flayed. Her jeans were torn and filthy, her exposed calves and thighs marked with scrapes of embedded pebbles, as if she had been dragged a long distance.

Mitch ran for the first aid kit. Lexie stroked Sharmalee's face with the back of her fingers. "Who did this to you?"

Sharmalee strained to speak, the effort it took clearly paining her. "Morloc."

"How many?"

Sharmalee's eyes rolled back in her head and Lexie smacked her cheek. "No, no. Don't pass out. Stay here, Sharm."

She whined again, and Lexie shook her. "Sharm, how many?"

"Twwwwww..." she strained.

"Two? Two Rares did this to you?" It was a miracle she was alive.

Sharmalee head lolled on the pillows. "Twwwelve."

14

"COME FUCKING ON, CORWIN!" RENEE yelled into her phone when Corwin's voicemail greeted her for the seventh time.

The Pack was assembled in the hospital waiting room. They were the only people there except for a janitor who lazily mopped the hall.

Though Sharmalee was stable, the nurse said they'd need to keep her overnight for observation.

When Corwin got there, everyone rushed to be the first to tell her how she fucked up by going on a date with some random boy. But no one could answer Corwin's first question: "What the fuck was Sharm doing out in the woods alone?!"

Corwin settled in one of the uncomfortable molded plastic chairs, and soon all the girls were snoozing in the glare of the buzzing fluorescent lights. All except for Lexie, who read and re-read the same three pages of *Things Fall Apart*, trying to find the irony but stuck in a pointless loop of distraction.

Soon after dawn, Renee and Jenna ran home to get decent coffee and snacks for everyone, while Lexie went outside to get some fresh air.

In the nearly-empty parking lot of the tiny hospital, a news van was raising its antenna. Two black sedans, parked diagonally across three spaces, idled behind the van.

A harried-looking assistant slathered makeup on a perfectly-coifed reporter by the van. Governor Blackwell stepped from the sedan, flanked by two young aides. They looked young and bright enough that they could be Milton students, except for the pressed suits and Ivy League haircuts.

A small crew adjusted a light tree, and the reporter began rolling before Lexie could even figure out what was happening.

"Governor Blackwell," the blonde, crimson-lipped reporter began. "Can you tell Miltonians about the horrific events of this evening?"

"Yes, Gretchen. I'm afraid that Milton has suffered yet another attack on a young woman by a Rare wolf. Tonight we thank the Lord that she survived, and that the terrific doctors here at the Rogue River Hospital gave her the attention she needed. I'm happy to report that she is in stable condition and is expected to make a full recovery.

"Attacks like the one on this poor young woman are unacceptable. I won't let the good citizens of Milton and neighboring communities be terrorized by these wild animals any longer. I continue to encourage citizens to arm themselves and take common-sense precautions when enjoying Milton's natural beauty, but remember that it's easy to underestimate these animals. So much of our population is comprised of seasoned outdoorsmen and women, but we've lost even seasoned hunters to these beasts. Rare wolves are aggressive animals and should not be underestimated."

"Governor Blackwell," the reporter continued, her big blond hair-do bouncing with each word, "are you concerned that your new highway project will put more citizens in harm's way?"

"Gretchen, I'm a Miltonian. I was born here, and I raised my three children here. It is not my intention to bring any more harm to my fellow citizens. Sure, the new highway will make everyone's commute to the capitol much easier, mine included." He chuckled, his bright smile bringing a blush to the reporter's cheeks.

Blackwell's smile faded into a grave frown. "It seems to me, from talking to wildlife experts, a project such as this new state route will divide the current Rare wolf territory. While it may be tempting to further assert our territory, I strongly urge Miltonians not to engage with Rares in any way. This young lady is evidence enough of that."

"Governor Blackwell," the reporter pressed, "is there any evidence the injured young woman was seeking out Rares?"

"It's not my job to speculate, but her fate clearly demonstrates the risks of vigilantism. For this reason, I am instituting a partial ban on all new weapon and ammunition sales. And until buck season begins in the fall, we will not be issuing any new arms permits. I believe that Milton residents have every right to protect themselves, but I do not wish for untrained citizens to engage with these animals out of vengeance or bravado."

Lexie couldn't stomach any more. She ran inside and found Corwin with her laptop perched atop her knees. Hazel and Mitch still snored in their chairs.

"Who do Hindus pray to?" Lexie asked.

"What?" Corwin said through a yawn. "Ganesha. Or Kali. Different gods for different reasons. Why?"

"'Cause Governor Blackwell is out front giving an interview, and I think he just thanked Jesus that Sharmalee survived."

Corwin made a face. "He what?"

As if summoned by the conversation, the automatic doors parted for Blackwell and his entourage. The Governor strode into the bleach-white lobby like he owned it. His lightly-tanned skin was eerily unblemished, and gray streaks ran at his temples among an otherwise dark brown head of hair. Blackwell's white teeth flashed in the harsh light as he directed his aides and the news crew about.

The nurse at the desk, who had been in the office watching sitcoms on her computer, rushed out to greet them.

Through a difficult and awkward phone call to Sharmalee's parents in North Carolina, Governor Blackwell negotiated a visit with Sharmalee, but no cameras.

Corwin stared aghast and rushed to intervene.

"What are you doing?"

"Pardon?" Blackwell waved off a black-suited man with sunglasses and a discreet earpiece.

"That's my girlfriend in there, and I don't think she'd be okay with you holding a press conference over her bloodied body."

Blackwell placed a large, well-manicured hand on Corwin's shoulder. "Don't worry young lady, I'm just going to give your friend some words of support."

Corwin shrugged off his hand. "My *girlfriend* doesn't need your support."

Blackwell ignored her and turned to address Gretchen and her news crew. His bulk blocked Corwin from view. "Milton is my hometown. I consider it my duty to take an interest in its citizens, which include the many vulnerable students at Milton College, one of Oregon's finest liberal arts institutions."

He turned and entered Sharmalee's room, accompanied only by his bodyguards and the nurse.

Corwin fumed. "That dude is using my girlfriend as a political prop. Fuckin' douchebag."

Lexie chattered to her, *This is the dude whose son you want to bone?*

"Shut up Lexie," Corwin said.

Lexie placed her hand on Corwin's shoulder, if only to maintain the illusion they were scared girls amid the chaos. One of Blackwell's interns stepped over. He was a skinny white boy who wore his hair and suit the same way: high and tight.

"He's here to help," the boy said.

Corwin glared. "Stuff it, Brown Shirt." The boy flinched and walked away.

Renee and Jenna returned with bags of food and a thermos full of French press. "What's all this about?" Renee asked, gesturing to the Young Republicans and the loitering camera crew.

Before Lexie could answer, Blackwell was back, straightening his tie for one more round of filming.

He started in with bravery, poise, blah blah blah. Lexie and Corwin ran into Sharmalee's room. They found her groggy and delirious.

"Are you okay, sweetie?" Corwin said, stroking Sharmalee's cheek.

"Who was that man?" she mumbled.

"Just our douchebag governor, hon," Corwin said. "I'm sorry I wasn't the first one to see you when you woke up."

"I was scared," Sharmalee whispered.

Corwin sniffled and wiped her eyes, then took Sharmalee's hand in hers. "I know sweetie, but we'll get you home soon. We're safe now."

"Are we?" she asked.

The sky was edging back toward darkness when the nurse handed the discharge papers to Corwin to sign.

"Make sure to stay on the main roads," the nurse warned. She traded Corwin the clipboard for three prescription slips. Corwin nodded and Mitch rolled his eyes. "Like that'll help anything," he whispered.

At home Renee and Mitch carried Sharmalee up the stairs.

"We should've asked for more sedatives," Hazel said.

"I did," Renee grunted. "The nurse looked at me like I was a junkie. Fucking racist."

"The nurse was black, Ren," Lexie said.

"Fine. Fucking anti-Semite," Renee clipped. She whacked Sharmalee's ankle on the banister. Sharmalee groaned. "Whoop, sorry sister. Eyes back on you."

Jenna fixed snacks, and the rest of the Pack tried studying in an attempt to ignore Corwin's sobbing as she held Sharmalee in bed.

Lexie stood in Renee's doorframe. Renee sat in a pool of lamplight, her back hunched over her desk. Sandalwood incense burned in the corner, and stacks of books and notebooks piled on her desktop and at her feet. She tugged on her hair with one hand and scribbled formulas in her notebook with the other.

"Not now, Lex," Renee said over her shoulder.

Lexie didn't move, waiting for Renee to put down her pen, rub her temples and turn to face her. Instead, she kept scribbling.

"What?" Renee said.

"I'm concerned," Lexie said.

"No shit, Lex," Renee grumbled. "We all are."

"So when are we going to try and find another half-blood to kidnap?"

"We're not," Renee said. "It's clear it's not the half-bloods we should be concerned about. It's the Morloc." She uncapped a high-lighter and struck it against some text. "I think we should lay low for a while."

"What?" Lexie almost laughed. "Weren't you supposed to be the solider? The general?"

"Leave me alone, Lexie. I have a test tomorrow."

Lexie stared at the back of Renee's head, her desk lamp silhouetting her like a cameo. She was so beautiful, and so opaque. "Sharmalee was almost killed, Ren," Lexie said. "We have to figure out what they want."

Renee slammed down her pen and turned in her chair. "Lex, lay off!"

"No!" Lexie shouted back. "I'm not going to go about business as usual when Sharmalee was almost murdered for some reason we don't understand."

"I understand. I understand that none of us are safe. It was do-able when it was half-bloods we were up against. We could have found them and picked them off, one by one, like we've been doing for years. But the Morloc? There is no fucking way."

"You just said the Pack needed to start playing offense."

"That was when we weren't totally out-muscled. You don't understand, Lex. You don't know. This is a game-changer, and one that puts us on our backs. I don't want this pack in any more danger."

"We already are. By living here, we are in danger."

"Then maybe we should go somewhere else."

Lexie shook her head. "What are you talking about?"

"Survival."

"Survival? Or complacency?"

Renee bit her lip and shook her head. "I'm not going to risk the lives of my pack to avenge a girl we didn't know."

"What happened to solidarity? Sisterhood?"

"*These* are my sisters. These women in *this* house." Renee slammed two fingers down on her desk. "I'm not going to force them to take on the burdens of all women anymore. It's a losing fight, and we need to win something."

"We can win this."

"How? By burning down the forest?"

"It worked once," Lexie said.

"For ten years. And now they're back. Twelve Rares should have rent Sharmalee apart in a half a second."

"But they didn't."

"Not by accident. They must have a different agenda for women like Sharm than whatever they had with Bree," Renee said.

"We've got to figure out what it is."

"No. Blackwell is right. We let your daddy and all his well-armed hunter friends be our first wave. They'll start bagging full-bloods soon, and it'll take the heat off of us. At the very least, it'll scare the Morloc back into hiding for a while."

"A while," Lexie snorted. "Another ten years for them to regroup and come back more murderous than ever?"

"Ten years is good enough for me. Long enough for the rest of the Pack to graduate and get out of this hellhole."

"You want to just walk away," Lexie scoffed.

"That's what I want you to do, right now. This conversation is over." Renee picked up her pen and turned her back to Lexie, going back to her frantic scribbling, alone in her pool of light.

Lexie closed the door and crept back down the hallway, thinking, or maybe just wishing, that behind the closed door, she heard Renee start to cry.

Lexie lay on her side, the window wide open, letting the half moon's white light in with the chilly air. She'd been having a hard time sleeping again. She considered sleeping out in the treehouse, but the thought of the ghosts conjured there, the memories of love and love lost, was too much.

In the distance she heard wolves. Normal wolves. Gray wolves. Not the monsters who had overtaken the Rogue River valley, colonized it, brutalized it, claimed it as their own. She wondered what future any other creatures had here, humans included, or if this was just the start of a larger attack no one saw coming.

Lexie turned to her side to try and find sleep. A timid knock sounded at her door.

"Lex? You awake?" Corwin eased open the door before Lexie could answer. "Sharm's having a hard time sleeping. She wants to know if we can cuddle with you."

Lexie hesitated. Corwin rushed to explain. "She tends to run really cold for a Rare, and I can't always keep her warm enough alone. Do you mind?"

"'Course not. Come in."

Corwin retrieved Sharmalee, carrying her into Lexie's room and lowering her into the bed. They lay like spoons in a drawer, with Sharm behind Lexie, and Corwin behind Sharm. Lexie found a place to put her arm and Corwin shifted until her legs were in the right spot. Then they all sighed and settled into sleep.

Soon, footsteps padded outside Lexie's door, and Hazel peered in. "Hey girls?"

"Yep?" Corwin said.

"Can I join you?"

The three of them nodded, and Hazel curled up against Lexie's legs, a tiny L-shape at the foot of the bed.

Hazel started to snore immediately, and Lexie herself began drifting off when she heard Mitch and Jenna whispering at the door.

"Is there room for two more?" Jenna asked.

Lexie almost laughed, though a restive headache pushed at her forehead. Instead she beckoned with one hand, and Mitch and Jenna snuggled up to Hazel and Sharmalee's legs.

Nearly fifteen minutes passed. Everyone's breath deepened, and Lexie's muscles unknotted enough that she thought she might find sleep. Just as she was perched on the edge of dreamtime, she heard a final set of footsteps. Renee tiptoed into the room and slid her lithe frame into the narrow space left at Lexie's side.

The Pack adjusted and relaxed, and once again their breathing joined to create a soft sigh of exhalations. Lexie felt warm and safe, her sisters by her side.

15

THE MOON WANED UNTIL ONLY a fingernail sliver remained. The girls sat on their hands for a week, waiting for Sharmlaee to heal and for the Pack to regain their fighting strength. But Sharmalee wasn't healing, not as fast as she should've, anyway. The waning moon had sapped whatever healing strength she had, and she was forced to rely on purely human functions. They all hoped the sliver of the waxing crescent, when it finally came, would help pull things in the right direction for them all.

Mitch was sulking even harder than usual. Late the next evening, Sharmalee finally told Corwin about the attack. She had been in the woods alone, armed with a simple blade for cutting herbs, collecting for Mitch. She'd been gathering goathead weed and snakeroot, the natural testosterone Jenna had been talking about. She had already gotten a few sprigs of each. She was excited, she had told Corwin, to put what she was learning in biochem to practical use. Then the twelve Rares attacked, and she had no hope of shifting. The next question everyone wanted answered was the one that no one could ask.

"Sharm, you can tell me. We've been there together. It's not your fault."

"I know!" Sharmalee snapped.

Hazel, Jenna, Lexie, Mitch, and Renee all leaned around the kitchen island, listening through the floorboards to the girls speaking above. Mitch chewed on his nails. Hazel played with the ends of her hair. Lexie tapped each finger silently on the linoleum, and Renee stood straight, arms crossed over her chest, staring softly ahead. A single pool of golden light illuminated a bowl of apples, their red reflection glowing withing everyone's irises.

From upstairs, Corwin said, "But...?"

"They weren't like the Rares we've caught," Sharmalee replied. "The half-blood, men-types or whatever. It was like being attacked by twelve really smart, really huge, wild animals. I don't know what brought them together; they didn't seem to work as a pack. But there were just so many of them. So big. So...." Her voice trailed off, caught by tears. "I couldn't tell what was in their eyes, whether it was sex, or power, or hate. They treated me like a doe, not a woman. It was almost scarier that way.

"I started feeling..." Sharmalee choked back more tears. "I was flashing back. And all the training we've done...Fuck." Bedclothes rustled, and Sharmalee's voice when next she spoke was muffled, as though she'd hidden under the covers. "It was all slow-mo. I thought for sure they were going to rape me. I was so ready for it. I was processing it before it happened. Like, I was almost willing it to happen so it could be over. And for a second I thought it might go in that direction. But then they started chattering to each other, barking. I knew they were talking, but I couldn't understand it. It was a language I'd never heard. Then they started arguing. I guess. That's what it sounded like.

"It shook me back to presence, and I ran. I thought I could try and shift if I got some distance on them, but it was a mistake. I just got nauseous and dizzy and stumbled over myself. They caught up and were on me again. But I guess I'd run to a different part of the woods, near the sea cliffs, on the other side of the Burnout. I caught a whiff of something, and the rest of them did too. It spooked them enough that I managed to escape."

The girls downstairs shared questioning looks, and Corwin asked the question they couldn't.

"What was it?" she asked.

"I didn't know at first. I was just concentrating on running, but...it's something I've smelled only once before, when Archer came back."

Lexie froze, not wanting to hear Sharmalee's next words, but too far away to stop them: "We were in the territory of a pureblood."

16

"ARCHER'S NOT BACK, LEX," RENEE called after Lexie when she bolted out the back door and into the yard.

Lexie turned, defiant. "There's only one pureblood. Only her."

"She's not back."

"How do you know?"

"We'd know. Sharm would know. Maybe it was a stale scent," Renee said. "Maybe that's just her old hunting ground."

"A stale scent scared off twelve full-bloods?"

Renee crossed her arms and stood in the back doorway. Mitch, Jenna, and Hazel clustered behind her. "What do you want to do?"

"Find Archer."

Renee rolled her eyes. "Sharmalee nearly died, the whole pack is terrified, and you're running off to stalk your ex-girlfriend."

"She's the only one who can help us. The full-bloods are bigger and stronger, and they apparently outnumber us two to one. None of us have anything on them."

"What's it matter? As long as we stay out of their way," Renee said.

Lexie looked at Renee with an expression of horror and incredulity.

"We will always be in their way. This town is in their way," Lexie said. "When that highway is done, their territory will be even smaller, and where do you think they'll go?"

"For the easy targets. And I don't mean any of us to be one."

Lexie scoffed. "Weren't you supposed to be the warrior?"

"Weren't you supposed to be the scared one?"

"I am scared!" Lexie said. "I just don't see how pretending nothing's wrong will help anything."

"But you think praying to Archer will help?"

Lexie sighed, feeling so unheard she might as well be invisible. "Yes."

"So what would Archer do?"

Love me, hold me, take me away.

"I don't know."

Fight me, fuck me, tell me everything is going to be okay.

"But Christ, wouldn't you go? If there was a chance?" Lexie asked. "Or better, wouldn't you rather have me moping in the woods instead of in the Den?"

"No!" Renee said. "I want you here, safe, with the rest of us. Sulking in the woods looking for a disappeared girlfriend isn't going to make any of us feel any safer."

"I'm not trying to make you *feel* safe, I'm trying to actually *get* us safe, because you seem to have stopped caring about that. So, you can go back in there and tell everyone that you've stopped fighting and that they should just keep their heads down and obey curfew, but I'm going to investigate this. If Archer's out there, I have to let her know we need her help."

"I still care, Lexie," Renee snipped. "I just think you pining after an ex isn't going to help. Whatever is out there is an old scent. Archer isn't back."

Lexie glared at Renee. "I'm going out there, and I'm going to find Archer, and she's going to save all of our lives."

Renee raised her hands and backed into the house. The girls behind her stumbled back to avoid collision. "Fine. Your life. Just don't get yourself killed, all right? Especially not waiting for your princess charming. That shit never ends up right."

17

LEXIE KNEW SHE SHOULDN'T BE running, not with all that had happened. Not with a morning test she hadn't studied for. Not with twelve killer wolves on the prowl.

At the edge of Archer's property, tiny flakes of snow began to fall. She watched them, no bigger than grains of salt. They caught and pooled on her palm. She remembered the ash and soot that drifted down from the sky when the cabin burned. Those left gray scars on her skin, visible even after she washed them away. These flakes left no impressions, gone as quickly as if they had been born to die.

The stacked slate fireplace stood amidst a black cube of char. Though the southeastern wall still held intact, the other three walls were burned through, collapsed in awkward piles. The wood bore thick, black scales like a reptiloid demon. The gruesome scene was bisected by the fallen log that once held the roof. Finally relieved of its weighty responsibility, it had broken in half and now teetered on the cracked ends of the eaves. The remains of Archer's dining room table lay crushed underneath. Lexie shuffled through the ash. Her toe caught the handle of a tin mug. She lifted it and held it up in the fading sunlight. She remembered the taste of nettles and yarrow, Archer's breath, and the tea that made Lexie feel warm and safe. That first morning. The last morning before…

She lifted her chin, brushed the tip of her nose on the wood, the hearth, anything she could reach. None of it held Archer. She wasn't back. She wouldn't come back.

Lexie cursed her eagerness, her belief that Archer would somehow know the danger the Pack was in, that she would somehow help. No, she was gone somewhere far away. She was climbing mountains, fucking were-coyotes, or some such shit. The hole in Lexie's abdomen roiled. She didn't carry her sadness in her heart. It lived in her belly and her groin. Both wept while her heart kept beating, knowing nothing else but the mindless continued rhythm of life.

"Archer…" *I'm scared.* Lexie folded her hands over her belly. "I don't know what to do. What I am. I don't know anything anymore. What they want of me. I don't know if I can give it to them."

This change. It hurts too much. I don't want to be this.

She lied.

Lexie wandered the wreckage, stirring the ash, conjuring plumes so she could pretend there was still life here.

You ran. I should run, she thought, drawing a cold fingertip along the slate of the hearth. "I don't belong here."

She dropped to her knees and dug her palms into the ash. She hoped it would deliver an epiphany, some insight on whether she should rebuild, fight, or flee.

She leaned her face to the ground, pushing her nose into the sooty remains of her lover's home. Chunks of petrified wood stuck to her skin. She snuffed short and hard to keep the crud from choking her. She didn't smell Archer, or that seductive scent from the woods. She didn't smell power or revenge or sex or salvation. All she could smell was fire.

18

"RORY'S DAD HATED BREE," DUANE said, thwapping a wad of peanut butter onto his plate and grabbing two green apples from beneath the sneeze guard.

Lexie loved that the dining halls were unlimited. And she loved that Duane never seemed to balk at the quantities of food she packed away every meal. Indeed, he could nearly match her bite for bite. She wondered if Duane's sisters felt just as comfortable with him, or if it was unique to their relationship.

"Apparently Rory wanted to propose. His dad wouldn't let him."

"That sounds like jerk dad stuff, not hate."

Lexie hadn't planned on eating at the dining hall. She had drained her weekly meal plan already, and it was only Wednesday. Duane just gave her a look and said "Seriously, don't sweat it." They walked to their favorite table overlooking the quad, in the back corner of the dining hall near the kitchen door where few other students ever sat.

"But it's weird," Lexie said. "Even if Rory's dad hated Bree, the man's the Governor of Oregon. How would he convince—or like, train—a pack of wild animals to do the job? It's not like it's convenient."

"It'd make more sense to plant meth on her and toss her in a cheap motel."

Lexie pulled a face. "That's grim."

"But no," Duane said, contradicting his own theory. "That would mean a full investigation, which would clearly get back to him. There's no quicker way to solve a homicide than say a Rare did it."

"No kidding," Lexie said, shifting her gaze away as they slid into their booth.

"Maybe he made Rory take her out into the woods and leave her there."

"Hansel and Gretel style?"

"More like Jurassic Park," Duane said.

"That's sadistic." Lexie dug her fork into a mountain of mac and cheese. "Are we sure she wasn't dead before she ended up in the woods?"

"Not that I trust the cops in this town, or any town for that matter," Duane said, "but the coroner's report made it sound pretty clear. Open and shut case."

"How'd you get the coroner's report?" Lexie asked, aghast.

Duane smirked. "I *called* silly. It cost me, like, thirty bucks."

"You sure you want to be a doctor? You seem to be pretty good with the detective business."

Duane smiled, his eyes catching Lexie's for longer than she would have expected or liked. She half-smiled and looked away.

"Hey, I know this is going to sound weird, but thanks," Duane said. "I feel like this whole thing is giving me the confidence to find out more about my own attack."

That dragged her attention back. Lexie swallowed and poked at her meatloaf. "What do you mean?"

"Well, you know, I remember things. The nightmares have been brutal, but actually thinking about the attack—remembering the de-tails—has been helpful. It takes it out of the realm of monsters and horror films and turns it into a real thing that happened to me, a thing I have power over. It's like how my mom used to teach me to deal with nightmares: write the story, then give it a new ending."

"What's your ending?" Lexie asked.

Duane laughed and dug into his salad. "Dunno yet."

"What do you remember?" Lexie asked, monitoring her voice for odd tones or breaks.

"So much. I remember the way the Rare looked. Black with a brown chest, really intense dark brown eyes. Sentient, you know? Leggy, smart, agile. And female."

Lexie coughed.

"You okay?" he asked while Lexie choked on a piece of bacon. She nodded furiously and wiped her mouth with a napkin.

She asked, "Are you sure?"

"One hundred percent," Duane said with a definitive nod. "Maybe we were camping in her territory or something. Like she had pups."

"My dad says there hasn't been a female spotted in decades."

Duane bit his lip and took a long swig of his soda. "It was a female. A tall, leggy, dark-furred female with a bone to pick with frat boys."

Lexie tried a dismissive laugh, but she ended up squirming. "That sounds kind of silly, Duane."

"Lex, I know what I saw."

"But you were under duress. Frightened and all PTSD-y. How can you be sure?"

"How can you?" he nearly shouted. Lexie realized she was being callous, but she knew she had to be in order to protect Renee and the Pack. It was a good excuse, anyway.

"What do you mean?"

"You were attacked by a Rare, too. How do you know it happened the way you think it did?"

Lexie considered the attack on the hillside, Archer's heroics, everything she thought she knew about the Morloc.

"Because I fought back."

Duane's face dropped. "Right. I'm the victim, and you're the noble warrior," he said.

Lexie sat back, mirroring him, then went one further and let her head fall back. "I'm not saying that."

"Sure," Duane muttered.

"Dude," Lexie said. "You did what you had to. You did the only thing you could do." She leaned forward and reached her hand across the table, almost, but not quite, touching his wrist. "You ran, and you hid. That was a good choice. It helped you survive. You were the smart guy."

Duane's eyes fell on the tiny space between her fingertips and his skin. "But you weren't." Lexie couldn't tell if it was a question, and the look in Duane's eyes said he didn't know either.

"No," Lexie said, retracting her hand, hardening her gaze. "Never have been. I never make the right choices. I just take the only ones that I have."

Duane's tone grew cold. "Which in your case was to fight."

She pulled her hand back and crossed her arms, glaring. "Because I had to, whether or not I wanted to."

Duane steeled his gaze to match, but his jaw clenched beneath his sharp, umber cheek. "You think I could've chosen?"

Lexie jutted her chin and stared out the window, taking a sudden interest in the mundanities of the quad. "You could've," she said. "But you probably would've died. Sometimes running away is the only right choice."

Duane pushed his tray to the corner. "Yeah," he muttered. "You're the brave one, and I'm the one who had to run away." He packed his bag and stood. "Thanks for the reminder."

He walked away before Lexie could think of an apology, before she even realized what she had done wrong. As she watched him leave the dining hall and stalk across the quad, she still didn't have the words. She was right. She did fight back. She didn't run or hide like Duane did. Nothing she said was incorrect. It wasn't her fault if Duane was ashamed of himself.

Lexie looked back to her nearly empty plate and poked at her mashed potatoes. She had bigger concerns with Duane than his weird trauma-jealously. If she knew him at all, which she liked to think she did, he wouldn't stop because she called him silly. Despite the leap in logic it would take for a guy like him to start seeing the werewolves in the Rare wolves, she worried that it was only a matter of time before he traced his attack back to Renee. The likeness was too uncanny, if one knew what to look for. She knew it the moment she saw Archer in her wolf form. There was nothing more than a thin veil separating the two forms. Once she saw it, she couldn't ever unsee it. And Duane was smart enough to figure it out, which would be a disaster for everyone.

Maybe it was a guy thing. Fragile egos and whatnot.

"Hey, Lexie." Rory stood above with a tray in his hands, looking lost. "Can I sit?"

"Uh, sure," Lexie said, unwilling to demean any more traumatized boys.

Rory sat, and then he just...sat. They stared at each other for a long moment, Lexie trying to cover her reddening ears with her hair. Rory looked as though he was trying to screw up the courage to say something.

"I was wondering if I could talk to you about ..." He rubbed his fingers nervously against the frost on his glass of milk.

Lexie sighed. "Corwin's just going through some stuff right now. I can't really talk about—"

"Oh," Rory said. "I know."

"Oh," Lexie said. "Sorry."

They sat in awkward silence, neither looking at the other, both waiting for Rory to say something.

"It's about Bree," he said. "Corwin told me you were wondering what's up with that. She said you'd kind of been asking around."

Lexie fidgeted. "It's not really what you—"

"The night she disappeared," Rory interrupted, "I went to her room. Something looked weird. Like there had been a struggle."

"Did you tell that to the cops?"

"Yeah, but they didn't seem to take it too seriously."

Lexie saw anxiety in his eyes, and fear.

"Another thing," Rory said. "She was..." He struggled to find the word.

Lexie's curiosity was distracted by a blur outside the window. She resisted looking away for a moment, wanting Rory to feel respected by her attention, but then the blur caught his eye, too. He turned and blanched, and Lexie followed his gaze.

Outside the window raced the bent hulk of a Rare. He swung his head from side to side, lamplight reflecting off his cold, yellow gaze. He wore a snarl on his lips that turned into a growl, sending students on the quad scattering and screaming.

Everyone in the dining hall rushed to the windows, cell phones in hand. One of the chefs rushed to the campus phone and dialed security.

Outside, the wolf caught sight of a running student and lunged after him. The boy darted and dodged. His flight would have looked comical if it weren't so horrifying to watch. Students in the dining hall snapped pictures and recorded video with their cell phones, though the deepening evening and florescent lighting would certainly kill the images.

Rory looked around at the students and staff, all either ogling or hiding their eyes. He looked back outside and watched the screaming boy run. "Someone should do something," Rory said.

"Right," Lexie said, ripped from her shock.

Rory fought through the crowd to the exit. Lexie followed behind, gripping the handle of her knife, although she had no idea what help she could be.

When they reached the doors, an alarm like an old tornado siren sounded across the campus.

Lexie covered her ears. "What the hell is that?"

Rory ignored her. He burst into the quad and ran in the direction of the Rare and his prey, still twenty yards away. The siren pummeled Lexie's eardrums and she grimaced as Rory headed toward the wolf.

"Rory!" she shouted. "Stop!"

Rory waved his hands above his head and shouted. "Lexie! Run to the door there and hold it open for me." He gestured to the dorm on the other side of the path from where she stood.

He looked back to the wolf and continued to make a spectacle of himself. Finally, the Rare noticed and paused, sniffing the air. The boy he had been pursuing bolted for the student union, rushing up the steps three at a time.

The Rare, its attention fixed on Rory, took a step in his direction. His jaw hung partially open, his tongue lolling out the front between two meathook canines. He passed a bench, dwarfed by his grizzled mass. He snuffed at the distraction Rory was creating.

The Rare walked, then trotted, then burst into long, loping strides. Rory stood frozen for one, then two huge bounds by the wolf. Then he turned and ran.

The Rare closed the gap between them in seconds. He leaped, his claws spread to rend.

A sharp crack shattered the siren's song.

The Rare screamed as a spray of blood erupted from his haunch. From her spot in the dorm doorway, Lexie traced the vector of the bullet back to a security guard, crouched behind an electrical box near the library.

Another shot grazed the wolf's shoulder. He barked and ran toward the guard, who stood and unloaded two more rounds. One slammed into the wolf's chest, but the other passed harmlessly through the scruff at his jaw.

With a roar more deafening than the siren or the shots, the Rare dove at the guard, slamming his shoulders and skull into the grass. The wolf clamped his jaws around the guard's throat.

Lexie watched students and staff look away or cover their mouths in shock, silent through the glass windows of the dining hall.

Rory and Lexie shared a look. He exhaled. Then he started to cry.

"Was that? Was that one of the ones that…?"

Lexie wrapped her arms around him as he shrank. She stroked his back with gentle hands. "Yeah, Rory. That was one of them."

19

Amid eulogies for Officer Stanley, new rules for curfew, and class cancellations, was a single blog in Lexie's RSS feed that dared ask the question, "Why?"

Why, exactly, are Rare wolves coming onto our campus? To terrorize students? Looking for a twilight snack? All I know is I'm holing up at home from now on and carrying a silver chain with me. You know, just in case. ;)

"It didn't seem to have an agenda," Lexie said to the girls assembled around the kitchen island.

Renee picked at her nails, peeling black currant polish from them in tiny bits. "Other than terrorizing the campus."

"Well, it's dead now," said Hazel.

"That one is," said Corwin. "There are supposed to be, what, eleven more?"

Lexie nodded. "At least, according to Sharm."

"So, girl dead in the woods, multiple killers, no motive," Mitch said.

Corwin chewed on her lower lip. "Sharm's nearly killed, no motive. Full-blood wanders onto campus with claws out for anything ..."

"The males need a motive," Renee said.

"Haven't you seen any werewolf movie, like, ever?" Hazel said. "They don't need motives. They're just monsters."

"This isn't a movie, Hazel," Corwin said. "How can we be so sure there was no motive?"

"They're males."

"Who told us half-blood males lose control and memory when they shift?" Sharmalee asked.

"Blythe, obv," Hazel said.

"And Blythe never lied about anything," said Renee, rolling her eyes.

"It makes sense. I mean, look at the boys we go to school with," Sharmalee said.

"Stefan told me they forget because they want to," Lexie said. "I think they could remember if they chose to. Like us."

"Seriously?" Renee swept polish peelings into her palm and threw them in the trash. "It's one thing to be a privileged douche. It's another to be a vengeful monster. We're talking about the Morloc here. Full-bloods. There have to be differences. These guys have been living in this area for hundreds of years, and this is the first big ramping-up of violence other than the battle ten years ago. The half-bloods. They're—we're—amateurs. Party crashers. None of us intended to be this way, none of us knew what was even happening to us. The Morloc, though, they have to want something. Else none of this makes any sense."

"Then how do find out what they want?" Mitch said.

No one had an immediate answer.

"We turn one into a man," Sharmalee finally said, though it sounded more like a question.

No one responded, though Hazel stifled a grin and Corwin shook her head.

"I thought full-bloods didn't shift," Mitch said.

"They don't, as far as we know," Renee said. "But what the hell do we know. We beat half-bloods to turn them from men to wolves. So maybe we have to do the opposite to turn a full-blood into a man."

"What's the opposite of beating?" Lexie asked.

"Petting?" Mitch offered.

"Positive affirmations?" said Jenna.

"Folk songs?" said Sharmalee.

"All right," Renee said. "Let's get one. We can figure the rest out from there."

The girls looked to each other, waiting for someone to speak.

"So..." Lexie said. "Where do we get one?"

20

LEXIE PULLED ON BLYTHE'S OLD black leather jacket. Hazel sat on the stairs, and Renee leaned on the banister.

"My dad keeps a tranq gun in the house," Lexie said.

"Seems a bit excessive," Renee said.

"Until you need one."

"Like now."

Hazel buried her mouth in her hands and wiggled her feet. Lexie and Renee exchanged a look.

"How do you get it?" Renee asked.

"No idea. I don't think he's left the house in three months. Since Hal died, he hasn't even left to go to watch sports."

"Is that weird?" Hazel asked.

"It's my dad. He's always been a little...sullen."

"Even when your mom was alive?"

"Kinda. Quiet at least."

"When my mom left my dad," Hazel said, "he got drunk all the time and wandered around in his underwear. Then he got really into Rilke. It was weird."

"It sounds like your dad's depressed." Sharmalee said, coming down the stairs in her pjs.

"I don't know if my dad has feelings like that. He's from the John Wayne school of masculinity: Don't say shit. The more it matters, the less you say."

"So, how you gonna get the gun?" Renee asked.

Lexie waved a hand at her all-black attire. "I don't really want to have to explain anything. I'm just gonna have to sneak in and take it."

Lexie wished for the first time that shifting was an option. Paw pads would help ease her path over her house's creaky stairs. But she'd never navigated her house with her wolf body before. Best to go with the knowns. She clicked her cell to silent and saw the time, 1:35am. Her father would be deep asleep by now, his pain killers just kicking into full gear.

The guns lived on a rack in the hall closet outside Ray's bedroom. He slept with his door open.

Lexie had only snuck in once before, during her junior year at Rogue River High after the homecoming dance. Now, walking up the stairs at the edges, she wondered why she hadn't done it more often. The answer, of course, was that she never had any reason to.

At the top of the stairs, Lexie turned away from her closed bedroom door and toward her father's open one at the other end of the short hall. The closet door stuck; she knew that. She turned the handle completely before pulling, eliciting a short moan from the door jamb. She froze and waited to hear her father rustling. He didn't. She peered inside. Next to the fresh sheets and towels was the gun rack, and at the end was the dart gun. It had a narrow, black barrel and fake wood stock. The brass sight glinted in the meager light. She reached for it. Somewhere nearby would be the box of darts and CO_2 cartridges. Cursing the lack of moonlight for rendering her blind, she eased her hand into the darkness, feeling towels, sheets, and nothing more. She leaned in farther, hoping to catch the corner of the box somewhere in the mess. The back of her neck tingled, and she heard a click.

"Get the fuck out of my house."

Lexie whipped to see the barrel of a rifle aimed at her head.

Her father stood in the doorway to his room, pupils wide from trying to see in darkness.

"Dad!" She thought the word would come out easier, but it croaked from her mouth. The panic from being in the crosshairs froze her muscles. "No!" she croaked again.

He stepped forward, the barrel just out of reach.

A choked wail echoed in the hallway and died amidst the linens: Lexie's terrified, and failed, final attempt at communication.

Or not failed. Her father lowered the gun and squinted into the darkness. "Lexie?" he asked.

Lexie whined and nodded her head vigorously. She was flush with adrenaline, struggling to regain equilibrium.

"Christ, Lex! What the hell are you doing here?"

"It's my house!" she shouted, finally finding her voice. As if that really answered his question.

Ray flicked on the light switch, and they both flinched against the yellow burn.

Her father wore shorts, thank god, and the rifle was still in his hands. Lexie held the tranq gun, and there was no way to hide it now.

Her mind scrambled for a plausible excuse. Hunting club. Zoology paper. Evil professor. Tenacious stalker. Her vision blurred. Tears welled up in her eyes, and she choked on nothing, gasping for breath and trying not to drown.

She dropped the gun and fell to the carpet, her diaphragm heaving in an odd rhythm. Amid her anger at her father and his lies was her own shame for excising him from her life. The burst of adrenaline at being in the crosshairs swept along all the resentment and shame in a flood of hot tears.

Ray stood flabbergasted for a long moment before he figured out what to do. He lay the gun on the floor and stooped with a labored grunt. He crawled forward to her, close but not touching her while she sobbed.

"Lex. Baby. What's the matter?"

He watched her from the distance of a wary pet, waiting for her to calm.

She hated that she couldn't have just asked him for the gun, that their once close relationship had deteriorated so far. She pulled it to-gether after a few shameful moments and bit her lip, hard.

"I'm sorry, Daddy."

Twenty minutes later, Lexie and her father were sitting at the kitchen table, hot chocolates in hand, and she was trying to tell him something. Anything. The house smelled strongly of mold and dust, and she hoped it was her keener sense of smell instead of a sign that things for her father had taken a bad turn.

After a grueling five minutes of silence, Ray finally asked, "How's the quarter going?"

"Semester. Milton's on the semester system." Lexie got up from the table and started digging through the refrigerator, finding only moldy take-out and sour milk.

"Oh, right. Of course. That's half a year, right?"

"Yeah, Dad." Lexie shrugged. "S'alright."

"You like living with those girls?"

Lexie poked around the kitchen cupboards. They were equally bare. "Sheesh, Dad, when's the last time you bought groceries? There's nothing to eat."

"There's some tuna and pasta in the bottom cabinet," he said, roll-ing the muscles of his lower back with his fist.

"Classes?" he asked.

"Fine."

"Any boys?"

"Boys?" Lexie asked. "Oh, you mean...No." She buried her face in the pantry, finding an ancient can of peanuts and cloudy jar of olives.

"I'm thinking boys might not be a thing."

"What?" he said, loudly.

Lexie exhaled hard enough to stir up a bit of dust on the shelf.

"What?" he said again. "I can't hear you when you mutter into the oatmeal like that."

If, before she changed, Lexie had been soft-spoken like her father, she'd become even more reticent now that her ears worked ten times better.

"Never mind!" she shouted, withdrawing from the pantry. She

tried to recall all the words Blythe had said that night. About her mother, about her lineage.

I know you lied about mom. The words came so easily in her head, but they refused to find a place on her tongue. Calling her father a liar bit her with too much irony. She had to come clean at least a little bit.

"There is—was—a woman."

Ray waited for the rest of the sentence, and when it didn't come, his brow furrowed in the same configuration of puzzlement as when he did crosswords.

Then the solution dawned. His eyebrows rose once, then all expression disappeared, replaced by his normal stoic face.

"Huh," he said at last.

"What?" Lexie said.

"Nah. I mean, sure." He looked away, thinking, weighing the possibilities, then returned to her. "Yep. That sounds fine."

"Fine? What?"

"Yep."

And that was that.

Ray's answer to her unspoken question was an eyebrow twitch that became a deep furrow. He took a long swig of his hot chocolate.

He swallowed and said, "That school of yours finally delivered your stuff."

"Stuff?"

"From your old caved-in room. I forgot to tell you about it when they came a couple weeks ago. I had them put it all in the basement."

Lexie swung open the door, scattering paint flakes at her feet. A wrong, sour kind of smell wafted up the stairs. She grimaced.

Two cardboard boxes sat at the bottom of the stairs, casting long shadows in the light from the upstairs. At her first step, she heard squeaks and the scattering of mice.

The stench of mold, dust, and mouse shit caught her by the throat. She grabbed for the basement light string and gagged as it clicked, warming the dingy place with its sulfur-colored light.

Lexie knelt at the nearest box and pulled out some moldy notebooks and her first semester syllabi, the pink highlighter bleeding over all the pages like watercolors. Beneath that was only clothing, crumpled and musty.

She reached for the other box. More books, two woefully overdue from the library, and beneath them, softness. Her quilt.

She pulled it from the box in a flourish of odor. The batting had been chewed through, and the whole of it had become a mouse nest. Bits of fabric and turds fell as she shook it.

"Dammit dad," she muttered. She shook the quilt again, hard, whipping as much filth and regret from it as she could.

"This place is disgusting!" was all she could think to shout.

No response from her father upstairs. The man never fought back, even when he was being insulted. "My quilt's full of mouse shit," she said. She climbed the stairs with the quilt in her arms, tugging off the light behind her. "You let my stuff get trashed down there."

"You left all that stuff behind, kiddo. Dean Fern had to get your RA to pack everything up and send it to student affairs. It sat there for five months and you never once asked about any of it. You never treated that quilt with respect."

"It was my blanket for my whole fucking life! It was one of the only things I had from Mom."

"Well you seemed happy to be rid of it."

"Well you seemed happy to be rid of mom."

Ray glared in the shape of a question.

Any more would be a confession, any less a cruelty. Lexie chewed her lip and spilled.

"I know what happened to Mom." Lexie stared at him, quilt cradled in crossed arms. "I know she's dead."

Ray stared into the brown depths of his mug and rocked his head in a facsimile of a nod. She couldn't tell if he was trying to lie again or come clean. His thoughts lived locked behind his stoic face.

His non-reaction was terrifying. She told him she knew he was a liar and she hated him for it. He took it all without so much as a raised eyebrow. She gripped her knife, hoping it would keep her from shifting and eating him right then.

"I'm sorry," he said to his mug. "I didn't want you growing up afraid."

"Of what?" Lexie asked. "Rares?"

He pressed his lips together and nodded. "Them. And your genes. Your ma wasn't in her right mind the night she died. She was having …what I guess you could call an 'episode'. I didn't know how to talk to you about it. Especially since Nana had died so soon before. It was just too much to explain to you, kiddo."

"I deserve to know the truth."

"I know you do," Ray muttered.

They sat in silence again, Lexie stroking her thumb against the tiny bubbles in the ceramic of her mug, Ray chewing the inside of his cheek. Neither looked the other in the eye.

"I want to kill the Morloc," Lexie said.

Ray gave her a confused look.

"The Rares that live up in the Barrens." Lexie picked up their mugs and put them in the microwave for a reheat. "That's what the gun was for."

"The tranq?"

Lexie wasn't ready to come clean either, it seemed. "No one's bagged a live one. I thought maybe I could catch one. For…science."

Ray stroked the white stubble on his chin. "You're talking about an animal that's as tall as a horse with the bulk of a tiger. I think you're gonna need at least two solid shots with those darts to take one out. Three would be better. And I think you're out of your goddamned mind."

Lexie watched the mugs whirl in the flickering microwave light. "So?"

"So?" Ray asked. "You're not fucking doing it 'so'."

"Dad."

"Oh hell no. No no no. You can be a smart-ass, you can be a college student, and you can be a queer. But there's no way in hell I'm letting my only daughter hunt Rares."

"Dad, I have to."

"Like shit you do."

"They're after everyone," Lexie pleaded.

"So, you do what everyone does. Keep your head down, stay alert, and stay the hell out of the north woods."

"Mom was a Rare hunter!"

"She was not!" Ray's face burned purple and his eyes bulged. "Your mama had mental problems, just like your Nana. And probably her mother before her."

"She wasn't crazy. She was trying to broker peace between the people of Milton and the Morloc. They're more than just animals."

Ray rubbed his temples. "Honey, I don't know where you got this stuff, but it's all bullcrap. Your ma was delusional, end of story. She hated it when white folks attributed all this magical mumbo-jumbo to Indians, even before she went 'round the bend. I wish I could say the stuff she came up with was insightful or symbolic, or magic or something, but it wasn't. It was just a string of nonsense followed by more of the same. Every shrink and brain doctor we could afford said the same. She had nightmares and took to drinking just before she died. These Rares, they aren't skinwalkers, or an organized society. They're barely even intelligent. They're just big, mean, dumb animals. Nothing more. Your ma died like that Curtis girl did—in the woods alone at night, for no good reason, all but asking for it. That's not sinister or supernatural. It's just a bad fucking idea."

"I've seen it."

"You've seen what? A wolf become a man?"

Lexie bit her lip. In a word? No, she hadn't. But she had seen six women become wolves, and she'd seen a wolf become a woman, her lover.

"That's just an urban legend, Lex. It's been around since I was a kid and it never got true. You don't think if that were real it'd be all over the internet by now?" Ray sighed and rubbed his forehead with a thick and heavy hand. "I'm real sorry I lied about your mama running off. That was a bad dad move, and it wasn't fair to you. But you can't hide from the truth by believing in fairy tales. It's not going to serve you. It'll just get you dead. I don't doubt that Curtis girl was chasing after some sort of rumor either. Don't do the same."

"Dad, these Rares killed Bree Curtis. They killed Mom. They've killed dozens since I've been alive, and they've controlled us with curfews and gun racks and decades of fear of the woods—our woods! And they'll keep killing. Why can't you let me do this?"

"Your ma had twenty-five years of experience on you. And she faced a Rare. One hit and she was dead. No way, kiddo. No goddamned way."

"I've seen them. I can handle them."

"You are just a girl, Lexie."

I'm not, though, she tried to say.

The microwave beeped, and Lexie brought the steaming mugs back to the table.

She placed Ray's mug in front of him, grabbed hers, and poured it on her hand.

"Lex!" Ray shouted.

Lexie grimaced with the pain as the chocolate buried tiny splinters of heat into her skin.

Ray stood like he was going for the sink, but Lexie grabbed his shoulder with her free hand and forced him back into his chair.

"No, Dad. Watch."

The rich brown liquid dripped away, exposing a bright pink, raw and throbbing hand. Her skin began to blister. Ray stared, nostrils flaring.

The burning sensation lingered, then died. Her hand paled and tightened, the blistered skin deflating, the ripples of damaged flesh regaining tautness and flexibility. Even the tiny, singed hairs regrew. In less than a minute, second-degree burns appeared, then healed.

Ray didn't say anything; he just stared agog at her healthy hand. He looked to Lexie's face, then to the hand she still had clamped on his shoulder. The puzzled expression returned. She eased back into her seat. He kept his eyes trained on his shoulder, and when Lexie finally sat, he rubbed and stretched it.

"The wolf that Hank Speer shot at, the one that killed him defending me, was my girlfriend." Lexie took a big breath before the plunge. "Daddy, I'm a werewolf."

Ray choked, and a vein like a swollen river pulsed along his temple and across his stubbled head. His eyes rested on the table top, and from across the table she could hear his pulse quicken. His face turned white and his ears red. He looked like she did when she was fighting off the wolf. But all he seemed to be fighting were tears.

Lexie's own throat tensed watching her father's pained face. He leaned on the back of the chair, eased himself to standing, and shuffled toward the stairs.

"Dad?" Lexie called after him.

In barely above a whisper, Ray said, "I think you'd best talk to Shirley."

They didn't talk about Lexie's aunt much in the Clarion household. She'd been estranged since long before Lexie's mom's disappearance-slash-death. Supposedly, Lexie met Aunt Shirley once, years ago, but she didn't remember.

"She lives down south a couple hours, just outside the Wilder Springs Rez," he muttered. "Might give you some of the answers you're lookin' for."

"Dad?"

He didn't respond—he just stared off in front of him as though she had disappeared. He reached for the banister and pulled himself up the stairs. Lexie stared, watching an ally become a stranger.

21

LEXIE PARKED ON THE DIRT drive, two dusty ruts overgrown with tall grass. The tranquilizer gun sat in the bed of her Bonanza, wrapped in Summer's ruined quilt. Shirley's trailer stood among others just like it scattered randomly throughout the clearing. Rust sprouted between the siding, and the torn window screen flapped in the breeze. The slam of Lexie's door set a dog barking somewhere off in the distance.

After a few minutes of silence, a marmalade cat appeared at the screen door, staring with lazy eyes at Lexie.

A woman appeared and nudged the cat away from the door with a brush of a slippered foot. She gave no reason of the delay in answering the door, nor an apology.

"You must be Alexis." The woman's voice was raw wool. Her hair was gray and ragged, interrupted by glossy streaks of black. "Leon get off the fucking couch!" she screamed into the trailer. Somewhere beyond Lexie's vision, a tiny dog protested.

Lexie stood below the front steps.

"Well?" the woman asked, lighting a hand-rolled cigarette.

"I'm sorry," Lexie said. "I don't remember you."

"Well no shit. Last time I saw you, you were barely bigger than a ground squirrel."

She held open the screen door and dragged hard on her cigarette. "My name's Shirley."

Lexie stepped into the trailer, a narrow space with wood panels concealing drawers and cabinets. All she could smell was smoke and dog and cat.

"So you're hunting for answers then."

"The word I had in mind was 'fishing'," Lexie said with a half-hearted smile.

"Big difference. When you're hunting you're alert and on the move. Fishing, you just sit and let things come to you. And no one comes to Wilder for the fishing."

Lexie let her hair fall in front of her eyes. "I guess. But I don't even know what I'm hunting."

"Eh, you rarely do. Long as you got the chops, it don't likely matter, neither."

"You're my mom's sister?"

"Well, sure, start with the obvious. Seems a fine strategy." Shirley threw a wet cough into a tight fist. "Yeah, I'm her baby sister by two years."

Lexie looked askance at the deep creases in her tan flesh, her cracked lips, and her leathery hands.

"You know what happened to her," Lexie said. She felt high, so close to answers—real answers—about her mother's death.

"Depends."

"On what?"

"On what you know."

"I know that she's dead," Lexie said. "And I know she was magic or something." Lexie felt foolish to reveal how little she knew about her mother's death. That the near-stranger sitting across from her held more information maddened her. "What do you know?"

"The gist."

"Who killed her?"

"All of 'em," Shirley said.

"The Morloc?"

"Mostly, yeah."

Shirley pushed a chipped ceramic mug in front of Lexie and poured some tepid coffee into it. Lexie took a sip and struggled to swallow the bitter liquid.

"How?"

She shrugged. "Wasn't there."

"Why—?"

Shirley made to talk, but Lexie talked over her. "Why didn't anyone tell me?"

Shirley took a heavy drag and lifted her mug to her lips. She squinted through her cigarette's smoke and answered. "Your Pa tried to cut your ma apart from her family. Part of that was pretending we didn't exist. I suppose he felt it was safe for you to know about your Nana because she was so batshit by the time you popped out, she wasn't gonna reveal nothing sacred."

"She wasn't crazy."

"Oh hell yes she was."

"She was a peacespeaker."

Shirley's forehead formed uncountable wrinkles. "How'd you know about that?"

Lexie shifted in her chair, loose screws drawing squeaks from the aluminum struts.

"Well, she was that too," Shirley continued, "but she was as schizo as a syphilitic hound dog, and don't you think those two are the same things."

Lexie hid her face behind her coffee mug and forced herself to take another bitter sip.

"Why'd my dad keep me from you?"

"Cause he's a rat bastard."

Lexie flinched. Shirley softened. "I expect he didn't want you to follow the same path as your ma. He sure didn't like it when Summer and I started going to the gatherings, and he tried putting his foot down after our first meeting with the Rares, but Summer was always the bull of the family. There was never any stopping her."

Lexie squinted as the pins slipped into place. "My Dad. He knew?"

"Not much, hon, but yeah, he knew."

"He told me my mom had left him for another man."

Shirley held her coffee in one hand and her cigarette in the other, bringing neither to her lips. "You fucking joking?"

Lexie shook her head, her bangs hiding her eyes.

"That sonofabitch." Shirley slammed her fist down, making the cigarette's ash leap across the table. The dog yipped and the cat rushed to hide behind the bucket under the sink.

"He tell you about the peacespeaking bit?"

Lexie shook her head again. "This is all I've got." She hesitated before unsnapping her sheath and retrieving her knife.

"No shit," Shirley said with a dry grin. "Haven't seen this in an age."

She reached for it, and Lexie balked.

Shirley raised her eyebrows. Lexie handed her the knife.

Shirley wrapped her fingers around the hilt and angled it toward the light. "Yeah," she said, her eyes squinting with a smile as she seemed to trace the memories. "This is a good one." She rocked the knife in her palms, catching the overcast light in the blade. It reflected a white streak against her black eyes. She smiled, serene for a moment, almost sweet-looking, before catching Lexie's wary gaze in the steel's reflection.

"Son of a..." her voice cracked. Her wide eyes fixed on Lexie's face.

"No." Lexie said, leaning away. She hadn't expected to be outed. Certainly not like this. "I mean...it's not a...a real thing. Not me. Not more than once."

"I'll be damned," Shirley said, not shocked, but something else, something certain but wary. "When did you change?"

"I don't know. I mean, just the one time. In October. But I haven't changed since the first time. It didn't stick." Lexie picked at her fingernails.

"Four full moons, and you haven't changed?" Shirley rasped.

Lexie shook her head. "No. It didn't take."

"Bullshit." Shirley waved the knife between their faces. "Carrying this thing around on your hip like a totem. I'll bet you even sleep with it, don'tcha?"

Lexie looked at her lap, wanting to hide alongside the cat.

"This shit is getting sadder by the minute," Shirley said, taking a long drag from her waning cigarette. "You bleed last month?"

Lexie nodded.

"And the month before?"

"Sure."

"You crankier than usual?"

"Well, yeah, but it's not just PMS. I lost someone."

"Bunk. You feel it."

"What?"

"Your wolf. You feel her inside of you."

Lexie pulled her knees to her chest, fingering her keys in her jacket pocket. "It's my ex. She's inside of me."

"Bullshit," Shirley said, slamming the knife down on the table. "People live in your head and your heart. Maybe your sexy bits if you're real lucky or unlucky. They aren't in your ribcage, your jaws, and your gut. That's your wolf. And you best not confuse the two."

Lexie was too ashamed to meet Shirley's eyes. She glanced up through a veil of bangs. "You know that ain't allowed, right?" Shirley said. "A girl being both a peacespeaker and a wolf?"

"So I've heard," Lexie muttered.

"Get rid of this knife. It's holding you back."

Lexie's hand darted across the table. She grabbed the knife from Shirley's hand. She felt better immediately, squeezing it tight before returning it to the sheath. "It belonged to my mom. I'm not just going to get rid of it."

"Why do you care so much about this? It's just an artifact."

Lexie began to feel defiant of this strange and abrasive woman. "It's got magic. It keeps me...intact."

Shirley took a thick draw and arched her eyebrows. *You don't say,* they seemed to mock. "That magic ain't keeping no one safe. Least of all you. It's keeping you weak, locked in that skinny little virgin body of yours."

Lexie felt the instinct to protest but stopped herself.

A weighty moment passed between the two women before Shirley stubbed her cigarette out into a plastic ashtray.

"I always thought your pa was gonna make some woman real happy someday. But your mama wasn't just some woman. She never did like being told what to do, by our ma, by men, by me, by no one. I guess that's why she always preferred the company of wolves."

Shirley shook another cigarette out of her pack and offered one to Lexie, who shook her head. "I suppose you have that in common. How'd it happen?"

"I fell in love."

"Common problem."

"So I gather." Lexie picked at her fingernails and shook her head. "I tripped my tits off and drank from a paw print."

Shirley snorted. "That sounds more like it." Shirley finished her coffee and tipped the mug on its side, spinning it by the handle. "What exactly you looking for here, squirrel?"

"Answers," Lexie said. "The Morloc are responsible, either directly or indirectly, for another death. And they attacked one of my pack. I want to stop them before they kill or turn anyone else. My ma's the only one who knew anything about this. She's dead, and I got nothing but this knife to sort through all this Cree woo-woo."

"Ha!" Shirley smacked the table again and expelled a cloud of smoke. "Cree woo-woo? Shit, girl, you have all your shit messed up, and I won't even blame your daddy for that."

"Cree woo-woo," Shirley muttered and shook her head. "You don't need answers. You need results, because that's the only thing you and all the white folks who raised you seem to believe in."

"What kind of results?"

"Depends on what you're shopping for. But I have a feeling, since you're Summer's kid, it ain't gonna be peace and quiet, am I right?"

"I just want things to go back to normal."

"You think killing the Morloc is going to get you normal? Squirrel, you been on this planet for eighteen years. The Morloc been on it for eight-hundred. This is normal."

"Fine. I want our town to be normal-normal, not Wolf Creek-normal."

Shirley stubbed out her cigarette and leaned back against the fur-spattered upholstery. "Morloc been killing, girls been dying, townspeople been grumbling since long before you or I were around to notice. You might be strong, hon, but you can't change history."

"The Morloc are getting organized."

"That's impossible."

"It happened once before."

"Yeah, but your mama's pack killed their leader."

"Maybe there's a new one. Multiple wolves mauled a classmate all at once. The Morloc have to be working as a pack. They already attacked one of my...sisters." Lexie nearly stumbled over the word, but it suddenly felt right on her tongue.

"If I fix this...

...*Archer will come back.*

...*My mother will come back.*

...*Renee will be redeemed.*

...*Duane will be healed.*

...*We won't have to be so scared anymore.*

Lexie knew none of these were true, but each vied for a place on her tongue, trying to trick her into their veracity.

"If I fix this..." Lexie said. "I don't know. I just know I need to. I'm following a trail, hoping it'll take me to the right place."

Shirley held her hand out to the cat that sat on the plastic carpet covering, flexing its paws. She opened her hand once, like describing a flash with her fingers, and the cat leapt onto her lap and lay down for a scratch.

"What'ya got?" Shirley asked.

"I have a pack."

"Of women?"

"Half-bloods."

Shirley laughed. "You may as well take on the Taliban with a slingshot while you're at it."

Lexie narrowed her eyes. "We can fight."

"I don't doubt ya. But don't get any grand notions of fighting the Morloc, cause a peacespeaker and a handful of ladies ain't nearly enough for those fuckers. We tried that already and got our asses handed to us."

"What would be enough?"

Shirley's laugh rasped, shrill and coarse.

"Hell if I know. We didn't have it ten years ago, and you ain't got it now. You need more manpower, that's for damn sure, and you gotta figure out a way to fight those fuckers where you actually have a chance to win."

"How?"

"Honey, if I knew that, I'd be with your ma at happy hour right now." She scratched the cat's ears and it purred in her lap. "Two things your ma had going for her that you could stand to learn though: conviction and resolve. You're torn in two. You think half your heart's with your lady friend, but that ain't true. Half is with your wolf, and the other is searching for a home. Maybe with your woman, maybe not. It means you don't know which side to fight on, or for, or for what. You gotta make a bold choice, squirrel. Cowgirl up, and ditch that knife for a bit."

22

THROUGH ALL THE INFORMATION SHIRLEY offered, all the warnings, all the history, only one thing burned in Lexie's brain: Dad knew.

Dad knew.

Dad motherfucking knew, and he lied to Lexie's face twice. When she gave him the out, when she laid it out before him and all he had to do was cop to it and come clean, the fucker buried his head even deeper in the pile of bullshit he'd been shoveling all of Lexie's life.

Rage burned under her skin and forced sweat from her brow. She ground her teeth until her jaw ached. She wanted to explode, to force her fist into someone's ribcage, to close her teeth around a throat and tear. Didn't matter whose.

Mom had been killed by Rares. Dad knew she was a peacespeaker, and he'd lied. He lied and lied and lied for eighteen fucking years. That patronizing son of a prick.

"Fuck you, Dad!" she screamed as she ran through the forest that had once been Archer's, far away from any ears.

"Fuck you, Dad!" she screamed again as she burst into the clearing by the river and launched herself up the cliffside leading to the treehouse. Her voice echoed against the rock face, and she screamed without words, until her throat seized and she coughed against her self-inflicted damage. Atop the cliff, she stripped off her jacket and shirt and tore into her sycamore, the branches scratching at her bare skin and tearing at her hair. She leapt into the tree, landing on the planks of the treehouse with a clatter.

The birds in their nest chirped loud and insistent, a warning, meager and pathetic. Lexie glared, and the birds peeped once and fell silent.

She stood at the edge of the platform. The glittering sea formed a narrow strip at the horizon. She drew her knife from her belt and threw it with all her strength into the trees. It caught the red sunset as it spun in the open air and dropped through the treetops. "Fuck you, Dad!" she screamed and grabbed her hair, pulling, tearing it from her scalp. Her face was wet with sweat and tears. "Fuck you, Archer!" each time louder, a seeping wound of rage and loathing. "Fuck you Randy, fuck you Brian, fuck you Duane, fuck you Mom, fuck you Blythe fuck you fuck you fuck you!!!" She choked on her voice, each scream croaking out of her.

"Fuck yoooooooooooooooooooooou!!!!!!" she howled.

And blacked out.

When she came to, a breath later, she knew.

Her chest felt heavy and full. Her breath came in gasps. She let her tongue loll out of her mouth and tug at her throat. She rolled her heavy skull on her neck and let her lungs fill up with one, two, three times the capacity of her human lungs. The inhalation was like the drawing of a syringe. She released a gurgled growl, drunk on the smells of the forest, of her body, of this treehouse. Scents too subtle for human noses now stood out starkly. They rattled her elongated sinuses, each layered scent bouncing at a different speed and angle, announcing their various degrees of import and interest.

Lexie stumbled, caught between standing on two paws and standing on four. She gripped the planks with splayed pads and righted herself.

She heaved a breath and stared at her paws. No more real than the first time she witnessed them in her love-drunk haze. Now, there was no moon, no love, only rage and betrayal and a need to let go. She had let it go, and this is what she got for it.

The knife had landed somewhere below, and with it a piece, so annoyingly obvious, fell into place. Lexie hadn't been willing her wolf to abate for these three months. Her knife had done that work for her.

Now, with three months of pent-up beast within her, it needed no incentive but her rage to spring forth.

Lexie curled her paw, claw tips reaching to prick at her forearm. Such drama over such a simple thing. Lexie admired her paw in the sunset's copper glare. The sun broke free of the clouds at the horizon, dwindling above the cliffs at the ocean's edge. Its yellow mirrored her own lightest hairs.

Why had she feared this beauty? Though Lexie loved Archer's human shape, she adored her in wolf form. It was the truest version of the woman she loved, free of subtext and subterfuge. Free of everything but love. Her shell was beautiful, but what was within was divine. Lexie might not have understood that if she had she not felt it herself. The shape her beloved took was simultaneously meaningless and potent. Lexie stared at her paw and wondered if she were capable of such a similar purity, free of the human world and all the bullshit it entailed. An elegance in comfort, an unloosening, naked, and for the first time really able to breathe.

A growl gurgled in her throat, the closest approximation to tears her wolf body would allow.

The birds rustled in their nest. Lexie glared at their cozy home. She stood on her hind legs, reaching her forepaws above where the nest sat hidden in the crux of the branch that held it. She dug her claws into the bark, securing herself for a long stretch. Her height titillated her. She stood two feet taller than her woman's body. She glared at the roosting birds, sniffing out their dander and dust. They stilled, sensing the danger in Lexie's notice.

Smart, Lexie thought, before tracing a single claw along the shell of the nest's lone egg. She left a thin gray line against the brilliant ecru. The female wren screeched and flew at Lexie, beating her wings and attempting, futilely, to scare Lexie off. She batted the bird away and hooked her paw around the male and the egg. The male bird trembled like a frantic heartbeat against her leathery pads, while the egg sat stoic and fragile, its small warmth seeping out. Lexie opened her mouth and shoved them both in, chewing just once, grinding the father and egg into a salty, crunchy paste.

The female darted and dove, then fled. Lexie fell back on all fours, grinding the bird and egg once more, then swallowing. The sweet crunch of the fetal bird and the salty, bloody fluff of its father washed down Lexie's gullet, and her stomach rejoiced.

Such delight made her muscles twitch under her skin. She had to do it. She shouldn't attract the attention. She couldn't resist. Say no. Stop.

Lexie tossed her head back on her neck, unfurling, uncoiling, stretching, easing.

Her breath, the great insane force of it, surged through her open throat like a banshee's wail. Her glottis caught it like a steam whistle, tearing the stream of air into two pieces, slicing it down the middle in ripples of pitch. Two ribbons, one low, one high, finding and fighting each other in the space beyond her muzzle.

They fled from her as though they had been waiting for months to do so.

Her eyes squeezed shut with splendid release. Her howl made the pine needles above her shiver. She howled as if she could cause the moon to rise, just with her voice.

Lexie lowered her head, spent. Just then, the white-horned crescent of the moon peered from between two boughs.

Sparks sizzled down her nerves, aftershocks.

A howlgasm.

She opened her jaws in a lupine smile.

Something darted through her like a minnow, another presence in Lexie's head. Where her paws connected to the floorboards of the treehouse, she felt it rattle her skeleton, ripple her fur. She couldn't name it or identify it. It felt like her human self, having traded places with her wolf, huddled and cowering in the recesses of her consciousness.

She smelled that other self, a dispersed sort of person-scent lingering in the treehouse, a layer of chemicals too thick to parse, foods, esters, synthetic simulacra of organic life, decay. A jumble of misdirections was the scent of people. Her smell roused the girl huddled inside her, and she knew she needed to get rid of what remained of her humanity, if only for the night.

Lexie leapt down the tree's side, paws scrabbling for purchase on branches and scraping against bark. The tiny meadow below was crisp with frost. Lexie bounded in the direction where she'd thrown her knife. She lifted her nose to the air, then lowered it to the ground seeking out the knife's scent. She couldn't find it. She paced forward, sliding past a birch trunk, black scars on white skin. She...smelled it, she supposed, but it was bigger than that. The scent started in her gut, not her snout. It trembled in her abdomen, like loud bass through a stack of speakers. It rattled her guts.

She leaned into the tree, stepping back and forth, rubbing against it like a worry stone. Its naked branches clattered overhead, and it oils warmed to her touch and sublimed.

The birch yielded the scents of cedar, sage, and river mud. Archer. Or a simulacrum of her. A stand-in made of earth and herbs.

Her muscles twitched in anticipation. While her human brain screamed threats, warnings, and pleas, the wolf-Lexie stared into the gloaming and only wanted to run. To take Archer's territory and make it her own. She was Archer's lover, and in that moment Lexie decided that was how territories changed hands. Screw it. She could Google it later. Now, she just wanted to run.

She tore off toward the south, following the Rogue River before it eased to the East. In her nose was a barrage of bright smells like colors, all of them shades of blue and green. Movements flashed to the left and right, blurry critters leaving a burst of fear behind them. Lexie ran onward, her own breath heavy in her ears, the sound reaching them on a new, slightly longer, odder path. It was like the sound from a film, added later, always just slightly uncanny.

She ran until her lungs burned and her tummy rumbled with hunger. She slowed in a patch of thick and mossy brush, sniffing out small animals, wanting to kill something else.

She followed the scent trail of a jackrabbit around low brush and to a taller stand of trees. It tore off, and she pursued, running fast, dodging and ducking under boughs and brush. When she lost it, she found something else to chase. She repeated the game for hours, sometimes eluded, sometimes giving up her prey for the sake of the chase. In the darkest hours of the night, deep in the southern woods, she found something new: the sound of a clumsy creature too stupid to know it was being stalked. It ceased its rooting and raised its head from the earth. A feral pig.

Lexie's mouth watered. God knew how much she loved bacon; she couldn't wait to try the real thing. She took a tentative step, and the pig's ear twitched, seeking her. After a frozen moment, the pig dug its snout back into the soil and resumed its rooting. Lexie took two more deliberate and silent paces, feeling each part of her paw ease into the earth.

The pig heard her footfall and froze again. It started to move, then stopped, listening. Lexie held her breath. The pig took off. Lexie chased.

She followed it around tree trunks and through bushes. It stumbled over a rock outcropping and she pounced, falling just short of it. It squealed as it ran, tromping zigzagged tracks in the frost-covered earth.

The pig fled toward the river. Where the water bent south, the foliage grew dense. The pig dove into the underbrush and Lexie slid to a stop before the branches snared her fur.

Lexie ran around the dense brush just in time to hear the pig's hooves tear across the frosty clearing beyond. She ran in pursuit, ending up in a stand of tall sequoias.

She took a deep breath to find the pig's scent, and found something else instead, something old and dead. Lexie looked around and realized she was standing on the ground where Renee killed the boys.

So little of the scent remained, but the memory of it was as fresh as it had been the day she stumbled upon it with Archer. Lexie retched, choking on the flood of memories of filth, bile, and tears. She should've known better than to let go. This time. Always.

Lexie slinked back to the clearing below the treehouse, sniffing out her knife. The dull throb returned, and the closer she got, the more nausea rose in her throat. The moon's sharp light glinted off the blade, half-buried at the base of a tree that wept sap.

Each step tugged at her throat, like the knife was a magnet pulling Lexie forward clavicle-first. When she reached the knife, she touched her paw to the handle and felt her body shift. Her cells and nerves reorganized in a cascade that left her brain in tumult for the tiniest moment. She lurched forward, her balance off as her arms tried to hold the weight of her torso. She collapsed next to the knife, her head against the tree trunk, watching it weep sap from its wound.

"Sorry, buddy," she whispered, touching the sap with gentle fingertips and bringing it to her lips. The alkaline liquid tasted bitter on her tongue.

She withdrew the knife and held it against her cooling skin, regret and shame filling in the places that joy had filled earlier. She shouldn't be here, in these woods, pretending to be something she wasn't, taking pleasure in such destruction. This wasn't her. It wasn't right. It wouldn't solve anything.

23

LEXIE DRAGGED HERSELF INTO THE house, wrapped in Summer's quilt. Its mouse piss and mold stink wafted in with her. Jenna was knitting in the living room, a mug of black tea steaming next to her, when Lexie walked in. The sunrise peeked through one small window over Jenna's shoulder, and she looked so warm and calm it pained Lexie to interrupt the moment.

"Pee-yew!" Jenna said, looking up from her knitting. "What is that?"

Lexie stepped into the living room, prepared to explain, but the tears won out. She was crying before she knew it.

Jenna gave Lexie a soothing shush and then pulled her into a hug.

"We'll get it cleaned up, sweetie. It'll be easy."

Jenna grabbed the quilt and shook it out, the crud gone but the smell clinging fast.

Four holes punctured the surface of the quilt, small rips following the delicate stitching and rows of multicolored fabric.

Jenna examined it carefully, holding it to the light and running her fingers along the stitching.

"It's salvageable. Handmade things can be unmade and remade. It's part of their magic. I'll separate the front piece, where all this detailing is." She ran her fingers over the crooked stitching. "And I'll add a new back piece, some patches, and new batting. No problem."

"It was my mom's," Lexie whimpered.

Jenna nodded. "It'll be fine. We'll get this piece of your mama back."

Lexie needed a shower. She plodded up the steps. Mitch was in the bathroom, fiddling with a roll of surgical bandaging.

"Can I?" Lexie asked as she poked her head into the bathroom.

"It's cool. Come in."

Lexie took off her clothes at the same time Mitch did. His breasts were shockingly large, especially since Lexie had never really paid much mind to his body. Seeing them now, released of their sports bra and undershirt confines, Lexie had a hard time not staring.

Mitch didn't notice—or he pretended not to. He wound the bandage around his chest, flattening the pendulous flesh into simulacra of pectoral muscles. Lexie ran the water and stretched.

"How was the woods?" he asked.

Shit, Lexie thought.

"You're going to have to start expecting that," he said.

"I guess it's hard to keep secrets around here."

Mitch snorted, a half smile digging a dimple into one cheek. "When I can smell everywhere you've been for the past two days? Yeah, you can forget about privacy." He bit his lip and looked away.

"You must miss her a lot," Mitch said, finally.

Lexie looked askance.

"You go to the cabin to think about Archer, right?"

Lexie fidgeted and shrugged.

"Do you see anything?" Mitch asked.

"Anything?"

Mitch bit harder on his lip, his dimples forming like forehead furrows. "Like of Blythe. Like blood, or fur, or anything." He forced a casual tone.

Lexie grimaced and shook her head. "No. I think the fire took care of all of that."

Mitch nodded and returned his attention to the mirror.

Lexie stepped into the shower and moaned at the needle-heat of the water. "I can go back there with you sometime, if you'd like," Lexie said. "To, I dunno. Say goodbye or something."

"Maybe," Mitch said in a grudging tone that made it sound like a no.

"Hey Mitch, can I borrow your hockey stick?" Hazel asked, her voice echoing through the bathroom.

"Why?"

"Professor Rindt is organizing a protest down at the new off ramp and I need to tape my sign to something."

"Why are you protesting?" Lexie asked, peeking around the shower curtain.

"Because paving a highway through an old-growth forest just to raise the state's bottom line is bullshit."

Mitch futzed with his hair in the mirror. "But it'll tear up the Morloc territory. That's a good thing."

"No it's not," Hazel said. "It's just going to squish them into a smaller space, which isn't going to be good for anyone."

The three stood still for a moment, contemplating that fact.

"Do you think?" Mitch said.

"That's why they're so pissed at Milton all of a sudden?" Hazel said.

Lexie pulled back the curtain so she could participate in the conversation without ending her shower. Her hair was piled on top of her head in a sudsy heap. "That'd piss me off."

"Do you think Bree...?" Mitch asked Lexie.

"Oh my god, she was!" Hazel shouted.

"Was what?" Mitch asked.

Hazel nearly leapt as she shouted, and from down the hall, they heard Corwin and Sharmalee shift sleepily in bed. "She was on the board of the environmental club! She's the one who brought Rindt on as our staff advisor. She was helping organize the protest!"

Lexie dipped her head under the stream. "You seriously just remembered this, just now?" Lexie asked.

"What?" Hazel said. "I was only at one meeting."

Lexie let the hot water wash away the past few days' anxiety and dirt. "Does that count as a motive?" she muttered to herself, forgetting the girls could hear her just fine.

"Probably not," Mitch said, "but it's a fair bet that someone out there didn't like her."

24

LEXIE PULLED UP TO THE back entrance of the Thorny Rose, easing her truck bed to the loading dock. The cold morning cast the
scene in a glaring gray. The building, which weeks ago hadn't left much
of an impression beyond industrial shabbiness, appeared downright
seedy in the daylight. The gravel parking lot extended for yards in all
directions, keeping the forest at bay. The red bricks had been painted
and repainted, the motley hues worn and peeled away, coloring the
warehouse the shade of a particularly brutal kind of vomit.

Randy greeted Lexie with a sheepish smile. "Is this how I make
it up to you?"

Lexie stepped down from the driver's seat and half-smiled. "It's a
decent start."

"I don't know if this will work, Lex," Randy said, leading Lexie
through the roll-up and into the dungeon. The cage lay deconstructed
on the wrestling mats.

"Well, it's the only plan I have," Lexie said.

The smell flooded Lexie's brain with memories of their night together here, and the awkward and shitty goodbye disappeared in the

fresh memory of their shared sensations.

"The hardware is all in this box," Randy said. It rattled when she kicked it. "My buddy emailed me the specs and assembly instructions. Here."

Randy leaned in close to show the paper to Lexie. She smelled of cologne, laundry detergent, and motor oil—the antithesis of the forest. That foreignness mixed with her sex nearly made Lexie swoon. She could feel Randy's tug on her, but she didn't care. She knew it was a bad idea, but she didn't care about that either. "The steel is stress-rated to forty-thousand PSI, but I'm not so sure about the fatigue life, especially at these joints. After reading about that Rare attack on campus, I really don't know if it'll hold one."

"It'll work," Lexie said in an attempt to convince them both.

"Just don't get yourself killed for a science fair project, okay?"

"I might. This could be the last time you see me."

"That's not funny, Lex."

It wasn't, and Lexie's face said as much.

"Oh," Randy said. "Then can I apologize again?"

Lexie was about to tell her no and turn away, but the gentle pleading in Randy's eyes held her gaze. It was the human equivalent of a tucked tail, and Lexie found herself excited by the submissive posture. She grabbed the back of Randy's neck and pulled the other woman's mouth to hers.

Randy flinched, then relaxed into the kiss. She wrapped her wiry arms around Lexie and pulled their bodies together, tight. Randy nearly matched Lexie in her leanness, and Lexie exalted their similarity. Randy felt different from the only other two bodies Lexie had held against hers. She didn't have Renee's round hips, or Archer's rolling muscles. Randy was scrappy, and Lexie delighted in the novelty.

"I thought—" Randy started.

"Shut up."

Lexie seized Randy by the arms, stroking her hands up her bare shoulders and burying her fingers in her cropped, grizzled hair. Randy let Lexie lead, looking as surprised as a teenage boy getting lucky for the first time.

Lexie pushed her to the ground, straddling Randy's body, and pulling off both their shirts. Randy was wise to keep her mouth shut, no doubt trained by a lifetime of loving complicated women. She seemed content to let Lexie take what she needed, and this time, Lexie was fully present.

The sunlight through the open loading dock cast white diamonds on Lexie's bare skin. Randy sat up, taking Lexie's breast into her mouth, stroking and sucking, rocking their bodies together, her thigh wedged between Lexie's legs.

They released one another only long enough to remove the rest of their clothing, and then they were back at each other, the wrestling mat serving as padding to cradle their crashing bodies.

Lexie dove onto Randy, pinning her down, biting her flesh, drawing her nails across her skin.

"Easy, tiger," Randy laughed, and Lexie relented just a bit before pressing into her again. Randy gasped, "You're stronger than you look."

Lexie smiled and traced paths with her tongue that she followed with her teeth. She caught sweat and sex in each taste, rolling it in her mouth, swallowing, and making it hers.

Lexie grasped at Randy's groin, which bore the same salt and pepper coloring as her hair. Lexie felt Randy's warmth move into her hand. Randy squeezed her eyes shut, looking both nervous and enraptured.

Lexie bit and scratched, gripped and pinned, searching out where Randy's muscles relented and where they resisted. Randy's small sounds became words: *Shit, shit, shit,* she repeated like a mantra. Then the words cycled back into sounds: *Shuh, shuh, sh, uh, uh, uh, uh,* in time with Lexie's stroking.

Lexie loved feeling the tiny muscles in her hands work so hard, as though she were learning to use them for the first time. The muscles fatigued but then re-upped to offer more cycles of pleasure and tension.

Lexie expected a burst, a scream, a singing moan. Instead, Randy's sounds faded to silence, and even her breath stopped. Her body clenched from head to toe, shaking like a seizure before falling into lassitude.

Lexie's hand didn't stop until Randy reached for her wrist. Randy's eyes were still squeezed shut, and she had yet to exhale. At Randy's touch, Lexie relented. Randy exhaled, a long, hissing sigh.

The weak sun had barely moved when Lexie eased into the driver's seat of her truck.

"We good?" Randy asked, squinting.

Lexie smiled weakly. "Nothing's good, Randy." The truth nicked her like a razor. "I'm a mess; you're a mess. I'd like to just survive the next month, and we can figure out where we stand after that, all right?"

Randy flinched, but she nodded.

"Just no more drunken aggression, okay?"

Randy reached into her pocket and pulled out a white AA chip.

"Good girl," Lexie said with a smile.

"Let me know if I can help in any other way, all right? And...thanks." She winked. Lexie returned it with a flirty smile and a nod. She eased her truck out of the gravel drive, the cage clattering in the bed like a steel skeleton.

25

TRANQ, MUZZLE, AND CAGE. THAT was the plan. They left the cage in the woods near the cave where the Pack would take their half-blood prisoners. It was accompanied by Hazel, Jenna, and the assembly instructions. Corwin had the topo maps and a satellite phone, GPSing as they went. Renee lubricated the spring mechanism of her crossbow. Lexie followed the new highway until it became the logging road it had always been, then they kept on going. She turned left into the woods and bounced for fifty yards until they were out of sight from the road.

Mitch stayed with the truck, awaiting Corwin's call for the pickup. "Double check with Hazel and Jenna that they've got the cage together," Lexie said.

They hiked in from there, up around the burnout, to the north face of Needle Ridge where Sharmalee had been herb hunting. Renee ran point, Corwin navigated while carrying the gear, and Lexie followed with the tranquilizer gun at her shoulder. All she had to do was shoot.

They followed a hunch and Sharmalee's memory of her path. Forty minutes after they entered the woods, the hunch paid off.

There was a scent trail of a full-blood, with faint dispersed scents of others.

They headed upwind and around the scent, like circling a stream.

The group came to a small clearing where the brush was as dry as the rocky soil. A small cave sat between some broken boulders, the scent of the full-blood thick in the air. They'd found one.

Corwin put down her cache and recoiled, stifling a yelp. A thorn embedded itself in her palm and she shook it without making a noise.

Renee grabbed her hand and walked her further back into the forest while Lexie watched the cave. She could see the shadows moving evenly, the deep sleep of a Morloc full-blood.

"What a weird-looking thorn," Renee whispered, yanking the brown star-shaped piece of plant from Corwin's palm.

"That looks familiar," Lexie said, also keeping her voice low. "Isn't that the goat's head thingy?"

"What goat head?"

"The plant Sharmalee was looking for. The herbal testosterone thing Mitch wanted."

"Seems appropriate," Renee said, "that a bunch of it would be growing up around these dudes."

Corwin sucked on her wound and dug through her bag for some work gloves.

"Hold up. Let me grab some. For Mitch," Corwin said.

The girls crept back to the edge of the treeline. The Morloc's den sat beyond, cold and quiet.

Lexie crept ahead, her tranq gun pointing the way.

"You smell him?" Renee whispered.

Lexie nodded. "He's sleeping."

In the clearing, Renee kept her eyes fixed on the cave opening, while Lexie scanned the setting for escape routes and cover. The only clear shot into the cave was from a small rise two yards from the opening.

Renee pointed to the rise and whispered, "On my signal, shoot from there, then bust a move back to the treeline. I'll cover you if you need a second shot."

"Let's hope one is all it takes."

Corwin waited near the trees with a coil of jute rope.

Lexie crept to the opening of the cave, where the earth dipped, eroded away by the full-blood's comings and goings. His fur rose and fell slowly with the rhythm of his snoring.

Lexie felt her heart in her throat. She swallowed twice against it. She braced her right foot and brought the gun to her shoulder. It felt too light, more like a toy than a weapon. She took two slow breaths through an o-shaped mouth and adjusted her position. She had about eight inches of exposed body to work with, and each step back reduced her window. Finally, at seven feet from the cave, she stopped and centered her sight.

The Rare's grizzled fur moved in the same steady rhythm. She only hoped she wouldn't hit a shoulder blade.

Renee stood off to the side, her nose in the air and her crossbow at her side.

Lexie took another three long breaths, trying to relax every muscle except for the ones gripping the trigger.

Lexie remembered this place, where her mind would go when she lifted a rifle to her shoulder, the straining calm that gripped her body, the gratitude for finding patience when faced with motion, and the small space of calm amidst a storm of panic.

One more breath, and she took the shot.

The tranq canister caught the Rare's trapezius. Lexie and Renee ran to the trees where they recouped and turned back to the cave. They sniffed and scanned for motion, their senses sharpened by adrenaline.

Nothing came. The wolf remained in the cave. They waited for the requisite twenty seconds, and the Rare's breathing settled into a slower, deeper rhythm.

After nearly a minute, the girls crept toward the cave, weapons still drawn. At the mouth of the cave, the beast still snored.

"No shit," Renee said.

Lexie shrugged.

Corwin dropped the rope and unfurled the tarp on the dirt. "All right, so now we just have to get him onto this."

The girls crept to the cave mouth just in time to hear the snore become a growl.

"Shit," Renee said.

"Shit. Shit shit fuck."

"Run!"

In a burst of snarling and slavering, the Rare leapt from the cave, skidding onto the tarp with four paws.

Renee fell back and raised her crossbow to release a bolt. It sank into the Rare's haunch and lodged in the beast's hip bone.

Lexie raised her tranq gun, trying to find a shot. The full-blood spun in circles, snapping threats at each of them.

"There's no flesh on this fucker!" Lexie cried. The Rare's skin was stretched like old leather over his bones. Fur was missing in chunks, replaced by scar tissue and fresh pink welts.

"Go for the neck!" Renee screamed.

"We don't want to kill him."

"Come on, Lex. Over here by the ribs!" Corwin shouted.

Lexie saw only more mangy fur stretched over bone. The full-blood leapt for Corwin, knocking her on her back. She screamed and threw punches. He grabbed her by the shoulder with his jaws, shaking her and tossing her onto the rocks. She fell like pruned branches, a broken crumple.

Renee loaded the next bolt and fired it, burying into his shoulder; the bolt jutted out like a gruesome piercing.

He roared and turned on Renee, staggering. All his movements were graceless. Jerky. At least the first dart was having some effect.

"Find a shot, Lexie!"

I'm trying! Lexie screamed in her brain, but her voice wasn't the first thing on her mind. She watched the arrow bob with the Rare's movements. *Fuck, the dude's all leather and bone.*

Lexie found her shot, eight square inches between the Rare's sharp shoulder blades. But the creature was taller than her, and she couldn't hit it from her vantage. She needed height.

The Rare snarled at Renee, who cranked the crossbow mechanism to load another bolt. "Lexie!"

"I'm climbing!" Lexie darted past the Rare's back legs, throwing the rifle on her shoulder and diving for the first boulder that comprised the Rare's den. The jagged pieces of broken stone scraped at her palms when she grabbed it.

She yanked herself to the razor's edge of the rock and leapt again to another ledge just above. The Rare dove for Renee. She jumped. The wolf caught her legs and sent her careening over his back. She landed hard on her side and groaned.

Lexie saw the flat point she needed on the boulder that formed the apex of the formation. She holstered her tranq gun and leapt over the gap, missed, then grasped frantically for a handhold as she slid. She dug the rubber of her boots into the rock, but it only slowed her fall. She flung her arms wide, the whole of her body pressing against the rock. She clung with every muscle, finding any tiny point of friction and dedicating her life to gripping it.

She pressed her fingertips down, but the rock slid like sandpaper beneath them. She curled her fingers, her nails dragging now. She cried out when her nails peeled from her skin. Her legs scrabbled for purchase. Her right foot caught on a tiny spur of rock.

She gritted her teeth through the pain in her hands and clawed her way up the rock, sliding on her chest and face until she caught the plateau she needed.

The Rare snatched Renee's shoulder in his jaws. Renee screamed and kicked at his throat. Lexie slid onto her belly and pulled the gun from her shoulder. She could do this. Like hunting from a duck blind, she thought, with a bigger, slower target, she told herself. Piece of cake.

Lexie put another tranq round on the tip and cocked the rifle. It sucked the air as the pneumatic engaged. Lexie took another breath, aiming for the flesh between the Rare's shoulder blades.

She exhaled and shot. The dart whizzed through the air to lodge in the tender flesh shielding the inside of his shoulder blade. The Rare released Renee and barked once. Renee scrambled for her crossbow. Lexie loaded one more dart, but she didn't need it. The Rare swayed, his heavy head lolling on his neck. Its weight disrupted his balance, and he staggered to the right. He tried to control his muscles, but his legs folded beneath him.

His nose hit the dirt, and he toppled to his side, eyes rolling into his skull and red tongue lolling to the ground.

One huge snuffle, and he was out.

Renee rushed to Corwin. She rubbed her head and stumbled to her feet. They all turned to the Rare, watching him warily for one long moment before rushing toward him. Corwin wrapped the rope around his snout, a tight muzzle, then bound his paws.

She favored her injured shoulder, and blood stained her sweat-shirt. Renee retrieved the tarp, and they eased it under the bulk of his body. "We need better weapons," she said, through heavy breath. "Crossbows suck."

"Call Mitch and have him hightail it up here," Lexie said to Corwin. "We've got maybe an hour."

26

THE GIRLS COULDN'T STOP STARING. The beast didn't pace like Lexie expected. He merely stood, heavy skull hunched below sharp shoulders, glaring. A makeshift leather muzzle fashioned by Jenna bound
its jaws. Corwin enjoyed buckling the muzzle onto the Morloc. She
punched him across the nose before the tranquilizer wore off.

Now, awake again, his yellow eyes tracked Lexie, fidgeting behind
the wall of her friends. No doubt he knew they were all half-bloods,
but she prayed he couldn't divine more.

They'd erected the cage next to the cave where the Pack, under
Blythe's rule, had brought half-blood males to beat into shifting.
Where Lexie had seen the violence these women were capable of, and
the hatred. She shivered and zipped up her hoodie.

The cave was too small for the cage, so they stood beneath the
haggard pines. They'd have to be extra careful keep the Morloc from
howling for his friends.

Gripping her knife in her left palm, Lexie stepped out from behind her friends.

The Rare went ballistic, throwing his weight at the cage with a horrific clatter. She held the knife in front of her, catching the Rare's reflection in the blade, praying both its metal and that of the cage wouldn't buckle. His yellow eyes glared back in the reflection of the blade. She looked back at him, squinting, trying to catch the sunlight, or maybe the shadow. She didn't know which.

Lexie stepped closer, and the Rare rolled a low growl. Despite being bound and muzzled, the beast intimidated still. His eyes were a putrid yellow, matching his teeth as he snarled. His ears were missing chunks of skin, and open wounds wept from his neck and back, two from the day's wrangle, and more from earlier fights and bites.

Lexie reached the knife into the cage, but it still didn't show a shift. The Rare was a Rare, no man to be found.

His growl fell to a steady roil. She placed the blade on his patchy fur. He shuddered like a horse deflecting flies.

She slid the knife under his fur, along his shoulder, and he snarled. Blood oozed beneath her incision, but his fur and fangs remained.

His eyes cursed her as she focused on the wound.

"Yeah, there's more where that came from," she said, wiping the knife clean on his fur and returning to the Pack.

"Well that's new," Lexie said.

"What is?" Hazel asked.

"When I wounded Blythe with the knife, she shifted back to human form. And when I held it on the full moons, it kept me from turning."

"So the knife should turn a wolf human?" Mitch asked.

"I thought it would, but it didn't."

"One test doesn't prove much," Corwin said.

"Maybe the knife makes them shift into whatever they are," Hazel said. "You cut Blythe and she turned into a person. You touched Archer with it, and she turned into a wolf. You cut mean animal over there, and he stays that way."

"Which means he's a wolf and not a man." Lexie sheathed her knife. "Which we knew. Or thought we did. Now what?"

The wolf's gurgling growls continued, rising and falling in tone, like the Pack's chatter, but muffled and incomprehensible.

"We're doomed," Mitch said, part question, part resignation.

"We can assume this guy was one of the Rares who killed Bree," Renee said.

"And attacked Sharm. If we can't get to the whole pack, at least we can kill him," Corwin said.

The girls continued debating what to do with the Rare now that their plan had fallen apart.

Lexie turned her ear to listen to the continued guttural noises from the Rare. She walked back to the cage, reached in, and ripped the muzzle from his snout. She snatched back her hand just before he snapped at her with his teeth. He bared them at her fully now, yellow against the black of his gums. He snarled once.

"What did you say?" Lexie said.

The wolf narrowed his eyes and snarled.

"What did you say?!"

His throat trembled, a chirping kind of growl. The pattern was familiar, strings of syllables with no breaks except when he took a breath. She had heard this language before, though she didn't know where.

Humans. This world is not for you.

Lexie jumped back. "Say what now?"

The syllables arranged themselves into lucidity in Lexie's mind. She struggled to stay present as fear flooded her, screaming at her with each shallow breath to run, to hide, to find Archer and dig a hole and wait out the rest of time together. She stammered, "We just want to know why you're killing us."

The wolf stopped growling.

She struggled to flex her throat around the awkward syllables, choking on the first, and dropping the second. Finally, she found the right tension to create the high-pitched gurgled note. She listened in her head to the words she sounded out in English while hearing her throat work on the unfamiliar. It felt like nonsense at first, or some trick from the freaky church down the road. Then sounds croaked from her throat without any analysis. They merely sprang forth.

"Uh…" Hazel said. The girls had fallen silent when Lexie ripped away the muzzle. Now they exchanged wide-eyed glances.

Lexie chattered until she could complete the awkward and stumbling sentence, a repeat of the question, "Why are you killing us?"

Does need motive spider to kill?

We are human, Lexie chattered.

The wolf stared at her.

*You attack humans...*she struggled to find the correct word...*not deserved.*

Who was here first?

Why two hundred years to... Another hole appeared in her lexicon. She stumbled. Revenge, she chattered.

We make attempts. We try new method.

Lexie scoffed.

Cities. Walls. You build to shield, to defend. But you bleed outside, on us, he growled.

Humans came from woods, you cannot banish us, Lexie said.

Not banish. Remind. Where human live in hierarchy.

"Why did you kill Bree?" Lexie spoke in her human tongue.

The wolf blinked in response.

The girl, why did your pack kill her?

Not a pack, the Rare said.

Why did you kill her? You killed child of...government man.

The wolf stared.

That's important!

To you.

To everyone! Lexie stumbled over syntax and construction, hoping he understood, as though reason was even an option. *They could burn forest. They could send in warriors.*

It we welcome.

Death?

Chaos. The humans destroy own walls, always. We survive, always.

"I don't know," Lexie mocked in English. "You look pretty haggard."

The wolf responded with another long stare and a small snort.

A flash of an earlier conversation appeared in Lexie's mind, walking with Renee, smoking the cigarettes: *I'm mortal Lexie, and so are you. So are all werewolves.*

Then, months ago, Archer's weak joke that at 185 her age was catching up with her. These Morloc, they were older than Archer, by far. This one certainly looked it.

Good at survival? Lexie thought. *No way.* The Morloc had no legacy. Archer was the only pureblood, and there had been no report of a female werewolf found, ever. This haggard wolf and his kin were likely the last of their kind—no mates, no pups. They had nothing but themselves.

What do you plan?

Take what is ours.

What is yours?

Our xouitihanou.

Lexie shook her head, not understanding the word.

Our blood survives after our bodies are dead. We create young to carry us on. Your females are ours as long as you live on this land.

"Well that was weird," Lexie said, stepping back to confer with the Pack while Mitch guarded the cage with the tranq gun at his shoulder.

"What did he say?" Hazel asked.

"A lot of things," Lexie told the Pack. "He made it sound like they're the ones on the defensive."

"That's insane," Corwin said.

"He seems to think his territory is under threat, and he and the other Rares are merely defending it."

"Well..." Jenna said.

"Well what?" Corwin asked.

"It's kind of hard to argue with that logic," Jenna said. "I mean, the highway..."

"They killed an innocent woman," Renee said.

"Who was inexplicably in the woods alone in the middle of the night," Jenna replied.

"That's victim-blaming," Hazel said.

Jenna held fast. "It's suspicious."

"You may as well be asking what she was wearing," Renee groaned.

"Well, what was she wearing?" Jenna asked.

"Oh my god, Jenna!" Hazel exclaimed.

"It could be a clue! I'm not saying she asked for it. I'm just finding it very suspicious that a pack of full-bloods felt the need to defend their territory from a eighteen-year-old girl."

"Because they're *lying*," Hazel said.

The girls looked to Lexie, who just shrugged. "I could barely understand him. I don't think sarcasm or duplicity would track with me right now."

"Never mind," Jenna said, waving her palms in front of her. "It's just suspicious is all. That's all I'm saying."

Lexie chewed on her lip, her gaze falling on the dusty ground at her feet. She knew the answer to Jenna's question, and knew every moment she didn't answer was a new betrayal to her pack.

"Jeans and a green turtleneck," Lexie muttered.

The girls shared a curious look. Renee said, "What?"

"Bree was wearing jeans, a green turtleneck, and a jacket. Some makeup. Diamond stud earrings. Boots with a low heel. She looked nice, like she was going on a date. But not too nice, like it was the first one."

The girls all gaped.

"I found her in Archer's territory. I was the one that called to tip the cops," Lexie mumbled. "She was in Archer's territory."

Lexie looked back toward the cage. Mitch fidgeted, straining to hear the conversation, his gun slack at his shoulder. The Morloc stared straight at Lexie.

The girls were dumbfounded. Lexie expected a barrage of questions but none came. On her sisters' faces were merely looks of horror and disbelief.

Renee shook her head. "Did you…?"

Simultaneous sounds struck them—a rifle blast, and a howl. The howl rattled their collective bones like the bars on the Rare's cage. It soared in all directions, a tsunami of sound. Lexie and Renee ran for the cage. The other girls took cover.

Mitch had missed; the shot gashed the metal bars and nothing more. The Rare stared at Lexie with hateful eyes. *Do not mistake, peacespeaker,* the Morloc said. *We will kill you, your families, your progeny, your mates. We will kill everything you love. And our blood will survive.*

27

THE GIRLS RAN SOUTH ACROSS the river to scatter their scent trail, should any of the Morloc get the idea to pursue.

Lexie stumbled on roots and rocks, wishing she was on four feet again. She let her mind slip into her wolf, even if her body wouldn't follow. A strange solace filled her as she gave herself over to the imagined sensations of her wolf instead of resisting them. The girls waded into the icy water and followed its shallows upstream, where they emerged on the other bank and shook their feet dry. The cold water sliced at Lexie's skin like a thousand tiny scalpels. The hideous cold faded into the brutal burn of damaged flesh. She sucked air through her teeth and rushed for the opposite bank.

When she emerged, the girls formed a semicircle around her, arms crossed and glaring.

"What. The. Fuck," Corwin said.

Lexie wiggled her toes to coax some blood back into them. "It wasn't some nefarious plan."

"No," Renee said. "It was just a dumb-shit one."

"It wasn't a plan at all," Lexie protested.

Jenna pleaded. "Why didn't you tell us you found Bree?"

Lexie looked to the faces of her sisters and saw the angst of betrayal. "It didn't seem..."

"Stop it, Lex," Renee burst. "You don't get to decide! You don't get to tell us what matters and keep to yourself what you think doesn't. This isn't just about you!"

Lexie fumbled for something to say in her defense, but no words came.

"You are a member of this pack," Renee said, jabbing her finger toward the other girls. "You are no longer one friendless girl skulking to class and avoiding eye contact. Every choice you make has real repercussions for the women standing right here in front of you. If you can't handle that, feel free to run off on your own and chase down Archer. But don't stay here expecting us to care for you when you deny us the basic courtesy of telling us what's going on in our woods."

Renee's eyes burned with fury, but more, with that maternal disappointment Lexie had grown up only hearing about. The gaze squeezed her soul in a vice of regret. She wanted to throw up or bury her face beneath the icy rapids.

"I'll take you to where I found her, Renee," Lexie squeaked, looking at her feet.

"No," Renee said. "Tomorrow, you're taking all of us. We do these things together from now on."

Sharmalee was lying on the couch when the girls burst in. She eased herself to standing. "What did you see?"

"We got one," Renee said.

"What'd he say?"

"Nothing good," she replied, dropping her crossbow on the kitchen table.

"They think Milton is theirs," Jenna said. "They want everyone out, full-stop."

"How do we know they won't start with us?" Sharmalee asked.

"Oh they will," Renee said.

"Here? Are we safe here?" Sharmalee said.

The girls looked warily to one another.

"We should be vigilant," Jenna said, trying to sound optimistic.

"We'll start keeping night watch in shifts," Renee said. "Jenna, can you draw up a schedule?"

Jenna nodded.

Hazel whispered, "Don't forget I'm at Luscious on Wednesdays and slim-moon nights now."

Everyone else exchanged glances. Lexie had the feeling there wouldn't be much going out in anyone's future.

"We'll talk about it later, honey." Jenna patted Hazel's hand, and Renee bit her lips.

Renee's room was a space in transition. The room hadn't quite completed the shift from Blythe's ice queen austerity to Renee's own preference for bold colors and worldly artifacts. As least the smell was right—a million different spices too tightly-linked to parse.

"I'm sorry," Lexie said, standing in Renee's doorway.

Renee lifted her filthy white tank top over her shoulders, revealing her bare torso and the seven gnarly puncture wounds that encircled her shoulder. Her skin was purplish and swollen, dried blood caking on her skin like rust on bronze. While the wounds had begun to heal, she still needed some cleaning up.

"I know you are," Renee said, cracking her neck. "I just wish you'd start thinking like a member of this Pack instead of some free agent hanger-on."

"I'm trying," Lexie said. "It's just so new to me. I want to trust you guys; I just don't know how."

"You could start by paying attention to how we trust you," Renee said. She plucked a brown bottle of hydrogen peroxide and a bag of cotton balls from a cabinet below her mirror.

"Would you do me a favor," Renee asked, "and hose me down with this?"

"Will this be strong enough?" Lexie asked, taking the cotton and dousing the first wad.

Renee sat backwards on her desk chair, leaning her bare chest against the backrest. "Couldn't hurt."

"Is that gonna…you know," Lexie said, gesturing to the wounds, "change anything?"

"Werewolves aren't a disease, Lex. Once you're dosed, that's all there is. I'm not going to switch sides 'cause I got bit by a douchey full-blood."

Lexie pushed aside the stacks of books next to Renee's bed to make room for the cotton and peroxide bottle. The books formed a ladder of famous warlords and strategists. Starting with Rommel on the bottom, the spines climbed through the names Patton, Joan of Arc, Nemirovsky, Boudicca, Fu Hao, Tamar of Georgia. Atop them all, a tiny black book rested open, face-down.

Renee leaned on her bed, and Lexie leaned over her.

"Studying?" she asked, pressing the cotton to the first wound on Renee's lower back. Renee sucked air through her teeth. The wound fizzed.

"Not really. First time I've gotten a C since freshman year."

"What's all this, then?"

"Strategy, I hope."

"Could be useful. For all sorts of things."

Renee reached onto the bedstand and retrieved some surgical bandaging. "Could you do this, too?"

Lexie tended to the wounds on Renee's back, then Renee flipped over and leaned back in her chair, giving Lexie access to the ones on her abdomen. Lexie tried not to stare at Renee's breasts, tried not to think of how she could have felt them pressing against her own if she hadn't chickened-out at their first meeting five months ago.

No, she focused on the caked blood and deep puncture-wounds marring the soft skin of Renee's belly. She wiped the cotton against that damaged skin. The wells foamed over like science fair volcanoes.

"The whole not-telling-us-about-Bree thing aside...good job today," Renee said.

"Thanks." A tentative grin stirred at Lexie's mouth. "What part? Aside from...you know."

"Saving my ass was a good start. But facing the Rare. That took chutzpa."

"Is that Yiddish?" Lexie padded Renee's wounds, and each time Renee sucked air through her teeth.

"Yeah," Renee said. "I only allow myself to say four things in Yiddish, otherwise I feel too much like my grandma."

"What are the other three?"

"Nah, it has to be organic. You'll hear them someday maybe. Speaking of languages," Renee said, shifting in her seat, "you seemed to have an impressive handle on them today. How did you do that?"

"Speak to the Rare?" Lexie shrugged and wrapped up the cotton balls in a discarded plastic bag. "I don't know. It felt like the words were locked in a part of my brain I didn't know existed. As soon as I heard the Morloc speak, they just started falling out. I wish I'd had more time to talk to him before he called for his bros."

"Well, it's good to know, at least. Maybe it'll help us learn things." Lexie bit her lips hard. "It already has."

Renee snorted. "Nothing we didn't already suspect."

Lexie released her lip. She couldn't keep this secret. Not after Bree. "There was one other thing the Morloc told me. I didn't have the right translation for it, and I didn't want to scare anyone."

"What was it?"

"Roughly translated," Lexie said, "all females are theirs."

Renee weighed the words. "What for?"

"What do monsters ever want with women in stories like these?" Renee studied her hands. "So Bree was..."

"Supposed to bear pups," Lexie whispered. "Yeah, I guess so."

"Why'd they kill her then?" Renee scratched her scalp and sighed. "Though it explains why they didn't kill Sharmalee outright."

Lexie let grizzly images flash in her mind, trying to shake them away but only finding them compounding in flashes like a medley of slasher films. She shuddered and made a sour face.

Renee slammed her fists down on her desk, making Lexie jump. "Why is it always fucking forced pregnancy with these assholes?"

Lexie tore at the gauze tape with her teeth but Renee reached for her hand and held it. "You were right not to announce it to everyone. It'll scare the girls into submission. They've barely coped with their own attacks, let alone the idea that these Rares are actually targeting women for rape. It's just too grim." Renee sighed, hard. "We have to kill them. All of them. Soon," Renee muttered. She leaned forward and inspected Lexie's handiwork.

"What can I do to help?"

"Conjure a miracle?"

"Okay, what else?" Lexie laughed and blew the stray hairs off her face as she put away the peroxide.

"I'm not kidding. We know two really good things about you. We need to figure out if there's anything else for us to..."

"Exploit?" Lexie said with a half-grin.

"Utilize," Renee said. "Yes. Starting with guns. You can use some of your connections to hook us up with firepower, yeah?"

Lexie shrugged. "I can try. Though it was hard enough getting my hands on that tranq gun. I doubt my dad would pull any strings that would encourage me to get in front of any more Rares."

"It'd be nice to not have to use them," Renee said, standing to assess her reflection. She picked pieces of broken leaf from her hair before tying it into a puff at the crown of her head. "God, it would've been nice to be able to turn today."

"Not for me. I'm no good as a wolf," Lexie said. Renee's bare chest distracted her from being too concerned about her admission. "I make a better human."

"The wolf is awkward at first. It almost always is," Renee said. "There's a part of yourself you just have to relax. It's like learning how to belch or orgasm. There's a tiny, intangible part of you that's also the strongest part you have. It's like a cage, or a safe, or the blackbox on a plane. Indestructible, but very heavy. Eventually, you figure out how to open that box, and once you do, you get a good look at everything inside. No matter if you thought it was a dream or irrelevant or healed. It's all there."

"And you get to decide if you keep going back to let everything out. It gets easier as you do it, but the first times are the worst, and the best, I guess."

"Can't you just burn the thing?"

"Could, but it's also the part that keeps your back straight. It's the part of you at the center of everything. Burn that, and what good are you to anyone?"

Lexie thought of her dad, of Duane. She thought of the possibility of her doing right, and the consequences. She allowed herself a tiny, optimistic look down the road. It felt nice, if foolish. What good was there in hoping for a future that couldn't be?

"It didn't feel good the last time," Lexie admitted.

"Bullshit," Renee laughed. "You were fucking." Renee pawed through her drawer for a clean white tee and eased it over her fresh bandages. She stood tall, stretching her shoulders, once again the gazelle of a woman Lexie was so struck by at their first meeting.

Lexie shook her head, knowing she had to come clean. "Not last time. Last week."

Renee glanced over her shoulder. "What now?"

"I did."

"Last moon?"

"Last week."

Renee grabbed Lexie's arms. She flinched. "Seriously, Lex, if there is *anything* else you're keeping from me, now is the time to come clean."

Renee was right. Lexie looked to the ceiling and scanned her memories, trying to find any other secrets than needed revealing. She shook her head. "There's just this."

"How?"

"I don't know. Not really. Something to do with my knife holding me back. And, I guess, a bit of a freak-out."

Lexie wanted to take it back, to save herself from the deluge of questions for which she had no answer. But she shouldn't, couldn't, and didn't. And the questions poured out of Renee. Lexie tried to answer with as much truth as she had in her, but the real question, which Renee repeated too many times to note, was beyond her ability to answer: "How?"

She could say it was her anger, her sadness, her willingness to be something else, but none of that was necessarily true. Lexie replied to all Renee's questions with the refrain she had been growing accustomed to: "I don't know. I was angry. I threw away my knife. And it just spilled out of me." Lexie wrapped her arms around her body, too confused to offer anything of worth, and ashamed of that fact.

"We have to figure out a way to do that again."

"I don't want to. It hurts. I can't."

"We need the muscle, Lex! You can't just say you don't want to when all our lives are on the line!"

Lexie's pained face contorted, on the edge of tears, and Renee softened.

"Sorry," she said, taking Lexie's hand and sitting next to her on the bed. Renee studied Lexie's face and stroked her cheek. "I went into my first fight not being able to turn."

"When?"

A soft frown stirred Renee's lips, but she closed her eyes against Lexie's curiosity. Renee rubbed her lips together and sat up straight. "I didn't know you mother. I never met her, even that night. I saw her between burning trees. I never even spoke to her." She released Lexie's hand and stared ahead. "I'm sure you would've liked to have known more. I'm sorry I didn't tell you earlier."

"You were there? The night my mother died?" Lexie said, the words catching in her throat.

"I guess we've both been keeping secrets from each other." Renee nodded. "I guess that makes me a bit of a hypocrite. I'm sorry."

"That happened when I was just a kid."

"I was too, in wolf years. A newborn. I had turned the first time, taken by surprise of course. But I didn't change that second moon, the night of the fight. I guess there was a part of me that was resisting, that was scared."

"You watched her die."

Renee nodded. "Though I didn't know what it was. I was far away, and fully human."

"How did you survive?"

Renee stood and lit some candles on her bureau, making the room feel warmer in spite of the chill running through Lexie's heart. "I fought. Most of them didn't want me to. Archer okayed it at the last second. It was a day before the moon and I couldn't turn, but I was a good shot. I ended up sniping from a boulder. Three injuries, no kills. Clearly not enough. But I fought. I had enough rage inside of me to tap like a fresh keg. Once I found it, it just poured out of me. Later that night, when we assessed the damage that had been done, I shifted for the first time. Unexpectedly, unwillingly, and only for a few precious seconds, but it happened."

"How many of you died?"

"All of us, save Blythe, Archer, and me. Nine total dead, including your mom. If we had had equal numbers we still would have been outclassed and outmuscled. There was never anything we could do about it."

"How bad was it?"

Renee played with the live flame of the candle. "Their eighteen to our twelve, plus a peacespeaker and a pureblood on our side. We took out four. They took out nine. Exeunt all."

"Dire."

"Devastating."

"Then why does Archer blame herself?" Lexie asked, trying not to sound more concerned about her lover than her mother.

"She always blamed herself for everything," Renee said, returning to sit beside Lexie on the bed. "For why the Morloc came to Milton, why they were turning men and raping and killing women. She wore all that shit right on her shoulders. I only knew what I was there for that night. The Morloc were mean fuckers, but the half-bloods they make are worse. They're the ones that gave Milton its reputation, that created Corwin and Sharm and Hazel and Jenna. Or at least turned them into who they are now."

Renee leaned to look Lexie dead in the eyes. "You see why, when Blythe told me there were wolves that needed killing, I didn't think twice?"

Lexie pulled away. "And now?"

"We're outnumbered, outclassed, and—"

"At the top of their to-do list," Lexie said, rubbing her temples. "What do we need?"

"Strategy. Muscle. Flamethrowers," Renee sighed.

"Can we settle for feminine rage and some shotguns?"

"If only. We'll never be as strong as the ones who created us, and that alone is infuriating."

"Physically, you mean," Lexie said.

"Sure."

"There are other ways to be strong," Lexie offered.

"I know. But none are quite as useful in battle."

"Maybe you should keep reading," Lexie said. She stood and lobbed *The Art of War* onto Renee's bed. "Maybe something in here will prove you wrong."

Renee smiled and scratched her head. Lexie had a momentary flash of memory, the feeling of Renee's hair beneath her palms, scratching her scalp. A tingle ran up her back and she shook it out.

"Call your daddy," Renee said. "Let's get us some guns."

28

THE NEXT MORNING, DUANE CORNERED Lexie in the only other dining hall open for breakfast. He didn't hide his hurt, and with a surly tone told her he needed to do the experiment to write his Abnormal Psych midterm.

Two hours later, Lexie was feeling sulky and ashamed, sitting in the psych building in a rolling office chair with conductive goo in her hair.

"Can you close the door?" Lexie said, the first words she spoke to Duane since he started.

"We're supposed to leave it open."

Lexie looked down the gloomy hallway of the psych building. "It just freaks me out, all strung up and exposed like this." She cast a wary glance down the hall, wondering how she would muster the courage to call her dad later if she couldn't even bear to be seen like this now. But she had to call, to ask for the guns, to tell him she knew he was a liar, and maybe just to say goodbye.

"I'll leave it ajar. How's that for a compromise?"

"Fine," Lexie said, blowing a stray hair out of her eyes.

Duane picked through her hair like he was looking for lice, a tube of conductive gel in one gloved hand and an electrode in the other. Despite the chilly gel, his touch felt nice, and once again Lexie was caught in a memory of the nurturing touch of Archer. She told herself she'd have to ask for that from the Pack. She'd often see them giving each other head scratches and foot rubs, but it always made her just a little too uncomfortable to make the request. But feeling Duane's touch now she realized how essential such touching was to her survival.

He dotted seven swirls of gel across her skull. She kept her eyes on a monitor that looked straight out of the 90s.

"Okey dokey," Duane said. "That's that. Now for the solenoids."

"The what?"

"These little coils," he said, holding up plastic cylinders that resembled old film canisters, or something you'd glue to your neck for a Frankenstein costume. "They'll create a small magnetic field around your temporal lobes. You won't even feel it."

He slipped an elastic band over her head and positioned the cylinders. "The EEG is going to measure your relaxation."

"I get to relax?"

"I told you it'd be easy."

Lexie leaned back in her desk chair, ready for the mini-retreat the solenoids would offer.

"Oh," Duane said, making a face. "I'm gonna need you to…uh, remove your knife."

Lexie pulled the bottom of her sweater over the sheath, blushing.

"No, seriously. Metal like that could screw up the experiment."

Lexie gave him a wary look, then slid the sheath off her belt, handing it to him reluctantly. He set it on the file cabinet behind him, safely within her view.

"Ready?" Duane asked, and Lexie gave a thumbs-up.

He pressed a button on a machine that looked like a hard drive from the 80s. A monitor displayed a path of wavy lines that looked like future music.

"Okay," he said more to himself than Lexie. "Got a clear baseline. Now the solenoids." He flipped a small toggle switch on the machine in his lap.

"Ah!" Lexie grimaced when a jagged pain rushed through her head like a metal serpent. "This hurts."

"Don't worry about it. It's an incredibly small amount of magnetism. You might feel a little dizzy, but nothing more."

Lexie took a deep breath and tried to relax into the sensation, but the buzzy, creeping feeling stayed. "This doesn't feel good."

"Just keep breathing. It's really not much."

Not much. Like trying to keep her ribcage closed. Like trying to keep her skull in one piece. Like trying not to let her teeth erupt from her skull, her blood sizzle her nerves, her nails tear at her fingertips. Not much, not much at all.

"Duane..." Lexie grimaced.

"Lex, you're stable, just relax. Let your brain drop in. Like meditating. It'll be over soon."

Lexie considered for the briefest moment that she might be overreacting. No. No. She knew this feeling. No, stop. STOP!

A fever flooded her, sweat bursting from her brow and running down her face. Her shirt soaked through as she tried to lash together her insides with nothing more than force of will. She squeezed her eyes shut. Her wolf was here, but not inside, not where it usually lived and paced. It was perched on her shoulder like a daemon. Then it was pacing behind her. Then it sat across the room, lounging on the file cabinet like a library lion. It scattered throughout the room like a phantom, then fell back together atop her chest, making it hard to breathe.

She moaned through gritted teeth.

"Okay," Duane said, focused on the instruments. "We should be calibrated and ready to go. How you doing?" He turned and paled. He clamped a hand over his open mouth.

Lexie was frozen in mid-shift, her body oscillating between two brutal forms. If she could only let go of her muscles, she'd surely vomit, but all she knew was the clench of electrocution forcing all her muscles into the ON position.

Duane yelped and tore the wires off her head. The machine protested with a tiny beep. Lexie slumped in her chair. Duane stepped gingerly to her, reaching his hand up to comb her hair from her forehead.

Before he could touch her, she retched, a flood of vomit drenching his legs and feet. Lexie followed it to the floor, falling in a crumpled heap, Mary Magdalene washing Christ's feet with her own sick.

Duane stood, frozen in shock as Lexie moaned at his feet. Footsteps echoed up the marble staircase outside the lab, and Duane slammed the door shut.

Lexie lay on the blessedly-cold floor. The marble wicked away her wolf and her fever.

"Lexie?" he asked meekly, leaning to her with an open palm. He almost touched her head, then flinched. "Are you okay?"

"Don't take me home," Lexie mumbled, her eyes swaying in their sockets.

"Don't?"

Lexie tried to shake her head but it merely lolled to the side.

"Stefan," she said. "And water."

Duane grabbed a fire blanket and eased it under her head. His palms were cool, soft, and trembling. She liked his touch. It was so gentle. He'd make a good doctor someday—if he survived that long, if any of them did. He steadied his hands and stepped away, reaching for his cellphone and hesitating at Lexie's knife. He left it where it rested on top of the cabinet.

Lexie tried to focus her eyes on him as he paced near the window that looked out onto the brick wall of the neighboring building. He unlatched the window and slid it open on its old, squeaky casing. The room filled with cold air, and Duane took a deep and calming breath. With his ear to his phone, waiting for Stefan to answer, Duane turned from the window to look at Lexie, still curled up on the floor.

"I'm just gonna say you passed, okay?"

29

STEFAN ARRIVED WITH TAYLOR AND Otter. "What do you want us to do with her?"

Duane was still pressed against the window, the farthest point in the lab he could stand from where Lexie was curled on the floor. "She told me to call you."

"We don't have a car," Otter said, his voice a jagged melody always ending on a sharp note. "What are we supposed to do with her?"

"I don't know, but I'd like it if my professor doesn't check in on me and find four dudes hovering around a passed-out girl."

Lexie mumbled from the floor. "Mmm...not...passed out." She squinted at the boys' faces from her awkward vantage. Her eyeballs felt like they were going to burst.

Taylor made a face. "What did you do to her?"

"Nothing," Duane sighed, his arms crossed tight against his chest. "It was just an EEG experiment, and she had a seizure, and...stuff."

"And stuff?" Taylor said. "Okaaay, creepy man."

"I'm not a creep," Duane said. "She...her body did...weird things."

"Weird girl things?" Otter said with a grimace.

Duane fidgeted. "Not exactly."

The fear in his voice confirmed that he'd seen it all. It wouldn't be long before he put the pieces together.

"Just pick her up, Otter," Stefan said.

Otter rolled his eyes and lifted Lexie in a fireman's carry, her torso dangling over his back like a cartoon cavewoman's.

She groaned, and Otter matched it.

Lexie watched Duane upside-down. He stared with a perplexed frown at the skinny boy holding her as though she weighed no more than a half-filled duffel bag.

"What?" Otter said.

Duane shook his head and waved away the question.

"All right," Stefan said. "Queers out."

The three of them walked down the hallway, leaving Duane alone with the beeping machine.

Lexie woke on Stefan's bed wearing an old but fluffy terrycloth robe. A cup of peppermint tea sat in a pool of condensation on his bedside table, filling the air with fresh-scented steam.

Stefan was at his desk, staring at a textbook open on his lap, his hands clattering furiously on the computer keyboard in front of him.

Lexie groaned and looked at her hand, reassured to see smooth skin instead of fur. She sighed.

"Morning sleepyhead," Stefan said over his shoulder.

"What...day is it?"

"Still Tuesday. Still shitty."

Lexie groaned assent.

Stefan clicked 'save' on his paper and turned to face her. "You alright hon? Hungover? Preggers?"

Lexie snorted and rubbed her eyes. "I shifted."

"You...?"

"Shifted. Yeah."

"Like, just now? At like 4pm on a fucking Tuesday afternoon?" Stefan shouted.

"Halfway. Like, both. In-between."

"In front of Duane?!"

Lexie couldn't muster any expression more than weak exhaustion. First, she narrowly avoided outing herself to Randy, and now this. "I am bad at the secret identity thing."

"What did he say?"

"Nothing." She shrugged.

"Nothing?"

"You heard him. I don't think he realized what was happening."

"He was in shock."

She shrugged again.

"My god," he said finally, assessing her face, "You look like you've been doing bong rips for days." He went to the bathroom just outside his bedroom door. From the hallway wafted the smell of anywhere between four to seven boys, various permutations of beast, boy, and hustler. She sipped the tea and rubbed her forehead.

Stefan threw a bottle of mouthwash and a vial of eye drops onto her belly.

"I couldn't let him take me home. I'm afraid he'll figure it out."

"Figure what out?"

"Renee is the one who killed his friends, mauled the shit out of them while making Duane watch."

"Oooooh," Stefan said. "I heard about that last semester, but I never made the connection. Poor Duane."

"Yeah, but also poor us if he puts two-and-two together." Lexie eased herself to sitting.

"You think he will? That's kind of a big logical leap to make."

Lexie swigged the mouthwash, swishing and swallowing, the heat ripping off the first layer of esophageal lining, cleansing her from the inside. "I've got to stop hanging out with normal people."

"You don't think he'd go to the cops?"

"I don't know where he'd go, but crazy is probably one tick above cops on his list. And neither of those will be good for anyone."

"Speaking of cops…" Stefan said.

Lexie groaned. "What now?"

"They came back yesterday, asking about you."

"What? Me? Why?"

"Some speed trap cop ID'd Randy's bike near the scene. They already talked to her, I guess. They wanted to know where you lived."

"Fuck," Lexie said. "Can all the bad things just slow down so I can handle them one at a time?"

Stefan shook his head. "Never."

"Do you think she told them?" Lexie asked.

Stefan chewed on the end of his pencil. "I doubt it. But Christ, Lex, how many normals know about this werewolf shit?"

Lexie fell back on the pillow, wanting to suffocate herself with the terrycloth bathrobe. "I don't know anymore."

From the side table next to her tea, Lexie's phone buzzed twice. REMINDER: LING. REQ READING & ORAL REPORT DUE TMRW 10:15AM

"Take this from me before I throw it at the wall," Lexie said, handing her phone to Stefan before burying her face under the pillows and pulling the covers up.

She stayed that way for a few long minutes before Stefan finally said, "Lexie, honey, you are going to have to leave my bed eventually, keedoke?"

30

LEXIE WAS LEARNING TO HATE the library. The smell of the place drove her insane. Each step through the stacks was like trying to dig nose-first through layers of oily fingertips and mold. She learned to carry tissues or else risk sneezing a trail from the bound periodicals on the ground floor all the way up to the first editions on the top story.

She gave up searching the computers for language dictionaries and eventually took her query to the circulation desk. After fifteen minutes of awkward, half-formed questions, the librarian finally sent her to the fifth floor to browse the local texts. He had scribbled some call numbers, although he warned her that most of the books up there didn't fit into the standard organizing system and that Lexie would have to "follow her instincts." Lexie groaned on the inside, tired of having to rely on her instincts for every damn decision she was making these days. Just once, she wanted to be able to rely on cool logic and deductive reasoning to get her out of a situation. But no. She was part animal now, which meant all her earned human faculties were relegated to the background as she learned to listen to an entirely bizarre part of her brain that told her when to flee, fight, feed, and fuck, with no room for negotiation.

She took the stairs three at a time, tiny leaps, over and over, carrying her to answers, or at least a passing grade.

Deep within the recesses of the fifth floor she smelled more mold and some sex. Clearly this part of the library was used for only storage and midterm quickies.

She wove her way through the stacks to books with no spine titles—just quiet rows of simple burgundy leather bindings shelved tightly together. She pulled a thin one out and flipped through it. The pages rustled like dry November leaves, more at risk of cracking than tearing. She landed on a page that delineated varieties of meat and matched them to words with some recognizable characters and other foreign ones. Lexie tenderly turned to the first page which read "Icelandic Language Guide, United States War Department, 1944." She replaced the book and pulled out another, this one in Russian. Each book she pulled down was a different language guide, seemingly written entirely to teach soldiers how to communicate with native speakers before they killed them.

She laughed bitterly, realizing this was exactly why she needed her own language guide.

Knowing no one would care much, Lexie pulled out every text that had sigils of any kind, whether true sigils or merely characters foreign to Lexie: Norse, Voodoo, Kabbalah, and Santeria piled among Russian, Old English, Dutch, Farsi, Arabic, and innumerable indigenous language guides.

The light through the sliver windows waned and her stuffed nose became too much. With the same frustration as when she tried on ill-fitting clothes for hours, Lexie quit her meandering search. She stood at once and walked, nearly ran, away from the pointless stacks of dead words.

She grabbed three of the texts at random and took them to the front desk for checkout.

When the librarian scanned her ID card, he said, "Clarion. We've got another book on hold for you. One sec."

He wheeled his chair to the shelves behind him, pulling down a tiny black leather-bound book and adding it to her stack.

"I didn't order that," she said.

He shrugged and handed it to her.

Lexie packed the rest of the books away in her bag and walked to the student union, the mystery book in her hand. She flipped through its pages while waiting in line for the cashier to ring up her coffee.

It was a smallish book bound in plain black library binding. The pages were thin, almost like parchment, and the text was clearly from a typewriter, one of the old ones before they became electric.

She thumbed back to the first page. In faded patchy script, Lexie read Miss Lucille Shoal. Anthropology, Milton College, Milton, Oregon, 1888. She flipped past an etching of a sunset over a forest scene and let her fingers glide along the smooth pages, finding the tiny indentations beneath each letter strike. Words she'd never seen before, and hand-drawn sigils and symbols that seemed so odd as to be alien, covered the pages. Every so often was a plate of weaponry, home life, or portraits. On page 74 she found a woodcut of a wolf. A large, fierce wolf. A Rare.

Her fingers grazed the image. The creature's fur was detailed to the point of obsession. The animal's face was crude, though, resembling more a Chinese dragon than any wolf she'd known. Its tongue slavered out of its mouth, a serpentine creature in its own right. Lexie tried not to laugh at this caricature.

Two pages later she found another etching, this of a person, some sort of shaman, their hands palm-down above a table covered with bowls and pottery. The shaman's head was tilted back, looking at the sky. The inscription below read: Berdache shaman conducting rite.

Flipping further, Lexie found a slip of yellow paper wedged between two pages. On it was fresh, new print: a series of sigils perfectly drawn. She removed it, flipping it over, searching for meaning.

A few pages later, she found its mate: a codex. The sigils were paired with sounds written in the standard alphabet.

"Next," the checkout lady called, giving Lexie an impatient look. Lexie slipped the paper back into the book at the codex page and rushed forward to buy her coffee.

31

BREE'S DEATHBED WASN'T HARD TO find, just a fifteen minute run into the south woods. After giving Lexie shit for being two hours late, Hazel, Renee, Mitch, and Corwin ran alongside her in silence, while Jenna and Sharmalee stayed behind.

The cracked leaves that had caught Bree's blood were crushed and scattered as though scavenged by small animals in search of sustenance.

Lexie pointed. "There."

Renee and the rest walked to the spot and dropped to their knees, sniffing the ground, trying to glean clues.

"Whoa," Mitch said.

"Yeah." Hazel nodded. "Weird."

Renee sucked in breath over and over, finally letting it all out in one big bellow. "Did you smell this when you found her?" she asked.

Lexie shrugged. "Yeah. She smelled sour, pungent. I thought it was just death. Or maybe...you know...sex...stuff."

Hazel shook her head. "No. It's not that. It's her. But it's...different."

Mitch stood and wiped his hands on his jeans, searching the scene for clues. Renee and Corwin followed, but Hazel remained glued to the ground.

"She smells familiar," Hazel said, more to herself than to Lexie, who hovered a ways behind. "Like something I've smelled at Luscious."

Lexie stifled a snicker, a myriad of snarky responses darting through her head. She kept them all to herself.

"Oh no," Hazel said.

"What?" asked Lexie.

Hazel called, "Renee?" and the girls hurried back to her. "I know this smell," Hazel said, her face tight, flinching. She dug her hands into the dirt and let her black hair fall over her face. "It's all circumstantial, but…."

Renee crouched to Hazel and placed her hand on her back. "What is it, Hazel?"

"She smells like Octavia from my work. Thick and creamy and kind of like, yeasty, you know?" Hazel sniffed again. "Like…nutrient-rich."

Renee rubbed Hazel's back.

Hazel shrugged Renee's hand away and flipped her hair from her face to expose tear-stained cheeks and red eyes. "Bree was pregnant."

32

LEXIE NEEDED TO SCREAM, HOWL, or bleed. She burst past the treeline, to the river where Archer had found her when the water was cool but not deadly. Back when things made sense.

She carried her knife on her hip, though it wouldn't do any good against the Morloc. It felt better to trust the knife than herself. She ran along the river and over the deer path into the cabin clearing. Snow blanketed the cabin remains, the meadow, the rocks, and the lowlands beyond. She found her wall, her first great challenge that she no longer even noticed, and bounded up to the plateau, and from there into her tree. It was a return, but it felt like the first time. Tiny flakes of snow found their way between the boughs and dusted her hair and shoulders.

Lexie skulked into the treehouse and looked darkly at the empty nest. She felt ashamed for the memory of the pleasure the birds gave her tongue. Lexie sat facing the east where the trees thinned out. She held the knife to her chest like a ritual object. The snowflakes clung to her, before their tiny sublimes.

Bree had been pregnant.

The girls would be lucky if they were killed when facing the Morloc. It was better than the alternative, the thought of which made Lexie sick. She remembered Bree's body, blue and red. She imagined a Rare hunched over her. Imagined him picking up the same scent Hazel had picked up on. She imagined his rage, slashing not just Bree's throat, but her belly also, as if her pregnancy had been an affront to him and his wants. He must have believed he was entitled to her. She shuddered against the thought and gritted her teeth. This, all of this, was too unfair, too perverse, too sordid. It was too old. Lexie was tired of this story. Tired of women in peril, tired of being reduced to her womb and what monsters and ideologues thought should be done with it. She was so angry she spat and watched the wad fall four stories to the ground. She wasn't mad at her father anymore, or her aunt or mother. She was mad at the world that put her in this position. It may as well jab a meathook through her shoulder and dangle her aloft like a chicken over an alligator pit. She was mad on behalf of the families of Bree and the other victims, for people who couldn't or wouldn't ever know the depths of the grotesqueries that had killed their loved ones. Then again, maybe it was better that they didn't know.

Tiny snowflakes fluttered their way through the boughs to land on the platform. The grayed and sodden sheepskin grew white again, flake by flake.

Lexie hugged herself. She felt slight and weak. But her body was hers. Hers to carry and to crush. Hers to abuse and maybe someday exalt. In her head scrolled the interminable list of things she hated about it, but when she looked at them, she found the words in another language, so indecipherable as to be irrelevant. She took a breath, let it fill her lungs, expand her ribs, loosen her shoulders, stretch her neck, open her belly, plant her feet. She spread her arms, rotating her hands on her wrists, wiggling her fingers, swinging her arms at the shoulder, hinging at the elbow. She shifted her weight from foot to foot, feeling as surefooted as she felt on her four paws. Another breath. She stood on the balls of her feet, feeling her weight there, her toes spread in her boots, gripping, tendons like suspension cables, distributing support. Another breath, and she shifted her balance to one foot, pushing her support up onto the ball of her foot and her toes. She rose taller.

The stretch of tiny muscles around her moon toe lead to other tiny stretches: her jaw, her lips, her forehead. Her tongue lolled out of her mouth, her jaw hanging loose and wiggling. She was sure she looked like a Chinese dragon, all bug-eyed and slavering. She didn't give a shit.

There in her treehouse, Lexie moved, feeling her body as if for the first time, discovering new quarries and springs, new joint pops and small patches of pleasure. Rocking her body in space, Lexie felt a slash of shame. She knew neither of her bodies at all, but she felt so much more seduced by her wolf form. It made sense in a way Lexie didn't like to admit. It fit right in places she hadn't known mattered.

She ran from that shame, darting and dancing over the platform, exploring span and grace. But it found her at the tree trunk beneath the empty birds' nest. She couldn't reach it now like she could as a wolf. Lexie grasped the branch and pulled herself up to face the cold, dark nest. A few tiny, downy feathers remained, but the rest was falling to pieces, twigs jutting out at haphazard angles. A spiderweb wound itself around the top of the nest—a tiny, silken trampoline. Hiding beneath a twig, she saw the spider twitch, its forelegs folded in front of its eyes.

Lexie dropped back to the floor and wrapped her arms around her chest. "Mine," she whispered. She lowered herself to the snow-dusted planks, curling up tight. *Mine*, she thought.

Lexie was jolted awake by an invisible something, a strange sound from the ground below. A rustling, guttural communication.

She held her breath and listened.

The night was as smooth, black, and cold as onyx. Scattered clouds glowed white from the waxing gibbous moon. Her heart froze along with the rest of her.

What was she hearing? Wolf chatter? A Morloc? It didn't sound the same. It was more guttural, straight from the chest through the snout. Resonant and deep. Heavy. Whatever was there stood upwind so that she couldn't catch its scent. But she understood its muttering, or thought she did. She could swear she heard the grunting voice say, "Excuse me."

An odd thing for a wolf to say.

She strained to listen either with her mind or her ears, still unsure which was which.

The voice sounded again, like the clearing of a throat.

Lexie blinked opened her eyes and scanned the branches overhead, finding nothing unusual. She listened again to something that sounded like a polite but increasingly impatient sigh. She crawled to the edge of the platform and peered through the furry boughs down to the forest floor. A shadow slanted against the pine needle carpet, hidden by lower branches.

"Hello?" Lexie called.

The shadow rustled and the sound of heavy footsteps followed. They were not the sounds of paw pads, but something harder, like a wood-soled boot.

Into a dappled beam of moonlight stepped a creature. Curly white fur covered it from hooves to horns. Its nostrils heaved like bellows from a nose the color of beach rock. A white buffalo. The buffalo swayed its heavy head once and looked up with wet black eyes, meeting Lexie's, which were frozen open, wide and unbelieving.

The buffalo snorted with a swing of his head, beckoning her down.

Lexie stared, frozen in wonderment, before rushing down the tree and cliffside. She landed at a safe distance, watching suspiciously.

The buffalo watched her movements and snorted.

"Who are you?" Lexie asked.

The buffalo swayed his head heavily to the right, then to the left. He glottalized and snorted and his form started to give way. Flickers of flesh and tangled hair traded space. The buffalo receded to the comparatively small body of a man, crouched.

Then a long exhalation, and he stood.

Tall, lean, with flax curls brushing his shoulders, the young man stood before Lexie and offered a gentle smile. He let her take in his presence, his transition, all about him, in stark silence before speaking.

"I'm sorry," he said, finally. "But I think you may be able to help me."

Lexie stared, too shocked to laugh.

"I'm looking for Archer Racine."

Lexie nearly choked.

"She sent for me. My name is Sage. I'm her brother."

33

Sage waited for Lexie to speak, but it barely occurred to her to do so. Her breathing was labored and her balance swayed.

"You're her brother?"

The boy smiled faintly.

"You're a pureblood."

He made no motion.

"Why are you here?"

"My sister said my help was required."

Sage's frank tone felt like an artifact from a different era. Lexie wanted to laugh to ease her nerves. The water rushing in the stream beyond was the only sound. Sage stared at her with unblinking amber eyes. Like Archer's, there was a hint of perpetual bemusement, though his gaze was more feral and prepared. Each sound from the forest elicited a small reaction: a glance, a pause. He seemed to look both at her and through her, taking in all the information the forest could offer at once.

His mauve lips curled ever so slightly at the corners, so that despite his solid gaze, he seemed gentle. Perhaps even content, in a wholly-inhuman way.

The returning silence reminded Lexie of Sage's nudity, and she took a step back. His skin was light, but not pale. He had been touched by the sun, but more easily reflected the moon, as if he were illuminated from within. He seemed utterly unaware of his nudity, and for this reason, if no other, Lexie wanted to stare, to take him in, like a statue at a museum. This was the first time a man had stood unabashedly nude before her, and she didn't want to squander the opportunity. She stole a look. When he didn't flinch, she scanned the whole of him. His muscles were long and slim, his stomach taut. Though he had appeared to her as a buffalo, so stocky and with such bulk, his human form was leaner and more sinewy than anyone she'd yet encountered, including Archer.

She sheepishly let her eyes drift downwards, finding the fine hairs below his navel and tracing them lower. His penis was darker than the rest of his flesh, reminding her of the tawny hue of Archer's own tender flesh.

His hair was curled and blond here as well, as though it were carved from marble in perfect ringlets.

She paused, then blushed, realizing she shouldn't be looking like this. But Sage didn't flinch, nor interrupt her perusal. He stood as if awaiting instructions.

She fought against a thousand stupid phrases that pressed at her mind.

"Thank you," Sage said finally.

"For what?" Lexie asked.

"For thinking I am beautiful." He grinned.

"Oh. Uh." Lexie said. "Don't think it's like…a thing…or anything."

Sage maintained that tiniest smile and stolid, unmoving gaze.

"How is this," Lexie said, gesturing to his body, "even possible?"

"Shapeshifting?" he asked.

"Archer is a werewolf. Aren't you supposed to be…"

"Technically, she's not. Archer and I are pureblood Rares. Though born as wolves, we have the power to be any creature we know. Most of us choose human for obvious reasons." He touched his abdomen.

"Though we all have our favorites."

Lexie cocked an eyebrow. "So you chose white buffalo. Inconspicuous."

"No more than a six-foot-tall wolf," he said. Lexie shrugged.

Lexie's earlier restlessness caught up with her. She had to move. "It's...late." The words came out more vicious than she had intended, residual bitterness that felt like it would never go away, because the world would never change, and it would never be safe for her to wander alone late at night. "I should head toward home."

"I'll walk with you," Sage said.

Lexie headed off without argument. Sage caught up with her. She could just see him out of the corner of her eye, but that didn't stop her from casting him several sidelong glances. "Are you cold?" she asked, her breath fogging the space between them.

He crossed his wrists in front of his waist and shrugged. "I'm fine."

Lexie led them on a quick-if-not-direct route to the Den. For several tense minutes, Lexie tried to figure out which question to ask first and finally settled on small talk.

"So you're here to help," she said.

"I believe so."

"To fight?"

"Fight?" Sage asked. "I can't imagine why."

Small talk may have been a bad choice.

"The Morloc. The full-bloods. You're here because Archer isn't. She sent you in her place."

"What will you be fighting for?" Sage asked.

"Our survival," Lexie said.

Stefan stepped the flat of his foot down nearly all at once, leaving footprints of consistent depth and making him walk as though he were ready at any moment to make a running leap.

"What makes that important?" he asked.

Lexie looked aghast. "You want me to justify that?"

"My people didn't survive. Few do. The most vehement defenders of one's right to live are the ones who survived various attacks against it. Why this town? Your pack? Why do they get my help?"

Lexie's ears grew hot. "Because this is our home!"

"It is also the home of the Morloc," he said.

"They're attacking us," Lexie said. "Unprovoked."

Sage's stare made Lexie question the veracity of her assertion. "Were they?" Sage asked. "Unprovoked?"

Lexie didn't like Archer's gift. She was ready to call to the heavens to have them take him back.

While Lexie steamed, Sage held her gaze. "I vowed over a century ago to never get involved in the troubles of humans," he said.

"This involves your kind, too!"

"Then why shouldn't I be fighting on their side?"

Lexie tried to calm herself despite the provocation. "Out of nowhere, they're getting all bloodthirsty, and we don't know why."

"So you want to preserve the boundaries," Sage said. "That's what you're after? Between you and the full-blood Morloc."

"Yes."

"Between you personally, or your people?" he asked with a cocked head.

"Both," Lexie said, growing impatient.

"Because you could preserve that boundary by leaving."

Lexie glared at him.

"Why not?" he asked.

"Because…my friends. My dad. My school. Everything I've ever known is here. This is my home." She gestured to the tree canopy, pieces of moonlit sky cutting through the leaves like shards of broken mirror. The scents were rich and familiar.

"And that's enough?"

"What do you mean 'enough'? That's everything."

"For you."

"Yes, for me!"

"I believe you. That's fine. But I don't feel invested myself," Sage said.

"Your sister commanded you to come here."

"Commanded?" He laughed. "She asked. Via postcard." He glanced to the sky, remembering the words his sister wrote: "'Gone to the desert. Was tired of trees. The trees don't brood here, they dance.'"

Lexie tried not to let that sting. A postcard to a long-forgotten brother, instead of one simple message to her recent, bruised girlfriend. Nice.

"This is bigger than me," she admitted, trying to convince herself, too.

Sage was silent, an invitation for her to continue.

"The Pack has taken on the task of defending this town from assault. The Morloc are raping women to continue their lineage. Walking away from that would be complacency, accepting a world that tells women our bodies are mere vessels for male motivations. That's bullshit. I can't let that happen."

Sage looked at her, assessing.

"I don't care who was here first," Lexie admitted. "Some things deserve to die off, like bullshit outmoded ideas of propriety and property. They want to rape us to continue their line? Then yeah, I'm fine killing them and watching their warped culture die with them."

Lexie breathed into that thought, now vocalized and impossible to recant. She worried that she had said something too brutal, too selfish, but she didn't care. Her own sense of rightness won out over her anxieties of saying the wrong thing.

This wasn't about land. This was about her right to live the life she chose, and the similar rights of all her sisters, werewolf or not.

They walked in silence for a long while, Lexie unable to shake the weight of Sage's attention. It was both emboldening and maddening. She quelled her mind by concentrating on the crunch of frost-covered leaves beneath their footfalls.

Lexie tried to tune into the invisible silver threads that clung to her chest like spider silk, reaching out to Sage. They pulled and drifted beneath her paces, flowing from her and catching and clinging to everything that passed. They drifted over low boughs, saplings and brush, catching in her hair and tangling together. They grazed Sage's torso as he walked alongside her. She tried to parse their meaning, or even their veracity. She tried to still her breath. She listened to each invisible thread as it floated on tiny breezes. Ripples of air sloshed at her ear drums, as real as anything.

"Who are your allies?" Sage asked.

Lexie arched a brow. "Besides the Pack? I don't really know. My father, but he'll try to stop me. And the boys."

"The boys?"

"Some guys that run in a pack here in town. Half-bloods."

"There's another pack here?"

Lexie nodded.

"And you cohabit peacefully?"

Lexie shrugged and nodded. "They're gay."

"While other rogue half-bloods just wander around willy-nilly?"

Lexie felt the need to defend her town against Sage's judgments, but realized she didn't have the patience.

"So another pack. That's useful," Sage said.

"If they'll help."

"What else?"

"That's it."

Sage stood silent, naked, his expressionless face belying what Lexie hoped was an active decision-making process. Then he started to walk again, and Lexie followed. They moved west, along the ridge above Milton, meager lights of civilization peeking through the trees. Smoke rose from chimneys, and the town felt as bucolic as a Christmas painting. They wandered in silence until they reached the edge of the woods where the trees gave way to the backyard of the Den.

Through the dense trees, Lexie's house glowed amber, and through the windows she saw her sisters moving about mundane tasks, as though nothing was wrong, nothing was dying, nothing was falling apart. "That is your pack?" Sage asked, and the answer felt further away than ever, yet completely and thoroughly true.

"Yes." Lexie nodded. Lexie watched the girls in the house, feeling a modicum of guilt for wanting to keep his arrival to herself. But atop that guilt was piled high the potential of having his answers, insights, and history. Crowning that pile of potential was hope. Somewhere she knew, or at least wanted to believe, that Sage was their savior, that he would be their secret weapon, the *deus ex machina*, the white knight.

Sage studied the house and said, "I'm a pacifist."

"All good people are pacifists until the wolf's at your door."

Sage smiled, gazing at the Den. Lexie let Sage's smell wash over her. She tried to dissect it in her brain, pulling the layers apart like the pages of a waterlogged book. In those layers she found black cherries, oak, oil, and amber. They caught in the back of her sinuses, heavy and rich, oozing like warm sap along the inner contours of her skull. She breathed shallow to keep the scent inside of her. She searched from the top to the bottom of Sage's scent for a trace of Archer. Some river stone or moss to prove that she was here. But Archer was nowhere in Sage, save, perhaps, his genes.

After a long pause where Lexie refused to look away, Sage finally spoke. "I'll help you," he said. "Of course I will. It is what I've come here to do. Though I think you need wisdom more than muscle. If you'll let me provide that, I will."

Lexie smiled and let her hand reach to his cheek. She expected him to flinch like any normal person, but of course he didn't—he wasn't. His skin was soft and smooth, so unlike the masculine roughness she'd expected. His cheek warmed her hand and she realized the intimacy of a simple act like touching. She wanted to withdraw her hand, but she resisted. Sage smiled at her. He opened his arms, and she stepped into his embrace. His skin was warm all over. Her brain was stunned into silence as it tried to make sense of her hugging a naked man in the woods. There was too much wrong with the idea to parse. Yet she felt drawn in, safe, held. A low thrum, like a steady heartbeat, held them. The energy inside her body began to swirl like flocking sparrows, diving and darting in an organized mess. Her cheek pressed to his shoulder. The sparrows rose and dispersed, finding their own paths along her nerves, pulling the electricity of her body into lightning bolts skittering beneath the surface of her skin. A sickening lightness fluttered in her belly. This wasn't her wolf, begging for release. This was something else. Her…woman, perhaps?

With that thought Lexie pushed away. Sage cocked his head, the corners of his mouth still upturned in a gentle grin.

"Are you alright?" Sage asked, arms open from the broken embrace.

Lexie nodded and tucked her hair behind her ears. "That felt…un-good."

"Is that the same as bad?" Sage asked.

"…No." Lexie thought hard about his question, wondering into the truth of her answer.

"Okay," he said, lowering his hands. "What would turn it good?"

Lexie stepped back a few paces. "Pants. Pants would make it better."

Sage looked down at his own nudity, then back up at Lexie. "Consider it done." He paused. "Where would I find such things?"

Lexie gestured to the lawn furniture with a nod of her head. "I'll leave the clothes on this chair. You can meet everyone tomorrow, okay?"

He nodded once. "I'll be back tomorrow. I'm going to head back south."

Lexie nodded, though a question stuck in her mind.

"This isn't my territory," he said, answering her unspoken query. "It's nothing personal."

Sage backstepped against a lolling pine and shifted, his lean limbs bulking up, his softness broadening, his height looming. Lexie wondered if she should enroll in a physics class next semester, because something about this had to make sense.

She took a deep breath, then another. She wanted to hide her eyes, his nakedness only more revealed by his shift.

"This will all make sense tomorrow," Lexie whispered to herself, as she watched his white form fade into the night.

34

"I SAVED YOUR QUILT," JENNA said when Lexie walked in the back door, dazed and lost in thought.

"What?"

"Your mom's quilt. I saved it."

Lexie had nearly forgotten about it, and she felt a stab of regret as she realized she was making a habit of that.

"Thanks," Lexie said, not stopping on her walk until she was nearly at the stairs, wanting to get in the shower before any of the girls smelled her.

"Don't you want to see it?" Jenna asked.

"Um…" Lexie waffled. "Can it wait?"

Though Jenna didn't answer, Lexie could feel her deflate. It had to be at least 2 a.m., and Jenna was no night owl unless the moon was in control. Jenna had stayed up, waiting for Lexie's return.

"I'm sorry," Lexie said, stopping on her trajectory upstairs and returning to the living room where Jenna sat. The quilt was draped on a clothing rack in front of the fire, the light of the flames lighting it as though it were a shadow theater screen. "That was really sweet of you. Thank you," she said.

Jenna smiled that same sweet smile. "Happy to help," she shrugged.

The orange glow illuminated the delicate stitching, giving Lexie a new appreciation of the beauty of her mother's handiwork. She forgot about Sage and Bree and Duane and all the other brutal disappointments and terrors that lurked beyond the walls of the Den. She breathed in a moment of simple beauty, her mother communicating to her across spans of death and age.

Jenna rested her chin on Lexie's shoulder and wrapped her other arm around her waist. "Your mother was a great craftsperson," she said. "This is some fine stitching."

"I was just thinking the same thing, but I don't really know what to look for. I'm glad you think so, Miss Expert."

Jenna smiled and gave Lexie's waist a little squeeze. She placed her finger on one of the cotton threads starting at the far left side of the quilt and running right. "Well, this was all obviously hand-stitched, and the stitches are so small and the curves so deliberate and detailed, it's pretty remarkable. See this part, here?" Jenna ran her index finger over a line halfway down the fabric. A horizontal line jumped into a peak and then down below the median level where it formed a U-shape, then up again into a loop that resembled a "p." The line followed this soaring and diving pattern across the entire quilt.

"It's really strange. Most quilts tie onto the batting just with some random loops or jagged shapes, depending on your style. This one mixes curves and loops with harsh angles and even some random little dots and hyphen-thingys, but all of it in these perfectly-spaced lines. It's really special."

Lexie followed Jenna's finger, her vision aided by the fire's backlighting. The stitches were silhouetted against the glowing orange of the rest of the quilt. She scanned the whole thing from top to bottom, appreciating Jenna's assessment. It felt strange, viewing this object she'd had since birth in a new light. She stepped forward to run her finger over the thread too, noticing only on the second line she traced that she was holding her breath as a puzzle revealed itself.

"You're fucking kidding me," Lexie muttered.

Lexie traced the thread that had held bits of filth only days before and now traced clean white lines across the quilt.

"What?" Jenna asked.

"What?" Lexie replied, ripped from the problem she was unconsciously trying to solve.

"You're spacing out," Jenna said with concern. "You've been running your finger over that same spot for a solid minute."

Lexie looked back to the quilt flickering in strange shadows. Her brain was caught like a rowboat on the rocks. The clues battered at her, while the angry waves of flame scattered her focus.

"These are...hold on," Lexie said. She ran up the stairs to her backpack and returned holding the small leather-bound book from the library.

"What?" Jenna stepped to the quilt and squinted as Lexie flipped through the pages, finding a page of script. "See?" Lexie said, pointing to scribbles in the text that resembled Arabic or Tagalog script, sharp angles and round bodies, soaring peaks and deep valleys. She looked back up at her quilt, which sported similar scribbles, all set with a single spool of thread.

Lexie looked through the pages to find the pronunciation guide, matching them from left to right. *Soo-too-kah*, she said in her head.

Lexie made a hard sound with her tongue. *Tka*, she corrected. Like a choke combined with a sharp percussive.

Sutka, sutka, she read.

"What's that mean?" Jenna asked, hands on hips, squinting at the quilt.

"Turn, turn," she whispered.

"What?" Jenna said with a short gasp.

Lexie ran her finger over the backwards "L" shape that fell into a lowercase "u" and into a peak with a dot over top it.

Sutka, sutka, fislume. Tan saong ritfoan.

"Turn, turn, wheel. All things change."

Jenna's jaw dropped. "Does it say that in the book?" She craned her neck to see the pages, but only found the script and pronunciation. "Where's the translation?"

Lexie continued, finding the sounds, closing her eyes and hearing the words reform themselves into the only language she thought she knew.

A gisaong knut, a gisaong xitkira.

"To something new, to something strange."

"Does that say that?" Jenna said, in a volume too loud for the semi-sleeping house.

Lexie nodded.

"Go on!" Jenna squealed.

Like jagged filigrees, the script unfolded.

"Nothing that be still or...something. I don't know that last word." Lexie said. "The moon waxes, the moon wanes."

"Oh my god. Sisters!" Jenna shouted.

The whole house came alive at once, and Renee rushed down the stairs. "Is everyone okay?"

"Yes, yes, yes!" Jenna squealed. "Lexie's mom. She's speaking to us."

One by one, the girls came down the stairs in various states of consciousness and dress.

Lexie stood in front of the quilt, reading the stitching like braille and speaking her stilted translations aloud.

"The mist, the cloud, will become rain. The rain to mist and again cloud."

She dropped to her knees and stretched the quilt tight to see the continued script. "Tomorrow becomes today." A long straight line connected that passage to the next. "Art is the child of Nature."

Some of the words weren't coming as easily as others. Lexie struggled to translate as much as she could. "Her beloved child, in...dunno dunno dunno. The something of the mother's face. Her something and her mood. All her something beauty. Somethinged and soft and something. Into dunno and with a human sense dunno. She is the greatest artist, then, Whether of pencil or of pen, Who follows Nature. Never man." She skipped ahead a line. "In Nature's footprints, light and quick, And follows fearless where she leads."

Separate from the rest, another line, smaller. *To my Daughter, whom I wish to live.* Lexie read the last line to herself.

The sound of the waning fire filled the silence as Lexie completed the translation.

"That sounds more like the *Tao Te Ching* than a battle plan," Sharmalee said at last.

Mitch nodded as he rubbed a heavy palm against his forehead. "Yeah, what does that even mean?"

"Are you sure you translated right?" Hazel asked.

"Hell if I know," Lexie muttered. "It's like some bastardized indigenous language plus eight other things I've never heard of. Well, not technically, but you know, cognitively. Or, like experientially, or, whatever. I don't know what the fuck I'm talking about. But, you know."

"I dunno," Mitch said. "It sounds too Hallmark-y to be meaningful."

Hazel rolled her eyes and walked to the quilt. "Oh my god, you guys. It's like you've never read a fantasy novel or a spiritual text.

"Change and the moon, right?" Hazel said, pointing to a line—the wrong line, since she couldn't read it. "She's talking about us."

Mitch peered at the quilt and rubbed his chin. "Renee, Sharm, you both speak two languages."

Renee held up four fingers above her crossed arms and shrugged.

Sharmalee nodded. "Seven-ish."

Corwin muttered, "God, I hate being American sometimes."

"Okay, you both speak multiple languages," Mitch said. "You know how to interpret a direct translation."

"Not really," Renee said. "It's all just context. Like Shakespeare more than Austrian or Bajan."

"To something new, something strange," Lexie repeated. "What's strange?"

Jenna frowned. "Our wolves."

"But different from the Morloc or other Rares?" Sharmalee asked.

"I suppose our ability to keep our heads even when we change," Jenna said.

"Which is a theory," Renee said.

"With good evidence," Mitch offered.

"What else?" Jenna asked.

"Maybe it means 'nature' in the literal sense," Hazel said. "Like our periods or something."

"We'll fight them with menstrual blood!" Corwin shouted with a laugh while Sharmalee grimaced.

"Knowing men, it'd probably work," Renee said.

The girls all studied the quilt, as though the solution to the riddle would emerge spontaneously from the worn cotton and corduroy.

Renee asked Lexie to repeat it aloud again, word for word, the crudest translation she could divine, while Renee wrote it down in small neat print on a lined notebook page.

When Lexie was finished, Renee studied the text and said, "Hm," once, percussive.

"Longfellow," Corwin said from the kitchen. While the girls had struggled over the translation, Corwin had grabbed her laptop and done some investigative Googling.

"What?" Renee said.

"'Keramos,' by Henry Wadsworth Longfellow. "Never man/As artist or as artisan/Pursuing his own fantasies/Can touch the human heart, or please/Or satisfy our nobler needs/As he who sets his willing feet In Nature's footprints/light and fleet/And follows fearless where she leads. 'Keramos and Other Poems'. 1878."

The girls cocked their heads and looked back to the quilt. "I guess that solves that mystery." Renee said. "A twice-translated, cryptic message that ends up being a poem by a dead white guy."

"It's probably a clue," Hazel said. "A message from beyond the grave."

"Sure," Renee said. "And our highly contextual, highly stressed reading will certainly yield accurate results." She buried her hand in her hair and scratched her scalp, staring at the glowing wall of faint text. "Well, good night again, everyone."

The girls scattered back to bed, leaving Lexie and Jenna alone again next to the quilt.

"A poem," Jenna said. "That's sweet."

Lexie shrugged. "I guess. But why translate an American poem into some random language? And why sew it into a quilt?"

"I do things like that. It's like spell casting. Weaving the words into intentions. Maybe she intended for you to find it when the time was right, and treat the words with some extra attention."

Lexie thrummed her lips. "Bummer," she said.

Jenna squeezed her shoulders. "Not everything has to be a symbol, I guess. Maybe you can just appreciate your mother's artistic eye and generous spirit." She took steps toward the stairs. "Try to get some rest. We've got a lot coming our way."

Lexie sighed. Right.

Jenna left her alone in the living room. Lexie stared at the flickering quilt for a long time, thinking back on the only two times she remembered her mother tucking her into bed. She replayed them in her mind, as though rehearsing a scene to memorize the lines and blocking. Lexie knew the memories were likely false or at least exaggerated, but that didn't really bother her. Only when the fire faded into embers did Lexie draw her attention away, remembering the book that now lay face-up on the low table beside her. She reached for it, the tiny yellow slip of paper floating to the ground. Lexie leaned over to grab it, and the translation came easy now: *Crow Moon. They Attack.*

35

Lexie had been typing a pre-morning-coffee email to her father when she was jolted by a shout from outside.

She looked out the window and saw a standoff in the backyard. Hazel had apparently caught Sage trying to retrieve the clothes Lexie left out for him, and now Hazel was screaming for the girls. Sage stood naked in the grass, holding his hands at his sides, trying to calm her down.

Everyone was home, but Renee got to the backyard first, crossbow in hand.

Shit. Lexie threw on her bathrobe and ran downstairs.

"You move, you die, fatherfucker!" Renee screamed as Lexie burst through the back door.

Sage said nothing, but kept his hands to his sides, proving nothing but his passivity.

"Renee, cool it. He's with me."

"He's with what?"

"Put down the crossbow and I'll explain."

Renee withdrew the weapon but kept her aggressive glare.

"Put on the clothes, Sage."

He wriggled awkwardly into Ray's rifle club t-shirt and the polka dot pajama pants Lexie had provided him. Hazel side-eyed Lexie. Lexie shrugged. "They were the best I had."

Back inside, Lexie filled in the Pack with what she knew and let Sage tell the rest.

"I said I will help you," Sage said. "And I will. But I vowed a long time ago never to draw blood from my brethren. Or sistren," he said with a glance to Renee.

"Some of your brethren deserve a little blood-drawing," Renee said.

Sage just smiled that smile. "I'll leave that to you."

"Even if we fight during the full moon, we're out-muscled," Corwin said.

"Especially if you do," Sage said. "The moon gives them strength that outmatches yours."

Sharmalee looked warily at the girls. "And that's different than the rest of the month how?"

Sage reached to the glass of water Jenna had set for him and took a long sip before speaking. "My kind lived in relative peace alongside humans for a very long time. Do you know what changed it?"

"Colonialism?" Hazel said.

Sage shook his head, the pale curls grazing his cheeks. "No. Not quite. The Americas at that time were experiencing settlement to be sure, but what drove that settlement was an arms race. We didn't try to reason or appeal to the emotions of our invaders. We just fought back. Wars of beasts are fought face to face. Claw to claw. No treaties or negotiations. Just blood.

"If you want to win, you have to think like animals but fight like men."

"Don't you mean 'think like women'?" Hazel asked.

Sage looked at her, unblinking. "No. I don't. That is what likely got your previous pack killed. You must fight with weapons and grit, but you must trade strategy for instinct."

"But you just said we're outmatched at the full moon, and we aren't animals the rest of the time," Renee said. "We can't change like you and Archer. Not at will."

"I did," Lexie reminded her softly, though she certainly hadn't willed it.

Sage nodded. "I believe it could be possible. Though for half-bloods like you it will always be painful and difficult to maintain. And forcing it for too long could undo you."

"Undo like insanity?" Hazel asked.

"Like pain, illness. Like death," he said.

Renee looked ready to explode, and an exploding Renee would sidetrack the rest of the discussion. "What else do we have?" Lexie asked before that could happen.

"Well, you are lucky in one respect. These full-bloods know very little of the human world. They know even less of turning than you do. They do not think like humans."

"This is a good thing?" Mitch asked.

Sage looked unblinking to him. "Quite."

Renee checked her phone, but didn't send anything. Lexie noted this and caught Renee's eyes as she slipped the phone back in her pocket.

"Do not ever underestimate that which is the boon of your species," Sage said, looking each of the four sisters in the eye.

"Which is what? Logic?" Mitch asked.

"Empathy?" Hazel said.

"Strategy?" Renee said.

Lexie watched Sage as a small, wily smile crept onto his face. He shook his head, his curls catching the firelight. He raised his hands to his cheeks and wiggled his thumbs.

Lexie snorted.

"Thumbs?" Renee said, with an are-you-serious glare.

Sage nodded. "Thumbs."

"But we can't be wolves and have thumbs at the same time," Mitch said.

"Such is your curse."

"Fighting the Morloc while human is suicide," Mitch said. "We're at our strongest during the moon."

"As are the full-bloods," Sage said. "As am I. The moon won't change your odds one bit."

"What would?"

"Using your distinctly-human advantage while the Morloc are at their mundane strength."

Lexie and Renee shared another long look. Both girls picked up their phones and texted—with their thumbs.

An hour later, Mitch had emptied the fridge onto the kitchen counter, preparing a legion of snacks, and Stefan walked in with Taylor and Otter.

"Lexie, I'm gonna be honest with you," Stefan said as he led the boys through the front hall into the kitchen. "I've got a midterm paper due tomorrow, and right now I'm thinking you are one crazy bi—"

He was interrupted by the entrance of Sage. "Holy..."

"...Man," Taylor finished.

The boys stumbled over themselves to get to Sage, who stood at the back door, holding some fresh logs for a new fire and looking confused.

Jenna, Corwin, and Sharm had arrived home with more groceries and were sorting them into "eat now" and "eat later" piles. They seemed intent on their task, working hard to ignore the strange men in their home.

"Open some beers, Mitch," Renee said. "Let's gather."

Renee led everyone into the living room. Sage deposited the logs next to the hearth and perched on the windowsill in the corner.

"Okay, honestly," Taylor said, "it feels like you guys doused the room in sex, and it's really distracting, so can we please cut to the chase?"

"It's Sage," Lexie said with a bat of her hand.

Sage shrugged. "Sorry."

"Don't be," Taylor flirted. "I'm just saying."

Lexie looked at the boys. "Where are the rest of them?"

"This is it, fuzzypants," Stefan said, grabbing the beer Mitch offered. "None of the other boys cared."

"They don't live here," Otter said, as though that answer was sufficient.

"We're at war," Lexie nearly shouted.

Otter rolled his eyes. "Okay, so what I don't understand is why you are suddenly deciding to declare war on the Morloc."

"They declared war on us," Renee said.

"By killing Bree Curtis," Corwin said, "and all the others over the years, and by coming onto campus in what was clearly a threat."

"So then why, out of the blue, are they declaring war on Milton?" Otter asked.

The girls looked to one another, no answers between them.

Sage spoke. "Because it was their land first."

"What?" said Otter.

"Surely you know that Milton wasn't already here?" Sage replied.

"Of course I know that, but there were First Nations here before."

"And they stayed clear of the Morloc too," Sage said. "It wasn't until the settlers made a deal with some other packs, to exchange defense for safety, food, and territory, that the land switched hands from Rares to humans."

"What other packs?"

"Female Rares have a storied past with this town," Sage replied. "Archer and her pack lived alongside the tribes here fairly peacefully. When the white settlers came here, they sought Archer's help to keep the wolves from the door, so to speak. For generations it was the female Rares who guarded this town, even as the indigenous tribes migrated or died off and the old ways disappeared, they stayed. It was their continued presence that attracted the Morloc, who saw them as an opportunity to continue their lineage.

"When Archer's relationship with the human settlers grew tenuous, my sister and her pack hid. The Morloc saw that as an opportunity to claim the land for themselves, and by extension, claim the females as well. That was the first war. Then the second, to which your mother bore witness, Lexie, and where Archer's pack was decimated," he nodded at Renee. "And now, it looks to be the third."

The packs exchanged uneasy looks.

"We're imperialists?" Sharmalee said.

"What do you mean, 'we'?" Lexie said. "I'm new to this pack."

"We all are," Corwin said. "Plus, you're white."

"I'm a quarter Cree," Lexie said.

"Funny. I've known you for nearly six months and I've never heard you claim Cree lineage until now," Corwin said.

"Corwin, you're a white girl with dreadlocks," Renee said. "I don't think you're in a position to talk about appropriation."

"Whatever. Lex, you look white, so it doesn't really matter what you actually are," Hazel interjected.

"How can you say that? You're white too!" Lexie exclaimed.

"But when someone thinks I'm Latina, they treat me like a Latina."

"You're white, Hazel. You can't just claim privileges as it suits you," Renee interjected. "You may as well be bisexual."

Hazel gasped. "How dare you?!"

"Now, now. No one's accusing anyone of being bisexual here," Jenna said.

"Except Corwin," Mitch chuckled.

"Except Corwin," Hazel nodded.

"Screw you guys," Corwin said.

"And Lexie has a thing for Sage," Sharmalee said.

"What?!" Lexie shouted.

Renee rolled her eyes. "He's a pureblood. He doesn't count."

Sharmlaee shrugged. "Whatever."

Stefan, Otter, and Taylor shared desperate looks and moved to sneak out the front door. Corwin caught Stefan by the backpack and dragged him back into the living room.

"Okay, okay. We're all guilty of oppression, and we're all oppressed," Renee said. "Can we acknowledge that and get to the point? This information is rather disturbing, as I think we're all learning."

"Yeah," Mitch said. "I don't want to be part of continued oppression of an indigenous group."

"Good point, Mitch. Any other thoughts?"

Corwin crossed her arms over her chest. "I want to live."

"Another good point, Corwin. I think we can all agree with both of you," Renee said. "The question remains, are these two goals mutually exclusive?"

"Land is traded in blood," Jenna said, solemnly. "History isn't full of peaceful exchanges."

"But if we believe we belong here, aren't we buying into the same imperialist philosophy?" Hazel asked.

Stefan raised his hand. "I'm just gonna interject, okay? Male oppressor here, commanding the floor. These wolves want your asses dead. We're past politics, and I don't think they're gonna trust a treaty."

"Can you really blame them?" Taylor muttered.

"Exactly. Let your white guilt play itself out in other ways, okay? By like, actually helping people, instead of passively resisting werewolves and getting eaten." Stefan said. "I think the choice you have is: dead or not dead."

"Yeah," Otter said. "Just because someone is part of an oppressed class, doesn't mean they're not also assholes."

"Or, what Otter said." Stefan said, rolling his eyes.

The girls were somewhere between sulking and lost in thought. Lexie looked across the room to Sage who gave her the slightest nod of support.

"But they're not killing us," Otter said, as though he just solved a riddle.

"What?" Renee said.

"We know some dudes have been turned. But as far as we know, the actual body count is all female," he replied.

"Yeah," Corwin said, her composure slipping toward ire. "What of it?"

"Why?" Otter said. "Why only females? I mean if this is a war, why not kill all the able-bodied men or whatever?"

"We have reason to believe the Morloc are trying to get a human female pregnant to continue their line," Renee said with a burdened sigh.

Lexie spoke up. "Because we're on their land. They think we belong to them."

"Though it seems that they're having problems with it," Renee said. "Hence the body count."

The boys shifted and glanced away. Stefan took a long swig from his beer bottle.

"So they're starting with you," Otter said. "It's 'all your females are belong to us,' but men aren't on the menu?"

The girls exchanged glances, feeling their stock fall. "No," Renee said. "Not yet, anyway."

"So it's a war on women, not on humanity," Otter said.

"A war on women IS a war on humanity," Renee snapped.

Otter made a face, unconvinced. The room fell quiet, both sides sharing wary looks with each other and glances to Sage, who stayed still and silent.

"Okay," Renee said, finally. "All in favor of killing the Morloc." She raised her arm high, nearly touching the living room ceiling. Each of the Pack's hands went up.

"Boys?" Renee asked.

"We get a vote?" Stefan asked.

"Two-thirds of one," Sharmalee joked.

"Shush, Sharmalee," Renee said.

"We're asking for your help," Lexie said.

Otter scoffed and the boys looked to one another. Taylor made a face and Stefan matched it.

"Do we have guns?" Stefan asked. Taylor and Otter shared an uneasy look.

Lexie replied, "We're working on it."

"So, what's the plan?" he asked.

"We're working on that, too," Renee replied. "We're arming up, planning traps. And we're deciding on a strategy."

Stefan grabbed his backpack and stood, placing his empty beer bottle on the coffee table. "Email me details when you have them. I want to know about weapons and attack plans before I kill anyone else."

"You're just going to sit by and watch the full-bloods attack?" Corwin shouted.

"Did I say that?" Stefan shouted back. "I'm not laying my life on the line when you don't even have weapons or a plan. You get those, and you call me. Meanwhile, I have a midterm to study for. Come on."

The boys grumbled some half-hearted apologies and left.

Lexie sighed heavily and rubbed her forehead, stopping when she realized it made her look like her father.

"Fuck 'em," Mitch said. "We didn't have their help this morning, and we don't have it now. Nothing's changed."

Renee nodded. "Exactly. Let's focus on what we can do."

"Like what?" Corwin asked.

Renee stared down Sage, who had sat impassively in the corner the entire time, the same eerie smile on his face. "We track down some weapons, and we learn to master our changes."

36

LEXIE WAITED IN THE HALLWAY outside the psych lab, Dr. Fern's book in her backpack, and another book splayed on her lap. She was failing Comp Lit, Spanish 101, and, ironically, barely making it through Professor Ritke's language class. New agenda item, Lexie thought, take easier classes next year. If she made it to next year. *Another agenda item*, Lexie thought. *If I make it to next year, start keeping an agenda.*

She struck her highlighter across a passage that sounded important, though she was only half-reading. Each tiny sound tickled her ears as she waited for Duane to arrive to set up the lab for his next subject.

Lexie reread the same passage for thirty minutes before she finally heard the soft soles of Duane's sneakers against the marble steps.

She sprang up and met him at the landing. He gasped and brought his hand to his face.

"Jesus!" he shouted.

"Sorry," Lexie said, surprised by her own energy, whether it was nervous or impatient or otherwise.

Duane rushed up the stairs, and Lexie bounced alongside him.

"You could've just responded to one of my texts," he said.

"I needed to see that thing again," Lexie replied.

"Are you serious?" Duane scoffed. "After what happened last time?"

Duane hurried up a second flight of stairs, clutching his books to his chest and avoiding eye contact. Lexie fought to stay apace.

"It was...a part of me." Each word eked from her mouth like a drop from a shut spigot. This wasn't going as she planned. "It was..."

"A Rare," Duane said, stopping at the landing and facing her.

"No!" Lexie protested, but she could hear the lie just as clearly as Duane could.

"I was nose-to-nose with one, Lex," Duane said. "I remember it all."

Lexie bit her lips and nodded, her bounces ceasing.

"Is that...how they all are?" he asked.

Lexie shook her head. "Some of them are all wolves, all the time. The bad ones are."

"But you're..."

"A good one," Lexie said, willing it to be true for more than her wolf. "And new."

"What about the one that killed—?"

"I don't know," Lexie interrupted. "I don't know what it was." The sentence caught in her throat but she pushed through it, a better lie than the last.

"I've been going through a lot." She rushed to fill the silence before he could examine her lie. "I know you have too, and I'm really sorry about scaring you and running off and passing out and, like, booting all over your shoes. It's just that there's a lot going on at home, and in my head, and none of it makes sense..." Through her babbling, she pleaded for Duane to find something, anything, to ask about other than his attack. She'd fill his brain with the volumes she knew about absolutely everything other than this.

He didn't ask anything else, but watched like she was descending into true insanity, aghast as she unloaded all the flotsam in her brain. He stood, quiet, and then pushed through the heavy door into the hallway. Lexie chased after him, wanting to scream.

"That electricity thing," Lexie said, catching up. "How did it work?"

"The EEG?" Duane asked, shaking himself into presence. "Um, it's just low amplification of your ion movement. It doesn't really do anything, just measures your brain's voltage."

"It has to do something," Lexie said.

"No, it's like holding a stethoscope up to your chest and blaming that for your heartbeat. It doesn't do anything but listen."

"You said it amplifies."

"Yeah, but it doesn't put the amplifications back in your skull. It measures, amplifies, and reports. There is no way this would make that...thing...happen."

"What about the other device?"

"The Octopus?" Duane asked.

"The what?" Lexie said.

"It's just what they call the solenoids." Duane shrugged, exasperated. He fumbled with his keys outside the lab door. "It's a low-level magnetic pulse that's supposed to stimulate your temporal lobe and generate a different sensation."

"What kind of different sensation?"

"A professor called it the God Helmet because he thought it inspired the feeling of another presence. Some people felt it was God, others thought aliens or ghosts."

"You hooked me up expecting me to see God, and you didn't tell me?"

"It was a blind study, Lex, the point is not to tell you. And no, I didn't expect you to see anything. I think it's bullshit; the guy's results have never been perfectly replicated. My starting thesis was that it's all placebo." Duane unlocked his lab and Lexie followed him inside.

"Well, I want one."

"One what?"

"The machine. The squid."

"Octopus, and no." He pushed through the door into the lab.

"Why not?"

"It's not mine to give! Besides, I saw what happened to you. I'm not going to just let you steal school equipment so you can ralph on more shoes."

Lexie gave him a look.

"And turn into a fricking wolf," Duane said, lowering his voice into a furtive plea.

"Just ask your prof!" Lexie said. "It's not like you aren't a fucking golden boy around here. Everyone loves you. Tell them you're doing an independent project, and they'll probably write you a check for funding."

"Lexie, I'm assuming you haven't noticed, but I'm barely holding on here. I never sleep anymore, my grades are slipping, and I can't focus on anything. I'm no one's golden boy. I'm just damaged." He turned away from her and busied himself with some files.

"I need that machine, Duane."

"Why?!"

Lexie hesitated. He was another potential body to put on the front line. But no, Duane didn't need more trauma in his life. "I can't tell you."

"Compelling argument."

"Dammit, Duane, this is a life-or-death situation! I thought you were my friend."

Duane rolled his eyes. "I'm beginning to think you don't know what that means."

"How can you say that?"

"Because every time we hang out, it's about what you need from me. You want me to investigate Rory, to help you with your home-work, to listen to you bitch about your roommates."

"I saved your life!"

"Yeah well, thanks for that. Now I get a life where everything triggers me into near catatonia, and I get to relive the evisceration of my friends every night. You really got me out of a bind."

"You're the one who chased me down, Duane. You're the one who's always wanting to hang out, inviting me out, wanting to spend time. Don't blame me for coming to you when I need a friend, and don't blame me for not giving you more when that's clearly what you want."

"What? Who told you that?" Duane said, dropping the files and turning to face her.

"No one. It's obvious. You follow me around like a lost puppy."

"Because you're my only real friend."

"You have plenty of friends."

"None like you. They all talk shit about this place all the time. And if they're not hating on my hometown, they're only talking about trying to get laid, or I don't know, sports teams I don't really care about. I just like spending time with you. You make me feel like not such a weirdo."

"You *are* a weirdo, Duane, because you like interesting things. And normal people don't like interesting things. They like simple things. And you're not simple."

"And neither are you."

"Fuck no."

Duane and Lexie stood in the dark laboratory, locked in a stand-off of ego and hurt feelings.

"I do like you," Duane said, barely above a whisper. "I'm sorry if I've been a creeper."

"You haven't been a creeper, Duane. You're like the opposite of a creeper. You're one of the good ones. You're the kindest, gentlest guy I know." Lexie reached for his hand, and although she felt like they were two magnets pointed the wrong way, she fought the resistance and grasped his hand in hers. "It's just…that's not enough for me to like you back." She flinched at the harsh truth, but Duane didn't. He just smiled his shy smile and nodded. Lexie spoke again, "I'm sorry my complicated life is getting all over you."

Duane chuckled. "I was going to say the same thing." He squeezed her hand. "Can you please tell me what's going on? I feel so alone in this."

"I will, Duane. I promise. Just not now." Lexie pulled her hand away. "I will tell you one thing: that Rare isn't going to hurt you again. And if any other Rare tries to, I'll kill it. I promise."

"What?"

"It's what I'm here for Duane. You're my people. I won't let you get hurt again."

In light of their fight and reconciliation, Lexie felt bad for waiting until Duane took a bathroom break to root through his lab and steal the Octopus and a handful of the EEG electrodes.

She'd return them later. He'd understand. Duane was a nice guy.

37

From dawn until lunch the girls tried meditating, beating on each other, and making faces like comic book superheroes. No amount of straining, visualization, or face-slapping would do the trick. Not one of them had so much as a flicker of a change.

Corwin took most of the girls to the gym to hit some punching bags, while Renee and Lexie stayed at the Den to work more with Sage and the stolen Octopus.

He tried explaining the shift in every language he knew how, showing them over and over how he moved from man to buffalo and buffalo to man. Lexie squinted, looked at him in her knife's reflection, tried to tap her lust, her sadness, her fear. For the first time since his arrival, Lexie began to question the value of this boy, the truth of him, and his potential.

Renee popped fresh batteries into the Octopus and brought it to them. "Let's see if this'll give you the boost you need."

Lexie took it, and Sage looked askance at the device.

"If it works, it works," Lexie said, too close to giving up to be skeptical. She reached to yank her shirt over her head, but paused.

"Could you...?"

Sage cocked his head to the side, waiting for further elucidation. Lexie raised an eyebrow. "Sage?" He shook his head, not understanding. "I need you to turn around, please."

"Turn around?"

Lexie sighed and looked to the sky. "Sage, I'm going to take off my shirt now so I don't ruin it with vomit and/or werewolf. Could you please face away from me so I don't have to expose my naked body to you?"

"Oh," Sage said. "Okay." He turned around.

Lexie sighed and shook her head at the motley parade of circus freaks that were now her allies.

Ten minutes later, Lexie shivered topless, kneeling on the chilly grass, a towel draped over her shoulders. Renee slathered Vaseline on Lexie's head. "This doesn't seem...scientific," Renee said with an arched brow.

"I'm just trying to replicate the experiment as much as I can remember it, Ms. BioChem major."

"If Duane used Vaseline on you, I'm more inclined to call campus security."

"Whatever. I've never done this before, so let's just go with it." Lexie handed Renee the handful of electrodes she had lifted from the lab.

Renee stared at their end: the branches descended into a trunk of braided wires and ended in a frayed root system of exposed copper and steel wires.

"Are you serious?" Renee drawled.

"What?" Lexie asked.

"This is supposed to attach to something. Like an input for a computer."

Lexie jutted her chin and considered. "I dunno, I just grabbed it."

Renee exhaled heavily and stuck the Octopus' solenoids to Lexie's scalp, the Vaseline oozing beneath the surface so that they threatened to slip off. "Just don't move and they'll stay," Renee said.

Once Lexie was feeling good and humiliated, Renee got the scotch tape and placed the other electrodes against Lexie's bare arm.

"No," Lexie said. "Back of my neck."

Renee obliged and then Lexie said, "Wait. No."

Lexie pulled the electrodes from the nape of her neck and placed two on her temples. She stuck the last two on each side of her sternum.

"Yay for flat-chests," Lexie said sardonically, tossing her hair over her shoulders and re-sticking the gooey solenoids to her scalp.

"This feels right," Lexie said, smoothing the tape over her skin. She covered herself back up with the towel and shifted her shoulders and head into a position akin to that of the original experiment. "Let's do it."

Renee looked to Sage and asked, "You wanna help?"

Sage, who had been sitting cross-legged, facing away the entire time, turned and nodded. He walked toward them, taking the controls from Renee and sitting in front of Lexie.

He smiled at her, his amber eyes offering her the courage she needed. Lexie held each tail of the towel against her skin. "Okay," she said. "Here we go."

Kneeling in the grass with the EEG cords dangling along her spine and wires against her chest, Lexie felt like a scrawny cyborg. She placed her hands across the electrodes taped to her skin and took a deep breath as Sage turned on the juice.

At first she felt a tingle, like a feather tracing across her skin. Then the tingle buried itself, a parasite burrowing through her flesh, drawing a jagged line between the two electrodes.

The EEG wires dangled uselessly.

Sage raised his eyebrows in a question and Lexie nodded, taking a deep breath and sinking into the sensation.

He turned the dial, and the worm wriggled faster, a unidirectional race through her chest. Her skin warmed with a thousand tiny sizzles cauterizing her flesh.

"More," Lexie grunted through clenched teeth. She gripped her chest, her hands warming the electrodes, willing them to work.

Sage cranked it to the max. The pulse ran, a knife against her flesh, endlessly retracing the path of trauma. Warmth and wetness cut at her ribcage, and her pulse raced to match the electricity. In that har-monized rhythm, a third rhythm appeared. A cycle of heavy thumps, impatient and ready. The pacing of an animal.

Lexie remembered this feeling, the interface of pain and pleasure, girl and wolf that danced around each other at the club with Ran-dy. She remembered Randy's instructions to feel into the space, find where they met, where they resisted, and where they clung together.

Lexie tried to push into that feeling, release it, expand it, let go, unwind, unspool, break apart. She strained—pushing, pulling, twist-ing, and unclenching, but none of it worked. Her ribcage was as strong as steel, keeping inside and outside, wolf and human girl, clearly de-lineated and bound to different realms of reality. Her wolf paced and snapped at her impertinent bones. She forced a retch, gripping hand-fuls of grass and pulling her belly forward, hoping to force the wolf to spring forth along with the limited contents of her stomach. Her face grew red and hot.

"Turn it off," Renee said. Sage obliged.

Lexie panted. "I can feel it. It's right there, but I can't let go. I need to turn off my brain. It's in the way."

"Turn off your brain?" Sage said.

"Corwin's got weed," Renee said.

"Marijuana doesn't turn off your brain," Sage said. "It turns it on. Opens you up."

The three considered while Lexie cycled her breaths.

"An orgasm?" Renee ventured.

The girls exchanged a glance, and without a word, Renee walked into the house.

Moments later, an extension cord ran through the open kitchen window and onto the lawn. Renee's vibrator, an ugly, be-knobbed wand, sat in the grass, ready to work its magic.

Lexie had ripped the useless EEG nodes from her scalp. She kept one flat palm against her chest, needing to connect with the crude device that wanted to bring out the beast in her.

"Alrighty," Renee said. "You ready?"

Lexie looked at the white device in the grass and made a face.

"Sage, you're benched for this one."

He looked at her, another question. "Go inside the house," she said.

He nodded and trotted into the house.

"Christ, it's like talking to a robot," Lexie said.

"Or a puppy," Renee laughed. Lexie muttered assent.

Lexie eased the vibrator between her legs. She looked up at Renee. "Can you give me some privacy, too?"

Renee gestured to the Octopus control box. "Should I just..."

"Turn around."

Renee turned. Lexie took a breath and turned on the vibrator. Immediately it sizzled through her skin, a force like twelve of Randy's motorcycles battering at her nerves.

A moan escaped her throat before she could catch it, and she gritted her teeth against more overt vocalizations.

The Octopus worked against her chest and skull but she barely noticed, the jackhammer vibrations through her skeleton obscuring any and all other sensations. Another groan escaped as the sizzles became tiny claws, racing up the surface of her skin in fierce bursts. Restless pinpricks dug in and sprang away, running up her belly, along her chest, her neck, her face. They leapt from the crown of her skull like violent splatters of rain.

Lexie clenched and released, trying to let the vibrations carry her brain away, but it wouldn't be budged. She could feel the back of her brain monitoring everything, like an overeager cockpit with dials and gauges she didn't understand.

She drew the wand from her and leaned onto her hands, panting.

Renee turned and grabbed her chin. "You can do this," she said.

"How? By clenching real tight? It's not fucking working!" Lexie threw the vibrator and tore the Octopus from her chest.

"It will work. You have to stop running away. You did this once before. You almost did it twice. You can do it again."

"I don't know how it happened before!"

"You freaked the fuck out, Lex! That's how! Now sit your ass down, and let's crank this shit out," Renee said.

"I can't."

"You have to."

"Why don't you try?" Lexie spat.

"Stop being a spoiled brat and get your act together."

"What?!"

"You're taking up too much space. You're holding us back." Renee's anger rose with each shake of Lexie's chin. "You have to pull your fucking weight and stop acting like some princess who doesn't have to earn her keep."

"I'm putting myself out here to help!" Lexie shouted. "I'm fucking jacking it naked in the frozen grass for you."

"Bullshit," Renee shouted. "You're doing this for Archer. You don't give a shit about the Pack or this town."

"What? How can you say that?"

"Because we've all been living with it for months." Renee raised her voice, her frustration moving through her forehead and down her shoulders to her hands. "Your misery is SO LOUD!" She pushed Lexie away from her, and Lexie balked, never having felt Renee's hands on her like this.

"I can't help it," Lexie pouted.

"The hell you can't. You can grow the hell up, starting right now."

"How?"

"Change."

"I can't," Lexie whimpered.

Renee whipped her palm across Lexie's cheek, bringing forth a yelp and a welt.

Lexie brought her hand to her cheek. She tried to back away, but Renee's long reach connected again with her face. WHAP!

Lexie yelped again and shouted, "Stop it!"

"You stop it."

Lexie fell back, holding her face. Renee closed the gap.

"You're nuts," Lexie said.

"And you're weak."

"I'm not." Lexie glowered, tears swelling in her eyes.

"You're small, stupid, and naïve," Renee said through gritted teeth.

"I'm not!"

"You are. You are so small you don't even fight back. Not without your girlfriend to come rescue you. But your girlfriend isn't here any-more. Smart woman left you, just like your mother did. Like everyone will, because you're unlovable. Ineffective. Stupid. Worthless."

"Fuck you!" Lexie spat.

"Words are for ladies and cowards. Show me your teeth."

Renee scooped up the fallen vibrator, pressing it hard against Lex-ie's groin. Lexie yelped. Renee gripped the scruff of her neck, yanking her body while grinding the wand harder against her. Lexie didn't, couldn't, resist. Her eyes were blurry with tears and her ears burned with the prick of a thousand needles.

"Show me you're not just a baby, some kept woman, some tooth-less little virgin."

Lexie whimpered. Renee caught her wrist and yanked Lexie's thin frame into a half-crouch. She spat in her face, and Lexie flinched, her tears turning to sobs.

"No wonder your mama chose a bunch of strangers over her own blood. If she had been a wolf, she'd have left you alone in the woods to starve."

Renee squeezed the back of Lexie's neck. Lexie's legs began to fail, and she quavered in Renee's brutal grasp.

The claws on Lexie's skin became rain, which became a torrent. The wolf was searching for an out as Lexie searched for breath, and she couldn't deny one any more than the other. She needed to push back against Renee's attacks, defend her mother, defend herself. The wolf no longer paced; it clawed at her from the inside for its freedom. All she had to do was let it out, let it fight on her behalf. Part daemon, part animus, she had no control over it, and yet it fought for her.

She found a tiny lock upon a tiny door that existed at once in her sternum, throat, and belly. Like a door to a secret room in her house that appeared only in a dream—when she found it she realized she had known where it was the whole time. She didn't even need a key.

The door flew open, and Lexie's voice spilled forth upon the back of the deluge, a gurgled, howling shriek.

Lexie roared. Her vision drained, like a cinematic version of death. Her ears filled with static, and she experienced a sensation like falling or sinking, a weightlessness before the shock of impact. A gray space followed. And a black one. The same color in this hazy dark.

The static in her ears abated and her senses returned to the sound of her own pulse, even and forceful. She found herself staring into Renee's face from the wrong angle, from below. She looked down at her paws, digging into the soil.

Lexie gagged and stumbled, her balance off, her body wrong. Her heavy head pulled her off balance. Another sway sent her teetering in the opposite direction. Her throat trembled and hacked. She coughed and tasted bile.

The cough became a hack. Lexie retched, a great heaving expulsion that shook her heavy frame. The wolf form struggled to keep its tenuous hold. Renee rushed to Lexie and sucker-punched her across the snout, yanking the wolf into sharper relief. Lexie snapped, and Renee jumped away.

She swayed back again, the world rolling around her, her muscles struggling to find equilibrium.

Lexie's human form flashed in and out, pushing her center of gravity up and down her frame, like a magnet trying to find true north. She squeezed her eyes shut, trying to hold onto the wolf even as it was wrenched away. She opened her eyes to catch sight of Sage running toward her just as her human body fell backwards to crack the frozen ground. Her ass hit first, then her skull. False lights dazzled at the periphery of her vision.

Renee crawled over, pressing her face to Lexie's. The icy grass on one of Lexie's cheeks mocked the warmth of Renee's face pressed to the other.

"There you go," Renee said. "Hold onto that. Whatever that is, seize it with both hands. Let your heart bury roots there. We're going to use that righteous rage for every drop it's worth."

38

LEXIE AWOKE ON THE FLOOR of the living room, wrapped in her quilt, a crackling fire her company.

When she sat up and stretched, Jenna swooped to her side with peppermint tea and a warm hand on her back.

"How do you feel?"

Lexie stuck out her tongue, a quasi-zombie face. "Queasy."

"Like food poisoning?"

"Like period cramps."

"Ooh!" Corwin shouted. "Now I can help!"

She ran upstairs and returned with a tin lunchbox embossed with a picture of She-Ra. Inside was a small glass pipe, a metal grinder, two lighters, and a jar full of marijuana.

Lexie laughed weakly and let her head fall back onto the pillows.

"You'll be alright," Corwin said. "This too shall pass."

She packed Lexie a bowl and left her to it.

"You need anything else?" Jenna asked.

Lexie shook her head, remembering every time she was sick and her mother sat at her bedside. She wanted to ask for a song or a back scratch, but she didn't. Instead, she smiled.

"You want me to carry you to bed?" Corwin asked.

Lexie shook her head. "I'm liking the fire. I'll be good down here."

Jenna swept her fingertips across Lexie's forehead and down her cheek. Renee's quick footsteps thudded down the stairs. She replaced Corwin and Jenna at Lexie's side.

"How you doing?"

The orange firelight made Renee's face glow like polished rosewood. Her expression was stoic but gentle. The hurt of Renee's words dissolved in the wake of the truth she had forced Lexie to face.

"Will you scratch my back?" Lexie asked, meekly. Renee smiled and eased to her elbow, tracing her fingertips against Lexie's skin.

"We're going to bed, Lex," Mitch called from the kitchen. "Just holler if you need anything."

Renee stayed next to Lexie for a long while, until the house echoed with the whispers of girls slipping into sheets and the heavy breath of sleep.

Finally Lexie said, "We're out of time."

Renee shook her head and stared into the flames. The same fire had danced in her eyes when she stood over Blythe's bloodied corpse.

"The Crow Moon is in three days. They'll come for us. We know they will." Lexie curled herself around the pillows on the floor as if they were a lover, or at least a friend. Lexie sighed and leaned back on the pillows. "I think I'm bleeding."

"Band-aid?"

"Tampon."

"That doesn't bode well." Renee went to the downstairs bathroom and returned with a small box. "I don't like not knowing what all this electro-mess is about."

Lexie cracked her knuckles one by one. "Me neither." Then, after a long pause: "Are you going to try it?"

"Of course," Renee said.

"Can I be mean to you then?" Lexie asked.

Renee chuckled. She sat again, but she left a space between herself and Lexie. She stared into the fire and scratched her head. "I'm sorry that I went there. You okay? For real?"

Lexie shrugged and rolled onto her back, facing Renee, who loomed above her. Their position reminded Lexie of the autumn, when the scariest question Renee could ask was *Can I kiss you?*

"I guess that's what people call 'tough love'?" Lexie asked.

Renee replied with a grunt.

"I didn't really have that growing up. The love I got was quiet and passive. Sulking, almost. Not tough." Lexie grabbed a tampon from the box and weaseled it under the blanket and inside of her. She edged toward Renee to curl up tighter next to her body. Renee combed her fingers through Lexie's hair, scratching her scalp.

"Tough love was the only kind my father seemed to know about," Renee said. "My mama, too, in a different way." Her fingers stilled in Lexie's hair. "I guess that probably says a lot about me."

Lexie chuckled and nudged her head against Renee's hand, demanding the other girl continue the dance of fingernails over her ears and cheeks.

"Does that mean you love me?" Lexie asked, hiding the vulnerability of the question behind a playful tone.

Renee cocked an eyebrow. "What do you think?"

Lexie nodded and edged the blanket up to her chin, giggling. Maybe she was being foolish, but she didn't care.

"Of course I do," Renee said, tickling Lexie's neck, playing back. She cupped Lexie's neck in her hand, coaxing Lexie to stillness. "You think you're nothing special, Lexie. Sometimes that makes you distant and cynical. But you gotta let yourself be loved if you want to have a chance at loving anyone else. And you have to start it off with believing you're worthy of it."

Lexie wrapped her fingers around Renee's lean forearm. "It feels so unsafe. Like I'll look weak or something."

Renee shook her head. "Big difference between being strong and being tough. I learned that a long time ago. Toughness is just a layer—the leather on a couch or the bark on a tree. You're strong. You've proven that over and over again. And you're going to have to keep proving it as long as you want to walk this world. But strength means pliability, tenderness. The willingness to wear your insides on the outside and to change, mold, and move."

Lexie released Renee's arm and hugged her pillows tighter. It made sense. It also sounded exhausting. And terrifying.

And maybe just a little bit exhilarating.

Renee sighed and rubbed her forehead. "Try to get some rest. Big days ahead." Renee put her hand on Lexie's belly. Her fingers swept to Lexie's hip and down her leg. Feathers danced on the surface of Lexie's skin. She smiled up at Renee.

Renee left, taking the stairs two at a time, and Lexie watched, contemplating her lithe frame, her wiry muscles, her firm skin—layers of tender strength.

All things must change / To something new, to something strange.

Lexie stared at the fire for a long while. The fluttering in her belly steadied and roiled in turn, over and over again. She tracked Renee's footsteps from her room to the bathroom and back, the whisper of the sheets as she pulled them over her body, and the heavy sigh as she tried to ease herself to sleep. Moments later, Lexie heard the click of Renee's desk lamp and the rustle of pages.

Lexie took a puff from the pipe and let the smoke find the crevices in her chest that needed sloughing. Like a creeping incense, the smoke filled everything and made her feel clean.

Outside, the moon waxed gibbous inside a rich blue halo of clear sky. She felt it tug on her chest, silver threads snaring like spider silk, seducing her into the woods. But she resisted. Out there was Sage, were Morloc, were a million things she didn't want to face. Inside there was a fireplace and food and marijuana. Fuck the woods. Just fuck 'em.

Lexie let her mind wander, watching the firelight and letting all the trauma and worries dribble out her ears. The tendons in her neck relaxed, as did the tiny muscles behind her eyes. She took a deep breath and let her jaw dangle open. This body. She would learn to love it, even if it killed her. She snorted at her gallows humor.

She brought the pipe to her lips and flicked the lighter, holding the flame to the herb and inhaling. Smoke filled her mouth and lungs. The firelight flickered against her skin, and she saw her second form appear and vanish. Her wolfish hands held the pipe and lighter, translucent claws curled around the curved glass of the bowl. Half-swallowed by her large paws they might be, but the two tools were still held firm between her dexterous fingers.

Lexie lowered her hands, held her breath, and considered. She raised them to the light again, squinting, capturing her secondary form in her vision. She wiggled her thumbs.

"No shit," she whispered. "Thumbs."

39

THE PHONE HAD BEEN RINGING for thirty seconds without going to voicemail. Lexie sat at her desk, wrapped in her mother's quilt. Frost clung to the outside of her bedroom window, and fog clung to the inside. Finally, when Lexie was two rings away from hanging up, Lorelei Koda picked up. Her voice was small, a whispering monotone. At Lexie's request, she put on her husband, George. Lexie hadn't seen him since the day Archer killed Hank Speer.

"Mr. Koda?" she said.

"Hello, Alexis Clarion," George said, friendly and frank, as was his way.

Lexie tried to make small talk, but George wasn't the loquacious type and she ended up feeling stupid.

"Mr. Koda," she finally said. "I have a big favor to ask." She wanted to sound matter-of-fact, like her father, like there was nothing weird at all about asking a buddy to borrow his pump-action shotgun.

She wasn't sure of the words she used, but she tried her best not to stumble over the request, like a neophyte telemarketer desperate to close. There was a long silence at the other end of the phone. Lexie strained to hear George breathing behind all the static and squeals of the telephone connection.

"Alexis Clarion," he said. He always used her full name in a mystifyingly patriarchal yet endearing way. "What are you getting up to?"

"Hunting," she squeaked.

He sighed like he was accepting a great burden. "I don't really know. I remember what happened the last time I saw you."

Lexie walked to her window and saw Sage in a circle with the women, leading them through movements that looked like Tai Chi.

"It's not like that, Mr. Koda. My friend and I. We just want a way to defend ourselves."

"I can respect that. But why aren't you asking your father?"

Lexie bit her lip, wondering if the truth might be useful in this scenario. "We're not talking," she said.

Another interminable pause. "Come by around dinnertime. Mrs. Koda will be here. She'll loan you a pair."

Lexie's next breath came in a half-squeal, half-scream. "Thank you, Mr. Koda," she eked out.

"Mm-hm," Mr. Koda sighed. He caught her before she could hang up. "Alexis Clarion, I trust your father so I trust you. You understand?"

"Yes, Mr. Koda," Lexie said, her ears growing hot. He hummed again and hung up.

Downstairs, Renee was sipping coffee, watching Sage and the girls through the kitchen window.

"What's this about?" Lexie asked, shuffling into the kitchen wearing pajamas and her quilt.

Renee blew the steam from her mug. "He's trying to show them how to find the space between thoughts."

"How's it going?"

Renee shrugged.

"Why aren't you out there?"

Renee sipped her coffee, made a face, and shrugged the question away. Lexie looked askance, but let it slide, eager to share her revelation.

"I've been thinking about the poem. 'Something new, something strange.'"

"Okay," Renee said.

"What if it's not werewolves, but something else?" Lexie asked.

"What, like a change of attitude?"

Lexie eyed Renee's coffee covetously. "Well, maybe not like that, but what if it's the space between that Sage talks about? Not the woman or the wolf, but the shift itself that has power?"

"I dunno." Renee noticed what had drawn Lexie's attention and passed her the mug. "The in-between place, when I've paid attention to it, just makes me feel nauseous."

Lexie took a healthy gulp of the coffee and felt it work its magic on her bloodstream. She passed it back to Renee. They passed the mug back and forth, watching the Pack balance and sway in the yard.

"Any word from your gun-toting buddies yet?"

Lexie grimaced. "Yeah. I can pick up two tonight from one of my dad's friends, but no replies from high school friends yet. Not that I'm surprised. I was kind of a weirdo in high school. How you would you feel if the spaz from Spanish class emailed out of the blue to ask for your Browning?"

Renee returned her gaze to the window, and Lexie knew the answer.

Renee stared at the girls as they strained against their bodies, willing them to bust open, to undo everything they grew up learning.

"Do you know how to work a pair of clippers?" Renee asked.

"Yeah, I used to cut my dad's hair...when he had hair."

"How would you feel about shaving my head?"

The upstairs bathroom got nice light through the skylight, but Lexie still spent awhile bringing in two extra desk lamps and Hazel's makeup mirror. She was nervous.

"I want this," Renee said. "It's cool."

Lexie took a deep breath and shook it out. "I've just heard stories..."

Renee cocked an eyebrow.

"...Of the way black girls feel about their hair."

Renee laughed.

"Promise that if I fuck it up, you're not going to toss me out to the Morloc first?" Lexie asked.

Renee sat facing the mirror and mock-narrowed her eyes at Lexie's reflection. Even sitting, her head came to Lexie's chest.

Lexie placed her hands on Renee's head and let her hands sink into the black suds of her hair. She sighed with the delightful sensation. "Ready?"

Renee stared herself down in the mirror, took a heavy breath, and nodded. "Fire her up."

Lexie pressed the clippers to Renee's scalp and skidded them along the curve of her skull. Her hair fell off in clumps, like lamb's wool.

Renee ducked and bolted out of her chair. "Okay, never mind."

Lexie laughed. "It's too late now. I just took a chunk out of your head."

Renee fanned herself with her hands and paced. "Okay. Hold on." She rushed down the hall to Corwin and Sharmalee's room. Lexie followed.

Renee snatched up the bottle of Cuervo Corwin kept on her desk and took a healthy swig. Lexie poked around and found the DVD of the porno they'd been watching on repeat.

"I don't get it," Lexie said, reading the back of the case.

Renee wiped her mouth and exhaled. "That's better." Renee offered it but Lexie waved it away.

"I think it's about redefinition and community," Renee said, swirling the tequila around in its bottle.

"Porn?" Lexie asked, unbelieving.

"That kind, I guess," Renee said. "Like with Hazel and her stripping. The porno is probably Sharm and Corwin's way of playing with new ideas, too, while feeling not so freakish for having the desires they do."

Lexie snorted. "Desires like dudes?"

Renee shrugged. "Sure, why not? Dudes are fucked over by the patriarchy, too. I think it's great that Corwin's letting herself explore. Just like Sharm and Mitch for that matter."

Lexie nodded and stuck out her bottom lip, considering. Renee took another swig.

"I guess it just flies in the face of the things—"

"—Blythe taught us," Renee interrupted. "Right?"

Lexie nodded.

"You came into the Pack at a weird time. We were tighter than ever, but that meant shutting out the outside world and any new ideas that might come from it. The outside world is a scary place, and we all needed to heal. Together. Now we don't have the luxury of living in an echo chamber. Which means we're going to in-fight and disagree. If we live to have that privilege, that is."

Lexie chewed on her lip and propped the porno on Sharm and Corwin's pillows, like some sort of pervy teddy bear. "That'd be nice."

"Okay," Renee said. "I am officially buzzed enough to face my bald future. Let's do this."

Back at the mirror, Renee kept her eyes trained on her reflection. Occasionally she'd daub tears from the corners of her eyes with some toilet tissue. Sage's commanding and soothing voice outside provided a muffled soundtrack as Renee had a moment with herself. Lexie felt honored to be a part of it.

"How's the book?" Lexie asked, gesturing to the tiny black book wedged in the back of Renee's pants. She was enjoying her role as mock hairdresser.

"Good," Renee said.

"Want to read me some?"

"It's a short book."

"This haircut won't take much longer," Lexie smiled.

Renee fished out the book and flipped it to a highlighted passage.

"Thus we may know that there are five essentials for victory," Renee read. "One: She will win who knows when to fight and when not to fight."

Lexie snickered at Renee's on-the-fly gender reassignment.

"Two: She will win who knows how to handle both superior and inferior forces. Three: She will win whose army is animated by the same spirit throughout all its ranks. Four: She will win who, prepared herself, waits to take the enemy unprepared. Five: She will win who has military capacity that is not interfered with by the sovereign."

"Well, we've got that last one covered," Lexie said.

Outside, yelps and shouts interrupted Sage's soothing instruction.

They ran into Lexie's room, which had windows that overlooked the yard, to see Hazel flickering back and forth between girl and wolf.

"Hold onto it!" the girls below shouted.

Lexie ran down the stairs and out onto the porch. "Let it go, but catch it before it falls away. Like that slidey-pole drop you do."

Hazel squeezed her eyes shut and concentrated on Lexie's directions.

"Like Pilates," Jenna whispered, in awe.

"Or Kegels!" Sharmalee shouted.

Hazel struggled and sweated, but she did it. Like a zoetrope, Hazel released and caught her wolf. The transition disappeared, leaving only her flickering form released, chased, and caught, over and over.

"Good, Hazel," Lexie said. "Now grab it and let go just a little bit. Hold onto it as light as you can while still holding it."

Hazel whined and grimaced, contorting like Proteus as she struggled to obey Lexie's commands. Her eyes squeezed shut. Her jaw clenched. Muscles and tendons corded her usually soft limbs as she strained.

"There!" Lexie shouted.

The girls gasped together.

Hazel stood on two legs, two feet taller than her usual height, her back curled forward, and her arms like forelegs, covered in a mottled gray coat. Her snout was wolf-shaped but shorter, her tail still curled behind her back. At the ends of her arms were her paws, half human, half wolf. Five sinewy digits—four fingers and a thumb—ended in scythe-shaped claws.

The Pack and Sage stared agog.

"This is it. Something new," Lexie repeated.

"Something strange," Renee finished.

40

THE LIT BUILDING WAS ONE of the oldest on Milton's campus, and
the professors' offices were shoved into the basement level, each boast-
ing a sliver of a window at sidewalk level. Rindt's office was at the far
end of a dark hall.

Lexie suspected the literary types on campus liked this subterra-
nean lifestyle, cozy in their caves, safe from the glares and blares of the
outside world. Walking the dark and echoing hall, Lexie thought she
might like it too. She briefly contemplated a literature major, which
would mean three more years of reading, Lexie thought with a grimace. Then she recanted; three more years of anything would be nice.

Lexie's homework had done itself, or at least it felt like it had.
She had copied down the script from her mother's quilt, character by
character, and then—in a different font—typed out the translation.

As an epilogue to her paper, she explained the origin of the quilt
and tried, obliquely, to describe her translation process. Her least am-
bitious hope was that it would impress Rindt. Her greatest was that
it would make him trust her enough to admit he left her the book
and the note. Some small part of her believed that if she ingratiated

herself to him, he'd pick up the phone and call off tomorrow night's Rare wolf attack. He spoke their language; he must be able to level with them.

Lexie was too caught up in her absolution fantasy to notice the scent bathing the hallway. Werewolf senses were ineffective when distracted by the imagination of a desperate girl.

Rindt's office light cast a rectangular shaft through the frosted glass of his door. It slashed across the flecked linoleum floor like the harsh cut of lamplight in a noir film. Lexie was the troubled dame—she couldn't cut it as the femme fatale. All she had to do was walk through that door and dump her problems into someone else's lap.

"Professor Rindt?"

She knocked first, and then she turned the knob. Her imagination was no competition against the scent now. The ammonia of piss, the musk of sweat, but most of all, the metal tang of blood, pummeled her.

She flinched, not against the scent, but in preparation for the gory sight sure to follow. But there was no body, only a splatter of fluids on the floor and bits of hair and bone. Lexie bent to her knees and peered into the puddle like she was scrying. Smooth streaks of clean floor interrupted the brownish-crimson puddle. Tongue marks. The blood was licked clean.

Lexie staggered to her feet, choking back bile. Professor Rindt had been eaten. She reached for the door and slammed it. She sniffed hesitantly. It had been over a day since the Rare had been here. She scoured the room for clues, skirting around the puddle. Beneath the bookcase she found a tooth. With a grimace, she pocketed it.

The upper-left drawer of Rindt's desk was locked. Lexie jimmied it. When it wouldn't budge, she took her knife and slid it into the latch, torqueing it. It popped open with a metal clang.

Lexie half-expected to find another coded note when she opened the drawer, a posthumous set of instructions. Instead she found a pewter letter opener, two hundred dollars, and a photograph. Lexie flipped on the desk lamp. The photo was self-taken; Rindt's blurred bare arm filled the left side of the frame. He was shirtless, his vividly-colored tattoos even more elaborate than Lexie would have guessed.

He whispered into the ear of a young woman nestled in the crook of his free arm. She wore a white bra and a bright smile. Bree Curtis.

41

"THE CROW MOON RISES ON Friday evening at 6:48 p.m.," Renee said. The girls sat in a semicircle on the floor of the living room. They each wore sweat- and mud-stained clothes. Mitch cracked his knuckles. Hazel spread her legs and stretched, a warm washcloth draped over her neck. "We will attack on Friday, at dawn."

"Er, what?" Corwin said.

"They're planning on attacking us at the moon," Renee said. "Archer's pack fought under the moon, too. Each time. Rares are nocturnal. We need to use the element of surprise and turn their biology against them. With the sunrise at our backs, they'll be at a disadvantage."

The girls looked to one another and shrugged.

Renee continued. "Here are the things we know about the Morloc: As full-bloods they're stronger at night in nearly every way: eyesight, stamina, strength. Each of them is roughly twice our size and twice our wolf strength, eight times our human strength. They're smart, but they are wild animals more attuned to hunting prey by picking off the slowest of a pack and defending territory. We know they cooperated to kill Bree, but we don't know to what extent they can work together otherwise."

Lexie nodded. "We don't know if they know we're prepping for a fight, but it's best to assume that they do."

Renee nodded. "And if so, they have every reason to expect we will come at them as wolves. Because of that expectation, they will undoubtedly prepare for a moonrise attack. We're going to get the jump on them. Questions?"

"How fast are they?" Corwin asked.

Sage answered. "Fast, but like a giraffe or an elephant is fast. They're fast because they're big. They span space in a different way than us. In a straight footrace they'd win."

"But in an obstacle course, we'd have the upper hand," Lexie said.

"So how do we make it one?" Mitch asked.

"The Morloc live dispersed throughout the Barrens, just a big rubbly open space," Lexie said. "We need to draw them into the woods."

Renee continued, "We'll use Lexie's guns as humans, deliver as much damage as possible, and then shift for close combat."

"That's fine for Hazel and Lexie, but the rest of us can't stay human the whole time," Corwin said.

"Yeah, they'll be too strong," Sharmalee said. "Five of their six ends are pointy. We wouldn't stand a chance."

"That's why we need to practice our shifts," replied Renee. "Hazel got there today, and I think we all can do it."

"You *think*?" Mitch said.

"We'll practice tomorrow. And Friday we fight."

"One day?" Jenna said. "One more day to train?" Jenna's voice cracked. She blinked back tears.

"And prepare," Renee said. "I need three of you to go to the edge of the burnout and start digging trenches, running trip wires, anything we can do to make the space more complicated for the Morloc. And I need one more to go with Lexie to pick up the guns. We need as much firepower as we can gather."

"What have we got?" Mitch asked.

Lexie shifted on her feet. "One pump-action shotgun, one bear rifle, and one over-under."

Only Mitch acknowledged the paltry list. The others didn't know what any of it meant, but Mitch's dismay was easy enough to read.

"That is insane!" Jenna said.

Renee crossed her arms over her chest and nodded, looking at her feet.

"Renee, we can't. This isn't a plan," Jenna pleaded. "You can't send us in there without any training. Lexie's the only one of us who's even shot a gun. We'll be eviscerated."

"Jenna, I understand your fear, but we don't have the time."

"We don't know that," Jenna said, tears flowing unimpeded now, her ears growing rosy and her curls sticking to her cheeks. "Why couldn't we go underground until after the moon, wait it out?"

"The Morloc aren't going to wait," Sage said. "When the moon comes, they will draw blood on a scale larger than this town has ever seen. We are Milton's only line of defense."

Jenna covered her eyes and tried to calm herself. Hazel reached out and stroked her back. "Do you realize what you're asking of us?" Jenna whispered.

Renee nodded. "I do. And you all should know this now: we may all die on Friday. We may lose, and then our teachers and our friends and our families will die too. But if Lexie is right about their plan, it's better for us all to die than to survive a war that they win."

Jenna tugged at her hair. "What if you're wrong? What if it's not about us?"

Lexie and Renee exchanged a pained look.

"Bree was murdered," Lexie said. "Whether she was supposed to be a sacrifice, an offering, or a sex slave, we don't know. You can hide behind our incomplete information, or you can take a stand to help stop it all.

"That's why we have to fight," Lexie continued. "Because even if we don't play, we lose."

Jenna brought her hands to her face, a grimace tugging at her mouth, but she was only giving expression to the horror that all the girls were feeling.

"I'm in," Corwin said. "These fuckers are going to pay for what they did to Sharm."

"No way am I going to be a character in these monsters' rape fantasy," Hazel said. "I'm in, too."

Sharmalee nodded. "Me too."

"Yep," Mitch said, rocking his body with his nod.

Lexie looked to Renee. "It's what I'm here for."

"Me too," Renee said, with a smile.

The Pack looked to Jenna, who clasped her hand over her mouth, her eyes bloodshot and heavy with more yet-to-be-cried tears. "Oh god," she whispered. "I'm so scared, sisters."

Hazel crawled to Jenna's legs, hugging them. The rest of the Pack stood and joined her, embracing Jenna from all sides.

Jenna let the Pack's hugs squeeze out the sobs. She choked on her fear as it tried to strangle her from inside. "Okay," Jenna gasped. "Okay. I'm in. We can do this," Jenna said it to convince herself, and it sounded familiar to Lexie. She once had to force herself to abandon uncertainty, too. Now she had shed it completely. She would not miss it.

42

Hazel led the girls through the shifts like she was choreographing a dance recital. "One, two, three, four. Keep breathing. Here we go."

Lexie followed along inside her head. She sat on the deck in front of a spread of five guns: three from George Koda and the other two the result of begging every high school classmate she still had in her cellphone. She took a break from cleaning them to type an email to her father. It offered an incomplete apology for what had transpired, and what was about to. It begged his forgiveness and, supposing she survived, his mercy. Before she could talk herself out of it, she hit 'send.'

At Jenna's instruction, Sage had taken on the Pack's usual full moon ritual: washing towels, packing sandwiches, checking the heater on the hot tub. Pretending everything would work out, or just praying it would, Lexie was beyond judging. She smiled at the illusion of normalcy Sage conjured.

Raising the first rifle to her shoulder and adjusting the scope, she shouted, "All right! Who's up first for target practice?"

* * *

Jenna made a big dinner, and they all ate heartily, even Sage, who never rid himself of his cautious, semi-feral behavior. He looked like a tiger in a bow tie, resisting the urge to bury himself face-first in his dinner plate. Lexie found herself stealing glimpses of him. His eyes were the same, warm amber of Archer's right eye. The color she missed the most.

"Where do the trees dance?" Lexie asked, interrupting the cacophony.

The girls gave her puzzled looks.

"Oh yeah," Sharmalee said. "What's that place?"

"Joshua Tree," Renee said, snapping a green bean with her teeth. "Why?"

"That's a thing? Dancing trees?"

"Not really, but they look like it," Mitch said. "All prehistoric, *Flintstones*-style trees. It's a cool place. Lots of artsy hippies and crazy vistas. Blythe took me there on our way to visit her folks a couple Christmases ago."

The girls smiled at Mitch's shared memory, and Corwin squeezed his shoulder as he let his gaze fall on his mashed potatoes.

For a reason none of them could explain, they left the candles burning all night, letting their slow diminishment count down the hours until the Pack's departure. The house fell quiet, girls peeling off in ones and twos to find their last night of comfort.

Lexie sought solitude instead on the back deck, staring into the woods, trying to keep herself from tearing off her clothes and running away from everything.

"Shouldn't you be sleeping?" Sage asked, interrupting her angst.

Lexie glanced back at the house, where sounds and scents declared that nobody inside would be sleeping for a while-- most of all Sharmalee and Corwin, whose giggles and moans bled through the walls. "You think I could?" Lexie snorted. "What about you?"

"I'm more of a four-to-eight p.m. kind of guy." His joke felt like a too-awkward attempt at fitting in with her community, her era.

Lexie joined him by the Adirondack chairs, the white of the moon cutting through the patchy clouds to rain down silver light on them. "I don't think I've heard you call yourself that before. A 'guy'."

Sage smiled. "I thought it was more of a generality than a gender."

Lexie considered. "Okay, that's fair." His scent, which she'd been trying to ignore, curled around her like threads of moonlight. But the threads were made of more than scent; they stretched in front of her like antennae or cilia, sensing and grasping, reaching and pulling close. Batting them away like before would be fruitless, so she let them linger, drifting toward Sage when he breathed in, and back to her when he exhaled. It went like this for long minutes, her wolf curled in her belly, resting, cozy, readying, breathing with him.

"Thank you, Sage," she spoke, and when she did it was a whisper, in a language custom-made for her company.

Sage stirred at the Rare vocalization. "It is my honor."

Lexie took his hand, letting the moonthreads weave them together, binding them with an ineffable truth.

His warmth crept beneath her skin. It was too much— his hand, his smile, his touch— the sounds coming from the bedrooms above pushing her down a road she wasn't ready for. She shook herself free of the grip she'd initiated and walked to the wooden rail, looking to the black forest and the white moon, trying to find meaning for what was happening inside of her.

Sage stood and followed her.

"Are you all right?" he asked.

"That's a silly question." Lexie turned to face him, leaning against the rail.

"No," he said. "Circumstances are dreadful, that is obvious. Fates are unknown and blood will soon be shed. But you, here." He pressed the flat of his palm against Lexie's sternum, seemingly holding all her weight, that of her body and the rest that stacked invisible atop her, in that small connection.

She felt into the space where his hand held her. His touch wasn't the invasion she feared, but instead a call that stirred a new animal within her, one she had not yet encountered. Her instinct was to name it, but she resisted. That animal was not afraid nor preparing for war. It just was.

The tension between their bodies thickened. She placed her hand over his, reaching to his face with the other. She stroked his cheek as she had upon their first meeting, but this time not from curiosity or disbelief.

His skin was velvet and his lips so perfectly mauve. A flutter started in her chest and rose up her throat to her mouth, tickling her lips. She didn't know if she wanted to, but she would, she did.

She pulled Sage's lips to hers. Unlike her kiss with Archer a lifetime ago, Lexie was lucid. Every detail was indelible. Every sensation was drawn into such sharp relief, the rest of the world may as well have been beyond the edges of the photograph containing this moment.

The moonthreads of their bodies mingled, faint tickling like static electricity, not only where their bodies met but where they longed to.

Lexie pulled Sage into her, as though she could open her chest cavity and have him fill the space that felt crowded with emptiness. Their mouths matched their rising pulses, tongues pressing, muscles flexing. Sage held her, and Lexie let herself be held. She pushed him and he relented. Lips and hands grappled, kissing like it was the end of her world.

She took in his breath, and it felt ancient and strange, and she gave it back to him, new and transformed.

Lexie could stay in this place forever, treading and retreading the waters of this desire manifest.

She held him, drank him, pulled him. Her wolf didn't threaten to overtake or shift blame. This was all Lexie.

All her. Lexie stopped. Lexie prayed for one of the girls to wake and interrupt them, to rescue her from her betrayal to the self she'd thought she'd known.

Whatever had opened in her slammed shut. The wrongness of it caught her like a swipe across the face. It was her consciousness, her humanness, scolding her, shaming her.

She shoved away from the embrace, pulling her threads back in, tying them across her chest.

Sage searched her face.

She shook her head.

"What?" he asked.

"No. This is. No."

His brow furrowed; his lips parted on a question.

"This is wrong," Lexie said, as unmoored as the first time her hands became paws.

"It's not." he said.

"It feels wrong."

"Because of my touch, or what you think my touch means?"

Lexie shook her head. How could she answer his questions when all her mind said was 'flee'?

Sage pressed one hand to his own heart. He reached the other toward hers, not pressing, barely touching, proving his delicateness. "Meaning is between things, not within them."

"I don't know what that—"

"Everything is a cocreation. Everything."

Lexie lunged at him and smashed her lips against his, hoping it would shut down everything: his gentleness, her shame. And it did, for a moment or two. But then the voices resurged, the ones she thought dead with Archer's love. Dead with her mother.

But they weren't her elders, her ancestors, her ghosts. They were all echoes of her own voice, her own ideas of right- and wrong-doing, with eighteen years of reinforcement behind them.

They tore her away from the immediate pleasure of desire fulfilled. Loudest of all was the voice of the recent past, of all she was learning about the world and her identity, turned back on itself to mock her in her ignorance. Lexie knew nothing, but now she finally knew it.

She pushed herself away. "I'm sorry."

"Is it my form?" he asked. "This body?"

Lexie wished she had an answer for him. She forced herself to try, hoping the truth would catch up to her words.

"Ish?" she said. "If you were a woman, I would still desire you, but I would fear it more."

"More?"

"Your power. Or the idea of your power. Women are … ever-changing." Lexie smiled at the tiny irony. "I feel helpless with women. I don't feel helpless with you."

"Some might consider that a good thing."

"Someone like me," Lexie said. "That doesn't mean I'm ready for it."

"And if I became—"

"Don't. No. That's unfair. If this is the you that you're choosing to be, it's dishonest to be anything else."

"Don't you understand? I am not this man's form, nor the buffalo, nor the wolf. I am the space between."

She tried to imagine that space where there were no forms, no egos, no ids. She felt into it but it felt like a fiction, a pleasant lie.

"Go," she said finally. "Find my treehouse. Sleep there. I need to be alone with my sisters tonight."

Sage nodded and turned, waiting until he was in the shadow of the woods to doff his clothes and toss them on the lawn chair.

"Tomorrow morning," he growled, in a language only they understood. "Dream well."

Lexie tried to sob, but when she found that she couldn't, decided to shift all night instead. She stabbed her belly with whatever emotion she could concoct, and watched her hand in the candlelight, her fingers flickering from woman to wolf, and back, so easy, so painful. The flickering candlelight allowed her to pretend she was hallucinating. Another memory of a life before. She wiggled her fingers, enjoying the shapes they made, their shifting geometries.

One by one, the girls stopped pretending they could sleep, stopped forcing themselves to try.

In Corwin and Sharmalee's room, they murmured and shifted in bed. She heard Sharmalee giggle, and then the whir of Corwin's laptop. They were watching that movie again, all giggles and sighs.

Hazel slow-danced alone in her room, her breath on an eight count. Mitch was listening to music in bed. Renee scribbled in her journal, soft pencil on linen paper. Jenna was in the kitchen, ninja baking. Lexie knew that Jenna wanted to make sure they had food for when they returned. Lexie heard Jenna's sniffles and knew her tears would be part of everything she made tonight.

How would you spend your last night alive? Lexie asked her right paw, watching it shift on her impulse.

How will you? she thought, dancing her hematite dark claw to her lips, teasing at her flesh with its hard point. Mourning the loss of first love? Yearning, warily, for the touch of that love's brother? Fearing her death? Listing all the things she'd done and the things she'd never do? It all seemed so trite filtered through the lens of certain death.

So Lexie lit another candle, lit the joint that Corwin rolled for her, and kept on changing, knowing there was nothing else to be anymore, except for something in-between.

LEXIE MOVED THROUGH A FOG the whole morning. Part of her remembered the old fishing ritual of waking before sunrise, packing thermoses and tackle boxes, filling coolers with ice and sandwiches. Except now the ice was for injuries, the tackle boxes replaced with arrows and ammo.

They packed the back of her truck first, then the hatchback of Renee's car. Blankets, ice, water, bandages, ammo, arrows, guns, and bows.

Renee insisted on coffee, even though the rest of the girls were worried about the shifts and losing the contents of their stomachs.

Bleary-eyed and furtive, the girls, Sage, and Mitch climbed into the cars and drove to the Barrens. Halfway to the highway, Mitch asked from the middle seat, "Lexie, can I borrow your cell? I want to text Stefan again."

Lexie knew better than to protest his earnest attempt at salvation and handed him her phone.

They pulled off at the edge of the new highway and clattered over roots and rocks deeper into the woods, Renee's hatchback bouncing and scraping behind them. As they disembarked far past the treeline, Renee asked again, "The boys?"

Mitch merely shook his head. They were on their own.

Renee put on her game face and gestured for the women to gather around her.

"This truck," Renee said, pointing, "is our line. We do not lose it. Understood? We are not fighting to the last woman, we are fighting to win."

The girls nodded solemnly.

"If we call a retreat, you retreat. We are faster and fewer and we can run if we need to. Jenna, you'll take the Bushmaster and cover the field from that tree. Sage will corral and distribute the Rares for ease of attack. We will all do as much damage from long range as possible. Reload and replenish at Lexie's truck. Shift when you can, but only engage if you have to. This fight will not last long. We have to keep at it one hundred percent for as long as we can."

Jenna was staring at her feet and shaking her head. "I feel like this is dress-up. We're imposters. We're not warriors."

Renee jabbed a finger in her face.

"These wolves *made us* warriors. We are all here because we *chose* to be. In this battle and on this planet. If you were a lesser woman, you would have let their rage end you. You'd have become a hollow shell of a person, the empty doll they all want us to become. But you didn't. You chose life. You chose to fight. And you found your wolf.

"Other women have experienced the same violence as we did, and they didn't come back from it. They either died or spent the rest of their lives blaming themselves. We learned mercy, that being a woman wasn't a fault that begged for punishment. We forgave ourselves, and we became stronger for it. Each one of us. And for that we should be proud. Now we will offer some of that mercy to these assholes—in the form of a swift death.

"Each one of you asked after they got you: Why me? Why us? Why this world? The answer is here right now. To make us into the warriors that will destroy them. We are the monsters they made us become.

"Are you with me sisters?"

"Yeah!" Corwin shouted.

"Are you with me?!" Renee shouted louder.

"Yeah!" the Pack screamed together.

"Are you with me?!!"

"YEAAAHH!" the Pack screamed, half howl, half war cry, woman and wolf.

Their shared howl echoed and died, and the girls shared one last look; conviction replaced fear.

Sage stepped to them and said, "Sunrise is in twenty minutes. Take your positions."

Renee looked at the faces of her sisters, satisfied. "Jenna, get up in that tree and get ready to shoot these fuckers down."

Jenna scurried to the tree, slinging the semi-automatic rifle over her shoulder and carrying herself up branch by branch, until she found a sniper position and hunkered down. Mitch took a midpoint and passed up one of the ammo boxes.

The girls scattered along a line, hiding behind boulders and tree trunks. Beyond their line was the Barrens: an open land of jagged rocks and dry brush. The forest would be their defense.

Once in place, Sharmalee waved at Renee. "How do we get their attention?"

Renee thought. "Hazel, do you want to run?"

"Thirty miles before a fight? Hell no."

"I'll handle it," Sage said, stripping and tossing his jeans in the back of the truck. "Is everyone ready?"

"Wait," Sharmalee said. "Let me."

Renee gave her a wary look.

"I've been bait before," Sharmalee said. "I know how to make a dude think he's got the upper hand." She ran forty yards into the field, tossing her thrift-store mumu over her head to the ground. She wore a simple bra and underwear, brilliant white against the chestnut of her skin. She walked in the fog of her breath, her hips moving in slow circles with each step across the broken slate.

Lexie could hear Sharm breathing slow and steady and whispering affirmations to herself that she could survive once more.

Alone on the soon-to-be battlefield, Sharmalee lowered herself to her knees, looked skyward to the gray dawn, and howled. It was a small howl, like her voice—soft, feminine—fading too quickly before being reborn with another strong breath. She delivered her howl as a dare to herself and to her attackers, letting them know she was alive and ready for a fight.

For a while, the girls stayed still. The last of Sharmalee's sweet howls carried away on the cold breeze and she sat, waiting.

When the first of the growls came from over the rise, it almost surprised the Pack, as if this wasn't what they were waiting for. A haggard wolf stepped into view, his patchy fur matching his hoarse and gravelly growl. His rumble was joined by another, then a third, and two more wolves appeared over the rise. Sharmalee stood and froze. The three took stalking steps toward her.

"Run," Lexie whispered. She looked to Renee and Hazel, who both seemed to be willing the same.

Run, she thought. *We need to draw them to us, not go out there and get slaughtered.*

Renee caught her eye, a desperate look.

Run, Sharmalee. Come on.

But Sharmalee didn't run. She stood stock still, frozen. Triggered and shut down, Lexie supposed.

The three full-bloods seemed to find this amusing, their slavering jaws parting in menacing grins.

Come on, Sharm, Lexie pleaded, her lips silently speaking the words as though reciting a prayer.

The wolves closed in; Sharmlaee didn't move. Renee took a step beyond her hiding place, readying to run and shift.

Hazel stripped off her clothes and dug her feet into the ground, making sure Lexie and Renee saw. She gestured that she was going to run. Renee signaled up to Jenna in her tree that she should prepare to fire.

The wolves were now only three paces from where Sharmalee stood frozen. The largest one leapt, his claws spread and ready to rake out her guts.

Hazel and Renee both launched across the barrens. Yards to the left, a pale blur bounded into the field. Sage shifted as he ran, his wolf beginning at his snout and scudding down his skull and spine. At once, he ran on lean legs, pale gray and beige, as graceful as a ballet dancer and with the speed and heft of a bounding elk.

He bellowed a growling snarl as he rammed into the neck of the first full-blood. The animal toppled and rolled, and Sage leapt over it as the two other wolves set their eyes on him. A clatter of barks shook Sharmalee out of her inertia, and she fell over herself to run.

To Lexie, it almost looked as though she were running in slow motion, her skin rippling over her thick thighs each time her feet hit ground. She couldn't outrun them.

Sharmalee disappeared beneath a mass of fur and growls. Lexie bolted after Renee and Hazel, all strategy forgotten. She was only yards into the field when a growl greater than the full-bloods' bellowed from beneath the writhing pile. Sharmalee burst from beneath them, feral and fur.

Sharmalee's fur gleamed blue-black with the same sheen as her human hair. Her brown chest mirrored her skin. She looked beautiful, and enraged. She leapt onto the back of the closest wolf and bit down hard on the scruff of his neck. He yelped and shook to dislodge her hulking body from his own, but she held on.

Renee launched a bolt into his haunch, attracting the attention of the three other wolves. They raced toward her. Renee ran to meet them, tossing her crossbow to the ground.

The forward pair swiped out to slice across her chest. She released a cry more fierce than anything Lexie had ever heard from a woman. Renee seemed half-banshee, her mouth stretching beyond rational bounds, a caterwaul erupting in a torrent of rage. She leapt, shifting fully in midair. Her wolf form erupted out, catching the full-bloods at the apex of their swipes and stifling the power of their blows. She landed behind them. The wolves scrabbled to a stop. Renee didn't pause to let them recover. She charged, battering them aside with her shoulder and swiping at their ribs and bellies with her claws.

Hazel and Lexie ran to her aid. Lexie raised her shotgun to her shoulder and fired, catching one of the Morloc at the shoulder. She followed by slamming the butt of her weapon into the shredded meat of the wound. Hazel aimed her shotgun at the neck of the wounded full-blood, but the third, fresh full-blood slammed into her with his pointed snout. Lexie pulled her knife and ran to Hazel's attacker, slicing his haunch. He turned and snapped. Lexie dropped to her knees and rolled under his belly, dragging her knife across it. He sprang away in a storm of blood and squeals.

Lexie heard a crack from the treeline. Jenna released a shot that drove deep into the yelping wolf's ribs. Lexie leapt to her feet and was blindsided by the fourth, unwounded Rare.

Lexie's vision went white, then star-filled black, the feral noises fading in and out as her body fell to earth. Another crack from Jenna's tree shook her awake. The beast above her teetered and fell. His skull slammed onto her ribs, the bones in her chest grinding, her ribcage bowing from the impact.

With a quiet moan, Lexie let her own wolf breach her flesh. Her ribcage expanded beneath the tonnage of the felled wolf. She pushed him off. He snarled, not dead, not nearly. There was a bloody gouge where his ear should be, his skull exposed by the bullet's path. His lips pulled tight from his teeth. He snapped and licked his maw, saliva and blood intermingling, pink foam dripping from his jaw. He dove for her and she swiped him aside with a clumsy paw. He snarled and snapped his jaws closed around her shoulder. He gave her a fierce shake and tossed her to one side. She lost hold of her wolf form and landed in her girl shape. The Rare bounded after her while she struggled to right herself. Lexie shouted for help, but her sisters were all busy when their own fights.

The Rare jumped on her, seizing her once again in his jaws, shaking and tossing her aside. She fell to the ground like a crumpled heap of dirty clothes.

Another shot from Jenna sent the Rare stumbling back with a low whine. Across the field, Renee rammed her heavy wolf skull into a beast that threatened Corwin. Sage returned, pursued now by five Rares. He barked, sharp, three times. Sunrise. Time to shine.

The yellow light breached the treeline. Lexie scrambled to her feet and ran for the trees to regroup. The others broke from their fights and did likewise.

All of the Pack—except Jenna, who was laying down covering fire from her perch aloft—collected their breath behind the treeline. Her shotgun lost on the field, Lexie grabbed the last rifle and reloaded alongside Hazel. Renee cocked a new bolt.

"Are we ready?" Lexie whispered through heavy breaths. The girls nodded, and Mitch wiped sweat from his face.

"Let's go," Lexie said. Those who had guns slung them over their shoulders. Lexie stepped to the field in a ragged line with her sisters, took a deep breath, and shifted. From the corner of her vision, she could see the others, shifted to the height of their changes, towering tall, balanced on two legs.

Renee struggled to maintain her equilibrium, her center of gravity higher than she was used to. She gripped her crossbow in her right paw, fingering the trigger with a long and fearsome claw and screamed "GO!" in a howling, bestial croak.

Lexie ran, teetering and stumbling a few steps before catching her stride and leaping over the tripwires that defended their front. Jenna shot a few more suppressing rounds. Dust and rock burst in the wake of her missed shots.

The Morloc squinted and flinched at the glare of the rising sun, and didn't seem to notice the furies bearing down on them. Lexie stopped to aim her rifle at one of the newcomers, her wolf-finger pulling the trigger so hard that she jerked the gun and skewed her aim. The bullet whizzed above her target, but it got his attention. The Morloc's jaw dropped in shock as Lexie ran to him with gun raised. She unloaded a second shot square between his eyes.

The shocked expression stayed on his face as he dropped, snout first, into the dirt. Lexie threw back her head and howled for the first kill of the battle, and her sisters joined in.

The other Morloc gaped as the howling, bipedal she-wolves ran at them. Hazel chased after the slowest, bulkiest one, running full-tilt with her gun at her side. She roared and sunk her teeth into his haunch. He fell, and she lost her grip. The bulky Rare recovered and ran at her, ramming her with his head. She flew and fell onto a pile of broken rocks, her hybrid form dissolving into her tiny human body.

The eight remaining Morloc scattered, the four healthy ones attacking anyone that crossed their path with swipes and bites while the wounded wolves from the first wave snarled and snapped and licked the hurts they could reach. Sage tried to lead the Morloc in confusing circles, but rather than bank with him, they held their ground and used his dexterity against him, waiting for Sage to cross their path and leaping to harry him instead.

When Sage showed no sign of tiring from that game, the healthy Morloc grew impatient, darting and dodging with increased antagonism while the wounded sought easier prey.

A whipping paw caught Renee across her thigh. A battering ram of a skull shoved Mitch face-first into the slate. A Rare's paw caught Corwin under the jaw. His swipe knocked her over. She hit the ground with a heavy thunk. Sage darted in her direction. He lifted her, but a Rare rammed Sage in the back, forcing the pureblood to drop his cargo.

"I'm out!" Jenna's call rang over the field of battle. Sharmalee ran to the truck, retrieved another box of ammo, and threw it into the tree to Jenna. Lexie zigged and zagged around Rares, trying to get to Corwin, trying not to get killed in the process. Her chest burned with the furious pain of her broken ribs. She wheezed and pressed her hand upon her sternum. She hoped the healing had already begun, though it didn't feel like it. She forced a half-shift and looked at her chest; her honey-colored fur was matted with dirt and blood. She found the faces of her sisters, bloodied, battered, tears and sweat intermingling, as though they were the same. The sun bathed the battlefield in yellow light, illuminating the thick dust that filled the air.

With the chaos of battle, most of Jenna's shots were hitting only rock. Hazel slashed her paws wildly at anything furry that passed by her, and Renee bared her teeth and ripped at flesh and fur. Mitch, a burly and short hybrid, ran at one of the Rares assailing Sage, launching himself at its throat and latching on tight.

Lexie looked back to the Barrens and saw the tall, mahogany-furred Renee unload an arrow into a Morloc's eye, then fully shift and force it deep into his skull with her paw. He staggered, and his jaw went slack. She shoved him to the dirt with a swipe across his snout and howled her victory.

The answering howls were a little more ragged this time. Hazel ran two more Rares in circles, dodging around a boulder, then leaping atop it. She half-shifted in midair and landed on one of her pursuers, claws digging into his skin as he bucked like a rodeo horse. She reached her paw into his mouth and pulled his head back, contorting his neck until it snapped. The second wolf snatched her forepaw in his jaws and clamped down with an audible crack. Hazel yelped and staggered away, gripping the injury.

Jenna dropped from her perch and tore across the barren land, each footfall clattering on the broken slate. She shifted fully and drove her skull into the Rare's shotgun-shredded shoulder. She followed him to the ground, clawing and biting in a flurry of adrenaline. Hazel limped back to the woods, shifting back to human, holding her arm and crying.

Mitch joined Jenna, and together they tore the throat from the wolf.

Sage darted through the knot of remaining wolves and the Rares followed him, frustrated with his games.

Sharm stumbled toward Corwin's prone form. Lexie took the reprieve to run to Renee's side. She retched as her form returned to human-shaped. "How many did you count?" Lexie asked, bracing herself on her knees.

Renee shifted back to human form, spitting a wad of blood onto the dirt. "Nine total," she said, gulping in breath. "Four kills." She picked up her crossbow and loaded another bolt.

"There were supposed to be twelve," Lexie said.

"I ain't complaining," Renee replied.

Lexie looked at her with doubt and hope, but mostly doubt.

From back in the forest, Lexie heard an odd sound. Bicycles. She pushed herself to standing and groaned at the pain that thrummed in her chest. Three tiny bicycle lights bounced behind the trees. Lexie limped to the forest and found Stefan, Taylor, and Otter dismounting from their mountain bikes.

"I'm pre-med," Stefan said, out of breath. "I can help. I think."

"The rest?" Lexie asked.

Taylor shook his head. "Sorry," he said. "We tried."

She cursed and briefed the boys. "Can you shift?" she asked.

"What?" Otter said. "Now?"

Stefan shook his head. "Of course not."

Lexie led the boys to the truck. "Here then," Lexie said to Otter. "Take my gun. Ammo's there."

"I've got this," Taylor said, pulling a katana from a sheath on his back. "It was my grandpa's. Never used it, though."

"Now's your chance," Lexie said, too exhausted to be hopeful. She ran back to the field and stopped, turning to face them. "Thank you."

"INCOMING!!!" Jenna screamed. Seven Morloc stood on the horizon, ready for blood. Lexie recognized one of the new ones by the bloody knife wound festering on his shoulder. She squinted at him—it was the wound she'd cut into the caged Morloc two weeks ago. It hadn't healed. "Fuck yeah," she whispered. Lexie drew the knife from her sheath and narrowed her gaze on the Rare. She charged.

Taylor and Otter followed her to join the fight. Sage ran past the ridge, pulling some of the Rares back over the crest and temporarily thinning their ranks so the girls stood a chance.

A Rare—the one with the sagging belly, courtesy of Lexie's knife—bounded toward Jenna. She aimed her rifle, but when she pulled the trigger, it only clicked. She was out of ammo. She raised the gun like a club and bludgeoned the monster on the snout. The gun cracked and broke apart on impact. Renee ran to help, arriving in time to watch the wolf strike so hard that Jenna landed yards from where she had stood.

Sharmalee found Corwin's shotgun and lifted it to her shoulder, standing her ground, waiting. Stefan ran to Jenna, lifting her from the rocks and carrying her to the truck bed for care.

The battlefield was bedlam: Otter and Taylor together, shooting and slicing at the beasts; Sage running interference; Renee shifting back and forth, swiping and snarling; Hazel tumbling about with her acrobatics, taking jabs wherever she could find them; Sharmalee nude with a gun, looking for a clean shot; Mitch throwing fists and rocks in equal measure, rage burning red on his cheeks. This didn't look like the battle Lexie had imagined—instead of armies, strategy, lines and ranks, it was chaos.

Lexie drew her knife and stood in the field, seeking out the full-blood she wanted most to kill—the one the Pack had caged. They saw each other at the same time. He ran at her, and she dropped the knife and shifted. He stopped dead before making contact. He snarled and swiped, but didn't connect, trying to intimidate her into running. *Just like gray wolves,* she thought. She snarled back. He kicked onto two legs, trying to dominate, but Lexie shifted back halfway and met him. They grappled, each trying to wedge their snout into the other's neck. The Rare's breath was rank and muddy. Lexie swerved her head left and right, snapping at his matted fur. He roared and pushed her. She grabbed his forepaws with her wolfish fists and pushed back. She dug her feet into the rocky ground, bracing. They were deadlocked, pushing against one another like wrestlers in a clinch.

Lexie shifted back to human, the change oversetting his balance. She somersaulted under his chest, catching her knife and swiping it across his ribs. The gash rained blood on her face. He snapped and wheezed, but she was already rolling out past his tail. She ran, tossing the knife aside and shifting once again to all fours. She tore across the Barrens, feeling him close behind her. He closed in and leapt, sinking his claws deep into her haunches. She stumbled and tried to drag herself free, but his claws dug further into her muscles. She yelped.

Then, just as suddenly, she was free. She bounded away and turned to see Mitch, then Hazel, then Sharmalee, then Renee pile on. Their tails wagged. They buried their faces in his chest and neck then returned to the sunlight drenched in blood. Mitch and Sharmalee shifted back to human, vomiting and choking. The Rare burst from under them, his filthy coat matted with glossy blood. He stumbled, limping, back over the horizon.

Lexie looked at the sky, expecting stars and dusk but finding that the sun had barely moved. It could have been midnight or it could have been May, for all her muscles knew. It was all exhaustion, strain, and stress, none of which she allowed to broach her brain. The girls looked just as weary, but the Rares kept coming, chasing down the girls who had come to Lexie's aid.

In the field, Sage shifted from wolf to buffalo, running, ramming, and corralling the Morloc for the girls. But the girls were growing weak, needing rest, water, a moment to recoup. It didn't come.

Lexie looked at the bed of her truck, where Stefan tended to Jenna. He raised his eyes to catch hers, shook his head, and returned to work.

They couldn't keep this up much longer. The early kills had been heartening, but most of their attacks had only wounded the Morloc. Six foes—four of them unhurt and barely winded—stood in the field, tails aloft, heads aligned with shoulders, gums curled back over sharp teeth.

The remainder of the Pack, plus Taylor and Otter, gathered at the forest's edge, preparing for a final melee. The Morloc charged, and the Pack fully shifted together, a motley collection of fur colors and heights. Tight together, they ran as a pack. Taylor's eyes widened and Otter choked up on his shotgun. Each Morloc footfall clattered in their ears, bits of slate and dirt exploding into the air beneath each step. *Hold onto it, girls,* Renee chattered. *3...2...1...*

At the last possible second, the girls shifted to hybrid and scattered, the Morloc shuffling over themselves to attack their suddenly-wily targets. Each girl ran, pursued by a Rare. Renee struggled to nock a bolt to her crossbow, her unwieldy paws fumbling it. The Morloc who pursued her smashed it beneath a heavy paw. Hazel tried to leap into a tree, but the Morloc caught her by the ankle and tossed her to the ground. She landed with a yelp on a scatter of sharp rocks. The Morloc trampled her. Sage darted to distract the wolves once more, but they ignored him, so he shifted into a buffalo and began ramming each one with his horns until they paid him mind. Taylor ran past the individual skirmishes, slicing his katana against the tough hides of the Rares, drawing blood wherever he could. Otter followed, picking off a Morloc and chasing it over the rise. Mitch tried to run but turned his ankle and was set upon by another wolf. Sharmalee swung her empty rifle, battering her pursuer's snout, but he didn't relent, pushing her to the ground and snapping at her neck.

Lexie saw their undoing. One by one, the girls fell, scratching, kicking, and punching in desperation rather than fury.

"Fall back!!!" Renee shouted.

Lexie sobbed, rejecting the notion. They couldn't yield. Not now. Not like this.

She sought and found Sage's eyes. They steadied her. He nodded and broke for the trees and the truck. Lexie bounded after him, as did Hazel, Sharmalee, and Mitch. Lexie's legs and lungs burned. Her vision blurred with unformed tears, and her breath broke around jagged spurs of pain. Jenna was in the truck bed, where Stefan tended her. But where was Corwin?

She caught sight of Corwin across the field, slumped and neglected in a rumple on the rocks. How long had she been out of the fight? Lexie couldn't recall. There was too much to keep track of. The dawn's glare glinted off the steel of Lexie's blade, abandoned on the shale halfway between the treeline and Corwin's body.

Lexie's wounded Morloc limped back over the ridge and spotted Corwin at the same time. The look in his eye shifted from animal to villain. He loped down to her, kicking up bursts of broken slate beneath each hateful footfall.

Lexie dove back onto the field. Halfway to Corwin, Lexie snatched up her discarded knife. She stretched every muscle to its limit, forward, forward, forward. She was in a footrace with a monster.

Lexie edged out the Rare, grabbing Corwin beneath the shoulder and lifting. Each breath drove a dagger into her heart.

She heard the footfalls, the eager snorts. She held her breath to dull the pain so that she could keep ahead of the threat that loomed only a pace behind her.

It felt like being hit by a speeding car, Lexie imagined, steel at sixty miles per hour. She flew.

She imagined wings spreading from her torso, like she was an angel, an eagle, or a goddess. But the body that crashed to the ground was the one she knew best. The girl, unarmored.

She saw Mitch run for Corwin, lifting and carrying her to the treeline, disappearing just as Renee came into view, gun raised and shooting.

Powerful jaws clamped around Lexie's shoulder before the blackness took her. Each dull, jagged tooth pierced her back and breast, pinning her like a butterfly. The Rare's hot, fetid breath warmed her skin.

Blindly, she squeezed her knife. She wanted to die with it in hand, she had decided. A goodbye to her mother. Proof that she had tried.

A stanza from the poem her mother had stitched into her quilt resurfaced in her mind: *Thine was the prophets vision/ thine The exultation/ the divine Insanity of noble minds/ That never falters nor abates/ But labors and endures and waits/ Till all that it foresees it finds/ Or what it cannot find creates.*

She would have laughed if she could, the thought of her mother venerating a white, male, New England poet. But the last words stuck, as though she were conjuring an epitaph.

Her heart fluttered like a fly against a closed window, too weak to fight but driven to try, to create the proper ending. The Morloc released his bite, rearing back to tear out her throat. She squeezed her knife tight and threw her fist into the Rare's mouth, down his throat. Her arm slid down his gullet. From somewhere deeper even than her wolf, she dredged up enough energy to drive the blade downward. She pushed through resistance, cut cleanly through esophagus, trachea and tendons. Her arm and shoulder emerged from the slit; she wore his face like a fur muffler.

The Rare may have tried to howl or squeal, but she'd already destroyed that in him. He crumpled into a silent heap atop her, his blood flowing onto her wounds, his weight compressing her until she felt part of the earth and part of his death.

Lexie swallowed some of her own hot, salty blood, feeling it flow into places it shouldn't be, suffocating her.

She sighed. Okay. Over. Last breath. Here we go. She drew her last breath and held it, waiting for her heart to slow too much, to stop. But at the bottom of that breath, she found something. Her wolf, sitting, patient but alert, waiting for her signal. The dead Rare pinned the knife to her hand; she couldn't release it. Her wolf was waiting for her, but she couldn't beckon it. The knife prevented it. Her wolf whined, over-tamed, waiting for the knife to go away.

Okay, she said. *Come on then.*

Its ears perked up, and its tail thumped. It glanced at the knife, and its ears flattened back against its head. She licked blood from her lips and said, "C'mon. It's okay. It doesn't matter," in the nicest voice she could muster. Her wolf stepped forward and Lexie transformed. Puncture wounds closed, organs mended, blood surged through her veins. For the first time Lexie felt the divinity of her wolf, its victory and sanctity. She lay, belly bare to the full morning light, paw drenched in the blood of her foe's throat, still curled around her mother's knife.

She drifted into a silent, painless place. No temperature, no light, nothing at the bounds of her body, no body at all. She expanded, dissolved, each atom falling away, an aura like the moon's halo evaporating around her. She exhaled and let her life go with it.

A crack shattered her peace. Two cracks. Three.

Shots fired from all directions, above, beside, behind.

She lay on the cold ground, the hard ground, the solid, present ground, returning to her body. Time passed, seconds ticking like her heartbeat.

Lexie's eyes cracked open. She rolled her head back, the trees and sky where her sisters took refuge flipped in her vision. In the trees, people perched like angels, rifles at their shoulders.

Everything was wrong, upside down, painful, twilit, and cold. Then she felt something familiar. Something from years ago, and it sparked a feeling she only experienced a few times, and treasured all the more for it. Heavy arms dug their way beneath her back and legs. Something heaved and grunted, and she flew again, this time warm, this time held. Not supported by wings, but by strong and solid arms.

She watched the too-bright sky disappear into the black of treetops. Grunting, pained breaths replaced the wails and yelps of her sisters.

Then she sank again, lowered onto a cold, metal bed, and the grunts became a whispered mantra: "You're all right, Lexie. Daddy's here. Everything's going to be okay."

44

ELEVEN MORE SHOTS RANG OUT, seizing Lexie's consciousness and dragging it back to the light. She groaned and rolled to her side, watching her father's friends, the hunters she'd grown up with, sink bullets deep into the felled wolves' heads.

"Corwin!" she heard Sharmalee cry. "Oh god, oh god, oh god, oh god!"

Lexie raised her head to see the Pack and hunters run to Corwin, who lay flat on the ground at the treeline, wheezing.

One of the hunters shouted, "Get me a kit!"

Renee's voice countered: "Get her into the forest!"

The hunter shouted back, "Don't move her!" but Renee and the other girls ignored him, picking Corwin up like a saint or a martyr, holding her aloft in their arms.

"Come on, come on, come on," Renee said.

Lexie slid herself off the truck bed, finding her torso wrapped in gauze and her arm in a sling. She hurried to Renee, taking part of Corwin's leg and shuffling along with them. "What are you doing?"

"If she changes, she might be able to heal. We need to get her away from the full sunshine."

Lexie looked through the trees, but there was no moon, and wouldn't be for many hours.

The girls lowered Corwin to a bed of pine needles. Renee's whispers emerged like an incantation. "Turn baby, turn baby. Come on come on."

Sharmalee was already crying, and Mitch held Corwin's hand to his mouth, kissing it like a prince trying to break death's curse. Lexie strained as though she could will Corwin's wolf to life. It wasn't praying, but it looked like it; it wasn't pleading, but it felt like it.

Lexie couldn't help but note—inappropriate though it might be—the beauty of their disparate colors: Corwin's skin too pale, too gone, too spent, and the melted, dewy brown of Sharmalee's as she draped herself nude atop her dying lover.

Ray and the hunters stood in a loose circle, watching in wonder as the girls negotiated with any deity or force they could, pleading for Corwin's life.

Corwin's face lost its pink, and her breath stilled to silence. Sunlight broke through the pine cover, casting yellow light on her blonde dreadlocks and deep shadows beneath her eyes. The girls put their hands on her, keeping her warm. When Corwin's breath stopped, no sound followed.

Then, only the faintest squeak from Sharmalee as she suppressed a sob.

Mitch wrapped his arm around her shoulder.

Renee placed her hand atop Lexie's, which rested on Corwin's sternum. Neither wanted to move, even long after it became clear that Corwin's last breath was expended.

The dappled sunlight warmed them all, as they sat as though in shiva alongside their fallen sister.

A moan broke the silence, followed by a gurgle. And a breath. Movement beneath Lexie's palm.

Without knowing why, as though it were a new sensation, Lexie held Corwin's chin, looking at the wolf inside like she did when she looked through the reflections on her knife. She called to it, inviting it to emerge but not to take hold. She held its gaze like an alpha. No.

Like a peacespeaker, the pack member charged with making the disparate parts into something more than just their sum.

Corwin's breath hitched in a ragged gasp. Her golden wolf silhouette teased at the edges of her body. She groaned as it twisted her injured innards. Lexie lay her hand on Corwin's furrowed brow, shushing her like a sister, calming the wolf that fought to emerge, while encouraging its power to heal.

Wordlessly, Lexie called to Corwin's wolf, asking it to lick the grave wounds, to seal the fractures in her flesh and mend the broken veins that filled her abdomen with blood. Corwin's wolf heeded Lexie's request out of a willingness to, not obey, but please. It understood contentment through allegiance and the power in submission.

Corwin's chin lengthened, the soft scruff of fur tickling Lexie's finger. Corwin groaned again, but a sigh soon followed.

Her wolf's chest pressed up against Lexie's hand. The other girls backed up to give Corwin more space. A cracked rib grated with each breath, and Lexie held her hand above it without touching. She coaxed the wolf further, to take on its full form, and as it did, the rib mended, Corwin's chest swelled, and the purplish bruise of blood receded.

Sharmalee held her hands around Corwin's temples. Corwin's yellow eyes opened once, wide, and then squeezed tightly shut.

Lexie scanned the length of Corwin's supine body, looking for any wounds left unmended and finding none. She crawled to Corwin's face, covering Sharmalee's hand with her own.

"Corwin, sweetie," Lexie whispered. She smiled when Corwin opened her eyes again. "Your body is healed, you can send the wolf away again now."

Corwin's eyes were blank with remembered pain. She shook her head, her muzzle not constructed to form words. Lexie stroked her fur.

"Thank your wolf for coming to you and send it back inside. She'll always be there, she's yours to call forth when you need her. But she is obedient to you. You have the right to decide how to claim your form."

Corwin nodded her understanding. With her next breath, she drew the beast within, leaving her honey-colored skin bare to the sunlight.

Hazel's wail broke the relieved hush that followed.

The girls ran to Lexie's truck. Stefan stepped away to allow Hazel room to throw herself upon Jenna's lifeless body. Lexie looked for Jenna's wolf as she had Corwin's, but there was nothing to call. No life there, nor had there been for some time.

Hazel didn't cry but heaved, a ruckus of overwhelming emotions, all of which fought at her throat to generate sound. What came out was a dry croak and body-wracking sobs.

The girls and Mitch stood in a semicircle around the truck, waiting for Hazel to expend or slow. Eventually, she wiped her hair from her face and glanced past her sisters to the nameless hunters standing like uncomfortable statues in the shadows beyond.

A rustling at the horizon stole everyone's attention. Ray reached for his rifle. Cresting over the hill was Taylor, face strained, Otter draped over his shoulder. Renee and Stefan ran to him. Renee took Otter, his limbs hanging like a broken doll's. Renee's eyes grew cold and dark, staring ahead, fighting tears. She lowered Otter onto the truck bed next to Jenna. Now it was Stefan's turn to break. His face fell into a silent howl of pain. He reached for Taylor and Otter both.

Lexie stepped away from the grief she could do nothing to assuage. She assessed the field. Twelve wolf corpses lay in the cold sunlight, individual red-black pools cradling their heads like oily pillows.

She had forgotten about her nudity, or perhaps she just didn't care anymore. Cold wind sliced at her skin, but she didn't care about that either. Nothing seemed to matter. She stood in a sad state of near-grace, buffeted only by her pulse, her breath. Memories and projections didn't enter her, they were wavelengths moving through a dead radio. It was all the present, and the sick sad rightness of it.

She heard the whip of a coat, and turned to find her father standing there, holding it by the shoulders, an offering. The coat was coarse wool with satin lining—deep green, handmade, leather hoops around leather buttons, and a hood. "This wasn't your mama's," he said. "It was mine."

Lexie expected Ray to avert his eyes, but there was nothing left to be ashamed of. She was his blood, his daughter, his pride, and his sorrow.

She stepped into the coat, pulling her bloody and sweat-soaked hair over her shoulder as he eased the sleeves up and over.

"I was skinny like you," he said. "And strong."

He turned her around and buttoned her in with clumsy fingers, starting at her sternum and working down. When he was done, he smoothed the fabric over her shoulders and held her. His face twisted into a pained grimace, and he began to sob.

Like a spark to tinder, his grief—or maybe his relief—ignited her own. She broke into sobs as well. His anguish was so true, so fierce, that she was powerless before it.

She stepped into her father's arms, and he squeezed her tighter than anything, ever. Her breath escaped on a wheeze and her bones protested. Her heart grew stronger in the effort to keep beating.

She sighed and let herself be held.

"Thank you, Daddy," she whispered and he just kept on crying, a squeeze with a sob to tell her that he knew.

"Do you want to sleep at home tonight?"

Lexie shook her head. "I think I need to be with the Pack tonight. We're going to have to figure out..." Lexie took a heavy breath, "...what to do with Jenna."

Ray nodded. "I'm sorry, honey."

Lexie wiped her eyes.

"No, I'm sorry about everything. I won't lie to you anymore."

Lexie laughed. "Sure, Dad. I'll try and hold you to that."

45

Ray offered to take Jenna and Otter's bodies to the coroner. He'd say he found them during some volunteer trail maintenance. The authorities would examine her injuries, come to the usual conclusion, and close the case. The other hunters dispersed. Renee drove the rest of the girls back to the Den, and Lexie gave a silent, huddled Stefan and Taylor a lift back to their house. She had tried to thank them, but they both ran from the parked truck before she could complete the sentence.

But she needed to thank someone, so she drove back to the woods.

Below her treehouse, she looked up, catching the faintest hint of Sage's scent. The cerulean sky looked like the sea from old paintings, too blue to be real, but beautiful. The air was cool, but it carried a tang of warmth, as though spring were making its presence known. She looked forward to warmth, longer days, shorter nights. She'd need a break from all the cold and dreariness for awhile.

Lexie climbed, but she hesitated before clambering onto the platform, wondering if this time her dream would be made real, and

Archer would be waiting for her. Maybe Archer had done what she promised and changed once more so that Lexie could try and love her in a new form. It was a perverse sort of thought, disturbing more than comforting, and Lexie shoved it back in its cage along with the rest of the unwelcome suppositions that populated her brain. She stepped into the tree and found Sage, nude and cross-legged, meditating in the center of the platform.

He opened his eyes at the sound of her footsteps, and she sat down in front of him, happy he found this place a pleasant one.

He held his palms out and Lexie placed her hands in his. Not knowing where she ended and he began, they breathed together.

"Thank you," she said.

He nodded with a warm smile.

"Are you leaving?"

"It's one of a few possibilities," Sage said.

"What are some of the others?"

"Staying." He squeezed her hands.

"Would you like that?" she asked.

"Would you?"

Lexie thought for a moment and answered, "Yes."

"I'll need your permission."

Lexie nearly laughed. "Why?"

"This is your territory now."

"Oh, I don't know about that," she said.

Sage shrugged. "Well, I'd still like your permission."

Lexie did laugh this time. "Why do you want to stay?"

Sage looked around and inhaled deeply. "I like it here. I've been wandering for a while. This place, this town. It's like a people-sized zoo. Very comfortable. Everything you could possibly need to survive in one handy little spot." He examined her hands. "It's an interesting concept."

Lexie nodded. "It is that." She reached forward and grabbed one of Sage's most perfect curls, sproinging it and smiling. "To the extent that you wish to," Lexie said, "I invite you to stay."

He smiled and leaned in to nuzzle Lexie's cheek. She grasped his cheeks, holding his delicate face in front of hers, and leaned to press her lips against his forehead. She felt a tiny sizzle and sighed.

"Thank you for your help," she said, pulling away.

She stood and walked to the edge of the platform. "Do me a favor?" she asked. "Don't tell Archer I was the one who let you stay. She might take it the wrong way."

Lexie was happy to be home. Standing in front of the Den, she realized what that word meant. Smoke rose from the chimney, and the scent of fresh bread wafted from the cracked-open kitchen window. She realized, for the first moment ever, she was happy to be here.

Inside, Mitch helped Corwin assemble an altar next to the fireplace, Sharmalee brushed Hazel's hair, and Renee sipped some tea. They all smiled wearily when Lexie entered.

"Where have you been?" Renee asked. "We were worried."

"Thanking Sage." Lexie sat next to Hazel, who touched her knee in welcome. She draped an arm around Hazel's shoulders, bolstering her with strength, warmth, or anything else the other girl might need.

"I should have stayed with Jenna," Hazel said, finally. "This is my fault. I knew she wasn't strong enough..." Hazel's voice broke off into tears, and Lexie stroked her shoulder. Hazel fell into her chest like a koala bear, clutching her flesh and hair, letting her sobs pour forth to fill the space between their bodies.

Renee padded over, sat beside them, and pulled them both into her arms. Sharm, Corwin, and Mitch followed, and for awhile, the soft echoes of sobs filled the house. But eventually the comfort turned to cuddling, and soon the Pack was lying together on the living room carpet, some sleeping, some just sighing into each other's touch. Lexie liked the weight, and lost track of where her body ended and those of her sisters began. She opened herself to the feeling of warmth, of belonging. She liked being among these women, her sisters. She belonged here. She was happy here.

She was home.

Acknowlegements

This book is dedicated to all the people who read *Lunatic Fringe* and hoped for a sequel. The emails, messages, and hugs I get from you have made this difficult and scary ride absolutely worthwhile.

To Alyc Helms. You make me see the best in myself. Each one of your edits teaches me a new way to be a better author.

To JP. Thank you for once again for sharing your creativity and talent with me.

To Rachel Gold. There isn't enough sushi in the world to sate my appreciation for you.

To Craig Cady. Thank you for transforming your burden into a gift for me. You do everything with intention, even capitalization.

To Rebecca Ford & Ashley Shepard, for your guidance and polish.

To Liz Upson. You're the tops, from the bottom of my heart.

To independent booksellers and book bloggers, for keeping it real.

To Shawna Hamic, who bears more than a passing-resemblance to an angel.

To backers of my Kickstarter, especially Matt Walker, Kirsty Heppenstall, Harper Jean Tobin, Donna Thomas, Keith Schwerin, Bucket, Jay Parry, Bran, Ash Miller, Dylan Cox, Sabrina Morgan, Monique Darling, Sonya Harway, Tobias Jaeger, Pauline Driscoll, Arielle McKee, Nikhil D. Majumdar, Sara & Ashley Vibes, and t'Sade.

To Mom & Dad.

To Nanny, for competing with Mom for the title of my Biggest Fan.

To Reid Mihalko, the rock that keeps on rocking my world.

And most of all, to Hans, who inspired me to get better at saying "Yes!" I wish I had said it more to you.

Made in the USA
Charleston, SC
18 March 2013